P9-BYH-989

Aftermath of DREAMING

wm
WILLIAM MORROW
An Imprint of HarperCollins*Publishers*

Aftermath of DREAMING

DeLauné Michel

HarperCollins books may be purchased for educational, business, or sales promotional use. For information please write: Special Markets Department, HarperCollins Publishers, 10 East 53rd Street, New York, NY 10022.

FIRST EDITION

Designed by Sarah Maya Gubkin

Printed on acid-free paper

Library of Congress Cataloging-in-Publication Data

Michel, DeLauné.

Aftermath of dreaming / DeLauné Michel.—1st ed.

p. cm.

ISBN 13: 978-0-06-081733-6

ISBN 10: 0-06-081733-X (alk. paper)

1. Women designers—Fiction. 2. Los Angeles (Calif.)—Fiction. 3. Triangles (Interpersonal relations)—Fiction. 4. Moving picture actors and actresses—Fiction. I. Title.

PS3613.1345A65 2006

813'.6—dc22 2005047180

06 07 08 09 10 WBC/RRD 10 9 8 7 6 5 4 3 2 1

For my mother
Elizabeth Nell Dubus Michel Baldridge—my greatest teacher

Acknowledgments

This novel would not have been written without the generous and kind support of Beaty Reynolds and Christopher Rice. Beaty Reynolds's friendship and editorial skills have been a constant guide, always steering me gently on the right course. Christopher Rice's clarity and insight were essential, as was the graciousness with which he gave them. I will always be happily indebted to Nancy Hardin and Elly Sidel for their early and unflagging belief in me as a writer. My agent, Eileen Cope, is not only a knight in shining armor, but a friend. Carrie Feron's quiet wisdom and thoughtfulness as an editor are gifts for which I will always be grateful. The immediate warmth with which Debbie Stier welcomed me to the fold, and her guidance, are deeply appreciated. I am lucky to have fellow Southerner Seale Ballenger's expertise and advice. Selina McLemore is always helpful and patient with my many questions. Christina Beck's experience and strength as both a writer and a friend have given me courage when I had none. Museum trips and conversations with John Swanger fed my soul. Hilary Beane's elegant, gorgeous jewelry was crucial inspiration; I am so thankful for the selfless and cheerful sharing of her time and expertise. Philip Brock brought his sharp eye and encouragement to the earliest burgeoning form of this novel with the patience of a saint and the humor of a comedy god. Regina Su Mangum, Mari Weiss, and Annie Weisman gave their time and keen observations to an early draft with indispensable results. My sisters Elizabeth Michel, Pamela Chavez, Maggi Michel, and Aimée Michel have all supported me with their love. Betsy Little's courage, grace, and humor is a constant light. Bruce Gregory was instrumental in helping me change my path—I am forever grateful. The audiences and writers of Spoken Interludes have created a community for me by generously sharing their stories, warmth, and lives that will forever enrich mine. And my husband, Daniel Fried, has given me a life of happiness beyond my wildest dreams.

1

I've been waking up screaming for the past three months. Not every night, God, no. Probably just three or four times a week. Three or four times a week in the middle of the night, I find myself sitting straight up in bed, eyes wide open, screaming from the depth of my being a sound so loud I never would have thought I could make, then suddenly it all stops. And a void is left, a hollow, like that vacuum thing they talk about nature abhorring, but here it is in my apartment, alive and full of air, sucking all the images and dreams out of me, and all I am left with is wondering what it is and why don't my neighbors ever do anything?

Because I really have been screaming—out loud. I mean, I know how confusing it can be when you sleep—there's that whole falling-down dream where you'd swear you're flying hard and fast through the air, then when you land, you've been in your bed the whole time, haven't moved at all. But these sounds are real. So real they wake me up every time.

I keep thinking I will mention it to my neighbors when I pass them in the courtyard or see them at the mailbox. "By the way," I could say. "Have you been hearing screams coming from my apartment on a regular basis for a few months now? In case you've been wondering about it, maybe waiting to see if it continues before you do anything—don't worry, it's only my dreams."

In the repeated fantasies I have of this exchange, it always ends in an empty, silent stare from them. Particularly from Gloria, the was-prostitute now-seamstress, whose apartment shares a staircase with mine. Not that she dresses like a prostitute, or that we live on or near Selma, the purportedly high-traffic street for that sort of thing in Hollywood, though I think her business was more a call-and-come-over kind. And I don't even know why she had to tell me about that part of her past. She's the last person I would have suspected, though she does keep her red hair *Playboy*-esque long, falling around her face and softening the lines around her eyes that are obvious when the sun hits her dead-on. Was-prostitute, near-fifty, now-alone. There's a terrifying dénouement.

One afternoon last year right after I moved in, I accepted her invitation for a cup of coffee and that was when she immediately began confiding her long sordid tale. As I sat on her couch feeling rather trapped, frankly, and listening to her cataloguing of the men and their particular predilections, her apartment's girlish, old-fashioned floral décor shifted in my mind from kitschy pleasant to purely depressing, as if it were meant to protect her from remembering her past.

Better protection would have been for her to not confide in me at all. Now that the knowledge rested also in me, it felt like my unfortunately spontaneous thoughts of it added even more ghosts to the memories she had of her "visitors" as she called them, the men who traipsed up and down the stairs before the landlord finally put a stop to it.

The other night after the screaming happened—it was twice in a row this week, usually I get a night off in between—I drank some water and was lying back down when it occurred to me that maybe I should worry. I mean, my life is wonderful. I'm twenty-nine, single, and living in L.A. I'm happy and all that stuff. I'm fine.

I'm just screaming on a regular basis with no discernible reason or effect.

Which is kind of like living in the South, actually, where there are lots of big, dramatic actions full of urgency and despair that finally may as well not have happened for all the consequence they have. You can exhibit all sorts of peculiar behavior where I'm from, just don't expect your neighbors to talk to you about it. Probably because they are all too busy being peculiar themselves to notice or even care.

I grew up on the Gulf Coast in Pass Christian, Mississippi (pronounced pass-chris-*tchan*-miss-sippy, with the syllables folding into and on top of each other. It's a slow-hurry sound like your first two sips of a good drink), just east of New Orleans, where both my parents grew up in families going back many generations in Louisiana. My grandfather's secretary, Miss Plauché, used to walk to work through the New Orleans business district every day facing backward and would return home the same way, just facing the other . . . You get the picture. No one ever said a word. Not to her, not to anybody. But as Momma always said, "Well, it's not like she's hurting anyone." Of course, it did give new meaning to the expression "You know, I bumped into Miss Plauché today."

One early summer morning when I was young, my grandfather, in a gesture weighted with importance for its rarity, let me accompany him to his office. We sat in the serious-business air-conditioned quiet, he at his massive desk solidly engaged in the *Wall Street Journal*, and I on the thick, plush carpet, stomach down, head resting on my hands, as close as I could get to peer out the floor-to-ceiling windows way high above the city. The people far below, so many dark-suited men among brightly clothed women, moved in chaotic order like a game of marbles expertly won, until the flow was broken and a parting occurred. Then I saw Miss Plauché walking backward toward the big bank building. Her silver-haired head bobbed along like a sleepwalker meandering undisturbed toward her dream's destination. As I lay there watching her peculiar backward stride, I wondered what it was she was leaving behind in her past that she still needed so badly to see. And why didn't anyone ever ask her?

I had lunch yesterday with an ex- . . . Oh, I don't know. What do you call those people anymore, "boyfriend"? Let's be honest, "boyfriend" is for high school and, frankly, I never even had a boyfriend. When I was in tenth grade, I sort of jumped over that part and went directly to an affair with a thirty-two-year-old just-widowed man whom I definitely did not call my "boyfriend." So that word has never really worked for me, and "lover" just sounds so . . . Judith Krantz. Anyway, this person, Michael, that I was involved with for almost a whole year, we hadn't seen each other in nine months, but he called, so we had lunch. Well, brunch, really; it's such a prettier meal than lunch.

Particularly at Wisteria, a restaurant I had never been to before, just driven past it on Robertson Boulevard while always experiencing that dreadful wanting to slow and stare and somehow suddenly be one of the glorious people eating outside there, so I loved that Michael picked it for brunch, but considering its high prices in relation to his modest salary, I was shocked. Michael is the programming director of a local NPR radio station, but not *the* local NPR station, the one whose shows really are better than commercial radio, which is probably why it's so popular—the cachet of having your radio at the far left of the dial without having to listen to any weird-views-and-strange-music stuff. Michael works at one of those, but secretly wishes it was the big one.

Michael was nowhere in sight when I arrived at Wisteria a few minutes past our agreed-upon time. As I waited by the maître d' stand at the entrance to the patio, the California sun seemed to intensify, but without adding extra heat, only shimmer, so that everyone glowed luminously. Even the brunettes looked blond. Though I doubted my mane of dark curls did as I hurried behind the maître d' through a tight array of tables, faltering a bit on the patio's uneven brick floor. I wondered if it was purposely designed that way to reveal who was used to it and who was not. I reached the (decent, not great) table without fully tripping and sank into the refuge of the chair. All the women at the other tables had drinks. Red and full and tall with straws shooting out of them like stamens, their bee-stung lips sucking the nectar down. It made me want straight gin, but at brunch that's a bit of a statement.

"May I have an iced tea, please?" I asked a waiter, or actually a busboy I realized when he gave me an aggrieved look and walked away.

Michael had not materialized. The other diners' conversations lapped toward me, leaving a small gulf of quiet where my table sat. I wanted him here to fill it with me. With him. With an us that once-was and how-it'd-been, but now would be made radiant by the glittering sun and the exclusivity of this locale we'd be in.

I looked around for Michael. He still had not arrived. My gaze stopped at the far corner of the patio—the prime banquette, colonized by a family. A tiredly handsome man, not even trying to smile, just focusing on his food and the champagne he kept downing and that was then immediately replenished; an energetically conversing woman wearing a stunningly elegant straw hat with nonchalance—on anyone else it would have been too much; the oldest child, the daughter, silent in the security of her exquisite blossoming—the sunlight that landed on her surely never wanted to leave, so happy it was with that similarly golden home; and the son. The son who allowed them to be done—no third child after two daughters here—and who appeared as unaware of what he had saved his family from as he was, for now, of all the power that held. As I watched this family in their attuned nonengagement, the conversation from the couple at the table next to me invaded my ears. It was like watching a silent film with the sound from another movie piped in.

"Yvette."

I heard my name spoken by Michael before I saw him. He sounded calm, which always amazed me when we were together, this calm voice Michael has, unperturbed by daily life as if emanating from an ancient realm—and his looks are that of a Mediterranean god, the you-want-to-start-civilizations-with-this-man kind so they sort of match—yet his body is in constant action. I feel movement with Michael whether he is still or not. It sometimes used to make me think I might get left behind.

I half stood up and leaned forward to receive the kiss he gave me on the lips, a restaurant kiss, a kiss that hasn't decided yet if it will become something more or not.

"Michael, hi." I hoped I sounded wonderful in an ultra-me kind of way. Really present and happy to be there, but able to leave at any second without a regret in sight. I hoped the elocution of his name and short syllable of "hi" held all that.

Immediately, the heretofore nonexistent waiter rushed to our table, as if automatically summoned by the presence of a man.

"We're ready, Yvette, aren't we?" Before the waiter could offer his salutation and the recitation of the specials, Michael had forged ahead.

"Yeah, I'll have the grilled vegetable salad."

Michael looked at me like I was a small child whose favorite doll had been snatched away, then said to the waiter, "What's your salmon today?"

"Grilled with a peppercorn crust, served on—"

"No." The word deflated the waiter. "She can't eat pepper. Let's do poached salmon for her, I'll have crab cakes, and bring the grilled vegetable salad for the table, and two iced teas."

The waiter turned away, clearly pleased to have the order so easily. Michael took one of my hands and, smiling at me, said, "You love salmon."

This morning as I am telling my best friend about yesterday's Michael-brunch, it is at this point in the story that I get into trouble.

"Oh, good Lord." Reggie's voice carries out of the telephone, filling my living room. "He ordered you a piece of cold fish and you memorized it. This brunch has become mythic."

"It has not."

I am sitting on my couch—the couch from my momma's house, the home I grew up in, that I slipcovered with a pretty but sturdy dusty blue linen so I can flop down on it and not worry about the cream satin damask underneath—talking to Reggie on the phone while I try to make my way through a bowl of oatmeal, the heart-healthy food. We've been talking during breakfast on our phones in our homes for a few years now.

"Do you not want me to continue or what?"

"Yeah, no, let's hear it," Reggie says. "Have you eaten even a bite, 'cause I'm halfway finished over here."

His crunching of toast can be faintly heard. I know it is almost burned, buttered right when popped out, then quickly slathered with boysenberry jam to allow as much melding of the two as possible. Early on in our morning-call ritual, we described our favorite breakfasts to each other, making it easier to imagine the other person was there. Ever since then, I have kept my eye out for an all-in-one spread—like they do with peanut butter and jelly for kids—so I can buy a case of butter'n'jam and leave it at Reggie's door as a surprise. His breakfast ready in one less step.

"There's not a lot more to tell," I say in a voice that indicates how completely untrue that is, as I take the mostly uneaten oatmeal to the kitchen sink. "It was your basic nonmythic brunch." I turn the hot water on, causing a spray to shoot up from hitting the spoon. "Until the end."

"Yvette, turn the water off. You wash more dishes than any person I know, yet you barely eat. What do you do, take in your neighbors? Tell me what happened."

Michael's words were swirling around me in Wisteria's sun-drenched air. "There's definitely an increase in our listeners. The new shows I've started are pulling them in; the numbers are like nothing they've seen before."

"That's great, Michael, I'm so happy—"

"Yeah, so—thanks! So basically the station is where I want it to be right now. Okay, Tuesday nights—maybe Monday, too—could be better, though I think this new deejay I found is going to hit them out the park."

I was trying to stay focused on Michael's business talk, which I always loved. Michael makes radio programming sound exciting and revolutionary and capable of transporting you higher, like some perfect legal drug. But my thoughts were drifting. I kept trying to figure out if enough time-space coordinates had shifted in our relationship, so we could kiss, make out, whatever . . . and still have it not appear on the Relationship Radar screen. So it could go by undetected. By us.

"And the weekend morning shows still aren't doing what I know they can, but sometimes synergy takes time." Michael was alternating bites of crab cakes with bites of asparagus that he expertly extracted from the mound of grilled vegetables on the table between us.

"You're great at this stuff, Michael." I had no idea what to say about synergy, being unsure I'd ever experienced it myself. It always sounded unreliable to me, like an outfit that is fabulous one night, but two weeks later is boring as hell. "You'll be the Ted Turner of FM radio; soon every car will be cruising with your station on their dial."

Michael momentarily beamed, then quickly sobered. "No, no, I'm just doing my job." He speared the last asparagus tip nestled among the ignored-by-both-of-us zucchini. "So, You. How are You?" The pronoun sounded capitalized.

But before I could respond, Michael's cell phone rang, causing the couple at the table next to us to dance the win/lose two-step as they each grabbed their phones, then realized the call wasn't for them. Michael read the number on his phone's screen before clicking it on and saying, "What's happening over there?"

Michael's cell phone. Which is also a pager. But only for "extremely, extremely urgent messages," as the cell phone's voice mail tells you when you call, but the whole time we were together last year, everything I wanted to say to Michael felt "extremely, extremely urgent" to me, but I couldn't get rid of a terrible little feeling that it really wasn't to him, so in fact the only time I ever felt qualified to leave an "extremely, extremely urgent" message was when I called to say that I was constantly, all at the same time, both too urgent and not urgent enough for whatever it was that we were doing together, so maybe we should just not do it anymore and do something less urgent like . . . be friends.

Which we did. Quite easily, really. He even called a few times to see how I was. I still haven't been able to decide if that was a particularly good sign or a bad one, because tumult and despair are the only yardsticks I've ever known to gauge true love by. At least that's what I went through one time before when I knew it was true love. Not that my breakup with Michael had no ill effect on me. I do remember a rough couple of weeks when I was sure the only thing that would save my sanity and entire personal future history would be to drive to his home and just bury my face in his groin until both of us forgot the past we had together and could start a new one over, like some weird kind of prequel that makes the original ending obsolete. But I never did.

"Sorry about that." Michael put his phone down on the table near his hand. "Things at the station are just . . . Wow. You know."

"Right," I said brightly. I glanced at the salmon on my plate. It was so lovely, pink and firm, lying there ready anytime. I took a bite that was melty and soft, as if my teeth were unnecessary.

"So." Michael broke into my fishy reverie. "How are the accessories? I mean, jewelry."

"Great, it's—"

"Right. Rings, pendants, bracelets. Are these . . . ?" He reached out his hand, briefly touched my earring, and then cradled my cheek as he might a small bird.

"Yeah, they're me. I mean, mine. Uh, my design."

The rest of the brunch swept by in a blur of sensations: Michael's deep liquid eyes bathed my face as we talked about my new jewelry line, a soft breeze that seemed to be orchestrated by him as he stroked my arms, and the sun drowsed my body, making it softly enthralled from within.

The patio was nearly empty when Michael and I finally left. The red brick floor had become an old friend now, an easy passage to float out on with Michael just behind me. We walked down Robertson Boulevard and around the corner to where my truck was parked on a side street lined with large jacaranda trees. The late spring day was awash in soft gold light diffused by the trees' open umbrellas of tiny purple flowers and newborn leaves. I stood in front of Michael as he leaned his upper back against the passenger window of my late-model brown Chevy truck, his lower body jutted out toward me as small blossoms rained down on us whenever a small breeze blew.

"So, do you wanna make out for a while and have it not mean anything?"

I looked into his brown eyes as I said it, looked into his eyes so lit by the sun that my reflection was clear, a small me staring back, but me made lit from his inside.

Michael choked, then tried to cover it by laughing, then I guess he realized I was serious because I was just standing there waiting to see if he wanted to or not.

Finally he said, "Everything means something."

"Yeah, well, how about not something serious?"

He looked at me for a moment like a diver eyeing a pool, then pulled my hips forward to meet his, as our lips touched and we kissed.

It was like a dream, but not the kind I wake up screaming from. Time did that minutes-swoosh-by-while-seconds-spread-out-slow thing. And then it all stopped. Because I stopped. But there wasn't a void, there wasn't a hollow, there was only Michael's face telling me that he had to see me again this week and the next, and asking why did we stop?

Frankly, I was shocked. I hadn't expected that. Maybe I had gotten so used to the "no discernible effect" with my screaming that I figured every area of my life was like that. Or at least Michael, who is casual about everything, so casual that he practically sets a new standard for casual, and this in L.A. no less. But as I stood next to my truck, being held by him, watching tiny purple flowers float and twirl and land on our shoulders and hair while he kissed my neck and mouth and lips and hand, every reason I had not to see him again floated away and disappeared on the wind.

"Okay," I said. "This week."

"And the next."

And time swooshed by as we pressed together, until I roused myself to pull away.

Michael waited on the sidewalk and watched me through the passenger window while I turned the engine over a couple of times before it caught and started up. As I was driving off, I glanced in the rearview mirror and saw Michael wave at me as he walked backward away, a slow backward stride, waving and walking facing me, until I turned the corner and couldn't see him anymore, but I knew that soon I would.

2

"Wait a minute," Reggie says. It sounds as if he's practically in my kitchen with me now, as if his large frame is hovering protectively near while I lean against my fridge, the perfect vertical bed. "What's with this 'nothing serious' stuff? That's why you broke up with Michael, am I right? The whole mushroom incident was just an example, if I recall, of how completely nonserious this guy is and has been ever since you met. What happened to that?"

"I found out that mushrooms are not—"

"What, serious?"

"Yeah. They're like making your own wine kind of thing—natural."

"Honey, a man who finally gets away for a weekend with his girlfriend, then spends the whole time eating mushrooms *alone* is not natural. He's a freak. And dated."

"Okay, so Michael's a little groovy."

"Next to who? Jerry Garcia?"

"Reggie." I blow air out my nose to stifle a laugh. I don't want him to know that I think something that stupid about Michael is funny, but I'm sure he can tell I'm laughing anyway. "Look, maybe that 'serious' stuff was the whole problem in the first place the last time. Maybe I just need to see what happens and not be so concerned with some preconceived idea about where I think this should go and by when. Maybe this time I can just take it as it comes and, you know, have fun. I mean, he's incredibly—"

"Okay, honey, you know what? You're nuts."

"And you're not?" I leave the kitchen to pace my living room floor. "I'm sorry, I don't mean to sound all New Age-y about this, but Michael keeps coming back into my life—"

"So does your period; that's necessary, he's not."

"Reggie."

"Of course, he's also unpredictable and puts you in a bad mood."

"Are you done?"

"I just think you deserve better."

"Well, obviously, I don't. I mean, he is better. I mean . . . You know what I mean."

I wait for Reggie's response, but there is just silence on the phone. We listen to each other breathe for a while, as if waiting for our intakes of air and emotions to get in sync before we speak again. I imagine Reggie's face hanging in the black nonspace that telephone communication creates. His features appear smaller when he is upset, his kind blue eyes and Kansas attractiveness pull in, as if the energy required for that emotion takes so much effort that his physicality must go without.

Still silence.

Okay, I knew he'd probably pretty definitely be upset about this Michael stuff, but what was I supposed to do, not tell him? He's my best friend, for Christ's sake. Though sometimes he acts like he's jealous, which I mostly find hard to believe, then annoying the few times I do because we've always only been friends, and even though I know he's straight—he's had girlfriends and women are attracted to him, though he hasn't dated in ages—I just don't think of him that way, so I wish he'd remember that our friendship doesn't involve sex and stop getting mad at me when I talk about other men.

"I'm glad you had a good time with him yesterday." I can hear the decision in Reggie's voice to move on, to let the rhythms and sounds of our mutual morning ritual carry us back to how we are.

I sit down on the couch, relieved. "Thanks, Reggie." Our friendship has been one long conversation interrupted only long enough for us to have more experiences to tell each other about, and I don't want anything to stop that. Until Reggie and I talk about something that's happened, it's not real. It's still in our heads, swirling around, waiting to be interpreted and set down, our minds a journal of each other's lives. "So what's happening with the script?"

"A big fat bunch of nothing. I mean, it's great having you tell me about New Orleans, but I need to see the places ol' Kate was writing about for myself—something to reinspire me—not that that's going to happen with how goddamn busy work is."

Reggie's dream project is the film adaptation of a Kate Chopin story that he's been writing forever and that is sort of the reason we met over four years ago. It was an L.A. New Year's Eve, rainy and dismal, things either should never be, but maybe not so surprising for winter and my second one out here.

I had parties to go to that night with friends, but it was still afternoon, so I was browsing in a bookstore to kill a few of the year's final hours. I looked at art books for a while, then went into a fiction aisle where a copy of *The Awakening* caught my eye. Taking it down, I flipped through until I found the chapter where the main character leaves her husband, and I suddenly remembered the first time I read that part and how I had to put the book down and just breathe for a moment because I was so amazed that this woman in 1890s New Orleans no less could walk away from the one man who enabled her to live the only life she knew.

Then someone near me in the aisle said, "Do you like Chopin, too?" which immediately catapulted me back from the novel's world to L.A. where a pleasant-looking man was gazing at me like we had been in conversation all day. Reggie was holding a book by Dumas, one finger marking a spot as if it had been resting next to his bed. He was wearing a dark gray Shetland wool sweater, so I knew he wasn't from here. And not East Coast, either, but near. Culturally, at least. We stood for over an hour discussing Kate Chopin—he had read everything by her—and New Orleans—he had never been—while people milled past us, water to our rocks in a stream. And our friendship's conversation began. Every year on New Year's Eve, Reggie calls to wish me happy anniversary.

"Maybe you could get down there for a weekend," I say as my phone line clicks, but before I can decide to ignore it, Reggie tells me to go ahead.

"Hello?" I hope it's Michael, then immediately don't, so I won't have to say goodbye to one of them for the other.

"You haven't even left yet?"

If I were forced to read those words without hearing the voice, I could still identify them as having been uttered by my only sibling, Suzanne.

"I am having a major bouquet crisis over here."

"Hi, Suzanne. We said ten; it's only nine."

"No." Her word lasts three beats. "We said Monday, nine A.M."

I silently shake my head, taking my own three seats, as I remind myself of the advice I read in a bridal book after Suzanne announced her engagement and chose me as her maid of honor: "Remember, bridesmaids, however she behaves, this is her big day!" I wish I had never read that damn book, though wedding protocol is probably like traffic laws—you get punished for breaking one whether you knew it existed or not.

"Okay, I'm just finishing up a call, then as fast as the freeway is moving, I'll be there."

"Hurry," my sister says, then hangs up the phone.

I click back to Reggie and hear the alleluia of his iMac coming to life, as if announcing that instead of resting on the seventh day, God made Mac. I relay the interrupting interlude to him, sure that he will believe what I remembered and Suzanne forgot.

"Freud was—"

"A great man, yes, that I remember. I also remember Suzanne telling me ten o'clock, but my mantra for her wedding is 'whatever.'" I walk down the hall to my bedroom to start getting ready to leave. "How is your work going anyway?"

"The director's a nightmare, and the client wants more energy, which, lemme tell ya, this commercial is never gonna have. They fight it out while I wonder how they expected the actors they hired to impersonate live people. If I passed one of these freaks in the produce aisle, I'd turn and run."

"They're lucky they have you to edit. You always make something amazing."

"I should be making something amazing with my own script."

"You will. It's gonna be great."

"Breakfast mañana?"

Reggie ends all of our morning phone calls this way. He told me once that his therapist decided that Reggie doesn't know how to separate effectively from people, that he continues to stay attached to them throughout his day. The evidence of this, the therapist explained, was in the wording of Reggie's goodbyes—they always contained a reference to when he and the other person would connect again. I told Reggie I thought it was just being nice.

Some therapists want to take all the manners out of you and think they haven't done their job until they do. Like the phrase "I'm sorry," for instance. How often have I said that in the course of my life? A hell of a lot more than the therapist I saw for a year was comfortable with, that's certain. He would say, and rather gruffly considering he was a paid professional, "What are you sorry for? You didn't do anything."

Where I grew up in Pass Christian that phrase was an expression of sympathy and concern and solidarity with the person you were visiting with. Such as: "I'm sorry you had a bad day," or "I'm sorry the hurricane tore your house up," or "I'm sorry the Saints lost again." Although sometimes I wonder if the real reason we apologize so much down there is that we still haven't atoned for that truly horrible crime that we committed.

That apology enters my head a lot when I'm with Suzanne. Sometimes it feels like a spell was cast on me at birth that transforms anything

I say or do around her from loving-little-sister to stark-raving-brat. At least, it appears that she views my behavior that way—but maybe some spell was cast on her, too. Though this morning, she definitely will think I'm a brat if I am any more late for my maid-of-honor obligation than I already am, which I might very well be since I seem unable to get dressed.

I have changed my shirt three times. There is almost a gravitational pull from my closet keeping me here as the pile of discarded clothing grows. The phone rings. I imagine it is Suzanne, or at least her energy using someone else's call to yell "Hurry up!" at me from her house in Santa Monica clear across town. I look in the mirror inside the closet door and only slightly dislike what I have ended up in. All right, just go.

I hurry into the second bedroom that I converted into my office/studio. Morning light streams in, filling the room with a muted quiet, but the air is urgent with the anticipation of work that needs to get done. Sketches of completed and still-evolving designs are tacked to a Peg-Board on the wall above my worktable; tools of all shape and manner are hanging there too, their images outlined à la corpse in black Sharpie pen—a custom I picked up from my father's work shed which he mimicked from all the detective novels he read; my computer is on and humming with photos of my new pieces waiting to be priced, printed, and organized; invoices and order forms spill from a two-tiered wire basket next to my carat and gram scales; black felt-lined trays filled with seed pearls and toggle clasps and checkerboard-cut amethysts and silk cords and yellow topaz vie for space on the worktable next to loose color-copied pages for press kits that are begging to be assembled. Not everything can be left out before I leave.

Crouching down in front of the gunmetal-gray safe that takes up the whole far corner of the room, I spin the dial quickly three times, right-left-right. Its familiar clicking is such an old song to me now that I can hear if the rhythm is off. Getting the safe into the apartment was hell. I had to pay the landlord extra for a guy to come out and check the building's structure to make sure an object this heavy and large wouldn't fall through the floor and crash into the apartment below. The safe's weighty door slowly swings open, revealing trays of finished pieces that need to be delivered to customers as well as more loose stones; necklaces and earrings; rings, bracelets, and pins; lemony pale citrine gems; rare mint garnets and cabachon-cut red ones; a tiny pile of peridots, known as the evening emerald gemstone; tourmalines of blue, purple, and watermelon pink/green; pieces set and bound with braided eighteen-karat gold, all sparkling and blinking at me from the safe's squatting bulk.

I take out trays and select earrings, a bracelet, and two pins, then put them on while checking in the mirror on the wall. The peridots are a pale whispering green, the tourmalines a soft lullaby blue, and all are shot through with thin bands of gold cutting across the gems that are then held together and apart by braided embraces of deep yellow gold. Sometimes I wish I could live inside a piece of jewelry. Or at least in a place where everything was smooth and polished and set and the only cuts that occurred were on purpose to make the light more enhanced.

I fill a large fake Louis Vuitton travel case with trays of jewelry, return the other ones to the safe along with the trays of topaz and amethysts and pearls from the worktable, shut the door, spin the dial a few turns, then stand up to look around to see if I've forgotten anything. Price sheets, order forms, and business cards with the name of my line, Broussard's Bijoux, are already in the pocket of the travel case, and I am reminded, for the hundredth time, that I need to get a brochure printed up, as well as a Web site—does it ever end?—but finally I'm ready to run.

I grab my purse in the living room, lock the front door behind me, then race down the stairs and across the courtyard as the soft late May sunshine plays on my skin letting me know how it feels to be out in the clothes I am in that makes me turn around, run up to my apartment, grab my favorite black shirt plus a blue one, relock the front door behind me, run to my truck, and, finally, leave.

3

The sky is bright and clear. The air is erased of all imperfection and smog. L.A. is ready for its close-up. Traffic down Crenshaw is easy, thank God, because I should have left twenty minutes ago. Okay, forty-five minutes ago, if I was going to be there at nine A.M. As it is, I'll be there just before ten.

I live equidistant between two large boulevards that each have freeway entrances, so I am constantly deciding which one to take. The more westerly of the two, La Brea, is usually more crowded, since it is generally understood to be the last civilized stop off the 10 freeway for anyone to use, even though my neighborhood that Crenshaw leads you to is quite lovely—old homes, quiet streets, large trees (an anomaly in L.A.), with pockets of apartment buildings from the 1920s. But when giving directions to my apartment, I always suggest La Brea; people here get uneasy when told to use a freeway exit they never thought they'd have to.

I pull onto the 10 freeway and find a place among the westbound semirush. The vehicles in their lanes on each side of my truck remind me of customers on stools at a neighborhood bar. Everyone is perfectly spaced apart; all together, yet all alone. Until inevitably someone gets hit. But when that's cleared up, what returns is a kind of massive hurtling forward while being lulled all at the same time. A perfect mind-numbing leave from life.

I love riding the 10 freeway, or the Christopher Columbus Transcontinental Highway, which is the official name posted on the big green sign welcoming you from Highway 1 where the 10 begins. Though I was out here a good year before I noticed that sign and learned the freeway's real name. See, I grew up with the 10 in Pass Christian. Of course, down there it's called the I-10, like some kind of personal rating statement, never the 10 freeway, but to me it was only one thing: the way out of Pass C. and to New Orleans—which is why I've always loved the 10. And I knew it kept traveling west, Houston and all that, but I never really thought about where it ended up until I got out here and realized it was the same one, just looking better cared for and with a different name. Like some burgeoning actress from the Midwest.

There is no sign, however, at the end of Highway 10 before it merges into Highway 1. No sign to make sure you knew the name of what you were riding on. Which I find very odd—as if the ability to keep on going makes up for the lack of a goodbye. But maybe that's the whole point of L.A.

The street my sister lives on in Santa Monica is a few blocks from the beach, but in a canyon, so there is lots of privacy. It is easy not to know it exists, tucked out of sight the way it is, just past a deep curving slope. The street's somnolence hits me as I drive toward her home. The houses appear hushed: most occupants are probably at work, and the few left behind are deeply engaged in some Monday-morning task that is meaningless except for its ability to kick-start another week.

A famous female folk singer from the seventies lives next door to Suzanne. I met her brother once years ago while he was staying with a friend of mine whom I used to run with every morning on the beach. My friend told me later who his sister was, and that explained why his frank blue eyes were curiously familiar, as if they had reprinted themselves off his sibling's album covers from so long ago.

But I didn't mention that to Suzanne last year when she showed me her new home and told me who all their neighbors were, going on at length about the folk singer. I was surprised that she knew so quickly who everyone was. I wondered if there was a list somewhere, a grand seating chart of the neighborhood that helped people choose their home so they weren't stuck with the untoward, like a bad dinner companion, for life.

Suzanne opens her front door before I barely have my truck in park. I know she can distinguish its old American motor from all the new European ones roaming around especially since I've had it for years. I bought it because it was sturdy, cheap, and good to haul stuff around in. And because it reminds me of where I grew up. Not that Pass C. is filled with trucks, but it definitely is not filled with exorbitantly priced non-American sedans. Soon after I bought it, Suzanne told me that it makes me look like I am dating someone from the wrong side of the tracks and driving his truck—which made me love it even more.

My sister-the-bride is standing in the open doorway wearing a celadon-green silk sweater that plays up the same shade in her eyes and is light to the dark of her long, straight hair. That green has always been so perfect for her that I am unable to see a garment of that color without thinking she must already own it.

"Thank God you are here," she says as I walk up the sidewalk. "Was traffic a nightmare?"

"You know." I wave my hand back and forth. LA's love-hate relationship with traffic at its finest: hate the annoyance; love the sins it hides.

Suzanne reaches her hands out in what I think will be a hug, so I lean forward to receive it, but she moves behind me, causing me to almost lose my balance, then takes each of my elbows in her hands, and steers me through her living room, which has morphed into a maze of nuptial adornments. She could have just led the way. Finally, we arrive at her couch and sit down.

Suzanne and her betrothed, Matt, live in an all-white home. The only color is a forest of ficus trees in front of the living room's large arch-shaped window. With the wedding accoutrements squaring the already excessive amount of white, the effect is blinding. I stare down at my black pants for a moment to help my eyes adjust. It reminds me of when I was a kid and would go into the darkness of our daddy's work shed from the summer sun outside. I loved the not being able to see at first, the standing there only able to take in the strong wood and sharp metal smells, as my new environment accommodated me to it before I could illicitly enjoy its loot.

"Okay. Question." Suzanne's slender hands sort through the alabaster objects overflowing on her coffee table. "I want to carry Mother's prayer book, but I saw some lily of the valley that are just so perfect. Is it too much to carry both?" She holds up a small snowy tome. "Do they cancel each other out?"

"Oh, my God, the one from their wedding picture." I have never seen the prayer book in real life, hadn't even known it still existed, as if it might have intuitively combusted the minute our parents' marriage went kaput. I take it from her hands. The gold ink spelling our mother's maiden name is still crisp, the ivory leather pure except for a faint thumb mark on the back, like a print left behind on the safety rail of a sheer drop.

"Yes, that one." Suzanne takes the coveted object back, puts it on her lap, and folds both hands on top of it.

"How'd you get it? I didn't see it when we split her things up."

"Yvette, I got Mother's prayer book because I asked her for it."

"After the accident?" My mind is frantically reconstructing our mother's last days, trying to imagine a moment when a lucid conversation with Momma was possible, as she lay looking so unreachable in that hospital bed.

"No, God, I did not take a dying woman's prayer book. Honestly. I asked her for it ages ago when I was twelve and she let me have it then. I knew I would carry it before you."

"Oh." My sister has always had a propensity for planning ahead that seems to me a particularly unfair trait when it involves items that other people (meaning me) are not even aware they should be thinking about. She is the only person I know whose material here-and-now is abundantly affected by decisions made very far in the past.

"Okay, so." I try to push away the image in my mind of Momma handing Suzanne this book. The way Momma must have looked in 1977 when Suzanne was twelve and I was eight. Momma would have been wearing a crisp linen dress, no doubt, with small heels, just like any other normal day in her life, never imagining that in a little less than two decades, her life would brutally end. "What kind of flower?"

"Lily of the valley. They're white."

"Right, white." I take the prayer book back, and as I turn it over in my hands, the coolness of the kid leather comforts me. It smells like Momma. That keen, rich scent that permeated the air when I was a child as she'd hold my face in her gloved hands to kiss me goodbye before she and Daddy went out to parties and balls.

"That would look great, Suzanne. Just a simple spray behind the book, even cascading over a little, but not covering the front." I move one hand around in the air, trying to illustrate tiny flowers cascading down. Then another scent wave of Momma hits me, so I quickly give the volume back to Suzanne.

"Good, that's what I thought, too." She walks through the maze and puts the prayer book away in a cabinet drawer. I half expect her to lock it up and swallow the key. "You're great with this stuff."

"So are you."

"Coffee?" Suzanne is already leaving the room. "And how's my veil coming along? I need to see it soon, the wedding's in just eight weeks, for God's sake."

"Great, it's great, almost done. Just the detail work left on it now."

I am secretly thrilled to be alone. The objects on her coffee table are astounding, the buried treasure of some dreadfully fabulous betrothal dream come to life: garters and albums and place cards and champagne flutes and a heart-shaped ring pillow with a smaller heart in the middle.

"It means a lot to me that you're doing it," Suzanne shouts from her kitchen, as I pick up the pillow to examine it. "If I've learned one thing from Matt's family, it's that they show up for each other, and I want you to hear that I really appreciate you showing up for me."

I notice that "Suzanne" and "Matthew" are embroidered in cursive script on the white satin pillow next to ribbons that will hold their rings. I can't tell if the "Suzanne" ribbon is for the wedding band that she will receive from Matt, or if it is for the ring she will give to him and thus be wed. I wonder if she wonders that as well, but probably she already knows.

I quickly flick the pillow back onto the table as she enters the room carrying our family's grand and heavy silver coffee service, but easily, as if it were made of papier-mâché.

"Sure, Suzanne, it's not that big a deal."

"It is to me, considering how we were raised." Suzanne is using her "I am saying something loving that happens to be true, so don't challenge me" tone. I suddenly feel exhausted.

"Okay, well, good."

I push a mountain of tulle aside so she can set the loaded tray down. She has the same expression of determined politeness she had when we played tea party with our dolls as she pours my coffee and hands me the china cup.

"You know, Suzanne, our parents did show up for us—okay, fine, you're right, not after Daddy disappeared and Momma wouldn't leave her bedroom. But before that—the first fourteen years of my life and, hell, your first eighteen—they were good parents." I can't help myself. For years, I have felt like a portable tape recorder whose pause button my sister depressed during the last conversation we had about our parents when I was fourteen and I am sure that my words are picking right up where they left off. "Daddy used to take us to ball games with him, and all those trips to Grande Isle, remember the father-daughter days at school and the times he would—"

"I refuse to have this conversation," Suzanne says, her eyes hard on mine before staring off in the mid-distance as if the sister I should be is there. "You either want to show up for me in my life today or you don't."

"No, I do. Jesus, I just . . ." Not understanding why we can't talk about our parents, I want to scream. Considering that we are the only two people in L.A. who know them. Who know that they aren't just "parents"—that amorphous, only-exist-as-psychological-factors-in-your-life stratum that everyone's parents fall into out here because no one can actually meet them. Whenever I talk about my parents (to my friends or even that therapist I went to a couple of summers ago, right after Momma died, to help me with the grief), I can feel little parts of them getting cut away by the words I use (which is the worst part—the words I use) because they have different meanings to each person who hears them. The people my parents were—in the shadowy memories that hold together the love I have for them—don't exist where I live. Sometimes I long to be in a place where they still do.

Suzanne is staring at me and my untouched coffee.

"I'm happy to be in your wedding." I carefully push a lace garter aside and place my china cup on the table. I can't have something so fragile in my hands right now; the way I feel is breakable enough.

"Good, I am, too."

"Good. So."

There is not one yellowed or dead leaf on any of my sister's ficus trees or on the floor underneath. I understand this to mean that she has a maid.

"How are the anklets?"

It takes me a second to figure out what she's talking about. Our mother thought anklets were trashy—hooker jewelry. Not that Momma ever would have used that word, but then she didn't have to, with the expression she'd have on her face.

"You mean earrings, bracelets, rings, pins." My sister is the director of a small foundation that helps children with AIDS, a fact I have never forgotten, so why she can't remember what I make I have no idea. Talking about my designs with Suzanne is like watching the semiprecious stones and gold I use get transformed into colored glass and tinny aluminum. "It's going great, actually." I keep my tone light, refusing to let her see how pissed off her remark made me. "I've been getting new commissions, and at the gem show in Tucson, the prices were so much better, I was able to buy bigger stones, and, you know, size matters."

I laugh; Suzanne does not. I had forgotten that since she got engaged, all sexual jokes have become verboten, as if the road to infidelity is paved with chuckles.

"Okay, so." I move the tulle aside again to uncover my purse. "When am I seeing y'all?"

"This Saturday, three o'clock." Suzanne gets up. Even though I am the one who started to leave, I immediately feel dismissed.

"Right." I stand up in the gleaming, blinding whiteness of the room. She and Matt must walk around in here squinting at each other all the time, either that or wearing sunglasses. "Why's Matt coming anyway? Won't the ceiling of Bridal Tradition come crashing down on our heads?"

"It's your dress we're fitting, not mine." Suzanne is walking me out through her immaculate nuptial labyrinth. "I want him included. Too many men feel left out of their wedding plans." She opens the front door, stopping on the first step. "Our marriage is a partnership—we do things together."

"Oh, well. That's great," I say with no enthusiasm at all. I have a sudden urge to run to her couch, throw myself on it, and demand to stay. Instead, I lean in to give her a hug. She moves forward, arms out wide, embracing more a force field than my body. I stare at my truck over her shoulder, willing it to pull me away from her.

"Okay, so." I step out of her loose grasp. "See you then."

"Bye. And bring my veil," Suzanne says, and turning around, shuts her door.

The walk down the sidewalk is the exact opposite of the wedding processional in a church aisle: no family all around, no celebration, and no one waiting for me at the end.

4

"Jesus God," I say inside the refuge of my truck as I reach for my cell phone to dial Reggie to tell him about my sister encounter. I can't sit with this until our call tomorrow morning. But his phone rings the dreaded four times that means he's already left for the editing room. I leave a brief message though I doubt I'll hear back from him soon enough, as in now. Any other time feels too far off.

Driving down Suzanne's street, I resist the urge to floor the accelerator. All I want to do is rush and speed through this uneasiness since being with her. Talking to Reggie would have gotten rid of it. God, I wish he were home. Maybe I'll try him at the editing room. No, I'm not going to bother him at work. Okay, I'll take the more scenic route from Suzanne's—perhaps literally slowing down when I want to speed up will soothe my jangled nerves. I hope.

I turn right onto a street that will reach the PCH, then take a left onto the highway, driving past the bright, shining beach to get back to the 10 freeway. The ocean is completely flat, as if at rest, exhausted from its morning exercise of tides. Sometimes when I've been on my side of town for long stretches of time, I almost forget that L.A. is at the very edge of the country and has a beach. The ocean seems so regulated here, like a giant set they pull out when you drive by, to give the promised view with an endless supply of joggers and surfers and cyclists clamoring through as unwitting extras in the picture for you.

But the beach does extend its influence across town on clothing—very little of it is required in L.A. Unlike Pass C., which is also on the beach. In the stifling heat of that Gulf Coast town where I grew up, I was expected to wear panty hose and slips under all dresses and skirts to mass once I hit thirteen. Momma wanted me upholstered like a Baptist matron.

The first time she pulled this was on a warm spring Sunday morning when I was thirteen. I immediately decided to get Daddy's support against her absurd and unjust injunction. Usually I left him alone about stuff like that, but when one of Momma's dictums really crossed the line beyond all reason, he was my big gun. I ran to find him, dashing through the house, crossing soft rugs, sliding on polished hardwood floors, taking the sweeping staircase two steps at a time, until finally I found him in his study sitting in his large leather chair listening to an old, scratchy jazz LP.

I paused in the open doorway for a moment to collect myself. My father's head was leaning back, his brown eyes closed, his tall elegant frame looking completely at rest except for his fingers, which were tapping out the sax player's notes on the taut leather armrest. I wanted to jump on his lap and surprise him; then sit there curled up, both of us silent, him with his thoughts, me letting the music become colors and shapes in the air, as we listened to the jazz together the way we had so many times before.

But lately it had begun to feel weird. My body was changing, the dimensions of what was where were all wrong, and in the past few months an awkwardness had developed between us that I kept waiting to outgrow, the same way I had suddenly outgrown the easy affection we'd had. And I think he felt it, too. He looked so removed a lot of the time, like a verse in search of its refrain, and I was angry with my body for enforcing this change whose consequences I couldn't control.

"Daddy," I said, standing next to him and patting his arm high near the shoulder. He hadn't heard me walk in, my footsteps on the old kilim rug had disappeared under the sharp aching melody.

His eyes flew open and he saw me above him. For one chilling moment there was a question in his eyes—a "Who are you?" question, "Who are you and why are you here?" question—that made me doubt my entire existence. Then the thought shot through me that my very existence was intrinsically wrong and that the floor was going to fall away and I would be gone, and he could be rid of me and go back to that place where I could never join him. But the turntable's needle skipped over a scratch, abruptly ending the song, and the expression in my father's eyes shifted. The moment ended.

I almost felt out of breath again, as if the fast-paced, heavy brass number that had started playing had knocked the wind out of me. But my body took over and words about Momma's stupid rule were coming out of my mouth as I twirled in front of him, showing my outfit off to full effect—a pale pink skirt and blouse, his favorite color on me. It was a treasured outfit of Suzanne's that I'd finally grown into and wanted to wear that morning to mass, making at least that part of it interesting.

I stopped my pirouette and waited, all prepared to hear his "Why, you look beautiful, darlin" so I could run and tell Momma that Daddy said it was fine, but he just kind of stared ahead, not even noticing my clothes. In fact, he barely seemed to see me, which was a first. He pulled himself up out of the chair—when Suzanne and I were small, we'd each take a hand and pull on him hard, and he'd sputter and huff while he stood up, then tell us he'd still be sitting there if we hadn't come along—got halfway across the room, and said, "Listen to your momma, Yvette," in this vacant voice I'd never heard before, then he walked out of the study, leaving the jazz playing and me standing there all dressed up.

I stood in shock for a moment, unable to believe what had just happened. I'll run after him, I decided. He just didn't hear me with the music, that's all; he didn't understand. But by the time I'd searched the whole house without finding him, then finally gone outside, he was already in his work shed—the one place we weren't allowed to bother him—concentrating on a mandolin.

My father made musical instruments in his spare time. Not professionally—it was just a hobby. Beautiful glowing wood instruments, finely carved and individually detailed, that he'd give away to family members whenever we'd drive to New Orleans for a visit. No one played anything but the piano, so there they'd lie—violins, mandolins, and even a few banjos—sprinkled throughout our relatives' homes like a mute melodic detritus left behind.

I could see my father through the work shed's window. His back was to me and he was leaning forward over the worktable putting finishing touches on a mandolin, this fine object coming to life in his hands. Many times during the past few weeks, I had sneaked in while he was at his office to see the progress he was making. Now I had a sudden desire to run in, jump up on his worktable, and smash the instrument to smithereens in a dance of destruction in front of him. But my father continued his work, his small gentle movements obvious in the stillness of his back, so completely unaware of me standing right outside that I felt frozen in place, forgotten and dismissed.

Suddenly I could hear Momma yelling for me from inside the house. I didn't want Daddy to realize I was watching him, so I dragged myself up the steps, across the porch and into the kitchen, then allowed her to yell some more until finally she came through the swinging door and saw me standing there.

"How long have you been in here, young lady?" Her hands were tying a silk scarf expertly around her slender neck. My mother could put on clothes and makeup in the pitch dark and still come out looking like a million bucks. "Oh, never mind. Come on."

With Daddy in his work shed—out of reach, like the safety zone in a kids' game of cops and robbers—I had no choice but to follow Momma and endure her "light check," a procedure I had watched Suzanne put up with for years. I walked behind Momma to the back door in the den—the place she had long ago deemed best suited for this absurd and draconian purpose—and waited while she opened it wide. I went to the doorway, turned around to face her, and planted my feet hip-width apart. Momma stood glaring in front of me, squinting into the sun, checking to see if the light shining through my skirt was showcasing my legs.

"Go straight to your room this minute, young lady, and put a slip on."

I made a face at her behind her back when she turned to go off in search of her constantly misplaced car keys. Who cares if someone sees the outline of my legs; it's no different from when I wear shorts, I wanted to yell, but I knew better than to argue with her, especially without Daddy on my side. As I passed the den's picture window, I glimpsed his work shed and longed to be in there with him. Hidden in there with him. Never to have light checks or go to mass with just Momma and Suzanne again. Then seven months later, right after I turned fourteen, when Daddy left us, I didn't have to put slips on at all anymore because Momma barely left her bedroom.

But in the socially accepted seminudity here in L.A.—people go around as if they are constantly in the middle of a workout—I wear slips by themselves. Or used to. I'm actually more careful about that now, since an incident almost two years ago on a summer day right after Momma died, a day when the tears didn't so much stop as just sit right below the surface all lined up waiting for one errant memory to trip their flow.

I was browsing on Melrose—not in the crowded retail part, but farther east where a few fabulous shops dot stretches of nothingness—in a mid-century furniture store. The designs were vastly unlike those I grew up with, so I thought it'd be a good distraction. I was admiring a low coffee table, all curved lines and golden glow, when a woman came into the store who had my mother's forehead. The resemblance nearly knocked me over. The stunning widow's peak that urged you to look down at the perfectly proportioned expanse, then to the naturally arched brows and the bridge of the nose that demurely finished it off.

The woman did not have my momma's eyes—no one could. One of Momma's eyes was hazel, the other green, as if the light she emitted was so complex that her eyes needed two hues. Like dichroic tourmaline, gems that have more than one color when viewed from different angles; Momma's eyes did that, too.

The woman turned to face me so she could have a better look at a bedroom set near the golden curvy coffee table I still stood by. She was asking the store's owner questions, pulling out her measuring tape, discussing size, so very much alive, and with my momma's gentle brow and creamy skin, but on this perfect stranger, on her and on my mother no more. I turned too quickly to leave, bumped into an old hi-fi—good God, not memories of Daddy, too—and rushed to get out of the store before the crying started, but my tears raced ahead, beating me as I opened the door. I hurried to my truck parked just up the block, slopping along like an overfilled bucket, leaving water drops in my wake. The day's bright heat was like too many bodies pressed together for a hug, no affection exchanged, just suffocating my skin.

I was wearing a black slip I'd found in a thrift store that a thin, red-faced, elderly man used to run. It was a tiny space filled entirely with clothes that were jumbled and jammed everywhere, no discipline or system in sight. The elderly man sat at a desk in the front, guarding against the clothes' eventual onslaught.

Being in that thrift store was a huge hue challenge for me. Ever since I learned the color wheel in fourth-grade art class, I have been in love with the logic of light and the order of shades that result from it. Crimson becoming red turning into orange changing to yellow. White is all and black has none. It was exhilarating to discover that color—such an old friend, one of the first and easiest distinctions to make—was not what it appeared to be at all: there and solid, preexisting and depending on nothing for its tone; but, in fact, was waves of light traveling at different speeds.

Though I never could figure out how that made different shades, I'd try to imagine it. Would close my eyes and visualize light, would see its curvy cupid arrows moving through the air, but how that eventually made blue, I hadn't a clue. Yet it was comforting that something as basic as green was gloriously, magically formed. From that point on, I began putting my clothes into color wheel order. It made me feel part of the huge, silent rainbow dispersed everywhere all at once, and I could help, too, by putting the light waves in order of speed, a race always won.

I have never cared about being organized; I just like decorous hues, so being in that thrift store was an ultimate challenge visually. I had a brief, wildly unpleasant idea of color-coordinating it for him, a kind of corporeal act of retail mercy, but wisely decided to just never go there again. The next time I drove by, the shop was closed, the clothes and old man gone, as if the whole thing had imploded from within.

Anyway. On the day I wore the black slip and saw my mother's forehead on a stranger in that furniture store, I had finally reached the refuge of my truck and was letting the sobs come out. It was horrendously hot, as I said, so the windows were down, and I was crying freely, safe in the false invisibility that vehicles provide, when suddenly a man stuck his head inside the cab and yelled, "Are you all right? Where'd they go?"

I jumped in such fright it stopped my tears.

"You were attacked, weren't you, miss? I seen you walking down the street, half your clothes gone, shakin' and cryin'."

I tried to comprehend what he was saying. He looked about seventy, with clipped white hair on a dark head, and wore neat pants and shirt with a green sports jacket too heavy for the temperature. I glanced down at my slip. The strong sun made my legs completely visible through its thin inky silk, and it suddenly became all too clear what the old man had thought my crying was about.

"Oh, God, no," was all I could say. It was impossible to explain that an inappropriate clothing choice had happened to coincide with a really bad day, so I just threw my truck into gear and drove away, leaving him staring after me in confused dismay.

Thus began my own kind of "light checks." Not as stringent as Momma's, but not as lax as before. Though occasionally I will change clothes in my truck—or my shirt, I should say. Some days, when it seems as if every article of clothing I own has transformed itself into an item I suddenly loathe, I give myself backup. I go out in whatever is my current favorite—even though it doesn't feel like a favorite, like eating food you love with a cold and having to remind yourself the whole time how it really does taste—with a couple of options brought along in case I decide that I could be happy if only I were wearing that other shirt.

And I watched Momma do her own version of this while I was growing up. It wasn't unusual for her to change outfits three times a day. Every social function's attire was highly stratified, even a trip to the grocery store had its own code—Daddy didn't allow her to wear pants there. And in the small town that we lived in everything was so close, and Momma could just pop home, exchange one perfectly accessorized look for the next, and head back out. But in L.A., most places I go are a good twenty minutes away, so driving home is not an option.

Which is how I decided that if I really needed to, I could change my shirt in my truck. A bra covers just as much as a bikini top, I decided, so surely a quick switcheroo on a side street would not be that different from a swimsuit stroll on the beach past completely clad customers at a café.

Not that I do this a lot. Only once in a while, when it is absolutely necessary. Like now, today, after a morning with my sister-the-bride before an appointment to show my jewelry at a recently opened store. Rox is what it's called, for the owner, Roxanne, who previously ran a rock star's wife's store on Sunset before going out on her own, backed by the rock star's producer, Bill, whom coincidentally I used to work for and who very kindly set up this appointment for me. Which I'm thrilled he did. I feel ready, but also a little nervous.

Because I haven't really done this before. Sold to a store. I mean, I do have my jewelry in Tizzie's, a small shop in Venice. One day while window-shopping, I wandered into the store, and the owner admired my earrings and necklace, then flat out said she'd love to carry my stuff, even got me to give her the pieces I was wearing, so sure she was they would sell. And I was flattered since I had been designing jewelry for only six months. I've been selling pieces there for almost a year, but I haven't tried to sell to other stores because private commissions have kept me really busy. But when this connection to Rox appeared, I thought, why not follow it up? My goal is to sell to department stores and go national. And I guess showing my jewelry to the women who commission counts as practice somehow, but they have already seen one of my pieces on someone else and call me specifically to get something that will be at least as good as or usually better than their friend's.

But here I am, parked on this street off Beverly Boulevard, around the corner from Rox, with fifteen minutes to kill until it is time to go in, and the idea of changing my shirt is relaxing me a little somehow. I wish Reggie had been home when I phoned him after Suzanne's; he would have made me feel better about this appointment. With all that Michael-brunch insanity between us on the phone this morning, I didn't remember to tell him that my appointment with Rox was today, so he has no idea. Maybe I'll try him at the editing room after all. Stop. Now, just relax. The appointment's going to be fine. She'll either buy my stuff or she won't. Please, God, make her buy a ton. Now c'mon, focus on something I can control, like . . . which top should I change into? Black is the obvious choice, but dark blue accomplishes almost everything black does while still being blue. I take my pins off the pale pink top I am wearing that I hoped would subconsciously convey to Suzanne my happiness about her impending nuptial bliss and affix them onto the dark blue fitted knit one. I whip off the pink top, put it on the seat next to me, and as I am about to pull the blue one down over my head, I notice an elderly Hasidic man in a large station wagon watching me as he slowly drives by. His expression indicates that he does not equate my partial nudity with a day at the beach.

If sea water were a store, it would be Roxanne's boutique. Tiny, aquatic-colored tile descends the walls from pale to deep. Clumps of clothing sprout up in beams of light focused from below and above. Three aquariums, each a different letter of "ROX," hold languid blue angelfish. As I wait for the salesgirl to get Roxanne, it is hard even for me not to be overcome by the extensive color-coding, especially when it strikes me that the shirt I changed into matches.

Emerging from the depths of the store, Roxanne glides to the counter where I am waiting, puts her overly manicured hands on her hips, and says, "Let's see what you got."

No "hello" or "nice to meet you," so I quickly decide to forgo all that, too. I read somewhere once that mirroring the other person's behavior in a business meeting helps you establish a rapport—I just never thought that would mean being curt, but it's her store; I'm only selling to it.

I lean down, unzip the fake Vuitton travel bag, and start taking the black trays out. I bought the bag when I began going to women's homes to show my jewelry for private commissions and sales. I needed something large enough to carry the trays in, and I realized that with the amount of gold and gems (semiprecious, but still) coming out of it, the women would assume the bag was real, and the implied fiscal success might make them feel better about the prices they were going to hear.

"These are the earrings, bracelets, and rings I told you about on the phone." I have set three trays on the counter side by side. Straightening a ring in one of them, I glance at Roxanne to see which pieces have caught her eye, then unhook a bracelet since her attention is on the earrings, and lightly blow imaginary dust off it, turning it this way and that, as if to check its gems, but really to give her time to see everything without me staring at her or off into space. I put the bracelet back, wait a long moment, and then bring the last tray out.

"And these are the pins, though they can also be worn as pendants on a chain. See this . . ." I pick one up and turn it over to reveal a small loop on the back. "But I prefer them for what they are." I have jumped in, my words escaping in an air-bubble rush, like a sea diver adjusting his mask. "The whole idea is a further personalization of our clothes. That simple black top we all have, well, you put one of these on, or two really, and the odds of someone else . . . I mean, how many parties have you been to where thank God for different hair or we'd all look just alike."

Roxanne sees me see her blow-dried, dyed-blond, appears-everywhere hair. "Plus," I say, trying to fix my gaffe, "being pinned."

"Pinned?" Roxanne's eyes swim over my body, as if trying to find this new form of piercing that somehow slipped past her au courant antennae.

"It's an old-fashioned promise thing. A guy would pin his sweetheart with his fraternity pin before she got the ring. Of course, this is 1998 L.A. so the concept is pinning yourself instead of waiting for someone else to do it." I silently bless Momma's stories of Daddy's Sigma Chi days for this immediate inspiration.

A fish in the X is staring at me from one eye while his fins silently keep him in place. I have a sudden image of each fish in the alphabet tanks sporting one of my pins, yet still swimming—a mobile hydrodisplay.

"And the prices are?"

The make-or-break moment has arrived. I pull out a price sheet from the bag and place it on the counter in front of her. Every item in the trays is on it: listed, described, and priced. I figured out a while ago that a piece of paper is much better than pointing to each piece of jewelry while saying a number, then sometimes having to go back and repeat a price since people couldn't remember so many at once. And a tangible sheet of paper makes it seem as if the prices exist separately from me, so if a customer is teetering, I can drop the amount a bit, instantly becoming good cop to the price sheet's bad.

Roxanne studies the figures, looking from them to the trays and back again. I try to read her expression, but she just looks professionally guarded. A prayer for my jewelry to be in her store suddenly starts chanting over and over in my head.

Roxanne picks up one of the rings, puts it on, then holds her hand out in front of her, like the opposite of a palm reader, farther away will tell her more. She squints at it, turning her hand this way and that, takes the ring off, looks at all of the trays one more time, then glances around behind her, catching the eye of the salesgirl who has been standing in a far corner refolding perfectly stacked cotton tees.

"I'll take one of each of these four rings, plus an extra of this for me," she says, pointing at the one she had on. "These three bracelets, one of each of the ears, and one, two, three, four, yeah, these five pins." Roxanne's fingers skipped, landed, and hopped over my wares, as I quickly jotted notes of her selection, to transfer to an order form later on. "Figure out the details with Sandra here."

And as the salesgirl sidles up, Roxanne angles away.

5

"Reggie, can you believe it, I got in another store." I am holding my cell phone with my right hand, steering my truck with my left, and trying not to let my euphoria increase my speed as I weave through the choked lunch-hour traffic on Beverly Boulevard.

"It's that new one I told you about last week that Bill hooked me into and, okay, short version for now, but she bought tons of stuff, so now I'm in two stores. Well, Tizzie's probably counts only as half since Lizzie still hasn't paid me for that last batch that sold, but you know what I mean, and Jesus, I'm so happy, I feel so much better since this morning with Suzanne which, you know, fine, she's my sister and a bride so that's like everything annoying about either role multiplied, but who cares, I just made a sale, okay, sorry sorry sorry for the long message, but I just had to tell you, and call me later, I'll be home tonight, okay, I love you, bye."

I press the red button to end the call, then continue holding it down, turning off the phone. Suzanne always tells me I should leave it on in case of an emergency, and after Momma's accident, I guess I should, though maybe that's why I don't. Traffic has taken over the road. I crawl through two more intersections, then push the red button on the phone to turn it back on to check my voice mail at home even though I am on my way there. Maybe Reggie's left a message since I called him this morning after Suzanne's. Or maybe Michael called. Thank God Reggie got over our Michael contretemps. I hope. I punch in the number to autodial my home as I come to a dead stop behind a car that is double-parked.

The one and only message, besides yet another hang-up—a wrong number probably, but I seem to get those constantly—is from Michael, who is already back to calling himself "me." As in "Hey, it's me." I love "me." Love that he didn't identify himself, like he did the few times he called in the first months after our breakup, as if our not having sex suddenly meant I shouldn't know his voice anymore the way he could no longer know my body, nor I his. I play his message three times, listening again and again to him asking if he can see me tonight, and leaving his cell phone number (I guess he thinks I didn't keep it—I did), for me to page him so we can make a plan immediately. This clearly elevates our date to extremely extremely urgent, and that makes me extremely extremely happy, so I'll page him right now and make a plan for us to celebrate my sale and our reuniting. Jesus, I love life right now.

I punch in his Westside area code, and am about to press the first number of his cell phone/voice mail/pager, when I realize that maybe I should not. Maybe this gushy, happy, rushy feeling means I should slow down. With him, at least. Because the thing about starting to see someone I've already had a relationship with is, I can't just give him a kiss at the door. That would be weird because the whole how-soon-do-we-have-sex thing has already been done, so my only option for maintaining some control over not immediately falling headlong into him is to wait a bit before I see him. Dammit. I wish I hadn't thought of this. My body so loves the idea of him tonight. Okay, I'm just gonna page him right now and see him this evening, I don't care, what difference does it . . . No I won't. I'll wait until later to call him back—that won't kill me—then I'll figure out some night this week to hook up. God, I hate restraint. Maybe he can go to that opening of my friend's show with me tomorrow night. That'd be waiting long enough. Jesus, just kissing him yesterday was so divine. Maybe tonight really is okay. No, this is better (keep repeating that) because I need to focus on getting this order together, though I'd really rather see him instead.

Traffic has finally started moving now that I am east of La Brea and in the genteel pseudo–East Coast world of Hancock Park, which my neighborhood would be described real-estate listing-wise as "adjacent to." I've never had a jewelry order this large before. For Lizzie, I just take new pieces to her store every four or five months, leave what she wants, then get a check (usually) after they sell. As for private sales, the most a customer has ever purchased at once was when a forced-retired-because-she-was-past-forty movie star ordered a ring, two bracelets, three necklaces, and four earrings. That was great. She loved everything, raved on and on, and wore four pieces in a picture for a *Los Angeles* magazine feature about her comeback film that then came and went, but the magazine tear sheet looks great in my press kit. She's someone I should send a brochure to, whenever that gets done.

But first I need to concentrate on Rox, especially since I told Sandra that everything would be delivered in a month. And then they'll send me the check, she said. Jesus, that's different from Lizzie's. Paid before the stuff even sells. Like real retail. Maybe now that I'm selling to Rox, I won't sell to Lizzie anymore. But no, it is another store; I just wish she'd get better about paying me. Although I'm not going to worry about that right now, I'm too thrilled about Rox. I hope everything flies out of the store, selling so fast that they order more more more. I start a quick prayer about that, then realize that I said one just a little while ago for Roxanne to buy my jewelry in the first place, and now here I am with something else. I guess if I'm in that pray-for cycle, it never ends.

And I do pray about stuff, but mostly to Mary, because growing up Catholic in a South Louisiana family (which is redundant), when I first met Mary as a child, I picked her out of everyone in that crowd because

God was clearly way too busy and Jesus always looked so unhappy up there on that cross, but Mary was something else. I figured she had gone through so much: being pregnant, but still telling everyone she's a virgin; having to mother, of all people, God. But in spite of all that, she always appeared okay and calm. I wanted that.

Not that I pray to her in mass. I quit going when I was fifteen and I was seeing widow-man and was having premarital sex, which the nuns said was a sin that turns your heart black and the priest can see it in your eyes right before he gives you communion, then I guess the altar boys bodily eject you from the church, I don't know, but I didn't want to find out, so I just quit going and never went back. About four years ago I started studying Buddhism, so I meditate every day, but frankly I'm still a lot more comfortable around a crucifix.

I was first introduced to Buddhism by an artist friend of mine, Steve, who took me to a meditation session that was held weekly at a Buddhist monk's crummy apartment in West Hollywood. It was very informal, and En Chuan, the monk, taught for free, so I really have no business saying anything about the crumminess of his building, but this was 1994 and the whole of Los Angeles was wrapped up in that "if you are really spiritual, then you'll manifest in all areas; i.e., you'll be rich" bullshit, so at first En Chuan's large and ugly 1980s junk-bond-built apartment building was a shock. But then it was a relief—I never could believe that harmony with God always results in large bank accounts.

What did convince me of En Chuan's authenticity was his constant smile and easy happiness; I wanted that. He was a doctor of Chinese medicine, sending most of his money each month to his family in Vietnam, and was a personal guru to several low-to-medium-wattage TV stars plus a hugely world-famous pop singer who would call for immediate (and free) in-person spiritual teachings at all hours of the day, though mostly night.

The weekly meditation group consisted of six of us who met every Wednesday night in En Chuan's beige-walled, brown-carpeted, lots-of-plants living room. We sat on black meditation cushions in a half-circle facing him—though one woman brought her own special leopard-print pad—and En Chuan would talk to us about Buddhism. Steve and the rest of them had been going for months, so my first few sessions were mostly concerned with trying to get used to this higher level of cross-leggedness that everyone else was able to hold for what seemed hours on end, then stand up and walk around without charley horses or limbs that were asleep and half dead.

After a few months of going to meditation and getting inspired by the Buddhism, I decided to try not praying to Mary but to Kuan-En, the Buddhist goddess of love and compassion. Or I started meditating to her, is how I think the Buddhists would say it. I sat in my best effort at the lotus position and repeated her mantra (syllables whose vibrations engender love and compassion to yourself and all sentient beings, meaning animals, too, and plants, I think) over and over in my head.

A few weeks into this, once her mantra came easy and fast like a lullaby I could sing without knowing I remembered the words, a feeling would come over me, or up from within, of being comforted and held in Kuan-En's warm arms. It reminded me exactly of how I had felt as a child when I'd pray to Mary after waking up in the middle of the night from a bad dream. I'd be all turned around in bed, still terrified from the dream and of falling over the edge, so while I groped in the dark to find my pillow at the head, I'd say Hail Marys again and again, and that made me feel safe immediately. That was how Kuan-En's mantra made me feel—as if Mary were with me and meditating from within.

One night at the end of a session as everyone was putting their shoes back on, I pulled En Chuan aside and explained the familiar sense I'd get from Kuan-En's mantra while meditating.

"She's Mary," En Chuan replied, looking at me with his dark, twinkly eyes. "That's why Kuan-En's mantra feels like Mary's prayer—it's just different forms of one energy. If it's more comfortable for you to use Mary's name, do. It doesn't matter; either way, it will help you."

I was so relieved—to continue meditating, but to have Mary part of it, too, because I just feel better with her around. Even though I automatically use the word God, I'm really talking to Mary, not the Big Guy in the Sky. I like that I can relate with whomever (or whatever) I'm praying to from a female point of view; and she was a female who actually got it all figured out. Even as a kid, I always knew that there was no way my experiences here on earth could ever be as difficult as hers. Of course, she didn't live in L.A.

I decide to stop at the wine and cheese shop on Larchmont Boulevard to pick up one of their special mozzarella/tomato/olive paste sandwiches and a cappuccino to fuel my work this afternoon and into tonight. I'll turn some music up loud when I get home—I figure since Gloria's never said one word about my screams, music isn't going to bother her. Maybe I'll put on that blues CD Reggie gave me on the disc rotator, with Lucinda Williams and Roxy Music, and let the hours slip away in a harmonic reverie of working on jewelry that will keep me distracted until I see Michael again.

6

Downtown L.A. makes me miss New York. Or makes me try to pretend that I am there, depending on the way the light is hitting the buildings. Because on a really bright, flat-light day, there is no way around the fact that I am on the West Coast and not in Manhattan. Even though the buildings here were built by men from back there and from Europe who went through Ellis Island before coming to L.A. to create tall office towers and high apartment buildings with beautiful, scrupulously detailed work of marble, terra-cotta, and tile just like in New York. But once L.A.'s collective consciousness decided it should have its own style based on easy weather and roomy land, bungalows with courtyards sprang up and two-story stucco structures became more alluring than the Gotham-esque towers of downtown.

But not to me. One of my favorite aspects of designing jewelry is being downtown—daily, usually—in the jewelry district, a universe comprised of a few bustling blocks that looks like Manhattan's Midtown filled with an international community. I've been here all afternoon and still have one more contractor in another building to see before everything closes: Dipen, an engineer from India who learned how to cast jewelry when he came to California ten years ago. He just moved offices, and I hope to God that means his schedule isn't backed up.

As I make my way toward the tinted-glass double doors to leave 608 South Hill Street—a building filled with stall after stall and floor upon floor of importers, wholesalers, and retailers; diamonds and pearls; stringers, casters, and setters; gems and stones of all kinds; bronze, titanium, and platinum; wedding rings and colored gold all glittering—I almost don't notice my cell phone ringing. I manage to find it in my bag, push the green button, and shout a "hello" over the cacophony of sidewalk noise I have walked into.

"Are you still going to that show tonight?" Reggie says, jumping right in.

A sort of friend, Sydney, gave me comps to the opening of her one-woman show because I helped her find musicians for it. I had asked Reggie weeks ago to go with me, but he refuses to see anything live other than blues because he swears the musicians are all dead and only appear to still be breathing.

"Yeah, I kinda have to. Why?"

"I stayed up all last night reworking part of the script, and wanted to come by with some Manderette takeout and read it to you."

"I'd so much rather do that," I say, crossing Hill Street at Sixth to get to Dipen's building, which is over and down one block. The sunlight on Pershing Square looks like God adjusted his louvered blinds, reminding me that I need to hurry up if I'm going to catch Dipen still in. "I really don't feel like seeing her show—I couldn't even get anyone to go with me." I don't mention that Michael was the only other person I asked—he's swamped at the station, so we're hooking up tomorrow night. "But I promised Sydney I'd be there and, you know, bad friendship karma, so . . . Can I hear your stuff another night?"

"You love Sydney's shows."

"I know, but I could be working on sister-bride's veil or hearing your script. How's Thursday night?"

"Probably. Breakfast mañana?"

The theater in Santa Monica is a mob scene when I arrive. I am surprised at how momentous her opening night is, but I guess Sydney's film career distinguishes this from the normally ignored L.A. theater event. A local news crew is creating a vortex of hierarchy for everyone trying to get inside. The famous are stopped to comment toward the camera and smile, while the rest are passed over, our bodies so much scenery for the finery going by. The crowd conveys me into the auditorium, and I quickly jump out as it passes my seat's aisle. The chair beside mine is one of the few empty ones and its emptiness exudes a loud silence into the noisy air, informing everyone of the ticket left unused.

As people keep pouring in, I pick up the program to kill the remaining minutes before the show begins. I read Sydney's bio and the director's, glance at the credits of the musicians whom I know, then notice a list of people thanked for their help in making this show possible and am surprised to see my name on it—that was nice of her—near the top since they are alphabetically arranged. A woman jostles my leg as she sidles past me to reach her seat. The audience is mostly settled, just a few stragglers are wandering in. I turn back to the list to see if I know any other names on it when suddenly I get a strange sensation, like the building's about to explode. I turn around and in walks Andrew Madden, my ex-never-thought-I-could-breathe-without, whom I have not laid eyes on in almost four and a half years.

Oh, my God.

I immediately throw my program onto the floor so I can duck down to retrieve it, as chaotic gushing explodes in the theater. Andrew Madden is one of those particular people this town breeds who become internationally well-known. For almost four decades he has been a movie star, director, producer, studio head, and basic all-around grand Pooh-bah of

La-La-Land. I keep my head down near my feet in hopes that Andrew won't see me as he walks on by.

Please, dear God.

Audible commotion is erupting row by row, giving me a kind of auditory tracking system of Andrew's procession down the aisle, so I wait until it moves forward a safe distance before I finally peek my head up to look cautiously around. The back of Andrew's perfect head—and how is it possible for the back of a head to be so perfect?—is moving elegantly away from me, so I sit back in my seat, but hunched down low.

Thank you, God.

Okay, I'll be fine. He didn't see me, didn't even notice me. Now just stay down in the seat and pray that this horrible fiasco, all from helping a friend with her goddamn show, quickly ends—which it will. Then I can go home. Okay, just breathe. I'm all right—it's fine. Andrew didn't even notice me.

What is his fucking problem?

No, wrong reaction. Thank God he didn't notice me is how I feel. I don't want him to see me here by myself. It's good that he walked on by. But why couldn't Michael be with me? Damn his stupid radio shows. He should be here with his arm around me, all Mediterranean husband—I mean, handsome—next to Andrew's golden, incredibly fucking gorgeous-beyond-words looks. Michael who?

Fuck, that is not the right attitude. Not even how I really feel inside. It isn't? All right, stop. This is insanity. Big deal—Andrew's here. Who cares? Only every single other person in this theater. But not I. Andrew Madden—whoop-de-do. So he's here. I could care less. Here with Holly. His wife.

On the one hand, that pretty much says everything. On the other, this is the second time I have seen Holly, in person and live. I met her once years ago on the subway in New York, not long before I moved to California. I was with Tim, the man I was living with at that time, and she was with her husband—her first—and a female friend she would not stop hugging as the train rattled and swooped, stations passing by.

It was late at night, and the subway car was almost empty, so her husband easily spotted Tim when we boarded at the Houston Street stop. They had grown up together in the city; introductions were made all around. Holly lifted her head from the friend's shoulder, blond hair only then not hiding her face, and gave Tim and me a glance before putting her head back down. She had clearly been crying, but laughed for most of the ride, always leaned against her friend, as if clinging to the last known vestige of joy.

"She's drunk," Holly's husband mouthed to us as he stood above her, his hand on the rail steadying him. "Karen here is leaving tomorrow for a year in Australia," he went on in full voice.

Tim nodded as if that explained all, and smiled. Then the two of them caught up on each other's lives while I watched Holly cleave onto Karen. I don't think she was aware I was there, but I knew who she was from the local news stories she did, mostly movie premieres, fashion stuff, and celebrity interviews.

Our exit came before theirs. We said our goodbyes; Tim and Holly's husband promised to have lunch, Karen shook my hand, and Holly lolled against her more firmly—as if the departure of total strangers was too much a foreboding of what tomorrow held in store. When Tim and I were halfway across the platform, I heard through the still-open train doors a long trill of Holly's laughter descend into a distinctive wail; then the subway bell rang its two-note tone, the doors slid shut, and the train carried them off. The reverberation of that cry left me unsettled for days. Her husband had seemed like a nice man. I wondered what he was really like inside.

Anyway. Andrew and Holly have settled into their seats at the theater just a few rows in front of me and a little to the right. That's closer than I'd like, but safe, I decide, because I am completely out of their (Andrew's) view.

Okay, so I just need to make it to the lights going down, which should be any minute now, then the show will distract me, I hope, or at least keep me under the cover of darkness until it ends and I can get out and run. I am immediately grateful to Sydney for not having an intermission; at least I'm saved from that hellish interval of milling around. The outburst over Andrew has subsided to a low thrilling roar of whispers and nudges from an audience completely flustered since the most famous and talented performer is sitting among them and not appearing onstage.

The lights flicker once, then go back up, then flicker again. Just go down, lights, please, and plunge us into wonderful concealing darkness so I can't see Andrew and he can't see me and I don't have to look at Holly. Suddenly, as if my thoughts were his cue, Andrew turns around and looks at me.

Just looks at me. The way he used to gaze at me across his bed.

Then he waves. A fingers-up-and-down wave. Which I find odd, and wonder if it is a habit he picked up from his two kids. And still he is looking at me. A time-has-stopped look. A no-one-else-is-here look. Then he waves again. But I still haven't responded to his first wave, other than the fact that my eyes are unable to leave his. Unable to leave his the way the earth is unable to leave the sun. My hands feel glued to my lap and I am suddenly finding it very hard to get the muscles of my mouth to smile, and exactly what size smile do you use for an ex-never-thought-you-could-breathe-without anyway? I cannot figure this out, so I just kind of half-wave, half-cover my sort-of-smiling mouth and look away.

The houselights suddenly go down as if they were timed for him. Then Sydney comes on stage singing a big grand song and I try to stay focused on her, but I can't stop looking at Andrew. The patter Sydney does between the songs helps a bit, and her jokes are distracting to an extent, except that all I do during each one is compare when I laugh to when Holly does and try to figure out which one of us is more in sync with him. Then during what I guess would be called a "romantic number," Andrew's and Holly's heads lean toward each other in an aren't-we-enjoying-this-the-most-since-we're-married sort of way, which I have a strong little feeling is for my benefit. At least on his part. I have no doubt she doesn't even know who I am, much less that I am here.

Mercifully, the lights fall to complete darkness, signaling the show's end, then they come up bright, brighter, brightest for Sydney to receive her applause. The crowd is on its feet, clapping and whooping, and the audience between Andrew and me conveniently blocks my view of him, so his of me. The irritated looks I get from the people in my row as I trip and push past them to get out to the aisle as they try to keep applauding are worth the freedom I gain as I use this perfect chaotic moment to slip out.

The second I am outside the theater, I break into a run to my truck like I am being chased by banshees, then I quick get in, even locking the door behind me as if that will keep Andrew from seeing me from all the way inside. And Holly. That's an introduction I have no desire to repeat. Not that she'd remember me. Or that Andrew would even greet me in front of her, or offer an introduction. Though actually, he might. With him, who knows? He might think it'd be fine, no reason in the world not to.

Hightailing it out of the parking lot, thank you, Chevy engine, I remember that I was supposed to go to the opening-night party afterward, so I leave a "loved your show; can't—cough, cough—make the party" message at Sydney's home, so she'll know how sincere I am.

When I reach a secure distance from the theater in that barren part of the 10 near Centinela, I pull over to the shoulder, put my truck into park, and lift my hands to cover my face. I thought tears would come, but they don't. I am in too much shock.

There are moments right after something has happened to me, catalytic or catastrophic, when I am truly amazed that the physical objects in my life continue to look the same as they did before. Like when I was in the waiting room, right after the doctor told me and Suzanne that Momma had died, I could not believe that the hospital I was sitting in was still standing, hadn't shattered and crumbled to the ground, no longer able to hold itself up. "My entire world has just changed," I thought. "How can this physical object still be the same?" I figured maybe I had stumbled on a koan, one of those Zen Buddhist mysteries you meditate on, and supposedly after you sit still long enough, it reveals itself to you. The emptiness is revealed. You can finally see past the illusion into the truth. But I didn't know—I had never tried.

Sitting here on the side of the freeway with every privately held image of Andrew streaming through my brain, I'm just grateful my truck doesn't explode because it sure feels like my heart is going to.

Meeting Andrew for the first time was like getting pregnant—conception had occurred. And not unwittingly by me. Which is how I'd always thought it would be—to get pregnant. That somehow in that moment I would know. My body would know. And with Andrew, it did. I felt so deposited in. Like a bank. It made me wonder about withdrawals.

I was working and he was dining at a legendary restaurant in New York where I had managed to get a hostess job three months earlier, right after moving to the city at eighteen. "No daughter of mine will work as a waitress," Daddy had once said when Suzanne and I were young and the topic of future possible summer jobs came up. "Babysitting is just fine." Then he walked out of the room to go to his work shed to make another musical instrument, and that meant the subject was at an end. But I was all the way up north, it wasn't waitressing, and anyway, Daddy had been out of my life for four years at that point.

Andrew was sitting at one of a line of tables that jutted out from a wall of windows shimmering with the gold-draped chains that the restaurant used instead of blinds. Two catty-corner walls were of this: panels of glass sheathed with swings of delicate gold chains one on top of another, like a totem pole of invisible necks, the chains swinging and swaying against one another, then flinging their shine across the room to echo upon the opposite no-gold walls. Against this backdrop, Andrew sat. With two women. One was a famous actress; both were horrifically beautiful. He was on one side of the table; they were on the other.

The air around them seemed stunned. It created a special space; the molecular makeup of their force field was clearly different from that of the other diners—as if the air itself realized it was too coarse in its natural form for them, so had transmuted itself finer and sweeter for their delicate intake. Everyone could see this. The captain of their table, Jurgos, practically gasped each time he penetrated the circumference surrounding them, knowing instinctively that the air he needed to breathe was not like their own.

It was into this atmosphere that I was asked (told, really) to carry a phone—this being 1987. Something about a call and Bonnie Davis, a name I also recognized, but even if I hadn't, the urgency and importance with which Seamus, the Irish maître d', commanded me to do this—his brogue, already usually thick, now running all over itself—signaled its unusual significance. Which I found odd. Henry Kissinger, the Kennedys, and have-different-last-names-but-still-somehow-are-Kennedys, and all the New York gods ate here regularly, so why some silly movie star, for Christ's sake, was putting Seamus into such a state, I had no idea.

The dining room was full. It was a Saturday night, late August, meaning the habitués were in the Hamptons. The city cleared each summer weekend, and that was my favorite time. Getting off work at the end of the night—eleven, if I came on at four; twelve, if I started at five—I would walk most of the distance home. Set out on Park Avenue, but usually, quickly, take one of the blocks over to Madison or Fifth. Those were the best. They were deserted; literally, quite empty. Often I would walk in the middle of Fifth Avenue so I could see the odd bus or cab approaching as I headed downtown, and the buildings stood on each side of me like tall adults surrounding a child's first solo stroll, ready to reach out and hold me, if I were to fall. They felt mine in that dark, in that late-hour coolness, in that emptiness and uselessness they had at just those moments in time. Summer weekend nights made Manhattan a different country that I was able to enter by the sheer act of being there. I'd walk up Fifth, turn west at the park, and continue on, walking on the building side, passing the doormen at the restaurants and apartment buildings and hotels.

They were fighting when I got to the table. I was carrying the phone, the black streamlined (I think that model is called) phone with the funny push buttons on the receiver that were small and round and protruded like so many pegs. The dining room had the hushed buzz it would get—the vibrations of the diners' hopes and needs and desires and fears all rising, moving up over their heads until each voice met and mingled with the buzz of the others already there, then the hush would step in, blending them all together, and the gold swinging chains caught so many verbs and nouns that the words lay on them like air bubbles on a fisherman's net. I could only hear their conversation when I got up close.

"Because I don't want to," the famous actress, Lily Creed, said as I approached the table.

Andrew was looking down, fixing a forkful from his plate. A beautiful, fleshy pink meat from a lamb that once was small, had become smaller still, and now was being prepared smallest yet into calculated cuts to enter Andrew's mouth.

He stopped, mouth ready and open, fork midair, when he saw me. Then it all went back so quickly—lips together, hand down—but our first moment was that. Seeing him like that. Then it was gone.

I knew I knew him from before. Like a dream I didn't need to have, it was already so much a part of my sleep. So much that I didn't even know that part of him was me until I saw him. Looked him in the eyes. Mine on his. His on mine. Again. Because that's what it was—an Again. An "Oh, it's you," plus an "Oh, and that part of me I thought was me has been you. All this time, has been you."

"Is that for me?" Andrew said, looking into my eyes and able to see all inside me and all outside me all at once me.

It was clear in that moment that everything was for him, whether it was meant to be or not.

I had to answer but didn't know what to say. My mind had gone blank. I knew Seamus had said, "Take a phone to Mr. Madden's table—a call [something] Bonnie Davis." But I couldn't recall if he had said "from Bonnie Davis" or "for Bonnie Davis." That information had slipped away, as though my body had known ahead of time that something momentous was about to happen, and shut down my brain so it wouldn't get in the way.

But it did get in the way because the word was lost, the preposition was gone, my mind did not grasp its short sound. And it wasn't like I could turn around, go back to the maître d' stand, and say, "Seamus, hi, sorry, me again. Is this a phone call for Bonnie Davis? Or from Bonnie Davis?" That was not a possibility, so there I stood in front of them, holding the phone before me, clutched in both hands like some dead telecommunication bouquet.

Finally, I made a decision. "It's for Bonnie Davis,"

"For Bonnie Davis or from Bonnie Davis?" Andrew replied.

Jesus God, all of this because of one word. I just wanted to hide, but then I saw the smile in his eyes and heard the hint in his words replaying in my head.

"From Bonnie Davis, for you."

There was a pause. As if I had won. As if the contest were over and in one long, though barely perceptible, moment, we had shifted from crossing the finish line to celebrating the game.

"Thank you," he said, and looked at me with a smile held inside.

I rested the phone before him, then knelt down to plug in the cord. I had to crawl on the floor because the jack was underneath the table in the middle of their legs. Lily had daintily painted toes on huge feet. Now, I'm usually rotten at telling the size of anything, but I had to put my hand flat on the ground next to her shoe while I inserted the plug, so it was easy to determine the space her feet took up. They were huge.

The other woman was wearing clunky, closed-toe, hot-looking shoes of synthetic leather. I imagined neither of them thought while they were getting dressed that someone would be examining their feet from so close up. I figured Lily still would have chosen the strappy high-heeled sandals that she had on while the other woman maybe would not—they probably were stinky when she took them off. Andrew's black silk-socked feet were encased in black leather loafers; I could sense their desire to be free, like two large children swimming in inner tubes. I scooted out the step or two backward and stood up, sure that I was a mess.

I looked at Andrew again. I hadn't wanted to, because a small part of me has never stopped believing the one-year-old's truth that if I'm not looking at you, you can't see me. He had just said, "Bonnie," with the receiver to his ear, and I immediately pictured a lass wearing a full soft skirt, sitting on his knee with one arm around his neck and the other feeding him the lamb. Andrew turned back to me and slowly mouthed, "Thank you." His lips, teeth, and tongue formed each empty sound perfectly, trusting the air to transport and transform them into normal volume for me. I thought I should smile, but couldn't. It was like being stoned, when just thinking of a response makes me believe it somehow was instantaneously conveyed to the room. I think he got it, but I couldn't hang around to see. I figured Jurgos would soon notice me still standing there, so I walked away from Andrew.

My mind began its way with me on the walk down the long marble corridor back to the maître d' stand. *Oh, for Christ's sake, Yvette, you really are too much. Andrew Madden looking at you? Please. You are out of your mind and pigheaded to boot. No one is looking at you, missy-thing, in your polyester lime-green Nehru jacket uniform. You're practically a walking diaphragm against attractiveness, honey, he was not looking at you.*

But privately, away from that voice in my head, I thought of him constantly.

I thought of him so repeatedly that one week later, at seven-thirty as I went to take my dinner break at work, I wished it were the previous

Saturday night, right before I met him, so I could live it all over again. I took my plate to the private dining room behind the barroom where customers usually didn't eat on Saturday nights. When the three private dining rooms were full—during the fall social season or for Christmas parties—we were forced to take our employee meals in the hall, a long passageway that allowed for quick and hidden access from the kitchen to any one of the dining rooms. The few chairs not being used were lined up flush against the wall, like a no-view single-seat train that kept you in place, while waiters, table captains, and busboys streaked past, like the blur outside a windowpane, yelling to one another in the Romance and Slavic languages of their motherland. As I ate in the empty silence of the private dining room, I tried to imagine where Andrew was and who was holding his attention.

When I returned from my break, Seamus sent me down to the coat-check room, normally a prized position because there you could earn tips during your shift. Few to no people gave money for escorting them to their table or delivering a phone, and certainly not for writing down their reservation when they called, but coat-checking enabled us hosts and hostesses to dip into the pile of cash walking in the doors each night, from patrons whose monthly florist bills were the size of our monthly nuts.

Even though we weren't supposed to. The house got the tips, but the customers didn't know that; they assumed we did. They'd watch us working hard to keep their coats and scarves from falling on the floor; saw us smiling nicely as we handed their garments over after (usually) quickly locating them, so they'd gladly put a dollar or two down. The tips were then swept into a small square hole that had been cut into the top of the counter, and shot straight to the pockets of the owners via a locked strongbox. Except for the ones that we hid in our hands and surreptitiously slid into our pants pockets, being sure to take them out later to neatly fold since a bulge under the jacket uniform was a dead giveaway.

As was taking too much. We all went by a two-for-the-house, one-for-us rule of thumb mostly because of a notorious story about a former host who, on a freezing pre-Thanksgiving day in a burst of holiday-shopping need, took every single tip that graced the coat-room counter during an overflowingly full lunch shift. Unbeknownst to the host, the manager had emptied out the locked strongbox just that morning with the intention of doing a rare surprise check on it later that day. So when the manager found not even one lonely dime, he was forced to fire the host, as the thievery was too flagrant to ignore—which they did for the rest of us when we kept our take small. But that made it feel like the only ones who were really being duped were the customers, who kindly gave the tips thinking it was the hosts they were going to.

Lydia, another hostess, had explained the system to me on a rainy June evening about a week after I started working there when we were sent down to the coat-check room to work the early-dinner shift, which consisted of customers in from New Jersey and Elsewhere who arrived at six to eat from the fixed-price (meant to be cheap, but who are we kidding?) menu, then ran out by seventy-thirty to catch a cab for a Broadway show. So it was two time slots of hell. Once when they arrived and decloaked, and again when they descended en masse to be reclothed. Lydia had told me that night that she had no intention of handling all those drippy umbrellas and slimy raincoats without taking tips just to preserve my ignorance until they were sure I'd be cool. She wore her thick, strawberry-blond hair over one eye à la Veronica Lake, and would peer out the other eye under a perfectly groomed brow. She had moved to Europe with her mother when she was a small child, I was never able to ascertain why, and at five, she was put in a kindergarten in Germany though she didn't speak a word of the language. She said she'd always remember that year as bright shiny objects and finger paint smells mixed with harsh German sounds. I held out from taking tips for about a week, then joined in.

But in August, the clanging iron mechanical rack was empty, so there was nothing to do in the coat room but stand and smile politely as customers came in from the street, then direct them up the stairs. Unceasingly, first-time guests would point a hand and say, "Right upstairs?" As if my presence, a coat-room clerk, prevented them from taking action without my consent. This was doubly odd because other than the restrooms, there was nowhere else for them to go. I wondered if they believed that if they just stayed down there long enough, the entire restaurant would descend to them. I'd smile and say, "Straight up the stairs," and they would smile back as if they knew it all along, but had done me a favor by asking the way.

That Saturday night, I got to the coat room at twenty after eight, a perfect time to read a book or a magazine. The eight o'clock tables had arrived, the sixes had come and gone, the sevens hadn't left yet, and the nines still had forty minutes to arrive, so I was reading *The New Yorker,* a splurge of a subscription I had started the month before.

I had grown up reading the magazine in a family that had read it from when it was first published. The spacious attic-playroom of my grandmother's home in New Orleans was wallpapered with carefully cut and artfully applied covers of the magazine starting in 1925 and marching steadily along to 1953; then they stopped, but it was enough. I would stand for hours looking at them as a child. The different styles of the artists, each with their own separate worlds of the same universe, all on display for me to see. Rainy afternoons, of which New Orleans had plenty, found me with large drawing tablets and colored pencils, sketching my own versions of the scenes on the walls.

I was standing in the coat room with the left side of my body visible from the window and the other side hidden behind the wall. *The New Yorker* was held in my right hand so I could occasionally look out, nod, and smile if someone came through, then easily return to my place. I was in the middle of a lengthy article about bee-keeping written by a woman who wore long dresses with no underwear when she tended her hives, which I found brave and lonely somehow, when suddenly the awareness that I wasn't alone came over me. I averted my eyes from the page while lowering the magazine and looked up to find Andrew Madden standing in front of me with only the coat-check counter between us, as if he had been instantly dispatched from a celestial realm.

"The men's room is to the left." My mind was on automode, though I knew directions were not what he was after. I surreptitiously slid the magazine onto a shelf.

"Uh-huh, thank you. Are you Yvette Broussard?"

"Yes." The formal response came out on its own.

"I'm Andrew Madden."

I thrust my hand out before I knew what I was doing and he took it, spurring on the combined shock and habitual behavior I felt locked in. I pumped a couple of times with a firm grip, an I'm-responsible-loyal-and-hardworking, interviewing-for-a-job handshake and maybe I was. His hand felt wintergreen, freshening mine from the work it had done. I let go first and he looked surprised that I hadn't hung on.

"Nice to meet you," I said, finishing the routine and immediately understanding why it had been devised so long ago. I wanted to cling to formality like a dress whose straps had been cut to keep from being exposed.

"Are you an actress?"

"No." I hadn't lived in New York long enough at that point to know that that wasn't a strange question, nor did I understand that the predicate noun signified predictable dreams and, usually, eventually dreadful plan Bs. "I'm not."

"Do you want to be?"

It was palpable in that moment that he had given me a question legions craved from him. I watched his face after he offered it. An idol mask had slipped on and his features set themselves in a practiced, enigmatic openness.

"No." Then I smiled and shrugged. He clearly liked actresses, thought the profession a good job to have; I didn't want to appear rude.

"Oh." This seemed to escape without his consent because he followed it with a small little laugh. "Well, what are you, then, besides beautiful?"

Which made me blush. I didn't feel beautiful in that polyester lime-green uniform, and I didn't think of myself that way. With my father I had felt beautiful because he told me I was all the time, even though I figured he said it because I was his offspring, and with widow-man I had, but as a teenager around girls and boys my own age, I felt off, different, like my soul had been in a rush to get to earth, so had just grabbed the first face it saw, one left over from an earlier time, as if all the modern ones were off in a queue getting their magazine-styled, cheerleader-straight hair.

"Porcelain" and "cameo" are words I've heard to describe me—not such stuff as high school boys' dreams are made on.

"I'm an artist, a sculptor." I tried to ignore how absurd I felt saying this in Modern Art's hometown, and as a coat-check clerk, no less, though it had been worse in Mississippi. Back home, I could see in people's eyes the cute-kitten and sweet-puppy paintings they decided a girl artist would create. "Sugar pie, that's so nice," they'd say, patting my hand as if making a physical prayer to Jesus for his light to shine through my work.

One of Andrew's eyebrows shot up, and he lowered his chin to examine my face. I felt he was seeing every piece I had ever done.

"I'd like to help you."

He took no breath for a pause, but it existed nonetheless, disuniting everything preceding it and since.

"Call me tomorrow. I'm at the Ritz-Carlton Hotel. Will you do that, will you call me tomorrow?"

"Okay, but . . . What's your room number?"

Andrew smiled at me. Kindly. And it held me gently in place.

"Just say my name, Yvette, they know me."

I never wanted his smile to stop.

"Okay."

"Okay."

We looked at each other for a long moment, then he knocked on the counter between us twice with his forefinger crooked, like a substitute for the embrace that had begun.

"So I'll talk to you; we'll talk; I'll talk to you tomorrow. Right?"

I nodded.

"Bye, Yvette." And he turned and disappeared into the men's room just to the left.

There was a gasp in the air and in me. A loud but silent, all-encompassing "Oh my God" inhaled into space and body and mind. I was too excited to stand still, so I started walking a tiny track in front of the racks. An entire year's worth of experience had happened in that short exchange, and my mind was racing with its sounds and senses and smells. I noticed *The New Yorker* folded back to the article about bee-keeping. In that magazine, on that page, lay the sentence that was the point in time when Andrew Madden and I had met. I wanted to frame it. Every word I read henceforth would be infused with him. If I could read at all. My mind held only his words, a necklace of auditory pearls consisting of every syllable he had spoken, one I could listen to, look at, and hold.

Then I remembered he was still in the men's room. I immediately wished there was someplace else I could be, some option more elegant than being stuck in the coat-check room with the lime-green of my uniform vibrating off my body, a strong signal from the lighthouse of my nonexistent art career. I paced a bit more, than decided my only real choice was just to stand behind the counter as nonchalantly as I could.

Andrew emerged from the men's room, wagging his finger at me as he walked across the lobby's marble floor. "Ritz-Carlton Hotel, tomorrow; don't forget."

I smiled. A smile I had never smiled before. A smile attached to a retractable cord that he had installed inside me, that pulled out and grew more taut with each step he took up the stairs, only able to snap back and coil up by talking to him again.

I wouldn't forget. Was he kidding? I couldn't wait.

8

The minute Andrew disappeared up the stairs, my body jumped in the air. Jumped and lit up, about to explode. Fireworks were inside me lighting up my internal sky. Andrew Madden spoke to me. Came up to me, knew my name, said my name, spoke my name in his voice, which only belonged to him, but now a little bit to me, as well. Andrew Madden spoke to me.

I wanted to pretend he had intuited my name all on his own. Could tell just by looking at me the way he seemed to know me already so well, but it was Seamus, I was sure, who had told him. Then I wondered if any of the other hosts had been standing nearby when that information was exchanged. I didn't want them to know, wanted to keep this between Andrew and me (and Seamus, unfortunately), not become fodder for the restaurant's gossip mill. I started to go over in my head who was working that night and who might have been where, then I gave up. All

I wanted to do was relive over and over Andrew's voice in my ears, his eyes locked on mine, his body so near. When customers came in, I tore my thoughts away long enough to look at them. It was easy to smile, joy flowed out of me in waves. Then I'd start the reliving all over again: the moment I realized I wasn't alone, the looking up and seeing him, my eyes drawn directly to his, his first words to me, and mine to him . . .

And he wanted to help me. Oh, my God. I couldn't even imagine what he wanted to do, how he meant to, but just that phrase—"I want to help you"—was so astonishing, so extraordinary, so giving me a ring. "I want to help you." It was all I could do not to scream in exhilaration.

Then I realized that Andrew would have to come through the lobby again to leave. He must have arrived while I was on break, so that would mean the end of his meal should be soon and I'd get to see him again! One more time until . . . Tomorrow, maybe? It felt like we had a date. Him telling me to call, but also something else. Oh, my God, just to see his face again looking at me and mine at him.

But what if Lily Creed or that other woman was with him? Oh, no. Well, even so, they were probably just friends. They'd have to be or he wouldn't have come down to see me. Okay, so it didn't matter if they were with him or not. I hoped. I wished time would jump to either Sunday, when I could call him, or back to forty minutes ago, when he was standing there. Either one, but just me and him.

After almost an hour of alternately wondering why Andrew hadn't appeared and envisioning all kinds of dreamy scenarios between us, another host came downstairs to the coat room.

"Seamus wants you up at the stand," Tommy said. He was from Queens and was working his way through John Jay College studying criminal law. "Had a good time in here?" He nudged me hard on the arm as I tried to walk by.

"No," I said, pushing my way past. "It was boring, like it always is."

"Yeah, a certain someone boring into you," he said, and leered at me.

Oh, God, of all people to know about Andrew. Tommy was the weird little brother my parents thankfully never had. He was constantly making homoerotic jokes with two waiters from Yugoslavia, and I found that odd since his girlfriend waited for him every weekend night after work. I hoped he wouldn't include this in his repertoire.

Up the same stairs where Andrew had walked, I walked—if my body being propelled forward by sheer ecstasy could be called that—into the bar dining room where I took my place against the wall next to the maître d' stand. Another hostess was there waiting to transport customers to their table like some benevolent version of the boat in that Greek myth, ferrying people to the Kingdom of the Dead. She was new and looked overwhelmed. It was her first Saturday night, and I remembered what it was like in the beginning, trying to quickly figure out the system and how it all worked. Seamus probably had her taking as many tables as possible to get her broken in, so maybe only Tommy might blab. But then again, even if he did, who cared? Surely none of them. Andrew was just some Hollywood actor, for Christ's sake. What was I worrying about?

But it was all I could do to stay still and not dance around the large room. It was as if a group of fourteen-year-old girls had taken over my insides. They were giggling, whispering, and screaming their swooning delight. Maybe Andrew was about to come through! Would he look at me again? Smile? Transmit a secret message to me with his eyes? Andrew, please walk by.

The cavernous wood-paneled barroom was dimly lit, like a stage whose main spotlight had been left off. Seamus hadn't looked at me once—just kept his head bowed, looking down. He was built like a boxer beyond his prime, with a face that wasn't handsome but one you were glad to look at. Usually he was flirty in an avuncular way, so I figured he was having one of his wretched nights. Seamus would have Henry, the Scottish bartender, fix him "tea" in a glass that was mostly whiskey, then keep it just inside the kitchen door to sip on with a few fast puffs off a cigarette in between arriving customers. A wretched night was one that allowed little opportunity for that.

Footsteps were approaching down the long marble hall that led from the main dining room to the bar. Maybe Andrew! I kept my head turned away so I wouldn't be looking straight at him, but could turn, see him, and pretend to be surprised. Oh, you hadn't left yet?

Closer and closer the footsteps came until the last tattooing on the hard marble floor was heard, then steps were taken on the barroom's deep carpeted plush. I turned to look, ready to catch his eye, but an elderly couple had emerged into the shallow light. Goddammit. The fourteen-year-old girls inside me were silenced as the couple bid good night to Seamus, and he sputtered a goodbye to them with his Irish charm. So where was Andrew? He must still be in the dining room, having some marathon meal. Okay, at least he's still near, still able to be seen again. I'll just be sure to ferry the next party into the dining room so that I can.

A party of four came up the stairs; the men in dark suits, the women wearing Chanel. It was clear that only one of the couples had eaten in the restaurant before. One of the women was looking around as the other kept a running commentary in her ear. The taller man walked with authority up to the maître d' stand and gave Seamus his name, while the other stood back but away from the wives, who were admiring the large brass mobile hanging over the bar, a waterfall of shimmer dripping in the low light.

I practically jumped forward to get in place to take them, almost bumped Seamus's arm as he checked the slip of paper that was prepared for each party—table number, number of persons, if they were VIP, birthday cake, anything the captain needed to know—but Seamus deliberately handed the slip to the new hostess, signaling her to take the foursome away. My face openly fell, but Seamus was too busy heightening his accent to the realm of leprechauns (he got bigger tips that way), as he told the party to enjoy their meal, to notice my expression.

I sank back toward the wall, even allowed myself to lean against it for a moment, before the words of the manager, Mr. Claitor, snapped in my head, "No slouching! Haven't you got a spine?" Then he'd smile, which should have been anemic considering its size, but it could melt your insides. I stood up straight and away from the dark wood paneling. Seamus was busying himself with the remaining slips of paper that indicated how many more parties were arriving that night. I watched his large, stubby fingers move them around with practiced speed, this one to there, that one next, as I wished I was in the other room seeing Andrew. Which is when I saw them. Next to the slips of paper lay the keys for the side door; the door used only by special people who needed to avoid the paparazzi waiting for them outside the main entrance. Seamus had already helped Andrew secretly leave.

"Andrew Madden speak to you?" Seamus's dark eyes darted over to me before glancing off, as if checking to make sure he was right about what I had been thinking at exactly that moment. It was funny that the name had become Andrew Madden—funnier even in Seamus's brogue. Just last week it was Mr. Madden, as if now Seamus felt one step closer to a personal connection with him. I wondered if soon it'd be Andy.

"I told him your name. He came up to me, asked about you. Wanted to know your name, where you were from, and if you were here. So, he did talk to you." Seamus nodded his head twice, as if he didn't need me in this conversation. "Don't worry, I won't tell anyone." Then he looked at me and grinned before turning around and walking through the swinging kitchen door. I imagined the striking of his match burning bright in the all-white kitchen.

I wanted to ask how he knew that I wanted no one else to know, but by the time Seamus came back out smelling of cigarettes and whiskey, the new hostess had arrived from the dining room, the dining room that no longer held anyone of interest. Seamus gave me a quick wink, then periodically grinned in my direction for the rest of the night. I felt like I was fourteen, had just gotten my period, and the boy's gym coach, of all people, had found a pad for me—uncomfortable with, but grateful for, our inappropriate alliance.

One of my roommates, Carrie, was still awake when I got home after work. She was also from Mississippi, a school friend of Suzanne's, and I had found the apartment through her—a terrible three-bedroom on the Upper way-past-the-good-part West Side with rent cheap enough for me to afford. Another woman, Ruth, lived there, in fact had the lease and the biggest bedroom with the cheapest rent, I had a feeling. Ruth was a musical-comedy performer, as she described herself, and was constantly going off on cruise ships for months at a time, subletting her room to an endless line of performers she had met on the ships who wanted to try their luck on the Great White Way. It sounded exhausting. I had a tiny pantry-sized room in the back behind the kitchen that provided no space for my art—other than sitting on my bed and sketching—but it was a place to sleep.

And since I was so new to New York, sleep was the only familiar landscape in my life—my dreams were a visual refuge for me. Though one night right after I moved in, as I was succumbing to slumber on the twin bed I had bought on Broadway at 108th—the salesman's Puerto Rican accent more at home in the city than my Southern one, him waving off the delivery fee as a welcome gift to the city—I felt a small weight on my foot. I instinctively flicked my ankle, then heard a soft thud and the scamper of claws on linoleum floor. Immediately, I was up, running and screaming through the apartment to the living room couch where I hopped from cushion to cushion, still screaming. Carrie and Ruth came tearing out of their rooms in the front of the apartment, and Carrie bounded on to the sofa when she heard "Mouse!" But Ruth dismissed us with "I can't believe you two are so afraid of that," and went back to bed in her far-away-from-the-rodents room, though I noticed she didn't protest when Carrie came home the next day with a cat.

"How was work?" Carrie asked that Saturday night when I walked in. She was sitting with her back to me on the uneven and pocked living room hardwood floor teasing her cat with a small doll on a string. She had decided to train it to dislike everyone else, though I wasn't sure how the doll would accomplish that. The whole thing infuriated Ruth, but maybe that was the point. I liked the cat, liked having another living thing in the apartment that was smaller than me who needed care, feeling myself sometimes like a cat the city had taken in but wasn't doing a very good job of keeping. A half-empty bottle of wine and a small carton of milk sat beside Carrie on the floor.

Her question was perfunctory. She didn't mind hearing, so was glad to ask, but I could tell it was said as an intro to "good night." Carrie worked at an answering service for a psychiatry practice and had many tales to tell of Upper East Side traumas the patients called in crisis about.

"It was good." I hadn't crossed through the room yet, was still standing in the hall doorway watching her cat leap and flip through the air, a feline ballet. "I met Andrew Madden tonight."

"You what?" Carrie's short blond hair fanned out à la Dorothy Hamill as she snapped her head around to face me, pulling the doll too far away from the cat as she did. The cat jumped at it, but grandly missed, swiping at the air, as if a tree would miraculously appear that she could slide down to brace her fall.

"I met Andrew Madden." The cat banged to the floor, then got up and nonchalantly walked a few steps as if it that were part of her plan.

"Oh, my God." Carrie was staring at me so oddly that I wondered if my hair had taken on some strange shape during my walk and bus ride home, but I decided to ignore it because I was finally with someone I could tell.

"I know, it's pretty wild, but he's really sweet, and he wants me to call him tomorrow at his hotel, and oh, my God, he's so incredibly gorgeous, and I've only seen one of his films, but it was like I've known him my whole life, and he said he wants to help me, though God knows what that means, and he had asked the maître d' about me, then came down—"

"This is going to change your life," Carrie said in a low serious tone, her blue eyes searching mine to see if I understood.

"Well, I don't know about that." The color on my face deepened. "I mean, okay, he said he wanted to help me, which is really sweet, but what can he do? Pay for some classes? Which would be great actually, but I mean, you know, he's just some Hollywood actor movie star person."

"Just some movie star person," Carrie yelled, making the cat run under the couch. "Honey, Andrew Madden is also a producer and a director; he's won Academy Awards; runs a studio; and here's where you come in, he's also a renowned collector of contemporary art."

"Oh."

"Oh, yes." Carrie stood up and seemed to tower over me even from her shorter height. "Andrew Madden is not just some stupid movie star, honey; he's practically his own industry."

"Oh." I had to look away from her, as if the key to my understanding all this was on the other side of the room, but Carrie kept staring at me so I met her eyes again. "Wow."

"Exactly. Here." Carrie picked up the bottle of wine and handed it me. I looked at it for a moment before realizing I needed a glass. I went to the kitchen for the one I had moved with, had packed among my socks and underwear. I had also brought a fifth of Jack Daniel's and a bottle of Kahlúa that my cousin Renée and I made one afternoon from vodka and coffee. It was weeks after I unpacked that it struck me I must have thought it would be hard to find liquor stores, but in the neighborhood I had moved into, there was one practically on every corner.

"Tell me, tell me, tell me. I want to hear everything," Carrie said as I came back in the living room and sank onto the couch. She had refilled her glass and lit a fresh cigarette from an almost empty pack.

"Well, I was standing in the coat-check room and suddenly he was just there, saying my name, asking what I'm doing, and telling me to call him tomorrow at the Ritz-Carlton Hotel." Telling Carrie, finally saying it out loud, made it real. Real in my apartment and in my life, and not just in my head.

"You've been discovered," Carrie squealed, and her cat ran out from under the couch and flew out of the room.

Like America. I just hoped with the same lasting results.

9

The next day Carrie was meeting friends at the Cloisters, thank God, because the last thing I wanted was her on the other side of the curtain that I used as a bedroom door, listening to my conversation with Andrew so she and I could talk about it more easily afterward—her suggestion. I assured her I could never make the call that way but promised I'd remember every detail. Ruth was at a rehearsal for a showcase she was doing in Queens. Whenever I imagined her singing, it was always with an immobile smile on her face and her arms high in a triumphant V before she moved into the next lyrically specific choreography.

I sat down in my tiny room on the twin bed, the only size that would fit in the space, with the telephone book on my lap. I had decided to call Andrew at two. It definitely felt like an afternoon thing to do. One o'clock seemed desperate and three, lazy; so I picked two. Or ten after. On the hour would appear too obvious. It was almost ten after, so

I decided to give it just a few more minutes. And hopefully breathe for a bit, too.

I tried to think about how he had looked standing in front of me at the coat-check counter, to see if that would make calling him easier, make it feel like a normal thing to do, but that only made my heart beat faster.

Okay, it was time. As I looked up the Ritz-Carlton Hotel in the phone book, my hands like a stranger's doing a task of their own, I thought of my walk home from work the night before when I passed Andrew's hotel on Central Park South as I did every time I walked home, the large red square carpet that took up most of the sidewalk, the two epauletted, gold-buttoned doormen in front. Now it all meant something different. It was where Andrew was. And had been for how long? How many nights had I passed that building never knowing it housed him? Walking past his hotel last night and peering in, I had thought how simple it would be to go in and ask for the phone number, or at least nab a packet of matches that surely would have it. I imagined going up to the front desk and saying, "I need to call Andrew Madden here tomorrow, what's the phone number?" As if by connecting to his hotel early, I was connecting to him.

"Good afternoon, the Ritz-Carlton, how may I direct your call?" The voice was elderly in a formidable way, not weak and kick over-able.

"Mr. Madden's room, please." I tried to say it like I said it a lot, said it so much that I could do something else while I said it, said it and barely knew I was saying it. I tried to say it like that.

"Who may I say is calling?"

I wasn't prepared for that. Not that I didn't have the answer, but that question never entered my head in the zillion times I had practiced this.

"Yvette Broussard." I was afraid to not give my last name. Not that there were so many Yvettes calling him, although there might be a curious run on the name, but the operator sounded so officious that it was clear only one name would never do.

"One moment, please, I'll check."

Check? That sounded ominous. At least from her it did. She put me on hold, leaving me no idea what to do with the empty, controlled time. I pictured the hotel where it stood across the street from the southernmost part of Central Park. The hotel my call was buzzing through, on hold but still viable, while the operator did what? How long could it take to put my call through? I was waiting in telephonic purgatory.

There was a small pulsing noise on the line, the hotel's hold sound, rhythmic and thrilling, like step after step after step up a ladder to the high dive. I wondered what view Andrew Madden's window had that he might be gazing through. Or, oh God, maybe he wasn't there. Maybe I should have called earlier, maybe he meant this morning, and I had messed up. God, I hoped he was at his hotel. The nicest one I'd ever been in was the Monteleon, a century-old hotel in the French Quarter. My parents would take us there on special weekend trips when we didn't stay with one of the many relatives that city was filled with. I supposed Andrew's room at the Ritz-Carlton was a whole lot nicer than the ones at the Monteleon in a Yankee definition-of-luxury way.

"This is Andrew." His voice suddenly was in my ear, curling up in my head. I jumped, thinking for a second he had somehow appeared.

"Hi," I said, regaining my composure. "It's Yvette." He had used his first name, to direct me as to how to address him. I wondered if the operator had told him that I had asked for Mr. Madden.

"Yvette." He said my name as if he had been speaking it my entire life. "Yvette, Yvette." Fluid and comfortable and mellifluous. His voice made the two syllables more familiar while placing them in an atmosphere they had never before been, yet were at home. It was exhilarating. "Yvette from Pass Christian, Mississippi."

"How'd you know how to say it right?" My accent became happily heavier hearing him speak the name of my hometown.

"I did a movie down there once." His words sounded muffled.

"Oh."

I had a vague recollection of the one he meant, but I had never seen it. He might as well have referred to the Napoleonic Wars—I had the same uncomfortable sense that I should know much more about the topic than I did, but fortunately, he didn't pursue it. I had never been a big movie buff. When we were growing up, Momma rarely took us. *Bambi* had been too traumatic for her and that apparently sealed the fate for all the rest. By the time I was able to get out of the house on my own, a local bar or an illicit trip to the French Quarter held much more interest than images projected in the dark. Though I had a feeling my own little private video festival of Andrew's films was about to start.

"And, and, and . . . How old are you?"

"Eighteen."

"Eighteen." Andrew whistled. "Do you know what age I am?"

"No."

"Forty-seven."

I wasn't sure what I was supposed to do with that. Feel different? Hang up? As if there were a cutoff point. Widow-man was seventeen years older than me; twenty-nine didn't seem that much further a leap. "That's nice."

Which made him laugh, a lying-back-on-the-bed, chest-and-stomach laugh. I could almost feel how he looked.

"You are so fucking cute." I had never much liked the word "cute" before, but I sure did now. "How did you get so fucking cute?"

It was exquisitely embarrassing. I felt enveloped in his warm brightness, all of me by all of him, even places in me that I hadn't known before. Who had ever thought I was cute? Not me, not anyone, yet there he was naming and claiming and moving things aside to show me what was underneath.

"Tell me, I want to know . . ."

And then there was silence. For a long moment I worried the phone line had been cut. I was just about to say "Hello?" when . . .

"What are Momma and Daddy like?"

"They're, uh . . . How'd you know—"

"You're from the South; you say Momma and Daddy. I still call my parents that. Years ago my brother started saying 'Mother' and 'Father,' but that to me sounded—"

"Pretentious."

"Exactly."

"I know, my sister tries to remember to call them that, too. I think it's silly."

"What are they like?"

For so long, no one had asked. Parents in New York City seemed as evolutionarily unnecessary as wisdom teeth, and my friends in high school had had no interest in mine just as I didn't in theirs probably because we could see how they were, our parent's behavior marked our bodies like we were little Indians wearing the war paint or peace headdress of our tribe.

"Well, Momma doesn't talk, and Daddy just sort of . . . left years ago."

"Left? Where'd he go?"

"Sarasota, I think. That's in Florida. Momma heard from Cousin Elsie, a woman she hadn't talked to in years, just one day out of the blue gets this call from her that she was sure she saw Paul—that's my daddy—with some woman from the North, who had moved down there, and was making a career of buying rundown houses, fixing them up spit 'n' polish nice, then selling them for double the money, saw them at the Heart Ball out on the dance floor, him foxtrotting this woman like he had my momma at their wedding all those years ago, and what did she think about that? Like my momma would be surprised to know he wasn't in Pass Christian. Like my momma thought he was out in the backyard straightening up his tools one more time on the Peg-Board he put up to keep them in a row."

"When was this?"

"When she called or when he left?"

"Both."

"He left when I was fourteen. Momma heard that news a couple of years later, then got divorce papers in the mail."

"And . . ."

Another tremendous pause that had enough time in it for me to jump out of my skin, but at least I knew it wasn't the phone line.

"And what was he like before?"

"He was . . ." I had been gulping for air, so I tried to breathe through my nose for a second to slow the intake. "He was . . . what the Gulf took her cue from every night to bring the tide in, is what he was. He was my daddy."

And again there was quiet on the line and I felt as if Andrew's light, which had been surrounding me, had receded a bit, leaving me in a hollow of nonbrightness.

"He must be a very sad man to have left a daughter like you."

"Oh."

"You never thought of that?"

"No."

"Of course he is."

"Oh." And Andrew's light came racing back to envelop me.

"And Momma doesn't talk? Why not?"

"I guess so she won't scream. No, I don't know. She was normal enough before, but when Daddy left, she took to her room and really kind of rarely comes out, and of course, how much is there to say if you're looking at the same walls all day?"

I waited to see how Andrew would respond, but there was more of that silence, so I continued. "Though I guess she could find something, but she doesn't, it's like she just crumpled up, and pale as hell, as you can imagine, like a Kleenex, all soft and white and unwilling to stand unless she's propped up."

"Hmmm," Andrew said. That was followed by another long pause, which didn't bother me as much because it had felt good to get all that out. Suzanne had stopped trying to get Momma to talk once she took off for USC a few months after Daddy left. She'd just send a letter home from California to Momma every month, the stamp and postmark from a world where truant parents could be dealt with by mail, and every time I'd try to talk to Suzanne about it on the phone, she'd say, "I can neither save nor fix Mother," and change the subject.

"And you express yourself nonverbally like she's doing, but creatively—which is healthy and has a point. I can't wait to see your work."

It was like he had taken hold of my hands from deep inside where the muscles and sinew meet the bone to become the part of me that gets things done and greets life and feeds myself and puts clothes on; as if he had taken my hands so they could do all of that while he never let them go.

And we talked about Suzanne, and Ruth, and Carrie, and widow-man, and two more hours went by.

"When are you going to get here?" Andrew suddenly said. We had been residing together on a plane that hovered above our phones, wrapped in voice-filled, time-jumbled prose, so it was a jolt to think of seeing him live and real.

"I can come over now."

"I'll call you right back." He sounded suddenly in a rush. "I have to meet with some people for a little bit, but . . ." Then his voice dropped down to a place inside of me that no one's voice had ever been, as if he had built a door without my knowing it and now had the key to get in. "You'd better be there when I call because I want to see you tonight, is that clear?"

"Okay." The word must have fluttered through the line to him, it was so inseparable from my grin, and I gave my number to him.

"Good. I'll call you back."

"Okay, bye."

I hung up the phone and kept my hand on it for a while, my skin that touched it connecting me still to him where his voice had just been. I was going to see him tonight, oh, my God. I wanted to jump up, run through the hall, bang on Carrie's door, and tell her about the call, but she was still gone.

I felt deliriously separate from my surroundings and ensconced in the bubble of Andrew's attention, like I could glide forth without touching earth. I stood up and looked in the mirror I had propped on the two-legged side of a three-legged table that I had found on the street. I had pushed it up to the wall under the window, hoping that would support it, and if I didn't put too much weight on that corner, it did okay. I turned my face this way and that in the mirror, trying to imagine what Andrew saw in me, trying to see myself as if I were him, but I couldn't.

And what should I wear? I turned to study my clothes hanging against the wall on a rod that had been attached with a shelf built on top. I literally was living in a closet.

As I flipped through the clothes, increasingly disliking each one, I remembered how Lily Creed had looked at Andrew's table. She was perfection. Her dress was like the Venus de Milo's shell—supporting her form and heralding her beauty while adding the loveliest touch so that your eyes were continually drawn to her bare arms and neck and face. I had nothing remotely like that.

The bubble I was in, the image of my perfect night with Andrew, was about to burst, teetering as it was on a rocky precipice. I stared at my clothes, willing them to transform into something fabulous. They stubbornly would not metamorphose. I considered going down Columbus Avenue about twenty-five blocks to the fabulous part and splurging on a new outfit, maybe even going to Charivari, practicality be damned, but I was trying to save up money for art supplies and to rent some space in a loft, and Andrew had wanted to meet me when I was wearing a polyester lime-green uniform, for God's sake, so I decided not to worry about it. I put on an outfit I hadn't conjured up before: black leggings, black corset-style tank top, and a black open-weave pullover, then began the wait.

I sat on my bed. I looked at the phone. I worried that the ringer had inexplicably died. I considered going into Carrie's room—not Ruth's, she somehow would know—to use her phone to dial mine, but what if Andrew happened to call at exactly the same time, got a busy signal, and never called again? It wasn't worth the risk.

I had forgotten to phone Momma that morning because calling Andrew had taken up all of my mind's space, but the week before when I rang her, she had just gotten home from mass, as I had known she would, and was preparing her lunch. She sounded surprised to hear from me, like she always did, as though I hadn't been calling every Sunday since I moved. Like she'd had a daughter once, but that was in the distant past, though given enough time, she would play along in this pretend parental role. Every week, I would ask the same questions, desperately trying to come up with new and improved ones that would inspire conversation. Few did.

Though one time I did get to hear a few sentences about the art league tea she would not be attending that afternoon. Not that she hadn't been invited. My momma was famous for changing her mind. No event was etched in stone; any and all could be canceled, missed, reneged on at a moment's notice. Clothes and/or fatigue were the usual reasons. "I just need to *sleep*!" she'd say, as if the occasion had been specifically coordinated to conflict with her REM time, or the outfit so laboriously planned had unaccountably fallen from grace.

I didn't want to read a book or fix a meal or do anything really for fear that my involvement in a task would somehow send repeated signals of "unavailable" to Andrew, reaching him no matter where he was and preventing him from calling me.

An hour and a half went by. Still I waited for Andrew to call. I felt hungry and internally cold, even though it was hot as Hades outside. I stared out the open window in my room that led to a fire escape overlooking an alleyway between buildings that were shouldered closer together than any I had ever seen. Refuse and trash from decades past formed a giant mound. Had it ever been nice? Or did this neighborhood immediately sink into disrespect and despair, fulfilling an unspoken obligation for the city to cover all points on the socioeconomic spectrum. Smells of pork and spices from the neighbors' all-day meal drifted in. On summer weekends, with music blasting, they used a makeshift grill on their fire escape to barbecue all kinds of meat in sauces I was sure I'd never tasted. A couple of weeks after moving in, I had told Suzanne on the phone what it was like—she in Beverly Hills living with her boyfriend—and she had sent me a letter exhorting me to embrace the

Puerto Rican culture and indulge myself in their music and food. My sister, sometimes, is out of her mind. My neighbors had as little interest in my embracing their culture as I did. I felt alien enough in New York City without adding a language I couldn't speak, food I couldn't digest (had she forgotten I was vegetarian?), and music I couldn't dance to. Beneath the clamor of their barbecue, my apartment was still. The cat was probably sleeping in Ruth's loft, gravitating naturally to the spot she was wanted least.

Two more hours went by. Carrie still had not returned home. Ruth was burrowing in her room while Chinese food aromas and Mitzi Gaynor's voice wafted from her confines. The cat had been duly ejected. I was hungrier. And felt stale, like a piece of bread taken out to make a sandwich then forgotten, my surfaces resistant instead of soft.

"What are you doing?"

I had known it would be Andrew when I said hello. Had known it would be him when the phone finally, thankfully, mercifully rang a little after nine P.M. But his voice sounded altered from before; it was on a more intimate note than our first phone call had ended on.

I didn't know what to say. "Waiting for you" or "Hoping to die if you didn't call" did not seem appropriate, though accurate they were. Nor did I have anything fabulous, exciting, or even mildly interesting to report from the four and a half hours I had just lived through without him. There was nothing really, so a gap appeared on the line like a Nixonian tape, just blank.

"Umm, I'm . . ." I got that out, then noticed how similar they sounded in my accent while hoping more words would magically materialize, but Andrew rescued me, ending the conversational flummox.

"Why aren't you here yet?"

He said it so seriously that for a second I forgot he had only just called and wondered at my own delinquency before I remembered the sequence of events.

"I will be."

"Will be?"

"Ten minutes."

"Good."

We hung up.

The cab driver didn't flinch when I gave him the Ritz-Carlton's address, so I tried to borrow his nonchalance. Taking a taxi was extravagant enough without getting all I could from it. I wasn't surprised that I was nervous; what surprised me was that I wasn't nervous in any way I had ever been before. I felt keyed up and able to notice each moment and detail as if I were reading microfilm, so much information compacted in such a small space, yet able to be seen.

After crossing the iron curtain of my neighborhood and shuttling down Columbus Avenue, we passed brightly beckoning restaurants with clusters of customers in front talking and gesturing. They looked crucial to the neighborhood, an integral part of this Sunday summer night, sustaining the avenue as it stretched south toward Midtown.

The Ritz-Carlton Hotel announced itself in gold letters above an ever-revolving door and again with its logo, the regal profile of a lion's head, on a red carpet that flaunted itself across the sidewalk to the curb.

"Welcome to the Ritz-Carlton," the doorman said, as he held open the cab door while I counted out the bills, then put them in the driver's hand. He asked if I had any bags in the trunk, and I wished for a moment that I did. Luggage to spend my life with Andrew.

I had to request his room number. He hadn't told me on the phone and I had forgotten to ask, but as the front desk clerk called to get Andrew's permission for me to ascend, I realized they wouldn't have allowed me to walk in and go straight up without announcing myself first anyway. I wondered if this was the sort of experience that induced all those restaurant customers to speak to me in the coat-check room before they headed upstairs. I immediately felt less churlish toward them.

The elevator I took to the twenty-eighth floor was filled with an empty quiet. I had never been here before. Not just here-here, in the hotel, but Here, with everything that entailed. There was no reference in my life for it, so my mind had no idea what to think. It was experiencing a rare phenomenon, the completely new event, and my lack of knowledge of the circumstances I found myself in felt freeing. There was nothing for me to do. Nothing for me to think. Nothing but to give in. A bell chimed, the doors glided open, and I was released into a small hallway that contained the entrance to Andrew's penthouse door. I knocked.

I could hear footsteps approaching after what was probably a three-Mississippi wait, if I had been counting, which I wasn't, but I knew it instinctingly becase of all those games of hide-and-seek I had played with the other neighborhood kids, hands covering closed eyes, counting off numbers plus our state's name up to ten to give everyone time to find a spot. I had a sudden vision of a young Andrew being a master at that game.

Then he opened the door and we looked at each other without saying a word. It was different seeing him after our journeylike phone call and the subsequent hours I'd spent with him in my head. As his eyes looked at mine, it was clear that a part of him was all for me, as all of me was for a part of him, like a branch's relationship to the trunk of a tree.

"Hi." He barely said it; the word was fractionally formed.

I moved into his arms. Our embrace was the ending and the beginning and we stood still in the middle. Andrew had such solid arms. Arms you wanted to detach and keep and connect around you again and again, an armor of amour, every bit of sinew and muscle and skin involved in his holding. And tall. His shoulder was at the bridge of my nose, providing many options to lay my cheek against. I forgot we had to let go.

He kept one hand across the small of my back as he walked me into the suite's large living room. And I had been imagining him in one hotel room. Good Lord. At least I had been right about the Yankee-luxury part; this definitely was more extravagant than the Monteleon. It looked like an extremely upscale apartment vacuumed free of "home." Andrew steered me to a yellow silk couch that I sank into as we sat down. He took my chin in his hand and turned my head this way and that. It felt more supported than it did on my own neck.

"Look at you. You're perfect."

I really felt I was not, but his voice was so strong and radically different than the one in my head that the shouts of protest became disarmed.

"Do you know how many beautiful women I've seen? You—are—per-fect."

And he started talking, saying long things, trains of thought about himself that had to do with me, and his words became physical, bathing me, swirling around, lulling me into a state of relaxed happiness I had never known.

Then he paused for a moment and looked at me. "I'm going to be in your life for a very long time. I've been waiting for someone like you." And he paused again, making sure I had heard.

"Thank God," was what I thunderously heard in my head. Thank God, thank God, thank God. Because the empty space in me perfectly matched the empty space in him, and for some inexplicable reason, the two empties together made one whole, like that weird math rule where you subtract twice, but still end up getting an addition, which in class I could never understand, but now here it was in the form of him.

The sex lasted a couple of hours. I undressed in the living room's light before walking into his bedroom, disrobing as easily as removing a cap that had squished my hair for too long. We were on the bed, a bed whose multitudinous softness I couldn't before have imagined, and we moved together in the immense dense darkness that only hotel rooms have. I liked the blankness of the dark, the sole reliance on form and smell and sound and skin.

At one point, Andrew reached over me and turned on a lamp. I had no idea which way we were on the bed and was surprised at how accurately he had located the switch. In the golden light, he looked into my eyes.

"This is how you know I'm not just fucking you, that I'm making love to you." And his eyes stayed on mine as he moved.

Then he nestled against me, saying something small and low at the bottom of my ear.

"What?"

"You heard me."

"No I didn't or I wouldn't've said 'what.' What'd you say?"

"I said . . . I said . . ." More movement ensued. "I said . . . I love you." He sounded about to choke.

Then the edges of my body disappeared, the room tilted, lifted, and opened up until there was only warmth and light and motion and Andrew's head buried in my neck.

Afterward, while he lay still on top of me, I rubbed and kneaded and plied his back, the big muscles of his public life and dizzy-heights career that were hard and interlocked. Encouraging his torso to release into gravity, I felt his rib cage expand, his lower back drop, and with a deep expulsion of breath, he relaxed into me.

It was almost one A.M., just the beginning of Monday morning, and Andrew was sitting on the side of the bed, wearing a fresh black T-shirt, and shaking out his jeans. He had decided it was time we leave the bed, the bed it felt like we had spent three incredible years in during the two and a half hours we were there.

"What do you want to eat?"

I was in New York City with Andrew Madden so there were no limits to the answer for that question. The gleanings of the city had never been offered so openly to me, but I was distracted by trying to find my clothes. They appeared to have attempted some sort of freedom run during the interval I wasn't held in their restraint. By the time I recovered them, dressed, and walked back into the bedroom, Andrew was reading the sports page.

"What did you like the best?" I said, standing before him.

He looked at me over his reading glasses, his right brow heightening the surprise and question in his gaze.

"No, no, not . . ." I glanced at the rumpled sheets to finish the sentence, as I blushed. "I meant, when you played sports in college, like you told me you did, what'd you like the best?"

"Oh. For a second there, I wondered where the sweet Southern girl I was with had gone. Football. I liked football the best. But they all were great."

I didn't understand football. All I knew was that Daddy had gone to Tulane and screamed bloody hell whenever the LSU Tigers scored a point.

"Now, what are we going to get you to eat?"

"Pasta and vodka." I had come up with that menu selection hours before, while sitting on my bed during one of the interminable intervals in which I had kept deciding that surely in the following fifteen-minute period, Andrew would call. That was all so far away now. My closet of a bedroom, the sitting and waiting, my mind chilling itself to keep from processing the loud menacing question, "What if he doesn't call?" I was safe from that now, ensconced in Andrew's glow.

"Pasta with vodka sauce?"

"No." That sounded odd. "Just . . . pasta, somehow, and vodka, like to drink." I hoped the vodka part didn't bother him since I was underage in New York.

"I see."

Andrew briefly disappeared inside a closet larger than my bedroom. "Do you like this jacket?" he said, when he came out.

He had put on what is generally referred to as a sports coat, though that phrase has always made me think of the burgundy polyester numbers I'd seen at the business conventions my daddy sometimes made appearances at in Gulfport. Andrew's was of an entirely different breed. It was a silk cashmere, and each thin thread was a separate shade in a spectrum of mid to dark gray to black, creating an effect of a muted charcoal gloss fitted precisely to his frame.

"It's stunning."

"An old girlfriend of mine gave it to me."

I wondered who she was and how much of him and his life had been hers. I was envious of what the gift implied. She had been able to buy him a jacket, a perfect one for his body and wardrobe and style. I imagined her—exquisite—sitting in a quiet, elegant store, having the time and money and opportunity to give him this gift that had lasted past their relationship's end. I wanted to give him something like that.

"Let's go."

"Where?" I knew New York continued into every hour of any night, but now that my hunger depended upon it, I doubted it would sufficiently come through.

"I know a place, don't you worry."

Walking on the quiet, vacant streets with Andrew was having him enter my dreams. The buildings I so often passed alone in similar dark emptiness now saw me with him. I felt a novel lack of need for their reliable stability. The path he was taking us on, unbeknownst to him, was a backward retracing of the route I took as I walked home from work, before catching the Broadway northbound bus the rest of the trip up. Andrew turned us right out of the hotel, heading east along Central Park South, then made another right onto Fifth. The marquee of the Paris movie theater boasted a British film that was getting much attention for its "searing portrayal of human darkness." A smoldering blonde, cigarette dangling to ensure the point, peered broodingly from the glass-encased poster.

"Didn't see it—that's not my cup of tea," he replied to my question about it.

I wasn't much interested in the film myself, but I would have enjoyed hearing his personal review so I could see it with his words interpreting the images, like his private subtitles in my head.

Fifth Avenue widened in Andrew's presence. Buildings sat back; the sidewalk softened. New York turned itself into a reverent country for him.

P. J. Clarkes' on Third Avenue was barely inhabited when we entered. A white-aproned bartender stood still as a statue in front of the beveled glass behind the bar. Portraits of Lincoln and J.F.K. stared down silently above him. A lone man sat next to a dark wood wall with a pitcher of beer, a mug, and the *Daily News* on the table before him. Andrew and I walked past them without disturbing their gaze, and into the empty dining room where Andrew settled me down at a large round table.

"That table there is for parties of four or more." A waiter was striding toward us, delivering his directive to Andrew's back. "You're gonna have to move to—"

Andrew slowly turned his head. It was like being inside a cartoon; the waiter was immediately defeated by seeing who our superhero was.

"Oh, I'm so sorry, Mr. Madden, awfully sorry, sir, I couldn't see it was you, sir."

Andrew didn't say a word.

"Let me get you some menus, sir, and anything you'd be wanting to drink?"

"She will have a vodka . . ." Andrew paused for me to finish my request.

"Tonic with a lemon twist."

"Any particular vodka that would be?" the waiter asked.

I had never ordered a brand drink before. When I went to bars in New Orleans with my friends, I'd bring enough money for one drink, figuring that by the time it was empty, I'd have met someone who'd buy me more, but those guys only bought house brand. Andrew and the waiter were waiting.

"Smirnoff."

"And I'll have a Pellegrino, no fruit."

The waiter walked over to a large wooden stand, selected two menus, came back, and laid them with a flourish on the red and white checked tablecloth. Andrew put his reading glasses on before opening his.

I wished the restaurant were busy, wished there were people everywhere, on dates, in groups, to further cement my togetherness with Andrew. To make us a solid couple by being gazed upon as a unit. I figured the waiter's eyes would have to do.

I wondered if the waiter could tell I was underage. I had started going to bars in Pass Christian when I was fourteen, but everyone always thought I was twenty-eight. And that really is rather odd for them to all, but separately, pick that particular age to think I was. Unless I really looked thirty and they were all just trying to be nice. Though, actually, I did feel twenty-eight back then. At fifteen, I was drinking and having sex with a man seventeen years older than me, but in terms of my bar age, only what, four?

When I moved to New York, suddenly everyone could tell what age I truly was, as if some sort of regression had occurred as I traveled north—the years I had lived that counted for double in the South now did not in the brutality of urban reality. Any mature-beyond-my-years swagger I once possessed remained so firmly behind that I began to doubt it had ever been mine, and I thought of it as a Southern condition, like relinquishing to the heat.

The waiter deposited our drinks before us, then stepped back, holding his pen and pad protectively in front of his chest.

"And what would you like?" He had put a little smile into it, but I could feel the exhaustion underneath. I knew there were career waiters in the city who regarded the profession as solid and respectable, the filigree in New York City's culinary crown jewels. I also knew, after almost three months of working alongside them, the imprisonment they could feel in the locked servitude of the customer's meal. I wanted to tell him he was holding up well.

The choices on the page had barely registered on me, so I glanced quickly to find something.

"Pasta primavera, please."

"Very good, and sir?"

Then commenced a lengthy discussion between them of the shrimp scampi, and another even more detailed one about veal scaloppine. Andrew brought up the chicken marsala; all were deemed excellent choices with accompanying persuasive nods of the waiter's head. A silence ensued.

"Cheeseburger, medium rare, and a green salad." Andrew said, closing the menu, and allowing the waiter to pick it up from the table before he withdrew.

I turned my chair toward Andrew's and rubbed along the top of his thighs. I had read in a magazine once that you can tell how a man will treat you years past the honeymoon by the way he orders his food. Andrew hadn't really been rude. Just thorough and exacting. But it was like watching a dance instructor and a student on a floor where the tiles light up whenever the student misses a step. Though Andrew did leave an awfully nice tip.

The Monday morning light reaching into Andrew's hotel room high above Central Park exuded a richer glow than the rays that circulated down through the alley and air shafts that my apartment windows faced. The sky unfurled itself toward Andrew's bed. It reminded me of being at the Gulf, standing at the water's edge and seeing only the blues of sea and sky that were allowed by the yellow of the sun. Andrew was lying on his stomach, his head turned toward me, his face illuminated by sleep. I edged sideways off the bed, letting my weight gradually ease, not wanting to end his slumber. In the bathroom mirror, I unmussed my hair, and used his toothpaste on my finger to brush my teeth. I was back in bed, reliving the night before, when he awoke and looked at me.

"Are you going to take care of my back?"

"What?" I wondered if he had pulled it during the night.

"My back. I haven't woken up without pain in my back for years. Whatever you did last night when you rubbed it . . . Are you going to take care of it for me?"

"Oh, yeah, I will." I was thrilled.

"Good. Are you completely all mine?"

"Yes."

"Good."

I started to move against him, but he kissed my cheek, then jumped out of bed.

"C'mon, we're getting up. I want to see the slides of your work."

In the dizziness of being with him, I had almost forgotten that I'd brought them, as he had asked me to during Sunday afternoon's phone call. Sitting on the bed and facing the windows, Andrew held each square up to the light. There were ten of the last pieces I had done in Mississippi before I left. They were a series of sculptures comprised of driftwood, copper wire, and found glass in expressionistic houselike crosses suggesting our reliance on fallible structures. The sculptures ranged in height from three to four and a half feet and were being stored in the attic of Momma's house, covered by old flowered sheets from the bed of my youth. There were also some slides of wood pieces and a few abstract oil paintings I had done years before.

Andrew was quiet as he scrutinized them again and again, sometimes flipping one over as if to view it from the other side. I tried to distract myself while I waited for his response by counting the number of taxis I could spot driving through Central Park, tiny yellow objects appearing and hiding among the trees. Then he picked up the slides' small plastic cases and inserted each slide into it precisely without marring them.

"You . . ."

It was an eternity before the next word. The number of cabs I had left off on was even, a sign—I hoped—that he liked my work.

"Are going to be . . ."

Nothing? Forgotten? What?

"A Big Fucking Star."

Oh. Jesus God.

"A big fucking art star." And he nodded his head.

I had no idea what to say. It was like being spoken to in a foreign language, in words you've vaguely heard before, but never thought would be addressed to you and with the expectation of a reply.

"Can you leave these with me?"

"I can leave them." *I can leave everything with you,* I thought, *even me.*

"I want to let someone take a look at them." He kissed my forehead and nose. "You big fucking art star."

The phone in the living room rang, and Andrew reached for the extension next to the bed. "Hello?" He listened for a bit, and made small "uh-huh" sounds as the person spoke. "Hold everything a bit longer—give me fifteen. Oh, and when he comes in this afternoon, I want the other guys' pictures on the wall behind my desk facing him. Yes, even though he already has the—uh-huh. Okay, fifteen." He replaced the receiver, picked my pullover up off the floor, and handed it to me.

"Okay, sweet-y-vette, you are going to call me this afternoon."

I didn't want to leave. Ever. I felt giddy and renewed, but like I was being sent off to school. I wanted to stay with him and be next to him for the rest of my life.

"Okay, but . . ." I had no end to the sentence; it was all I could muster. My clothes had become traitors—their coverage of my body allowing me to leave. "But when will I see you again?" I sounded like a child who doesn't believe everyone will reappear in the morning after the night's sleep. "Will I see you again?"

He smiled at me, kindly, and put his finger on my nose. "Oh, you'll see me again. You'll see me a lot again."

Andrew put on his jeans and a navy blue T-shirt, but with an air of being temporarily dressed, then kissed the top of my head as I put my shoes on. I resisted the urge to try to leave something of mine in his room; that was too obvious and schoolgirlish. When I stood up, I saw him holding out a hundred-dollar bill toward me.

"Oh, no." I was shocked. Did he think I was there for that? Then I saw his eyes on mine. I obviously needed the money, that he could see, there was nothing more to his offer than that. I shook my head, and he put it away. I didn't want to need him for that or for him to think that I did.

In a whirlwind of motion, Andrew escorted me down in the elevator, had the doorman hail me a cab, and, settling me in, kissed my cheek while pressing the hundred-dollar bill into my hand.

"For the fare, so you'll have enough. Call me this afternoon, honey."

And when he shut the door, the cab moved into action, entered traffic, and left Andrew's quickly departing figure behind.

11

Driving home on the 10, getting farther and farther from the theater, I start coming down from the shock of seeing Andrew again after so many years. I think I just thought he was supposed to be dead. Or at least in Bel Air, where he lives. No, dead really, somehow. For me, at least. I mean, I knew he wasn't. He very clearly wasn't. I've seen indications of his continued existence in the media, but in terms of my own experience, I just really had decided he was dead. The Andrew I knew. Gone from my life while a carbon copy carried on in the world. But tonight at the theater, as we sat a few rows apart, it was horribly clear: Andrew is very much alive and so is everything I ever felt for him—full form, like a person who has been waiting for me and finally walks into the room.

As I lie in bed trying to fall asleep (and worrying that tonight might be a scream dream night—please, God, not that to deal with, too), I suddenly remember a conversation I had with Sydney last fall when she called to get referrals of musicians for her show. She was in a bad mood, perturbed (her word), because of a phone conversation she had just had with Andrew Madden—she had no idea I knew him—about getting money from him. Sydney had been in one of his films a year or so before and had felt comfortable enough to ask him if he'd invest in her show.

"And it's not like he won't get every cent back, Christ. I mean, it's gonna sell out." Her Canadian accent, which was normally under wraps, was on full display in that last word.

She went on to say that Andrew was considering investing some money—"a thousand dollars, like he doesn't have it"—but had been taking forever to decide. Weeks and weeks had gone by with no answer from him, so she had decided to call to say that she really needed to know, but instead of giving her an answer, all he had said was that he sure would love to fuck her, if only he wasn't married.

Big deal, I had thought as Sydney indignantly yammered on, that barely means anything coming from him. It's the same as a "hi how are you" from anyone else. I couldn't understand why she was so upset. If she knew him as well as she claimed she did, why was she taking it so seriously? I knew what Andrew would say when he really meant that, and what Sydney described wasn't it. He had told me once that most of the time he felt women expected that stuff from him, that some even got angry when he didn't flirt with or flatter them. I could imagine Andrew thinking Sydney would be one of them.

Then Sydney's diatribe suddenly drew to a climax. "He came on to me like I was some *waitress*." She decimated the word more than spoke it.

I had never heard such disdain. She should meet my father, I thought, they'd get along so well on this subject. Then I remembered that Sydney's career had gone great guns right from the start, that she had never had a lowly job of any sort—luck had protected her from the artist's usual fate. As she continued on, her Canadian accent a fuzzy moss covering her angry words, I imagined a secret restaurant system that transmitted customers' attitudes toward the servers slaving over the food, letting waitstaffs everywhere know who the nightmare customers were in advance.

But Sydney's willingness to be talked to like a waitress had paid off.

Andrew obviously had given her the money, then attended her opening night to see his dollars at work.

Why hadn't I remembered that conversation before I went to her show tonight? Though maybe I did somewhere deep in my mind; but I would have gone anyway, if I had remembered, because I never would have thought Andrew would go to the show. His fame is so huge, his persona so large, that a small theater for a one-person show is not a space or event big enough to hold him. Though it did. Crammed in there, his presence taking up the entire room, leaving no space for anyone else, which was fine, because no one else mattered with him there.

Now that I have finally seen him after all these years, the odds are probably back in favor of it not happening again—at least for a very long time. Like last year when someone broke the taillight on my truck; that was a drag, but living in L.A., a person can only go so long without having some kind of car contretemps, so I was grateful that my turn came up on a little thing. It's the numbers game theory. So I figure three rows apart in a theater after we haven't seen each other in four and a half years . . . I've probably got a good long stretch of time before I see him again, before any real dialogue happens between us. Unless of course hand-waving counts as dialogue, I don't know. But even if it does, I'm sure I won't see him again now for a really long time. Maybe even forever. Maybe Andrew will die, really clinically decease, before I get a chance to see him again, and tonight in the theater was it. The last acknowledgment from me he will ever see.

And me from him.

Oh, fuck.

Jesus, I miss him.

"How was Sydney's show last night?"

"Fine," I say too quickly to Reggie on the phone, making it sound like she'd laid a big one. "I mean, great. You know, it was what she does."

My voice sounds hoarse and thin. I've had four cups of coffee in the two hours since six A.M. when I finally got out of bed, tired of just lying there all night, unable to sleep. And the few times I did, the dreams I had of Andrew were so real—us at the theater, but wrapped up in each other's arms with the crazy crowd all around like bedclothes, keeping us warm—that I was even more exhausted upon awakening from them. But at least I didn't scream.

"And what else?"

"What else what?" Oh, please, Reggie, don't get all intuitive on me. Please be blithe and vague and unable to figure anything out. In short, please be completely unlike yourself.

"What else happened? Something did—you sound like you slept with someone and don't want to talk about it."

"No. God." I try to sound indignant to mask my shock at his accurate appraisal of my emotional state. "I just couldn't sleep, that's all."

I had decided not to make oatmeal—I couldn't face those goddamn grains—but I need something to cut the caffeine, so I take an apple from the fridge and get peanut butter out to spread on it.

"Thinking about the wedding?"

For one wild second, I think Reggie means my long-lost fantasy of mine and Andrew's, then I remember Suzanne's wedding and wonder if it's supposed to be weighing on me so heavily that a restless night would not be odd.

"Are you worried about Suzanne's veil, honey?"

"Oh, no, not really. I still need to work on it, but no, just . . . you know. What's going on with you?"

Hanging up the phone from Reggie has an emptiness to it, like I was talking to someone else. But the person who was someone else in our conversation was me, because for the first time, I didn't tell him everything. I couldn't bring myself to after how he was about Michael. And anyway, what difference would it make? So I saw Andrew for the first time in four and a half years—big deal. Okay, so I am slightly completely totally a mess about it, but this whole thing will blow over, retreat into the past, become an incident I barely remember, with no more significance or future impact than if I'd switched brands of dental floss. I saw Andrew again—big deal.

Yeah, then why didn't I tell my best friend? Well, I still can tomorrow when we have breakfast again. Just say very casually, "Oh, by the way, I forgot to mention that I saw Andrew the other night. Not 'saw' euphemistically, but 'saw' literally across a crowded theater with tons of people all around, including his wife, so it was more like being stranded on a desert isle and watching a glittering cruise ship go by than having any real contact, though it did feel like real contact for me, and for him, too, I believe."

Okay, that's exactly why I can't mention it casually to Reggie. Because it doesn't feel casual to me, and the words that would betray my true feelings about Andrew would come streaming out of my mouth as if my heart had found an outlet for them since Andrew's not around to get them, so telling Reggie would give them someplace to land, even though Reggie doesn't want them and would ban them from coming in, like they were boat people, uninvited and made to turn back around.

So I was right to not tell Reggie. Except that now, for the first time, a page in the journal of our friendship is blank.

The art opening where Michael and I are on our first postbrunch date is a vision of rousing yet mellowed expression: subdued black-hued paintings explode on the walls; subdued black-clad people throng the rooms. Through the mass of bodies, I catch glimpses of Michael at a table loading up a plate with food. His jeans and simple white T-shirt stand out in the crowd like a flare further highlighting his exquisite looks. I want to walk over and wrap myself all around him, but someone brushes past me, snapping my attention back to the paintings.

The artist is my friend Steve, with whom I used to go to En Chuan's meditation sessions. Steve is an old-moneyed WASP from back East whose personal style is mixing Zen with Ralph Lauren, making each the better for it aesthetically. His paintings emit a somber, elegant silence into the art opening revelers' din. Each one is surrounded by quiet admirers, gradually ebbing into the art crowd's hysteria in the middle of the rooms. The effect is like a wedding with beautiful caskets on view.

Steve's wife died from ovarian cancer seven years ago, and this is his first show since then. I went to his studio a few weeks ago to see the paintings before the opening. He made green tea on the Bunsen burner he keeps there and served biscotti, and we sat in the loft's large silence with his paintings all around. We talked and didn't speak and spoke and quietly watched the sunlight shift and wash across the large canvases of deep gray and black and dark blue as well as a few that had words painted on them, too. Tonight, when Michael and I walked into the loud and crowded gallery, I was glad that I had first seen the work in the sanctuary of Steve's studio.

Which actually is where Steve and I originally met. About four years ago, a gallery owner suggested that I check out the Santa Fe Art Colony, a group of old warehouses converted into artists' lofts on the edge of downtown, to find a work space to share. Sure enough, on a large message board in the courtyard of the colony were ads for lofts that people were looking to share. The handwriting on one of them caught my eye—it was one step short of calligraphy, but not fussy, just beautifully expressed. I figured if the loft looked the way the person wrote, it'd be a great place to work. I immediately called the number from my cell phone and Steve answered right off, then gave me directions to find his loft.

Two minutes later, he opened the door and welcomed me in. He was wearing jeans and a worn Brooks Brothers shirt, and the smoke from his cigarette curled up from his mouth toward his hair as if it were painting the few gray strands in the black there. He was the most relaxed person I had ever seen. I had a palpable feeling, while talking to him about rent and square feet, that just being around his energy would improve my work.

I don't know if it did, but the arrangement we had was great for a bunch of years. I had a nice sunny section where I pounded and soldered and fused my sculptures while he worked at the other end filling his canvases. We'd meet in the middle to share the lunches we had brought, items that always complemented each other although unplanned, and he'd smoke cigarettes afterward and we'd talk about music and art. It was how I always imagined it would have been if I had ever been allowed inside my father's work shed with him while he was working, and got to see that side of him close up. The same quiet, creative energy. Nothing mattered except the piece at hand. Then last year when I dropped art completely for making jewelry, I stopped renting his loft.

Not that I don't think the jewelry I make is art; I do. Sort of. But I'd never call it that because it would sound pretentious, frankly. A pin or a pair of earrings that someone puts on is just less precious than a work so uniquely produced it must hang untouched on a wall. The jewelry I create is definitely not for a museum or a gallery. Though I still sketch—I'm unable not to. But I have no interest in showing them to anyone. Except maybe Andrew. And wish I didn't.

Michael is still across the room, but now he's talking to someone—I can't see whom. I try to get a better view through the crowd, but people are crushingly close. I nudge past a woman next to me and catch a glimpse of a broad back and shoulders in front of Michael. Okay, he's talking to a man. I think. Or a drag queen who left her dress at home.

I seize a bit of unoccupied space in front of my favorite painting. It's a huge canvas, sprawling and almost barren, painted a deep shiny black with the word "epithalamium" in the darkest of grays written sideways, but straight up and off center to the right. When I first saw it at Steve's studio, he told me that the word means a song or a poem to celebrate a marriage and is from the Greek root "thalamos" for bridal chamber. Maybe I should buy it for Matt and Suzanne's wedding gift. No, I don't think she'd get it. She likes Impressionists, as I do, but sometimes I tire of paintings that conjure up a story of when and where and who. Though looking at a word referencing marriage is not evoking joy in me.

As I turn toward the next painting, Michael emerges through the crowd carrying a small plate brimming with food. "If these paintings were a voice," he whispers in my ear, "I'd call it monotone."

"Michael."

He kisses my neck and ear as I explain about Steve's wife.

"That's horrible," he says, holding the plate out to me. "Here, I grabbed the last shrimp for you."

As Michael puts it in my mouth, Steve suddenly appears, so I quickly finish chewing as we hug, then introduce Michael to him.

"Great stuff," Michael says, transferring the plate to me, so he can shake Steve's hand.

"Oh, thanks." Steve always appears vaguely surprised when complimented about his work, as if it were a particularly handsome dog that just happened to be following him. "I'm really trying to explore the nature of monotone in my work."

Michael looks momentarily nervous—did Steve overhear his remark?—then slightly abashed that his critique was so dead-on. I look around at the paintings and notice for the first time how acutely alone each one looks despite sharing space on the walls, then a woman steps in front of me, blocking further inspection.

"You," she says to Michael, planted before him like she is more art to view. "Are revolutionizing the FM experience."

"Thank you, I'm—"

"I know who you are. I saw the article in the *LA Times*."

I am surprised that Michael's fame has extended past the airwaves into the visual realm. I have always considered him famous, but in a concealed sort of way, a secret celebrity for the people at his station and the radioheads who were in on it, too. But here this woman is, great looking in a Kundalini-cum-collagen kind of way, gushing all over him like some love-crazy teenage fan.

"Since you took over," she continues. "The difference—you can't even measure it."

Steve smiles a goodbye at me as someone pulls him away. I wish they had pulled fan-woman away instead.

"That station is your voice, just lots of different conversations you're having all throughout the day, and let me tell you—"

"Wow," Michael says, his eyes enrapt on hers. "That's really wild you say that because that's exactly how I think of it."

She puts one hand on his arm, the other on her left breast. "You are reaching me on a very deep level."

Even through the silicone? I think.

"That's just great. I'm sorry, what did you say your name was?" Michael slips an arm around me, as he holds his other hand out to her.

The only thing preventing me from falling off my couch is Michael's arm encircling my waist. My head is turned at an odd angle, forcing me to look uncomfortably down to see his head resting on my chest. He appears to be asleep. At least it sounds that way. One minute, his personal noises were connected to ecstasy; the next, exhaustion, with no transition in between.

It started at my front door when he brought me home from the art gallery, as my key was finding the lock. Michael pressed against me from behind, making my legs weak, then the door opened and our clothes flew off, as if it were an indignity for them to be on, and my mouth found him, and the familiar and the now and the memories of all-other-times as he made me come again and again before he did as well, pulling us down into that lovely afterward drowsy spell.

Michael stretches awake on top of me, causing me to slip toward the floor, but he catches me in time. "God, are you all right?"

"I'm fine."

I reach out for the soft woven tapestry I keep draped on the couch and wrap it over us as I nestle against him. My parents got the tapestry in Paris on their honeymoon, its deep blues and sad yellows a prophecy of their marriage to come.

"That's downright scary," Michael says.

For a moment, I think he has somehow heard my thought, then I realize he is staring at my sister's wedding veil, which is perched on a tall iron dressmaker's stand in front of the large living room windows. The outside light is filling in the netting's empty spaces with a soft, pearly glow, making it look like a bodyless bride ready to proceed through the semidark.

"Yeah, I guess it is. Actually, it reminds me of a dream I had when I was really little, like in second grade." I turn to face him, wanting to gauge the interest level in his eyes before I continue, but he is just watching, waiting for me to begin. "I was in my house, in the dream, though it didn't look like the one I grew up in, and it was filled with tombstones, but wonderfully ornate ones like the mausoleums in New Orleans."

"Easy Rider."

"Exactly. And it wasn't sad or scary, just beautiful and homier because all my ancestors were there. Suzanne was standing next to me when suddenly this angel gravestone—the most beautiful one, very Gothic, one hand carrying a torch, long hair streaming back—came flying through the house—well, rolling, really, she was on wheels—and the house was a shotgun design, so all the doorways lined up in a row, and she tore straight through with sirens whirring and bells clanging. I looked at Suzanne as if to say, 'What's the deal with her?' and Suzanne very matter-of-factly said, 'She thinks she's a fire engine,' as if that explained everything, and in the dream, it did, like we weren't supposed to ruin her fantasy."

I look at Michael—who is now looking at the veil as if it sprang fully formed from my dream like Athena from Zeus's head—and wonder what he'll say. He's been known to just change the subject if he decides a topic has reached its end, unencumbered by conversational rules, yet communication is his life. But maybe that's why.

"An emergency rescue vehicle," Michael says. "That's a trip."

In all the years of remembering that dream, I had never thought of it that way. Maybe so I wouldn't have to wonder what I needed rescuing from. When I told Suzanne about it after it happened, she was just annoyed that I had her saying something that she thought was so dumb.

"Do you have any food?"

I know I do not, at least the kind he'd be interested in, but I go to the kitchen anyway, duly checking the oatmeal in case some miraculous conception had occurred and it had divinely delivered cookies. I am taking out two apples, plus the jar of peanut butter, when Michael walks in and peers over my shoulder into the fridge's brightly shelved almost-emptiness.

"Let's get in your bed," he says, then turns and leaves the kitchen.

I put away the apples and peanut butter, fill two glasses with water, and follow him into my bedroom. It occurs to me that the scream dream might be scared off by his presence tonight. I hope so, otherwise it would be kind of weird for him to wake up at three A.M. as I scream hysterically into his ear. Michael is already in bed, appears, in fact, already asleep when I walk into the room. I put the glasses down on the stack of antique suitcases I use as a nightstand, pull back the spread, and get in. With one sleepy reach, Michael pulls me close to him, his body like a pillow. His arm lies over me protectively, and I fall asleep more easily than I have in months, somehow knowing that there won't be any screams tonight.

12

The early morning air in my apartment is still tingly even though Michael is over two hours gone. My living room is ebullient with last night's mess strewn about. Clothes are on the floor, the couch's slipcover has been pulled off to throw in the wash, and the room is charged with the experience of us.

I'm spinning and twirling, even though I'm sitting still. I want to tell Reggie everything, leave out no detail, but I know that I can't, so I force myself to dial his number slowly, trying to keep my excitement held back.

"That's great, honey." Reggie sounds uninterested and annoyed. "I'm glad you and Michael had such a good time."

I have told him the most G-rated, no-threat-to-our-friendship version of last night's date that I could, but clearly that made no difference.

"Oh, Reggie, are you really that upset with me?" I can hear him vigorously cutting what I know is sausage on his end of the line. "It was a date, with someone who knows me and I—I—"

"And what? Someone who what?"

"Okay, all right, so Michael hasn't said the L-word to me—yet, but . . ." At least there's a chance of my having a future with him because, for one thing, he's straight, I want to say, but don't, because honestly I don't think Reggie is. At least I don't think of him that way. More neutral kind of. If not deep inside really gay. He told me a story once a couple of years ago about how he and this male friend of his used to kiss so much whenever they saw each other that they practically had their tongues down each other's throats. I had thought when I first met Reggie that he wasn't really into women, so I was relieved that he finally felt safe enough to talk about it with me, and I told him the truth. I love you whoever you're attracted to, I said, what matters is that you follow your heart. He was quiet for a moment then changed the subject. And ever since then, all he talks about is women. As if that conversation never took place. And he's had a few girlfriends, so I don't know what to think.

Not that Reggie wants to date me. Which is one reason I find his possessiveness or whatever it is so easy to brush off, though annoying because sometimes I think he thinks he should want to date me. Similar to the way I feel about beets. The idea sounds good, they'd be unusual on my plate, but once tasted, they're rejected and forgotten, as if forces other than myself had conspired to put them in front of me. So I understand, and besides, I've never even heard of a vegetable that Reggie will eat.

"Are we not going to be able to talk anymore because I'm seeing Michael again? You didn't hate him so much when I was with him before."

"I was building up steam."

"Reggie." I pick up my clothes to put in the hamper, returning my living room to its natural state. There is emptiness on the line, then a sigh that is so connected to how I feel that I wonder for a moment if it was mine.

"I just don't want to see you go through the same thing you did last summer, but you know what? It's your life and it's none of my business."

"Ow. Hello? You're my best friend—I want it to be your business. I just don't want you against it—or me."

"I'm not, honey. Really. I just want you to be happy."

"That's funny; so do I."

I stare out my living room window at the tree in the courtyard, wishing it could transport me away from all this Reggie-mess. It is a type of eucalyptus, silvery green and light brown, a habitat just out of reach but on display for me, along with the birds that nest there, the wind in the leaves. Sometimes I just sit and look at it, watching it through my living room window because even though it's not a kind of tree that I grew up seeing, it reminds me of home—the big branches shading everything, an intermediary between earth and sky. It makes me feel safe and happy having it there right outside.

"I'll try not to be so grumpy about Michael." Reggie's tone is musically sweet, wrapping its apology around me.

"Thanks, Reggie."

"How's Chinese for tonight before I read you the new part of the script?"

Even though it feels weird to have had such a short conversation with Reggie, at least it ended okay. He's my best friend, stayed practically glued to me when Momma died, his voice a constant in my life; I have to be able to tell him about Michael. Especially since I'm not telling him about Andrew. Not that there is anything to tell. Or ever will be anyway. And after being with Michael last night, I don't even care anymore that I saw Andrew the other night. Had almost completely forgotten about him and in fact only thought about Andrew because I still haven't told Reggie—which I don't need to because who cares? I don't. I'm not even thinking about him.

But I wonder if Andrew has thought about me. Since the other night. And in the four and a half years since we were together. And I wonder if he wonders if we'll ever see each other again, or if the other night was it.

The headpiece for Suzanne's veil is a nuptial nightmare come to life. It should be done, finished, executed exactly as she dreamed, for her to see at my dress fitting this Saturday. But it's not. From the sketch she has given me, what I have done so far fulfills all of her specifications, but not only isn't it finished, it looks half-baked somehow. She wants a jeweled effect without sparkles and not all pearls. I don't even know what that means. I realize I could have asked her, but I thought having her draw it would make her demands more concrete. The sketch she gave me is the most expressionistic rendering of a veil I have ever seen. Schiele would have been proud. Maybe my sister should have been the artist in the family.

I have moved the veil and the dressmaker's stand into my studio so I can spread out and work with my tools, but all that does is remind me that I need to get downtown in an hour to meet Dipen to see how the casting for Rox's order is coming so I can get that in gear. And then I need to drive clear across town to Brentwood to deliver a commission. I consider calling Suzanne and telling her that she just won't be able to see her veil this Saturday, but I don't feel like hearing bridal wrath, especially after this morning when Reggie was so cranky on the phone about my Michael-date.

I attach a few tiny glazed beads onto the headpiece to fill in some gaps. They look nice. And completely uninspired. Okay, my only option for salvaging this project is to employ the method I use when making jewelry: I have to put the goddamn thing on. This is not something I want to do. At all. Lifting the veil off the stand and holding it carefully in both hands, I realize that I have no idea how to get it on. I wish I had the attendants that brides have—getting into the costume looks more complicated than getting to "I do." After a few tangled attempts, it is resting on my head. The image in the mirror isn't so much me with veil, as veil with me. I might as well be an eight-year-old girl with a feminine pad—this accessory is that unnecessary on the body it is on.

As I glance around the room to ensure myself—illogically—that I'm alone, I half expect a matrimonial constable to appear with a citation for "endangering the welfare of a veil." I look into the mirror again. I have heard that some women upon seeing themselves for the first time in bridal gear burst spontaneously in joyful tears. Sobs of despair are more what I feel. I suddenly wonder what people who spontaneously combust have just seen.

The veil is floating down around me to the floor, billowing out in a soft silhouette. I look small inside all this white, contoured, like a negative version of the outlined-with-black-crayon pictures my cousin Renée and I used to draw. For the first time, I understand why the virginal color was picked; everything else recedes when the encapsulation is so pale. The bride's previous life is blotted out, ready to be renewed and transformed into a new woman for the groom.

The phone rings. It is probably Suzanne, conjured up by my wearing her veil, calling to reclaim her sole ownership of object and role, and to hasten my work along.

"Hello?" It is difficult to get the receiver near my ear through all this netting. I can barely hear the person at the other end, the veil is crinkling and rustling so. I push it back, like gloriously long straight hair, behind my ear. "I'm sorry, hello?"

"Yvette?" The female voice is vaguely familiar.

"Yes?" Maybe it's Roxanne about the order for her store.

"Hi, it's Sydney."

"Oh, hey." Seeing Andrew at Sydney's show two nights ago completely eclipsed my memory of her. "Your performance was amazing. I was sorry I couldn't stay for the party; I hope you got my message."

"Yeah, I did. And thanks again—the guys are working out great."

"I'm so glad." Why has she called? We're not call 'n' chat friends. I met Sydney years ago through a pop singer I used to be close friends with, but other than occasionally helping her find musicians for her shows, we rarely talk.

"I thought I should let you know." She stops for a pause I could drive my truck through. Holy Christ, what? Ever since I was fourteen and my mother called me at my cousin Renée's house where I was spending the night to tell me in two short sentences that Daddy had left, I have had mixed feelings about telephonically transmitted news.

"Andrew Madden asked about you."

"What?" I cannot have heard her right. For someone in my life today to not only know about but bring up this precious buried part of my memories and dreams is the colliding of the worlds I shuttle between.

"He asked about you. At the party, after the show. I was all over the place, talking to everyone—did you see my preshow crowd on the ten o'clock news?"

It takes me a split second to realize she is waiting for my response. Just tell me what he said, I want to scream. Inject it in me all at once, so this tedious trickling can end, then when his words are safely circulating inside, part of me and him-of-then, I can listen at a normal pace, decipher and decode what only I can know he meant.

"No, I missed it, but I saw the news crew outside." Whoever thinks manners are only important in the South has never tried to survive in Hollywood.

"It's getting great reviews."

"That's wonderful, Sydney, I'm so happy for you."

"Thanks. It's been a lot of work, and it just never ends, but you know how it is."

Actually, honestly, I don't. My work is small, viewed up close, almost in private. Standing in person before the hordes isn't something I do.

"Well, you do it great."

"He wanted to know if we are friends."

"What'd you say?" I jump right back in with her to Andrew-land.

"Yeah, you know. He asked about your art, if you were still doing it. I told him not that I know of, but your jewelry designs are going great."

"You said that?" As I move toward the chair to sit down, the veil and the phone cord encircle each other, binding me tighter to this call, so I perch on the edge with the receiver held in both hands.

"He was really happy to hear it; said something about that making sense with how personal and delicate your art was. He asked if you were seeing someone, but I didn't know, then he said, 'I care a lot about Yvette, and have for a very long time.' He wanted me to please tell you hello."

Hello, Andrew, I silently answer back with the wild hope that he can hear.

"Then a bunch of people came over to us. Christ, that man is never left alone, crowds kept forming and unforming around him all night like amoebas." I wonder if I'll hear that used about something else in Sydney's next show. "And his wife, Holly, is so beautiful. And such a great mom to their two kids. She's so nice; no one can hate her."

Oh, right, his wife. Well, hello, Andrew. And goodbye.

I crab-dance around Sydney's questions about how I met him and were we involved by saying—which is true—that I have to run downtown.

Driving on Beverly Boulevard in the late morning traffic to meet Dipen downtown, the word "care" reverberates in my brain. The way Andrew would say it. In his voice, in my mind. So maybe he has thought about me all these years. Like I've thought about him. God, I miss him.

13

The Monday that I woke up in Andrew's bed at the Ritz-Carlton Hotel in New York, I worked the eleven-to-eight shift at the restaurant in a state of tired ecstasy. The little sleep that I had gotten thanks to our late night and early rise proved to be helpful in muffling my expression of the shocked bliss I found myself in. I appeared extremely, privately glad, but nothing so exuberant as to warrant questions from the other hosts and hostesses, and especially from Lydia, which was good because it felt too personal to talk about at work. Seamus came on that night at six, but by then I was in the reservation room for the last hours of my shift, so I was able to avoid his knowing eyes, thank God, because I have a shot at being a believable liar if the person I'm fibbing to can't see me, but one-on-one, my truth-telling thoughts are practically pasted on my face, so readable is my countenance. I had the next day off, and on Wednesday was scheduled for the nine-to-four shift, so I figured I wouldn't be in real contact with Seamus again until Thursday night, and by then his mind would be too roiled with the chaos of the week to remember to ask about Andrew and me.

I called Andrew that Monday afternoon as he had told me to, sneaked downstairs to the restaurant's pay phone booth—an astonishing blessing that it had a real booth with privacy—and dialed the hotel number, already knowing it by heart like a code to my salvation.

Andrew's voice was immediately on the line, unlike the wait I had endured the first time. "Where are you?" he said, forgoing a hello.

"At the restaurant, at work."

"How are you?" The phrase was spoken so sincerely, it made me realize how rarely it is.

"I'm good. It was . . ." My temperature rose a hundred degrees. "Really nice being with you last night."

His voice did a sideways and down one shift, moving us into a more private place. "It was wonderful being with you, sweet-y-vette. Do you love me?"

"Yes." I was relieved he had asked. I hadn't said it to him when he said it to me, and remembering that had caused a lopsided, one-shoe-off sensation in my head. "I love you, Andrew."

"Good."

I thought so, too.

"I've got some people here I have to see. What time do you finish work?"

Oh, God, what clothes did I wear here? Was it anything I could see him in?

"Eight, I get off at eight."

"Call me then."

"Okay." I tried to keep out of my voice how ecstatic I felt about seeing him in only a few hours, to play it cool like it happened all the time.

"Okay?" His voice was patient and kind. Andrew's living room had people in it—the kind whose daily existence included sessions with him, yet in those few minutes, he gave me the implicit understanding there'd always be time for me.

"Okay."

"Bye, honey, I'll talk to you soon."

I walked slowly up the stairs and into the barroom. My task was to fill bowls with fancy mixed nuts (the nuts we illicitly wrapped in dinner napkins, hid in our pockets, and nibbled on throughout our coat-room shifts) to set along the bar in time for the predinner drinks crowd. All I could think about was how much time there was to endure before calling Andrew at eight, then seeing him when life would begin again.

Andrew and I spoke when I finished my shift, talked when I got home, talked again at ten. Then at ten-thirty, when he promised to call me right back, I knew I would collapse asleep before he did. In a small way, it felt okay not to see him. I was still overflowing from being with him the night before, and that experience could extend further before another encounter with him regulated it to the past.

The next morning, Carrie's timing to converse about the Andrew escapade, as she called it, coincided with my being in the kitchen preparing to bake bread. I had stopped at the grocery at the end of my daily five-mile run to buy the ingredients, lugging the plastic bags the two long and two short blocks home. I was dying to tell her all about it—especially since it was a whole two days ago and I still hadn't told anyone. Not that there was anyone else to tell. The only friends I had made so far, like Lydia, all worked at the restaurant, and that was way too gossipy a place for this information, so that left only Suzanne—not really an option. I could already guess how she'd feel about Andrew. She hadn't liked widow-man, not that she had ever met him since she took off for college soon after Daddy left and had stayed in California, never once coming back. But she used to call me specifically to fuss about my seeing widow-man, what a terrible influence he was, and what kind of real high school experience could I have dating a man in his thirties. I'd do algebra problems during these "You should be . . ." speeches, throwing in a few "uh-huhs" every now and then until she ran out of steam and hung up. So I had a pretty strong feeling that telling her about Andrew Madden wasn't going to be a happy sisterly chat.

But Carrie was great. Drinking her protein shake, thrilled to hear everything, wanting all the details, asking questions, squealing when I told her about leaving my art slides with him. Then she told me about Andrew's girlfriend, Lily Creed, the beautiful British actress who was at the table with him that first night he came to the restaurant.

"But he has always had others on the side," Carrie said, as if explaining a tricky but essential foreign language verb conjugation. "So you can't feel bad about her. There's no way she can think she's the only one. And as my mother always said, 'It's not like he's married.' "

Which is exactly how I felt, too. Besides feeling constantly like I was in a dream, the dream that Manhattan was meant to be. As if the real New York City had been unlocked for me by Andrew, and for the first time since I moved there, I felt connected to the city and all the energy it held. Every moment was lived in high gear with a perpetual fall crispness in the air, and I felt I could take on the world.

Andrew called as Carrie was in the shower washing henna out of her hair and I was filling the bread pans with dough.

"What are you doing?" he growled to my "hello," sounding like a lion disguised as a cub.

"I'm baking you bread."

"You're what?"

"I'm baking you bread; I thought I'd drop it by this afternoon." The oven door slipped shut out of my hand. I had had to stack the pots and Pyrex dishes we stored in there on my bed until the baking was done.

"No one has made me anything since I can't remember when. You are so fucking cute. When do I get my bread?"

I was so ecstatic, I almost dropped a pan. "An hour or so for it to bake and cool; I can come by around one."

"If I'm not in, leave it at the desk." His delight and warmth and protection were palpable over the phone. "You are in such big trouble for this."

I couldn't think of a better way to be.

I went to the hotel, dressed to see him, but when I reached the front desk, I was informed that Mr. Madden was out—would I care to leave a message? I opened my bag to take out the loaves. They were in Saran wrap, taped closed, then gift wrapped in pretty paisley paper napkins, and tied with silk bows. I had worried they looked too girly, but I decided it reflected more the giver than the givee, and who doesn't like to unwrap something? The desk clerk appeared nonplussed as he took the warm bread from my hands. I guessed they didn't get that very often.

"Do you know what I'm doing right now?" was Andrew's greeting when I picked up the phone later that afternoon.

"Asking me to come over?"

"Eating your bread."

"Oh! Do you like it?"

"Are you fucking kidding me? I've eaten half a loaf already—what's in this thing?"

The name of every ingredient flew out of my head. "Uh. Wheat." I might as well have said "cow" for the butter and milk. "I mean, flour and—"

He rescued me from the list. "This is amazing."

"Was it still warm?"

"No." He sounded like a child who found out his Christmas train didn't choo-choo. "Can it be? I want it warm next time."

God, he was cute.

Then he told me about the art gallery. About the lunch he'd had that day with Tory Sexton, the British owner and namesake of the space, while

I was delivering his bread. I knew about her SoHo gallery—everyone did. It was one of the top three downtown, farther outside the mainstream than the other two, but widely respected and reviewed. I had been there in June.

I had moved to Manhattan to apply to the School of Visual Arts by December and start my undergraduate degree there in the spring, but a couple of weeks after I arrived in New York, knowing no one in the art world, I decided what the hell, I'd go around and show the dealers my work just to see what they thought. I knew it would take years to get a show, probably at least until I graduated, but Daddy had always said, "God helps those who help themselves," and maybe some job would turn up or something, you never know, so I took a week-old copy of Ruth's *New York* magazine, pulled out the art section, and compiled a list of every gallery in town.

And off I'd go. Working around my restaurant schedule, every minute I could, I'd focus on one neighborhood at a time, walk into a gallery, and ask if the owner had a moment to view my work.

It was weeks of uninterested response. Many were arch and filled with disdain. A few were polite, outlining their gallery's procedures or simply stating they were, in no way, an open door. The rest fell somewhere unpleasantly in between. After the first few days, I didn't want to keep going. Each entrance was hard, every exit excruciating, but I consoled myself that I wouldn't have to lie in bed every night thinking I was in New York but not doing anything toward my dream while I waited to get into school.

The last group of galleries I hit was in SoHo, where, in reverse tack, I decided to start at the low end and work my way up. With only two galleries left to call on, I finally had a unique experience at Sexton Space. The assistant, a woman named Peg, explained that Tory would never grant me a meeting, but took the time herself to see my work. I showed her everything: color slides of my paintings, a small notebook of sketches, slides of my sculptures. As she studied each one, I imagined she was from upstate or Connecticut, close enough to Manhattan that her urban integration wasn't jarring or hard.

Handing all of it back, Peg told me that as my work developed, and if I got into some group shows, this might be a gallery I should come back to. She liked the construction of my work and thought I had a strong, unique vision that was clearly developing. "This is an extremely tough field, but don't give up."

And here was Andrew, a couple of months later, explaining Tory to me, the work that she liked and how what he saw in mine was simpatico with her eye. He'd known her from London back in the seventies when he was shooting a movie there. I couldn't help but think how funny it was that the one person on my self-ascribed door-to-door gallery tour who had shown real interest was Tory's assistant. Maybe this was meant to be in some big cosmic way.

"Call Tory tomorrow; she's expecting you."

"Thanks, Andrew. That was really wonderful of you."

"I just passed your work on; you're gonna do the rest, you big fucking art star."

Peg wasn't in sight when I walked into Sexton Space that Thursday afternoon. I was told by an exquisite pale man, whom I didn't remember from my summer visit, to wait; Ms. Sexton was on the phone. I studied the work on display in the prohibitively silent gallery. The air was filled with an admonishment not to speak, as if in the face of such nonnarrative images, words became obsolete.

After thirty minutes of looking about, I began to feel lulled by the intensity of the paintings—rage was a prominent emotional theme—and the quiet of the room. Adrenaline had pooled in me with no place to go, so I jumped when a hand touched my back.

Exquisite pale man told me to go in, as he pointed me toward Tory Sexton's sanctum. I suddenly wished I had something to hold on to—some object to derive strength from.

When I walked in, Tory Sexton was sitting inside a gigantic, ornately carved Chinese canopy bed, but with furniture in it instead of a mattress. It was a red-lacquered room within the real room that I had to walk up two steps then down one to get into. Low-slung leather stools were placed in front of a burnished wood table that Tory sat behind on a French rococo chair whose legs had been lopped off, guillotined victims of her revolutionary design. My slides were laid out in front of her like tiny children walking a tightrope in a row.

Tory's crimson lips were practically a separate entity. They floated above her black-suit-clad frame, pronouncing sounds, enunciating edits, and charting new courses with the air they exhaled. The conversation she was having at me was so previously unencountered in my life that my mind practically had to translate her words into ones I could believe. My sculptures were to be in her group show of new artists in December. I should talk with Peg to arrange the shipping of them here, the gallery would cover that, of course, and tell her now about where I was from that I was making such work at eighteen.

While Tory listened to me, her right forefinger goosed the edge of one of my slides, then she abruptly held out her hand, signaling our time was at an end. "Call Peg," she said as I stepped down into the real room. "There is much to be done."

Pushing out the gallery's door, I noticed "Sexton Space" painted on both sides in small ruby letters, their syllables shouting ownership of the street. I walked to the subway in a daze and waited for the train to take me to work as my Tory experience settled into me and became true, not just a dream. I almost had an urge to tell the people on the platform, shout out my good news—I didn't care to whom. For a second I considered calling Momma, but figured I should wait until my initial enthusiasm was over so I wouldn't need any from her, too. Carrie would be thrilled though, and Suzanne. But maybe not. She'd probably find some reason it wasn't good. And dammit, this meant she'd have to know about Andrew. Well, who cared, look what he had done for me. If that wasn't an indication of how he felt, what was?

After changing into my uniform at work, I called Andrew at his hotel, but had to leave a message since he wasn't in. I could hardly wait to tell him.

A few hours later, unable to stand it anymore, I slipped into the phone booth on an alleged restroom run and called Andrew's hotel again.

"Mr. Madden requested that I find out where you will be tonight, and he wants to know how did it go?" The operator's voice serving the information was like a tennis ball, impartial to whose point it is, but the only connection the players can have. I felt a sudden affinity toward her, as his messenger.

"Tell him I'm at work until midnight, and it went really, really great."

When I got home, Andrew's voice was waiting for me via the small red bleeping light on my answering machine.

"Hi." Mechanical sounding, but him after all. "This is your uncle Andrew." That was odd, but sweet somehow. As he took a breath, I imagined his body gradually materializing, each word contributing another layer to his presence there with me. "I'm out tonight, but I'll call you in the morning, okay, honey? Good. Bye."

I played it again and again, holding the machine in my lap, as I sat cross-legged on the linoleum floor, the electric cord pulled taut from the wall. I didn't know what to make of the "uncle" part, though it was sweet the way he'd said it, like a family member who has long been missing and is reconnected by claiming his role.

When we spoke the next morning, Andrew was so thrilled about my Tory interview that he told me to come to the hotel.

"Come around lunchtime—just call before you do. I'll see you in a little bit, sweet-y-vette."

Hanging up, I felt as if clouds were under my feet, soft and buoyant and lifting me up.

As Andrew opened his door at the Ritz-Carlton Hotel, opened his door to my seeing him again—since I left his bed four days before, left my slides, left his world with mine forever changed—it felt as if we had lived a year together. He was wearing a dark blue T-shirt, jeans, and no shoes, like a comfortably rumpled bed I wanted to crawl into. We stopped in the foyer of his suite, and his body pressed against mine, which was pressed against the wall, and my mouth pressed against his, but for some reason, he wouldn't allow a proper sexual kiss, so I was quick kissing his neck, cheeks, lips, and ears, while he moved his head whispering near, "You are so fucking cute; how'd you get so fucking cute?" over and over, until he took my hand. "Come on, honey."

I started walking to the bedroom, but he guided me toward the couch.

"I need to finish up a call. Pick out whatever you want." He pointed at a menu lying on the coffee table. "We'll order up."

And go to bed after lunch, I finished for him in my head.

He sat on the couch, reached for the phone, and motioned me to sit next to him.

"Okay." He returned his attention to the person on the line.

Watching him as he listened, I could sense he was talking to a man.

"Uh-huh. Uh-huh. Really. Uh-huh. Uh-huh. Hmmm."

I nestled up against the side of his body, his sounds resonating among the many minutes of the other person's words.

"I don't agree that that is the way to go."

Andrew leaned forward, elbows bent and resting on his knees, then he glanced over at me. The menu was still on the table. He looked at it, then back at me with one eyebrow raised, as if I were a nine-year-old refusing to clean my room. I laughed noiselessly, causing a smile of surprise on his face that disappeared when his attention turned back to the phone. I opened the menu, glancing through page after page after page of elaborately explained food. I was so used to ordering the cheapest vegetarian thing that the many options were like picking out candy.

"Uh-huh. Uh-huh. I would do that." Andrew appeared to be gathering and accessing information. There was so much space in his power—large open areas for other people to speak in while Andrew's mind reassembled things, organizing them in ways the speaker couldn't dream.

So this was how they talked. Men like him in spacious, quiet rooms—their conversations building and edifying so many aspects of so many lives. I imagined them all over Manhattan, points on a grid that extended out to Washington, Chicago, L.A., and beyond. The conversations in my father's and grandfather's offices had reached only across the state—their jurisdiction held close by map lines. Or if they did occasionally go beyond, the North was never involved, much less the entire country's entertainment. Here, in Andrew's suite, phone conversations impacted far points on the globe.

Andrew's friend, a famous actor whose films even I had seen, arrived after lunch, just at the moment when I thought we'd go to bed. At first I was annoyed at the intrusion, then thrilled to be meeting Andrew's (from what the press said) best friend. The maleness in the room multiplied exponentially when he walked in. Sitting between them, these men whom most of the world experienced writ large, and listening to the actor tell me stories about Andrew, which Andrew laughed at, was like being in a deftly orchestrated scene with them.

"She's perfect," Andrew said, after he had told his friend all about me. "An artist—beautiful, talented, and young. Name another with all that. Female ones, I mean. See? She's perfect."

The actor was looking me over. "I'll say."

"Okay, honey," Andrew said, as he stood up and took my hand. "Where are you headed to now?"

I didn't want to go. I wanted us to tell his friend goodbye, so we could have sex while the afternoon began to end.

But Andrew was looking at me, waiting for me to get up and go. The actor stood up and kissed my other hand. "It was a pleasure to meet you, Miss Broussard. I look forward to seeing you again."

But before I could respond, Andrew helped me up by wrapping an arm around me and pulling me away from the actor. I looked over my shoulder as we left the room. "It was nice meeting you, too."

"Call me later, honey." Andrew and I were in the outer hallway; the elevator button had been pushed.

"Maybe," I said. "I'm going out."

"Out? Where?" He sounded growly again. "Who are you going out with? I'll fucking kill him." The elevator doors opened. "Who are you going out with, Yvette?" I kissed his face and stepped inside. "You'd better call me. And you'd better not fuck him." Andrew's hand held the door open. "Call me. Okay?"

I nuzzled into his neck, grinning and kissing him quietly. "Bye," I said, moving backward, and the elevator doors gradually partitioned Andrew's face out of view, as I heard him say, "Call me, Yvette."

"Did I meet you this summer?" Peg asked, when I called her at Sexton Space that afternoon.

"Yes, I was in—"

"I thought that was you. When Tory showed me your slides, I recognized them and . . . it's so funny that it's you."

"Yeah." I remembered how short Peg was—one of those tiny girls who look capable of breaking a wild horse while keeping their cashmere sweater set impeccably clean.

"Well, this is great. I loved your work, but Tory would never take an artist on without them having a show somewhere first or someone knowing them. When can you come down here? We should meet to go over everything we need to do."

I didn't call Andrew as he had told me to. And that night, I let my phone ring and ring before listening to the machine click on, then hearing his barely audible, "Hmm, hmm," noises, as if he were able to ascertain my whereabouts by his voice infiltrating my room. He called five times. I liked having him try to find me, but being unable to, the same way I couldn't reach him physically when I wanted to. It was like letting some of my skin grow back on, a layer from the inseparableness I felt with him, especially since we hadn't had sex again. Not that that was all I wanted from him, but sex solidifies things, and with Lily Creed in the picture, I wanted the reassurance that he wanted me that way, that he loved me that way. Besides the fact that it was so out-of-this-world fucking incredible. I wanted more.

14

"Please tell me you're kidding me."

"Thanks for the nice reaction, Suzanne. No, I'm not kidding—I really am going to be in a show at a gallery in SoHo."

Carrie and Ruth were out of the apartment, so the curtain in my doorway was drawn back, the window overlooking the alley was open, and I was sitting in the middle of my room, drinking an iced tea while a summer breeze cooled me down. I knew I would need all that during my conversation with Suzanne.

"I'm not talking about that part—I can't even get there yet, I'm so flipped out about this Andrew Madden stuff. Andrew Madden, for Christ's sake, is the biggest womanizer in the goddamn world. How do you not know that? What'd you do—move to New York and completely lose any sense you ever had? I knew that relationship with that married man in Mississippi was going to screw you up."

"He was widowed, and it's not like that with Andrew."

"Not like what? So you're not having sex with him?"

"Yes, I am, but . . ." At least I thought we were, though he hadn't let us since that very first night, as if he suddenly didn't want to anymore, which I couldn't figure out why, but I wasn't going to tell Suzanne any of that. "Look, you don't know him, you don't understand. And besides, when did you get so small-minded to believe gossip anyway? You haven't even met him."

"Gossip? Oh, please. Yvette, where there's smoke, there's fire; that's all I'm going to say. Andrew Madden, for Christ's sake. Well, when you get exploited in this relationship, or whatever it is you want to call it, because you will, it is only a matter of time, don't say I didn't warn you. And you're not even in L.A.—how'd he get to you out there? Never mind. I knew I should have insisted you go to Tulane. You are still applying to the School of Visual Arts in the fall, right?"

I was too busy staring at the mound of refuse in the alley and imagining Suzanne's pretty little head sticking out of it, like a child buried in the sand, to respond to her needling.

"Right? Yvette, tell me you're still applying to college."

"You know what? I have a lot to do; I need to get off the phone."

"Uhhh, I could kill Mother for never coming out of her room. Just promise me you will—"

"Bye, Suzanne, I'll talk to you soon." I hung up, then immediately picked it back up to call Andrew. I wasn't going to tell him about the conversation with my dear sister, but just to hear his voice in my ear, so near, to refute her words in my head.

"Malaysia," Andrew answered when I asked him on the phone where was he going, trying to keep the panic and dread from my voice, though I doubted my success. "It may be hard for me to speak to you from there, but I'm not leaving for a while and I'll be back. Besides, honey, you're gonna be busy with Tory."

"Are you not going to be here for the show?" My emotions ran out ahead of my words, pulling sounds along in their torrent.

"I don't know. Maybe. It depends on how long this goes. I'm not leaving you, sweet-y-vette, I'll just be gone for a little while." His words were firmly bracketing me, but I still felt as though I were falling.

After he told me to call him that afternoon, we hung up, and I went for a run in Riverside Park to try to calm myself after the double whammy of Suzanne's phone call this morning and now Andrew's terrible news. Andrew leaving New York—fuck. Okay. I had known that Andrew was about to start shooting his film. Carrie had left a newspaper gossip column on my bed about *Paradise Again,* the movie he was directing, producing, and starring in with Lily Creed, but I had assumed it'd be here. He was here; she had been here; why couldn't they shoot the damn movie here? Malaysia, for Christ's sake. Maybe there'd be a dreadful hurricane that would prevent him from going, if they even had hurricanes there—I didn't know. Oh, Andrew, please don't go.

A breeze was attempting to come in off the Hudson, the park was full of people trying to heighten their August Saturday experience by being outdoors whether it was pleasant or not. I ran down the broad path past Ninety-sixth Street toward Seventy-second where I would turn around to head farther uptown than where I began, past Grant's Tomb—a surprise to me that the joke's punch line existed in my neighborhood—then over and up into Morningside Heights before returning to the awful stretch of my block.

Exactly two weeks before, I had run in this park and seen Andrew that night for the first time. One week before, I ran in this park—had a great run, actually, my timing nicely improved on the dreadful fifteen-block hill—and met Andrew that night, and in the short time since, he had so completely infiltrated me that not only couldn't I imagine life without him, I hadn't thought I'd ever have to. Oh, God, I wished he wouldn't leave. And he didn't even know how long he'd be gone. Don't movies have schedules to keep? Carrie had told me that Andrew lived in L.A., but I still had never thought that he would one day actually leave New York. Fuck.

As I ran past a pushcart hot dog vendor, the cooking infusing the air with more heat than it could hold and causing ripples of steam to move out toward the street, I tried to imagine being here without him, without phone calls to and from him three, four, five times every day, without him at the bottom of the park in the Ritz-Carlton, a sentinel of safety. It was like helium leaving a balloon; it was nothing without that vital energy inside.

I passed the homeless man who I saw on the same bench every time I ran. One morning, when my run was feeling terrible and useless, I decided to just go get a coffee and bagel to eat on my walk home. As I was leaving the park, I saw the homeless man sitting on a bench at the entrance. I had never seen homeless people in Pass Christian. The man was looking toward the ground as if he had lost something—which very clearly he had, lost a lot of things, but this more recently—and I suddenly found myself saying to him, "I'm going to get a bagel, would you like one, with an egg or cheese on it, maybe?"

He looked at me blankly for a moment, then said, "I don't eat bagels."

For a second, I understood. They were brand-new to me when I moved to Manhattan—biscuits or beignets being our breakfast fare. Then the oddness of his remark struck me. "It's just bread," I almost said but quickly realized that in a life so at the mercy of others, one would grab control wherever one could. I gave him a dollar from the ones I had folded and tucked in the hidden pocket of my running shorts, as I heard Ruth's voice in my head saying, "They'll just drink your money up." But what did she know?

Turning around at Seventy-second Street to head back uptown, I decided that I would do everything I could to see Andrew a lot before he left. I hated Lily Creed for getting to go with him. But maybe he'd get really sick of her there. And maybe we'd have sex a lot before he went, even though he seemed to keep avoiding us doing that, which I could not figure out. But maybe he'd change and we would. Tons of it. Tons of solidifying, unifying, glorifying sex that he'd think about nonstop while he was gone, so he'd come back to me, having forgotten all about Lily Creed, and we'd be together forever, in perpetuity. That's what I decided had to happen.

My hunger strike wasn't intentional; I just didn't want to eat. The late summer heat, I thought, was the reason, so I didn't give it much thought. Until the fainting began. It happened the first time at work in the coat-check room, so that was easy to hide and not tell anyone, but then a week or so later, it happened again.

I was downtown looking at arts supplies, and suddenly knew I had to get something in me—my skin felt cold and hot all at once, and my blood seemed to have turned to caffeine, so jangly and metallically I felt, so I went into the nearest deli. It was lunchtime and horrendously crowded around the salad bar and buffet, which had steaming trays of sticky sweet meats, vegetables that appeared too fresh to not have been processed in some way, shiny chunks of tofu, noodles swirling like snakes, and all of it revolting me.

I was trying to select a drink, wavering between cold tomato juice, or going up front for a hot tea because the one female waiter at work, a blonde from Wisconsin, had told me that a hot beverage in the heat makes you feel better, something about aligning your internal/external body temperatures. I had thought when she said it that it was crazy Yankee logic, but maybe there was something to it and I should give it a try. But suddenly I felt my eyes and head do a back flip while my legs gave out straight in front of me.

The next thing I knew a bike messenger from Brooklyn was encouraging orange juice on me through a straw, the wax-coated container sweating like me, as he kept saying how he had braced my fall. "Otherwise, that linoleum floor . . ."

It was humiliating. I was relieved I wasn't wearing a short skirt, but I felt dirty from being on that floor and shaky from the experience of my legs involuntarily not supporting me. When I was able to make my way out, the heavy woman behind the cash register stared at me stonily as if I were a junkie or something. As I hailed a cab, which would cost the earth to take me all the way home to West 109th, because I didn't have the energy for the subway, I realized that I had unconsciously formulated the idea in my mind that if I didn't eat, Andrew would stay. Jesus, that's so teenaged, I thought. Then with a shock I realized that at eighteen, I still was.

It was impossible not to tell Carrie: she was home, my bath in the middle of the afternoon was out of the norm, and a bruise had developed on the side of my leg where the corner of a milk crate had cut into it, so I told her, but left out the reason for it.

A few nights later, I came home from a party that Lydia had thrown—all of us crammed into the small one-bedroom apartment that she shared on the Upper East Side, drinking vodka greyhounds and Tom Collins—and was greeted by Carrie as soon as I opened the front door, as if she had been waiting for me or something.

"Andrew called," Carrie announced as I entered our apartment, stumbling a bit over the door's burglar bar, a long steel rod that when propped against the door and locked into place on the floor supposedly prevented people from breaking in, but I found it wildly unsettling.

"What?" It was late, I was drunk, and I couldn't believe she had listened to my answering machine while a message was being left on it.

"Andrew called, and he's very upset about you fainting." Carrie was speaking her words as if they were lines in a drawing room play that she happened to be quite brilliant in. I remembered she had taught high school drama in Mississippi for three years before ditching that and moving here.

The greyhounds were running through my brain and were not helping me make sense of what she was saying. Had I slipped up and said something about the deli incident to Andrew that he only now on a phone message was addressing?

"We had a good long talk all about it."

"Oh, my God, Carrie, you talked to him?" I couldn't believe what I was hearing. Maybe she had also thrown out all my clothes during her rampage into my life.

"Yvette, I'm sorry," she said, sounding not a bit in the least. "Your phone rang, I was in the kitchen, and this automatic response just kicked in—I swear I need to quit my job—so I picked it up and—oops!—it was him."

"Oh, Jesus, Carrie. Are you kidding me?" I tried to remember how much I had told Andrew about Carrie on that first marathon phone call we had had when most, if not all, of the important relationships of my life were uncovered and examined. "What did he say? What did you say? Fuck, Carrie, you told him about the fainting?" I wanted to kill her, but she was looking so unguilty and giddy.

"And thank God I did. We had a nice long talk about it—he's very concerned about you and was glad I told him. He asked me what you eat, that took all of two seconds to describe. 'She won't listen to me,' I told him. 'I know,' he said. 'I'll have a talk with her when she gets home.' God, he was just so nice and everything on the phone. Solicitous and polite. I mean, Andrew Madden, just like in his films, but talking to me." She practically pirouetted and leapt.

It reminded me of how Suzanne used to always play with my dolls instead of hers when we were small. As Carrie prattled on, saying the same stuff two or three times, she appeared so thoroughly resolute in the righteousness of her deed that a rebuttal was pointless. And Andrew was worried about me, concerned enough to talk to my roommate whom he hadn't even met, only knew about because of what I'd told him. It made me feel floaty and cozy, as though he had taken up residence inside my body.

Andrew wanted to see me. He wasn't happy about what Carrie had told him, but I was happy that he told me to come to his hotel room that night after work. It had been weeks since I'd had lunch with him and his actor friend, though Andrew and I talked tons of times each day. He'd call first thing every morning; I'd call later on, speaking first to the operator whose voice I now knew and tried to be friendly to, but she acted each time as if our communication were brand-new.

"How are you?" he'd immediately say on the phone if people were in the room, skipping the "Hi," that short sound he managed to brand all his own. Then after my answer, "Where are you?" It was giving my coordinates to him—he who could better read the map—the longitude and latitude of my emotions and self, fixed on a point, in relation to all the other marks of how and where I'd been. He was my navigational system, no longer did I need to rely on the distant North Star.

Andrew was sitting on the yellow silk couch, and I was perched on the coffee table facing him with my legs between the open spread of his and my chin once again in his hand. He picked up my hands, studying each of my nails. I was hoping he would drop the doctor routine and get romantic so we could get in bed, when he said, "I bet you're anemic."

I thought it was much simpler than that—I needed to eat.

"You vegetarians never get enough iron or protein. I want you to see a doctor this week."

"Okay." I had no intention of spending money on that. I hadn't opted for health insurance at work, and I could just as easily tell myself what a doctor would say—take iron and eat three meals a day.

I was ready for this topic to end, so I leaned forward to kiss him, my hands rubbing his legs down, around, and inside, and he started to move his lips toward me, but broke away.

"I want to show you something." He went into the bedroom and came back with a folder of large, glossy pictures, which he spread out on the coffee table next to me. I moved to the couch so I could see. "This is where I'll be."

It was wonderful and horrible to see the locale that would possess him. I pictured him as he was now—barefoot, black T-shirt and jeans, comfortable in his hotel-living mode—superimposed on each photo. I wanted his easily accessible phone to be going, too.

"It's beautiful. How long will you be?"

"I don't know, honey." Our heads were bent gazing at the landscapes, surely opposing responses to them in our heads.

"Are you excited to go?" I couldn't look at him when I said it. I wanted to be happy for him, but knew my voice would break if I saw his eyes, knowing they'd be leaving.

"Yeah." He tested the word. "More ready than excited." Then he looked at me seriously and touching his finger to my nose said, "I'm excited about your show."

"I wish you were gonna be here for it."

"I know, honey, but it's going to be great—you big fucking art star." And he grinned at me, drawing me into him, my face in his chest, my arms around his back.

"While you're there," I said, the words muffled a bit by his soft T-shirt. "Will you think about me?"

"Will you think about me?"

I looked up into his eyes. "Every hour every day."

"Good." He kissed the top of my forehead, seeming to end the conversation.

"But are you gonna think about me?" My words held down a wail. With all the things he'd have to do in that distant land and so many people needing him, was there still going to be room in his mind for me?

"Will you, Andrew?"

"Yes, Yvette, I'll think about you." He kissed me on the lips, quick, soft, and sweet, then turned his hands into fists, playfully swatting me while I moved and turned to regain our embrace.

The phone rang. It was past eleven on a Monday night, and the hotel had been slumbering when I walked in at ten, the beguiling stillness of Central Park extending across the street into the lobby.

Andrew listened on the receiver and said, "Send her up."

"Who's that?" I suddenly worried it was Lily; that he'd forgotten we shouldn't meet.

"A friend of mine. You'll like her; you'll see."

The elevator his friend took apparently was an express because the ones I took to Andrew's suite seemed to mosey along. Within seconds it seemed, there was a knock at the door.

He was in the foyer with her far too long. I looked at the pictures again. I killed some time hating the clothes I had on. I thought about going to the window to get a better look at the view, but decided I didn't want to give up the couch—Andrew most likely would sit on it, and I wanted to be closer to him than she would be.

Finally, they walked in. Andrew's hand was on the small of her back. I made myself notice it, this same gesture he used with me, to see it and decide it meant nothing about us that he was using it with her. A vision of being dropped off at school by my father on days I'd missed the bus suddenly hit me. Him being in an environment I wasn't used to seeing him in made his withdrawal from me all the more excruciating, so I could barely tolerate watching his Cadillac pull away. Sitting on Andrew's couch and seeing his hand on this other girl's back was like standing under the school's portico, needing to run to class, but forcing myself to watch my father's car recede.

She sat in an armchair. Andrew sat in the opposite one to the left of me, facing her. All we needed was a fourth for a game of bridge. One sweep of his hand cleared the pictures off the coffee table, then he slid them into their folder, and put it down on the floor. At least she didn't get that part of him.

Her name was Susie. Or Suzy, I guess. She was a writer, Andrew didn't say what kind, but I made a mental note to dislike anything written by someone with that first name, since I'd probably never know her last. She clearly was years older than me, six or seven at least, and was extremely pretty. When Andrew told her that she was, as I was certain he did, she probably took it as her due. There was an ease to that blessing gracing her face, uncomplicated to enjoy like hot chocolate.

I had no idea what we were doing. Why was she here and couldn't she now leave? I would just wait her out and reap my reward in Andrew's bed. Surely soon he would make her leave.

Andrew was telling her all about me—my art, at least—including the big fucking art star part, which I found equally embarrassing and a relief, with a bit of a "Ha-ha, he loves me" thrown in. Sitting serenely in her chair as she listened to him, she appeared powerful, yet submissive, like an employee the boss really needs.

"Honey." Andrew had gotten up and was reaching his hand out to me. Thank God, he's finally making her leave.

"I'll walk you down," he said.

My face dropped as I stood up. Andrew took my hand, and turned us toward the hallway to the front door. It was the opposite of that terrible dream where I need to get away, but can't move—I wanted to stay, but was forced to leave.

"Okay, well, nice to meet you," I said to her, instantly hating that I was so automatically polite. Couldn't manners have sensors on them—bells that would jangle to prevent them from being blurted out when I didn't want them?

She simply smiled back. A hot-chocolate milk-white-teeth smile. I hated her for it.

Andrew moved me along, and his foyer disappeared past us, but waiting for the elevator made us stand still. He started kissing my cheeks and hands, but I pushed him back, turning away. "Stop it."

"Are you mad?" The elevator opened while he waited for my response. "Sweet-y-vette, are you mad at me?" He tried to kiss me again, as the doors shut.

"Quit it. What is your problem, haven't I told you no?"

He gave me a look that was blankly innocent and unassailable, like a gentleman in a bad fix. "What did you think was going to happen when you came over here?"

"What did I think?"

He nodded, glad I was seeing his point.

"What did I think?" This time my voice was higher and my stomach got involved, forming the sounds with its loud emptiness. The elevator opened into the lobby which held a radiant hush and uniformed employees.

"I thought you loved me." I knew they could hear me clear out to the street; I screamed it.

Andrew blanched before turning red as the employees bristled to life while in their stand-still mode.

"Come on, we're getting you a cab." He was walking next to me, forcing me along, and my attempts to get away from him were contained and redirected by one of his hands on each of my arms.

"No," I shouted. "I can't afford one, and they won't take one of your stupid hundred-dollar bills anyway."

All of the employees stared when they heard that, then quickly looked away. Andrew stopped us at the front desk, pulling me close into him and holding me tight with his left hand, while his right reached into his pocket.

"Could you break this into small bills, please?" His words were lovely, efficient, and calm. The desk clerk hurried to do so without looking up. It felt like a very cordial bank robbery.

"Thank you." Andrew put all of the money into my palm. "And we need a cab."

Every employee leapt forward, moving through the revolving door in groups, running to the curb.

"I'll call you in the morning, Yvette," Andrew said, as we emerged from the revolving door.

"For what?"

"What?" Andrew either didn't hear me or was very confused.

"What are you gonna call me for?" We were standing in the carpeted sidewalk area, which was replete with hotel help waving down cabs or looking surreptitiously at us. "I don't understand what you want me for; you don't let me give you a goddamn thing." I turned into him and began hitting his chest. He pulled me closer, trying to disguise it as a hug, when a cab pulled up. A line of employees made a corridor to its door for us.

"Into the cab, there you go," Andrew said, while three employees held open the door. "Take her straight home," he said to the driver. "Don't let her go anywhere else."

"I'll call you tomorrow," he said, and leaned down to give me a kiss on the forehead. I refused to look at him, and when he shut the door, the cab jerked from the curb. A few buildings away, I sneaked a look over my shoulder, but Andrew and the many employees were already gone.

The next morning, when I picked up the phone, the first thing I heard was, "Thanks to you, I got to sleep early last night."

Andrew had said it sweetly, but I still wasn't sure. "What does that mean?"

"It means I sent Suzy home is what it means, sweet-y-vette."

"Oh." I was thrilled, but didn't want to show it.

Then he told me that he had people waiting for him in his living room, so call him back in an hour or two, and did I love him?

"Yes, Andrew, I love you."

I rolled out of bed, and pulled on some clothes to go for a run. So I had met one of the other ones—the ones Carrie had assured me existed, and that I had been pretending did not. But suddenly I realized that Suzy didn't matter—none of them did. They were everyone and no one to him. Had nothing to do with me and him. What I meant to him. What I was to him. As I ran through Riverside Park, I realized that even Lily Creed didn't matter. He was with Lily, but still needed me. If what he had with her had been able to fill that space in him, then it wouldn't have been empty and waiting to strongly pull me in when our eyes met at the restaurant, ready for me to fill it for him. Fill it without having sex. Even though we did have sex that first time, it was clearly an aberration. The other women were a backdrop to my relationship with him, not unlike the trees and grass I was running past. My jealousy of them evaporated like the late summer heat finally had.

A week or so later, I was at the restaurant working the eleven-to-eight shift. It was a chilly, rainy, early fall day, and the coat room had been hell during lunch. A dense, tangled mass of hats and attachés, wool and cashmere, umbrellas and shopping bags, even a pet carrier case that, thank God, was empty. A day destined to be a labyrinth of garments hiding for minutes on end while the owners waited impatiently for Lydia and me to find their truant coats. But at least we were doing the shift together. We had a good rhythm going, split the tips we procured evenly, and had fun talking about everyone and everything in between the customers coming and going—though I still had never told her about Andrew. Lydia had a full-length Russian sable coat that she wore the minute the thermometer dipped below fifty degrees. She'd hang it on the rack like a customer's coat, and would let me try it on when no one was around. I never asked where she got it and she never volunteered. I imagined it was the last vestige of a relationship with some European man, a relationship she had hoped would prevent her from being where she had ended up—working the coat-check room of a restaurant in New York. But she was young and there were lots of rich men. "All you need is one," she'd say to me and laugh as if she didn't mean it, though I knew she did. It made me think how I had gotten a rich man, but it wasn't like that with him.

The worst part of the shift that day came toward the end when a customer went upstairs and summoned the British manager, Mr. Claitor, to intercede. Claitor flew down the stairs, solidly upright like an animated arrow moving through the air, while the angry, uncloaked customer straggled behind, demanding that his sacred twenty-year-old Burberry be found. After much sorting through and crawling about, the cloak was discovered snuggling under a Persian lamb, as if the coats had taken an instant liking to each other and had colluded on their own. Claitor soothed the customer in his U.K. tones, like a male Mary Poppins calming a truculent child, as he held open the treasured trench coat. But once the customer was safely out the door, the scolding began. "If this happens again, there will be changes around here," he said, glancing at the hole in the counter to make it explicitly clear what he meant, as if Lydia and I didn't understand. "Are you doing your job or am I?" He was awful and wonderful in a *Night Porter* sort of way.

Finally at a little after three, I was able to sneak into the phone booth to call Andrew. His regular call to me that morning had been earlier than normal and brief, just telling me to call him that afternoon.

"Yvette, I have to go now."

"Okay, I'll call you later."

"No, I'm going now, leaving, for overseas."

"Oh, no." The tears were in my voice and on my face so immediately that I wondered if they had heard his words before me.

"I'll try to call you from there, but I may not be able to. Take down my address in L.A. I'll probably be back here, but I want you to have it just in case." I hated "just in case." "Just in case" sounded scary and him-without-me. "Ready?"

The phone booth mercifully had a pencil on a cord and neat pieces of paper in a wooden slot by the inverted hanging directory. I had refilled the scrap paper months before. I had liked that the restaurant supplied it, edges so neat, color so white, but now I hated that it was helping in this parting of Andrew and me.

Some words in Andrew's address were familiar, like "Bel Air." That was the brand of the first cigarette my cousin Renée and I smoked. I always imagined it was named after the car, not a land of enchantment where Andrew resided, and probably did four years earlier when I was fourteen and puffing my first cancer stick.

"And if you really need me while I'm in Malaysia, call this number." He gave me one with the L.A. area code. "Leave a message there and they'll get it to me wherever I am. Use it if you need to."

"Thanks, Andrew."

"C'mon, you're like a daughter to me."

And then it all made sense. No one else in his life had that special role, even with all those women circulating through. That "I'm going to be in your life for a very long time" role. Let the others be his girlfriends and then get dumped by him—I knew what I was to him and that was all that mattered.

"Your show's going to be a big fucking hit."

I couldn't think of doing anything without him. "I love you, Andrew."

"You, too, sweet-y-vette. And don't do any drugs. Promise me you won't."

"I won't, I promise." That was out of the blue.

"Okay, bye, honey. I'll talk to you soon."

He will? No, of course he won't.

"Andrew?"

"Yes?"

"Uhm, bye. Be careful and have a great time."

He laughed kindly. "Bye-bye, sweet-y-vette."

I let him hang up first, listening to the emptiness of the line. I knew the "If you'd like to make a call . . ." recording would come on in a moment, so I figured I'd let it shoo me off. I huddled forward over the hung-up pay phone, crying my goodbye to him, resisting the urge to quickly call back to make sure it would all be okay and I'd see him again, speak to him again one day, but he said I was like a daughter to him, so I knew I would. Andrew was going. Leaving. Gone. To a place far away—a devourer of our communication and physical reminders of us. Oh, Andrew, please think about me every day and come back quick. I wanted to shrink the Ritz-Carlton down to a tiny size and carry it with me all the time: him living there, the unfriendly operator, the yellow silk couch, the front desk clerk, the view from his room, the uniformed doormen, and mostly me with him. I took all of that, made a version I could forever see, and placed it in the foremost part of my mind so I would have to peer around it for anything else to be seen.

The morning when I was fourteen that I came home from spending the night at my cousin Renée's house, the night that Momma called to tell me in two short sentences that Daddy had left us and wasn't coming back, I went straight to his work shed before I entered the house. It was a late spring Saturday and the heat was already up and full and holding me in place, so to move at all required a going forward plus a breaking through. I abandoned my bike and let it fall against the porch railing, ignoring Momma's admonishment in my head that it would chip the paint, dropped my knapsack on the red brick path—where tiny bouquets of weeds and grass were popping up through the cracks as if they too had gotten the news that Daddy had left and were reclaiming ownership since the man of the house was gone—and went to stand in front of my father's work shed.

I knew he wasn't inside. But his presence seemed to radiate from the stillness behind the closed door and the window facing me. Like the sacristy in church, even when Monsignor Marcel wasn't there, it was so definitely his space—his authority hanging over everything—that you couldn't help but speak in whispers and say only good things. I opened the door and stepped inside. The work shed greeted me as it had the many times I had sneaked in while Daddy was at work to see what he was creating, to look at the tools, smell the leather, metal, and wood, feel the cool darkness around me, him around me, the sensations more my father than when he sat at the dinner table during the silence of our family meals.

I went over to the worktable and looked up at the tools still hanging in their spots on the Peg-Board, tools utterly left behind, and I understood. My daddy was gone. Not just at his office or on an errand to the hardware store, but gone. Like a dead body is how it was in the work shed, all the physicality was there, but the life was gone, the secret was gone, the not-supposed-to be-in-there was gone, my father was gone.

I sank down on the tall stool he never much used, and the cool metal seat was a slap to my bare legs, so I perched on the edge, just where the bottom of my shorts covered me. I could hear the buzzing of the spring day outside, dragonflies, air conditioners, the air so charged with heat it practically made a sound itself, but inside the work shed was quiet and peaceful. Had he come in here before he left? Considered taking some tools with him, but changed his mind? Where did he go and would he make instruments there? The last one he had been working on, a violin, was nowhere to be found. I couldn't remember if he had already given it away to a relative or not. Or not. Maybe he took it with him to give to someone who would be in this new life with him. The air in my lungs seemed to leave all at once and I couldn't get any more in. I grabbed my chest, gasping in the dim light, then felt dizzy and let myself crumple to the floor. The wood shavings and dust filled my nose with their scent, and I curled up under my father's worktable and cried myself into an exhausted sleep.

When I awoke, the sun was higher and hotter in the sky, so a couple of hours must have gone by. I got up and started taking down the tools before I even knew what I was doing. Scraps of leather, pieces of wood, musical strings, and all sorts of materials were in the bins my father kept everything so well organized in. It was mine now, the work shed was, as if in my sleep that information had been passed to me like waking up from a dream and instantly knowing a truth. It was a realm I could enter and stay in by the sheer power of using its tools.

I began working on an instrument of my own that afternoon—a mandolin, which seemed less forbidding than a violin—teaching myself to use the tools, work the wood, the hard and soft objects to be manipulated and changed into a greater sum than their parts, but finally had to stop hours later when I heard Momma's voice calling me. I guessed she'd called my cousin's house, then seen my backpack and bike lying where neither should have been. She yelled once more, then I heard her start back up the porch steps, and I knew I should call out to her. I opened the work shed door, saying, "I'm here, Momma, I've been home all day." I saw her eyes see where I was. They looked like someone was about to strangle her, the one hazel and one green seemed to view a horror that was invisible to me. Then she made a "huhnn" noise, a kind of "I can't believe it, yet doesn't this make sense," sound, then turned around and walked inside.

We never talked about my using the work shed. In fact, she pretended from then on that the entire structure didn't exist. Which was fine with me. The world inside the house didn't exist when I was in the work shed, which must have been why Daddy went there. At certain times, when using a tool or trying to figure out how to construct part of a piece, I'd hear his voice in my head guiding me. Saying things I knew he would say, but things I'd never heard him utter in real life. As if part of him was still in the work shed, and that part of him was talking to me, working with me.

That first instrument I tried to make came out looking more like a Cubist sculpture than a real mandolin, so I let it be that. I put it in a box I built and added some things of my father's that he'd left behind—cuff links, part of the newspaper that was lying on his leather chair, broken bits of an Old Spice bottle, a bill addressed to him, the sash to his robe, an old 78 LP he loved more than anything—and titled the whole thing

What's Left. I kept it in the work shed until I moved to New York, then before I left, I sewed a velvet bag for it that it has stayed in behind the clothes in every closet I've had since then. It's the only piece I've never shown anyone and probably never will.

Downtown L.A. on a Friday is a driver's nightmare. People are there only because they have to be at work, but they know that the traffic going out will get exponentially more terrible with each passing half hour after noon, so they all start leaving early. Which I think is what makes it worse. If they would just stay until the usual time, pretend it's a Tuesday or a Wednesday, then the traffic would be okay. But they've never asked me.

The only reason I am venturing here today is an emergency. I got a frantic call from Dipen this morning saying that the casting they did for the necklaces makes them not hang right. How many were done? I asked him, trying to stay calm. All of them, he replied. This is the only time I've ever been unhappy that he's done what he said he'd do on time. As I fight my way through the sidewalk throng to reach his building, I pray that this setback won't make my order for Roxanne late.

Dipen rents space on a high floor in the Los Angeles Jewelry Center building, an old office tower from the twenties fronted with gorgeous sea-green tile that stands in vertical waves that protrude up the front between rows of windows reaching into a peak that I have heard holds a penthouse suite where wild Prohibition-era parties were held. The bottom of the building has been disgraced with modern and cheap-looking jewelry stores that flank the still-gracious double and revolving doors into the lobby, and a large ugly sign runs the width of the building above the stores. I usually stop for a second before I go in, my hands shielding my eyes from the ruined bottom part, and gaze up at the majestic green—such a choice—and imagine how it was way back when it was built.

But today I am one of the many who are ignoring history as I push through the doors and wait with a crowd for one of the two ancient small elevators servicing the building. The elevators in the jewelry district are notoriously slow, which make the diamond and precious gems dealers on the upper floors nervous enough to hire private security men instead of relying on the ones the building provides. Robberies happen down here all the time.

Dipen's office is two tiny rooms that were partitioned out of a larger suite—most of the offices I pass in the long narrow corridor to reach his door are like it. People from all over the globe—India, Armenia, Korea, China, and the Philippines—are here in tiny spaces making jewelry for the United States. He grins at me sheepishly when I walk in, his dark hair falling over one of his eyes.

"He use your measurements from the sketch you left me, but no good, not working, come see."

I follow Dipen around his desk into the other room and see the pieces for the necklaces lying on a worktable. They are shaped like tiny thin saxophones, but smooth, and the part that looks like the mouth of the horn curves back to touch the longer arm. They are meant to be attached by one end to a bronze leather cord, then the other, the part that forms a hook of itself, will hold a big semiprecious stone—a tourmaline or a checkerboard-cut citrine—by clasping a bar that the gem will be suspended from. But the weight and curve of the gold make the pieces fall in toward the gem instead of holding it straight.

"I know this works, Dipen, the prototype did. How'd we do that?"

"I had Mahee for that. This new guy, he follow measurements exactly, but no right."

I remember how Mahee could take my designs and would instinctively shave off a little here, add a bit more gold and weight there, to make them all fall right. I wish to God he hadn't gone back to India.

"Okay, let's figure it out." I pull out paper and a pen and draw a new prototype by flattening along the back and adding more of a curve on the top. I know Dipen's going to charge me for the useless batch, and I imagine my profits on these pieces dwindling. "And he'll melt these pieces down, right, so I won't have to . . ."

"Same gold, same gold, and . . ." Dipen looks away for a moment, as if consulting some hidden oracle. "I knock a third off price for casting those."

"Thanks, Dipen, you're the best. And have him only do one first; I'll come back and look at that."

"Right, right, all fine," he says, smiling and walking me toward the door.

"And the other pieces, how are they coming?"

"Fine, no problem, we make many before. Next week, come back, see necklace."

As I enter the packed elevator to leave the building, I consider for a second getting a new caster, but then remember the horror stories I've heard from other designers: casters selling their designs to knockoff firms, casters being paid off by competing designers to stall orders so a talented new designer will fail, casters making pieces that are fourteen-karat gold instead of the eighteen-karat that was paid for. This setback with Dipen is deeply annoying, but nothing considering what it could be.

Sitting in traffic on First Street trying to get out of downtown, I decide to call Lizzie. Maybe I'll jump on the freeway, take it all the way to Santa Monica and go to her store in Venice to get the check for those sales that she owes me. Her store's phone rings and rings, no machine picking up, nothing. I know the number by heart, but I check it in my address book to make sure my fingers didn't forget, then dial the same digits again. Nothing. Jesus, Lizzie, what kind of store isn't open on a Friday afternoon? I am tempted to drive out there anyway—the really horrific traffic will be going the other way—and wait for her to appear, but that's a dubious shot. I start to call Reggie to complain about Lizzie, but then don't. He was so happy last night reading his script to me, sitting on my living room floor with Chinese food containers all around, then talking about Chopin and New Orleans and filming. It's been pretty much all about me this week so I decide not to bother him about stupid Lizzie—it isn't anything that hasn't happened before, and those other times, she always paid.

I am midscream, volume full throttle, eyes open and staring, in my bedroom. Then my sound disappears as I realize that what I was seeing is no longer there. I want to see it again so I can know what it is. It is two-forty A.M., and my apartment is completely quiet—now that I've stopped screaming, at least. I find it so weird that Gloria has never said anything. Unless she thinks I'm entertaining my own "visitors" who have really odd tastes—like scaring the be-Jesus out of me. The rotten part is that it's hell trying to get back to sleep after one of those dreams. I wish it would fucking end.

I go to the kitchen to make myself a cup of chamomile tea. While waiting for the water to boil, I lean against the kitchen counter in my antique silk slip and try to figure out what in real life does terrify me that might be causing the dream.

Cockroaches head the list. Particularly the huge flying ones I had to grow up with on the warm wet Gulf Coast; they continue to inspire in me a fear unequal to most.

When I was seven, I decided to take matters into my own hands about those fearsome pests since obviously the bug man (a regular visitor to every Southern home) and Daddy were unable to keep the horrible monsters away. Kneeling on the floor of my bedroom with my favorite teddy bear beside me, wearing an only-for-mass-and-certain-parties dress, I told God—out loud for double effect—that I was ready for a deal. I would let a roach—one of the big nasty flying ones that came in from the outside, like some true owner of our home whose generosity toward us could only last so long—crawl over my hand if for the rest of my life I never had to see another one. I thought this an extremely fair exchange.

No roach appeared. For once, where is one when you need it? I couldn't tell if that meant God was going to skip my part and, being all-loving, just do His, or maybe other people were praying out loud, too, and mine had gotten lost in the din. Or worse, maybe one crawl across the hand wasn't enough for Him. All right, I'd try again. I recited the plan, but this time upped my end, saying that the roach could crawl along my entire arm. Again, nothing happened.

Just as I was about to try again, Daddy stuck his head in and asked what I was doing. I explained the rules to him—maybe if I got him involved, the whole house could be an insect-free zone.

He walked over to me, sat on the floor, and wrapped me up in a hug. "You can't make deals with God, darling, it doesn't work like that."

As soon as he said it, I knew it was true. Our trading sides were so uneven—my offer so paltry to Him, never enough to alter the exertion of nature on my life, but at least I had Daddy's arms around me.

The tea kettle is screaming that its job is done, so I pour the water into a mug, letting the chamomile-infused steam waft in my face. The scream dream reminds me of those cockroaches, appearing out of nowhere and flying suddenly into view. But the worst part is that my mind, or subconscious, made the damn dream up. Created it, called it forth, brought it into being—for what? To terrorize myself through and through?

I get the pillow and blanket from my bed and head for the couch. The tree outside my living room window is lit up by security lights so its large branches and full leaves, soft brown and silvery green, are solid and shimmering in the dark. It is indifferent to the night—has no need to sleep, no pressure to lose consciousness so it will be alert for the next day's activities. I find that as freeing as not setting an alarm clock. Suzanne's veil is in the living room where I moved it this afternoon, like a marital ghost in the room's gloom. Before I settle on the couch to go to sleep, I get up and move the veil back to my studio, out of sight.

The dressing room's three-part mirror reflects an ungodly amount of pink. There should be a design ordinance against this, but I guess bridal boutiques would have to be exempt from that rule. I understand the color is supposed to be warm, soft, and flattering to one's skin, but the result on me is a heightening of green undertones I never knew I had. Or maybe that's a physical reaction to the maid-of-honor dress hanging on me. And I mean hanging. The distance between the fabric and my body reminds me of that blank space you see on children's pictures: earth and trees way down below—huge gap—then way up at the top, a line for the sky with the sun stuck in the corner; the space in between is unaccounted for, but caused by the other two.

Suzanne is so ecstatic about this tent I am wearing that it has almost made her forget that she was mad as a wet hen when she saw that I hadn't brought her veil with me for her to try on. She was also annoyed about my tardiness, but now her face is enrapt as she moves around me, plucking at the floral material billowing out from my frame.

"I'm sorry, but other than me getting one three sizes smaller, what is there to fit on this dress?"

"Hush, it's perfect," she says, still dancing around me, thrilled with the effect.

"Is everyone's like this, or am I just particularly lucky?"

"Of course yours is different—you're my maid of honor. It's beautiful, exactly how I pictured it. Go show Matt."

My blond and handsome soon-to-be brother-in-law has intelligently brought something to read on this shopping extravaganza he joined us for. Suzanne started to protest when he sat down in the store and immediately pulled out the *Wall Street Journal*, but he patiently reminded her of the murder mysteries she devours at Dodger games, so she turned her focus on me.

I stand in front of Matt for a paragraph before I interrupt his reading by saying, "I know, I look like a walking floral rectangle."

Matt lowers the paper. "No you don't. You look . . . Pretty."

"In a bathroom-wallpaper kind of way, yeah. But it's her day, and at least she's paying for it. She's probably going to use it later to slipcover an armchair."

"That's the sisterly spirit."

Matt moves his newspaper off the hot-pink tufted velvet love seat so I can sit down. The dress pools around my shoes.

"So, how are you? Seeing anyone? Are you happy?"

Pink walls will never be exempt inside a bridal store, but those three questions should be. Though I know Matt means well, and I like that he adopts a brotherly role.

"Work's going well. I got a new store."

"That's great."

"Thanks, and the commissions keep coming in, so I figure the next step is another boutique, and then a department store really is my goal, and getting into another magazine. A national would be great, so even with Momma's money winding down, if things continue as they are, I should be okay."

"That's good," he says, but without the same enthusiasm as before.

I can hear the financial-planning lecture Matt is calculating whether to give me or not, so I decide to keep the conversation moving along. "And I sorta started seeing Michael again."

"Michael?" IRAs and bonds are still cha-chinging in Matt's head. "The guy who drank out of his own flask at our Christmas party?"

I wish he'd forget that. "That was Rick. No, Michael, remember? We ran into y'all at the movie theater?"

"Oh, Michael. Radio, right?"

"Right." Recalling Michael's work is good. "So, anyway, it's nice."

"Right, this is the guy who canceled dinner after Suzanne cooked seafood gumbo all day. Now I remember, okay. So you're seeing him again—and he's actually showing up?"

I want to be annoyed that Matt mentioned that—didn't I bring Suzanne a flowering plant to apologize?—but I like having shared history with him.

"There you two are." Suzanne appears carrying two child-sized wedding dresses. "What do you think?"

"Yvette's seeing Michael again." Matt shoots me a look as if he got an extra turn picking Saturday-morning cartoons.

"Oh, that's nice, honey." Suzanne hands me one of the dresses to hold up. "Okay, which one? Now consider the music that will be playing—it all has to match."

"What, in God's name, are those?" Matt has finally noticed the objects of his intended's concern.

"The child bride's dress," my sister announces in a voice that I know means, "We've discussed this before."

"It's an old Southern tradition," I say for Matt. "A child bridal couple walks down the aisle first in the processional, symbolizing—what, Suzanne, do you know? I mean, other than the obvious."

"I don't know and I don't care; it's sweet." Suzanne puts down the dress she was holding and takes the other from my hands, holding it in front of her, as if it somehow could fit. "Which one?"

Driving away from the bridal shop in my truck, I have a wild impulse for a cigarette—I haven't had one in years, but a longing for the taste is there instantly. I have to keep telling myself that I don't really want one and definitely don't want that habit again. I know that desire is just to distract me from where I've been. Then an image appears in my mind of a long white coffin nail, as Daddy used to call cigarettes. It is lit, and the cherry at the end glows bright red. Then the long whiteness of the cigarette transforms into a bride with an aura of smoke obscuring her face.

Michael and I have turned the corner onto Fairfax Avenue, or Kosher Canyon as he calls it, and are walking toward Canter's Deli for a meal. It is Saturday night and the environment is divided—God's darkness pushed far above by L.A.'s lights bright below. I haven't seen Michael since Steve's gallery opening on Wednesday night. Since, all right, one night after I went to the theater and saw Andrew. Not that I'm thinking about him. I'm thinking about Michael, his hand in mine, as we walk down Fairfax on this gentle night; I just seem to have lost track of what he's talking about.

But before I can figure it out, what grabs my attention is the absence of clothes. In the far corner of Canter's parking lot is a man who appears to be in his sixties, each tired, difficult, meager year is collected on his pale face and paler body, which, save for a pair of dull baggy underwear, I can plainly see.

"Oh, my God, he's nekked." My hand flies to my eyes to save the man from disgrace.

"Naked," Michael replies.

"What?" I peek through my fingers. Maybe it was an apparition, a ghost from the street's past, but the man is still there, his body so white it looks practically lit from within like a battered-up lamp you never notice until it's turned on. The man is busy, precisely folding imaginary clothes, engaged in that most comforting of rituals—getting ready for bed.

"It's pronounced 'naked,' not 'nekked.'"

"Well, where I'm from, it's 'nekked.' Of course, growing up, I thought they were two different words. 'Naked' was when you were about to or just finished having sex, and 'nekked' was not having any clothes on, but for no particular reason really, like for running through the sprinklers or something."

"So, this guy's nekked and wishes he was naked."

"Michael." I wish he wouldn't try to be funny at a time like this.

The man is moving around, pulling out imaginary drawers, pantomiming brushing his teeth in his private-illusion bedroom-cum-bath, living in a master suite that only exists in the gap between his memory and time. "We need to call the police. Not that I think he's a criminal for doing his ablutions in a parking lot, but they could take him somewhere, get him off the street before someone comes along and . . . I don't know. He needs protection."

"Yvette, the only place the police take anyone is jail; this guy shouldn't go there. Wait here."

Before I can ask where he's going, Michael hurries away from me and, darting between cars, crosses diagonally through the parking lot. He stops near an SUV and watches the man from a short distance.

The man is now on his knees and looks to be praying. I can practically see the four-poster mahogany bed he thinks he is saying his nightly devotion next to. The Guardian Angel prayer that Suzanne and I said as children every night before bed is suddenly triggered in my mind. "Angel of God, my guardian dear, to whom with love, commit me here, ever this day, be at my side, to light and guard, to rule and guide. Amen."

The man makes the sign of the cross; I hope he said that intercession, too, and that his guardian angel isn't too old to hear. God only knows the dangers that this poor man has to be frightened of since he is sleeping outside, and yet he looks so calm as he lies down for sleep. I think about how nervous I am every night going to bed, never knowing if I'll awaken to a scream about something that isn't even there. In the real world, at least. Maybe I'll start saying a prayer before going to bed, too. Like the reverse of when I was a kid and, waking up from a bad dream, would say Hail Marys to feel safe while I got back to sleep.

Michael slowly walks around the SUV and disappears from my view for a moment, then reappears, and walks back. His jacket is no longer on him, and he looks over his shoulder a couple of times before he reaches me.

"That was so sweet of you. Did you put it over him?"

"No, I didn't want to get in his space and scare him. I just draped it nearby where he'll see it and hopefully figure out to put it on. I didn't see any other clothes around, but it's something, at least. He probably ran out of his medication."

"What medication?"

"He's a paranoid schizophrenic, delusional. He's clearly not living in the reality that we all see."

And for a moment, thinking of my Andrew memories, I understand the attraction.

When Michael and I leave Canter's at the end of our meal—towering pastrami sandwich for him, tuna salad on rye for me—we try to find Nekked Man to give him the half of my sandwich I didn't touch, or Michael does as I wait on the sidewalk while he goes to the far corner of the parking lot and looks around, but Nekked Man is nowhere in sight. Nor is Michael's jacket, which we hope is a good sign.

Driving away from Fairfax on Beverly Boulevard, we head east to my apartment in the Saturday night traffic's expectant rush. I am perched on the passenger seat in Michael's car, his late eighties BMW, which from the outside looks great, cream paint job still good, no dings anywhere, but inside it's a whole different world. The seat I am on rocks side to side whenever he accelerates, changes lanes, or stops, and putting my feet firmly on the floor is out of the question because it is covered with easily breakable CDs, partly filled soda cans, and a backpack that Michael explains is set and ready to go if he gets the urge to go hiking. The passenger door can't be opened from the outside, requiring that Michael never open it for me, as if the car intuited his feelings about chivalry and adopted a defect to match. His radio station is playing on the expensive and confusing-looking stereo that he takes out of the trunk and slides into a slot in the dashboard every time we get in. The stereo is much better situated in this car for an accident, or even just a drive, than I am. For the first time in my life, I long for a shoulder strap.

"So, I'm just going to do it. I sent them a check for the whole thing today," I say as I check the traffic to make sure there are no major obstacles that Michael needs all his attention for. "I've been wanting to do a Buddhist retreat for years."

"That could work."

"Yeah, and this one is for Catholics. Well, Christians. 'Zen for Christians,' that's what they're calling it. Some Jesuit priest who happens to be a Zen master is leading it. Three full days of silence. I think it sounds fun. Like running a marathon is fun. You get purged and excellent all at the same time. It's at the beginning of August, right after Suzanne's wedding that we're going to together, right?"

"Right."

Michael's head is completely turned to the left looking at a restaurant with lots of tables outside. The exterior is a deep bright yellow, making the profusion of black-clad patrons look like cross-walk safety sign figures come to life.

"I think it will be helpful in a merging kind of way. The last time I went to mass was Momma's funeral, and I stopped going regularly when I was fourteen."

"That's never going to work."

"No, I think it's perfect, really." It's sweet how passionate Michael is about this. "Dharma and divinity. Emptiness and redemption. What more could I want?"

"What?" Michael looks at me for the first time. "No, this show. I thought it was in better shape than this, but it's still . . . no one's listening, would you listen? Jesus Christ."

As Michael's car careens along, I think about the phone calls I used to have with Andrew. Hours of me talking and him listening, and him remembering practically everything. Andrew Madden with his huge career and insanely busy life always had time to listen to me, and this SOB sitting next to me can't even hear three sentences without getting distracted by his fucking radio. But Andrew's not around and Michael is. And maybe Michael can give that to me when things at the station settle down. Just stop comparing Michael to Andrew—as long as I do that, no one can win.

The cross above my bedroom door is the first thing I see when Michael wakes me hours later in the middle of the night. I nailed it up there last week, hoping its protection would extend from vampires to nightmares, but even though it hasn't worked, I can't bring myself to take it down. Maybe its protective powers just need some time to kick in; its safeguarding ability will emerge once God finally gets word it was hung.

I pull the covers back so Michael and I can get under them and sleep properly in bed. Our clothes are long off, and the protected interior air of my bedroom is a few degrees cooler than pleasant on my skin. I remember Nekked Man and hope he found more clothes somewhere tonight and is asleep someplace safe.

"That was the best sleep," Michael says as he stretches. He sounds oddly done. "I've only been getting like four or five hours a night since I took over the station, but, man, those three hours felt like nine. That was amazing." He kisses my shoulder and neck and arm. "You are amazing."

We kiss some more, and I am moving down his body with my mouth when Michael suddenly tells me he has to go.

"Go where? No. Stay here."

"I can't, Yvette, I need to be at the station really early tomorrow, and you know, traffic on the freeways is a bitch."

"On a Sunday?"

He kisses my mouth and hands. "It's important I'm there. Right now is a very—"

"Crucial time," I finish for him.

He looks so appreciative of my understanding that I feel bad that I didn't really mean it, so suddenly I do.

Listening to Michael's rhythmic footsteps going down the stairs, I wonder if the noise will awaken Gloria and bring flashbacks of her "visitors," but my screams don't seem to register on her, so maybe footsteps won't, either.

I wish Michael had stayed. Jesus, he's so into his work, but maybe he just needs more time and then he'll be like that about us. The outline of my body still feels nicely blurred from Michael's skin, weight, and hands on me. The pillow is under my head, the blanket pulled up right; bed, sleep, and me start combining, becoming an undifferentiated dream. Everything with Michael is fine; we're taking it slow, which is what I wanted to do. I hope going back to sleep at this hour will prevent the scream dream. Or thoughts about Andrew. Where did that come from? For God's sake, I was thinking about Michael.

But not anymore, I guess. Andrew is in my mind as solidly as a body in my bed, the way his hands felt on me, his eyes on mine. Fuck. Michael, why aren't you canceling out Andrew? Okay, I just need to see Michael more, that's all, get really hooked in with him, then Andrew will be a thing of my past, never to be thought of or seen by me again. I hope.

But really kind of don't.

Fuck.

16

The day after Andrew left New York for Malaysia to shoot *Paradise Again* with Lily Creed, a day that I wished his being on the other side of the world would magically end so he'd be in New York with me again, Peg called to tell me that I would be having dinner that Friday evening with Tory and seven men. She didn't say it quite like that—seven men—but as she rattled off their names, a few I knew from reading *Art-Forum*, I noticed they were all masculine. Dinner at an Italian restaurant in SoHo at eight-thirty, did I need directions or could I find it?

I had heard of the place and had passed it many times on my way to and from Sexton Space. It was garnering a lot of attention. The owner was from Milan and had a restaurant there that was famous and essential with the fashion and art crowd, and his New York location was just as instantly in demand.

I would have to juggle my schedule at work, though I didn't bother Peg with that detail, would have to beg Lydia to cover for me, which she probably would once she heard where I was going and what it was for. Lydia lived for the restaurant scene, and if she wasn't going, she was happy to live through it vicariously.

On the afternoon of my dinner with Tory and the seven dwarfs, as Carrie was calling them, she and I were sitting at the kitchen table deciding what I should wear. Carrie was suggesting outfits made up partly from her wardrobe and partly from mine while reading aloud personal ads in the *Village Voice*. We were almost settled on an outfit, though were still going back and forth about the shoes, when suddenly the cat jumped onto Carrie's lap, startling her into moving the paper which caused the fine corner of the front page to scratch my eye. It didn't require my going to an emergency room, but the result was a constantly crying left eye. No matter how long I kept a bag of frozen peas on it, a stream of tears kept pouring down, so my right profile looked fine, but from the left, I looked like a weeping Picasso come to life. The two sides of my face did not match.

It was horrendous and there was no way I was going to dinner like that. I was all ready to call Peg to cancel, but Carrie convinced me that would be a bad move—all those important men's schedules arranged for one night to meet me. Just go and explain what happened, they'll understand, she was sure. So off I went in an outfit that I felt great in, at least, because the left side of my face still had tears running down it, but hopefully it would be too dark in the restaurant for anyone to really see.

The loud, chic Italian restaurant was perfectly lit for the patrons to look great, but especially to be seen by everyone else since that, more than eating, was the point of the place. In the well-lit space, I had to zigzag through closely packed tables while everyone craned their heads to see who had come in, which added to the ersatz runway experience of walking in. Tory's table was in a private room in the back with two men in dark suits standing at each side of the door. They appeared to be on guard, and eventually I realized they were—one of the seven men was from a large prominent family in Milan that controlled all kinds of things, is one way to say it, and they belonged to him. Tory spoke to him only in Italian, and seemed to covet his bodyguards the way a person does a private plane. The seven dwarfs were all different ages and heights, but all horrendously sophisticated about art: a critic, a few huge collectors, a prominent artist, and a couple of curators at museums. At various times in the evening, each man turned to me, bearing down with his elegant and educated brain, and gave me a question or two, which I answered while doing my best to hide my still-tearing eye. Though to the man on my left, it was impossible to camouflage, and he kept glancing at the tears as if they were contagious, so I tried to explain what happened, but he was the Italian and didn't understand. He kept confusing "eye" for "I," thinking I was cut somewhere else, but only magically expressing it on one side. I gave up, and did my best to converse with him in the little English he knew, but it didn't go anywhere. Tory was ignoring my eye or didn't notice, so busy was she at the other end of the table talking in French, Italian, English, and sometimes in all three. Once she said, "From the South; Alabama, I think," among other words I couldn't discern, though I definitely heard "Andrew" a few times.

At the end of the evening as we were dispersing on the street, Tory came up to me, grabbed both of my shoulders, and said, "For God's sake, get some rest." I started to tell her what happened to my eye with the *Village Voice*, but she thought I was talking about getting publicity, then one of the men tapped her shoulder to say goodbye, causing her smile to be reborn when she turned to him.

My cab ride home was an exercise in reliving the whole thing and wishing it had gone a lot better—as in great. I told Carrie all about it when I got home. She thought it sounded fine, but I kept wishing I had been more "on."

"How much could they expect? You're eighteen, for Christ's sake, in a show at Sexton Space. That's plenty cool enough, and you looked great tonight. Okay, the eye, I know, but other than that, you did. They probably all wanted to have sex with you and were just putting up that disinterested front the way boys do. Don't worry about it." And she poured me another glass of wine.

Lying in bed that night, waiting for sleep to come, I wished to God that Andrew was at the Ritz-Carlton—or even just reachable by phone—so I could tell him about the dinner, get his reaction, hear his comforting voice, and his reassuring, "You big fucking art star."

Then for the first time, I doubted it might come true. Andrew had always made it sound so much a fait accompli that I hadn't really questioned it. Just trusted him and what he knew. And he was so confident about it, why shouldn't I be? But suddenly in the dark of my tiny bedroom on my lonely twin bed, I realized that there were a lot more hoops to go through than I ever could have imagined before that could come true.

On the following Tuesday, I went into work for the eleven-to-eight shift and found the restaurant in a state of total doom, as if the entire city of New York had died, and as I soon found out, it pretty much had. It was October 20, the morning after Black Monday, the worst stock market crash since 1929. Lunch reservations were being canceled nonstop, including standing reservations for men whose names held court on the pages of the long leather ledger every day of the week, representing a booth along the wall in the barroom or a table by the pool in the main room held only for them until and if their secretary called to let it go. None were coming in. Though a few out-of-towners showed up and I watched Claitor do his best job ever of hiding his disdain for that sort; tourists were not his thing.

One horrendously hot and humid summer day toward the end of lunch, an obviously touristy couple—looking as if they came from Nebraska, but had walked all the way—straggled up the stairs. The dining rooms had already begun clearing out, some tables were empty, and there was enough time to seat them before the kitchen closed. Claitor smiled in his most charming way, and explained that he would love for them to have lunch, but unfortunately, he couldn't seat the gentleman without a jacket and tie, house rules. A host who was very new and unused to interpreting Claitor's many tones immediately piped up, Wasn't that what all those navy jackets and striped ties in the closet were for? Claitor kept the same small smile fixed on his face as if no words had been spoken, and thanked the couple for coming in, then suggested they try La Chanteuse up the street. When the rejected tourists were well down the stairs, Claitor turned to the offending host, saying, "And did you *like* the way they looked?" Then walked into the kitchen to order his meal.

But Tuesday, October 20, made everyone in the restaurant suddenly extremely grateful for tourists. The city had come apart overnight. In the weeks following, tips for everyone fell to the ground, service-industry jobs disappeared, or if people were able to hang on to them, their income was cut. And the high that the art market had been on came crashing down.

"But none of this is going to stop your work from selling," Carrie reassured me in late November as my gallery show was looming. "You're new, starting out. Your prices aren't exorbitant. You're exactly what they need to be investing in."

Though I thought the whole problem with the crash was that so much money had been lost that people had nothing to put into anything, much less an unsure thing, I decided to believe she was right, and it wasn't like Tory was canceling the show. Which was a relief for tons of reasons, one being that I had missed the deadline to apply for the School of Visual Arts to begin in the spring. Suzanne's voice was in my head fussing at me about it as she had done on the phone the other day, but Carrie had said not to worry about it. "Your work in the show will sell," she said. "You'll quit your job, find a studio somewhere, and just make art all day long. Probably even be asked to teach classes at SVA eventually as a visiting artist, that sort of thing." I hoped she was right. And Andrew would be back soon from his film, maybe even move here from L.A., or I'd fly out there to see him, drop in for lunch on my way to meet with a collector I had sold to again. What was I worried about? It was all going to be fine.

Peg helped me find something to wear to the opening. I blew a whole week's paycheck on a black dress at Agnès b., a store I passed all the time to and from the gallery, loving everything in its windows. Peg said it was perfect, and I loved it more than anything I'd ever owned.

So I was on a high when I arrived at the gallery half an hour before the show started, wearing my new dress, about to see my art on display in a SoHo gallery in New York City just six months after I arrived, with Andrew Madden in my life. How much better could it get?

The other artists in the group show were standing around looking at one another's work when I walked in. I had met them before in the gallery. They were all men, all older than me, and had trained formally at Yale, Rhode Island School of Design, and an art school in Barcelona. We exchanged hellos, then I joined them in looking at their work—paintings that were exuberant, aggressive, and taut—before turning toward the middle of the gallery to see how my work had been displayed. The last time I had seen all my sculptures together was the spring before when they were exhibited at a small gallery in New Orleans. I had felt such pride then, but in a way that surprised me for that word. It felt quiet and having to do with me, yet not. It was a sensation that kept me happily comfortable and able to talk to anyone about my work, more like I had discovered the pieces than made them. Like they had always been around to be found, to be reached out and grabbed, like Keith Richards once said about songs—how they're in the air and all you have to do is grab them.

But in Sexton Space my sculptures were offered up on high white stands, not on the floor connected to the earth. And in spite of or because of the additional height, they looked diminished, as if they were floating in space. I found Peg, and tried to keep the panic from my voice as I told her that I hadn't known they'd be displayed that way, they were meant to be on the ground. I wanted people to feel above them, not the other way around, but she assured me that Tory had decided they would have been invisible without the added height—lost in the throng, knocked over even; it was better this way. But I wasn't so sure. Disassociated from the ground, up close to my face, the whole sense of structure I had created was gone. They might as well have been on burgundy velvet and bathed in black light, they were so far from what I'd envisioned. Then seeing my dissatisfaction, Peg said that it was too late to do anything now, the guests were starting to arrive. I tried to reassure myself that Tory, if anyone, knew how to display art, but I was angry that she had changed our plans without telling me first. It was as though the sculptures and I had lost our footing.

A huge crowd began swarming in, and in a short time the gallery was packed with collectors and critics, artists and actors, models and musicians from all over the globe. A perfectly divvied up demographic of the fabulous and known commandeered the gallery, sidewalk, and street, extending the party into the cold, deep SoHo night.

I was standing in line for the bar to get a glass of wine; the opening was in full bloom. Everyone knew so many there—there were shrieks and huddles and embraces. I tried to remember what I had thought it'd be like. Not this. I'd thought . . . smaller. Dispersed. People talking quietly. I'd thought . . . museum, I realized suddenly, not prom night, *Vogue,* and the Concorde rolled into one.

A six-foot-plus drag queen was in line ahead of me. When he/she had arrived, I'd thought, *What an exceptionally tall woman, but so nicely dressed.* I recognized the Oscar de la Renta dress from the window at Bergdorf's on my walks home from work, and there it was cinching a waist before cascading down in a profusion of flowered satin. "But look at the hands," the Spanish artist had said in my ear, nodding a couple of times. "That's how you tell." Then he walked away to meet him/her.

Suddenly I was bumped. Pushed, really, into him/her. And as I tried to right myself, the wine that was held up high in his/her hand poured straight down the front of my dress.

"My fault," a man said, as a cocktail napkin–filled hand started dabbing at and rubbing my chest. I wondered if it was the drag queen who had spoken, all decked out in grand femme style, but stuck with a deep voice.

"That's okay. I'm fine, really, thanks," I said, trying to end this invasive and ineffective toweling off, but it wouldn't stop, and the hands continued roaming all over my breasts, more touching them than doing any drying. Finally, I couldn't take the pawing anymore. "Please, stop," I said, but the "please" wasn't heard. My head was down when I said it, watching strange male hands have more interaction with my breasts than anyone had had since Andrew, which made me wish it was him, made me miss him, then my head had moved up for the word "stop," but no one had heard the word "please," so it came out a sharp command.

People all around suddenly hushed and stared. The man froze, leaving his hands on my breasts, as his eyes flashed first with puerile, anxious shame, then adult, vindictive rage.

"I was trying to help." His hands flew off me, the reverse of a slap, but having the same effect. The spectator circle had widened, more were tuned in. "You are a mess," he declared in a voice that carried well. Then people parted for him to walk away, leaving me standing in an ever-widening silent glare.

I spent the rest of the opening and that entire sleepless night regretting that I hadn't seen his face before I spoke, the face of a man I had met weeks before at Tory's dinner. He was an extremely influential art critic who was known for holding huge grudges and exacting revenge in his reviews, which were very well read.

His pen was mightier than a Glock, and the worst part was that I agreed with part of his review—the sculptures had looked displaced. God, what a depressing word. As if in their transfer to New York, their lease for one homeland was lost, while another never came through. Part of me wanted to call him up and tell him it was Tory's idea for them to be placed way up high on stands, but I knew I couldn't. I wondered if she would ever admit that she had messed up, but probably not.

The first cigarette I smoked gave me a head rush, or it might have been the strong coffee I had with it. I had walked to the Hungarian pastry shop in my neighborhood after reading the suicide-inducing review, not wanting to be alone in the apartment with it. A Columbia student engrossed in books was sitting near me, serenely smoking his cigarettes. The third time he lit up, he turned and silently offered me the pack, as if knowing my craving before it reached me. The cigarette occupied my body; the rush occupied my mind. On the way home, I stopped at a bodega, bought a lighter and two packs of Marlboros, and threw the newspaper with the review into a trash can that was brimming with empty bottles of beer. I prayed that with Andrew being halfway around the world, he somehow wouldn't find out about the review. But I knew he probably would.

Peg called the day after the review came out to say that Tory was heading to London and would talk to me in January. There was something to look forward to. If she was going to drop me, why not do it now? Part of me wished I could talk to Andrew to make me feel better about this, and another part hoped that he'd never find out and that the whole experience would disappear.

I stayed in Manhattan for the holidays, not wanting to be in my mother's house under the attic where my sculptures had been before their New York ravaging. And Suzanne as usual was staying in L.A. with her new boyfriend, so it would have been just the two of us, which sounded beyond dreariness. Working and running and smoking tons with holiday parties thrown in were all semiuseful in keeping me occupied, but mostly, I worried about what Tory would say when she returned and what Andrew's reaction was going to be when he found out about the opening. A big fucking art star I definitely had not become. I had a feeling that thanks to all the people working for him, he easily kept up with anything and everything that he spent energy on. And recommending me personally to Tory qualified as that.

Oh, God, I just wanted to go back in time and redo that opening. Redo that hour, that minute, that one little twist that screwed everything up, but as much as I prayed, time persisted in its forward path, carrying me with it in a dreadful agonizing march of days.

The bronchitis hit right after New Year's and put an end to all of my activities, except worrying. I wished it were the other way around, that the part of my brain that worried had the exhausting illness and was too tired to raise more concerns while the rest of me could go along merrily. Not that I knew it was bronchitis. I missed day after day after day of work, took aspirin to no avail, and wondered what never-ending nightmare of a flu I had gotten.

By the two-and-a-half-week mark, I figured I might have consumption. Suzanne had gone through a brief teenage period of wanting to die from that, so we had looked it up. And I was practically living in a slum—hadn't an epidemic started in apartment buildings like this in the early 1900s? Maybe I'd get sent to a sanitarium where I could quietly cough away my life. That'd be an escape from blowing my big opening. For a few delirium-filled afternoons, that sounded like the best idea I'd had in years. Carrie was still in Mississippi on extended holiday and Ruth was performing on a Caribbean cruise, her room rented out to a tall Danish woman who grimly set out each morning on open chorus calls. When I was able to, I worried how I'd make next month's rent, not to mention all the bills lying unpaid.

I was dreaming of being at a sanitarium. A blue stream was in the distance with sunlight flitting on its surface; there was a soft wind and rolling hills. Tory was in a wheelchair being pushed by exquisite pale man. He kept ramming the hard footrests into people's shins while she shrieked, "Off with their heads!" Decapitated sculptures appeared, the heads floating in space like paintings midair. I was running toward the stream, which had become the muddy Mississippi, trying desperately to get there, when a bell began to ring, the alarm that I had escaped! My pace quickened going up the hill, I was panting hard, unable to breathe, a stone appeared in my path tripping me, I fell and hit the ground, and that jarred me awake. I realized that the ringing bell was my phone.

"Hello?" I was still shrugging out of the dream, trying to get back to the real day despite my delirium.

"Hi."

I had a horrible feeling it was exquisite pale man with rotten news. "Who is this?"

"Andrew."

I immediately started to cry. Not audibly, thank God, because I sounded dreadful enough, but tears were streaming down. I wished they would cool my blazing face. "Are you here?"

"No, I'm still—are you okay?"

I wanted to throw myself on him and never let go. "I'm sick."

"With what? For how long?"

He wasn't happy that I hadn't seen a doctor, even more displeased when I finally revealed I didn't have health insurance, never had, so couldn't afford to go to one, plus all the work I was missing, and—

"Just hang on, Yvette, I'll call you right back."

"Promise, soon? Really right back?" I was terrified it'd be weeks or months before I heard his voice again.

"Yes, really, right back. Just hang on."

The long-distance clicking stopped, and the line went dead. I had to rest a minute before reaching down to hang up.

Andrew called ten minutes later, and told me that his assistant in L.A., Patrick, was finding a doctor in New York for me, and when Patrick called, to give him my checking account information for him to wire-transfer into. I cried through Andrew telling me this, it was like feeling his strong, safe arms wrapped around me from so far away. My thanks was a small arrow making an arc to reach him.

"You just get better. I'll call you when I'm back."

I kept myself from asking how long that would be. "How's it going?"

"It's . . . good. It's going well. I have to go now, sweet-y-vette. I'll talk to you soon, you just get better."

His voice was a blanket lying gently on top of me, swaddling me, and nudging sleep to come. I hung up the phone. Maybe he hadn't heard about the gallery opening. Or maybe he had and didn't care. Didn't care that I hadn't been turned into a big fucking art star. Loved me anyway and that was all that mattered. God, I hoped so.

Patrick was the epitome of polite solicitousness when he called an hour later waking me up. He spoke with an authority tinged with a disposition to please. The doctor he found arrived at my apartment that night, gave me a shot and left large capsules of antibiotics. The next day, a thousand dollars appeared in my checking account. It had never known a balance that high. For weeks, the wire-transfer slip stayed in my purse, and I'd pull it out on late bus rides home from the restaurant like a picture of a loved one.

Tory's imperative was that I needed new work. She made it sound like an item I could run across at a store for a really good price. The question that had concerned me for months—where to create this?—was answered during her spiel. One of her painters needed an additional assistant—I could have a small stipend or partial use of the studio that his ex-boyfriend had vacated when he moved to Rome. Tory made it clear what my choice would be.

Thank God she wasn't dropping me. Maybe a bad review wasn't the end of the world. Here was a chance for me to sculpt, to let my life in New York cut into my work. And maybe Andrew did know about the opening, and it wasn't as horrible as I thought it was. Tory wasn't dropping me—that meant something. As I went for a run in the park, difficult as hell from the cigarettes I had returned to after the bronchitis, I framed questions in my mind that I wanted to address in my new sculptures, and mostly, I felt relieved.

Suzanne pretended to be happy for me about the apprenticeship, but made me promise I would apply to the School of Visual Arts to start next fall.

"You need to go to college; this is absolutely ridiculous. You're already a year behind—what are you going to do, start when you're thirty? And don't think you'll get that money for anything else. At least Mother isn't in control of that, thank God. This man is ruining your life."

I didn't have to ask her who she meant.

17

The painter I would be apprenticed to was well-known to me from articles in *ArtForum* that I had read in Mississippi, the magazine an emissary from the world I longed to join. He was so renowned that I had even seen a feature about him in Momma's *Vogue*, heralding a MOMA exhibition. Most of my interview for the position was with his chief assistant, or C.A. as he referred to himself in the third person while describing the duties required of me. The painter, Raul, appeared midway through and sat down close to C.A., who massaged his massive hands, while I recited again for him where I was from and how I had gotten there, all information I figured Tory had already given them.

"When's your birthday?" was the only thing Raul wanted to know, then he and C.A. looked at each other for a moment after I gave the date.

"Not a bad fit for this group," C.A. finally said. "And her Chinese year is excellent."

I had no idea what a Chinese year was, let alone that I had one.

"Figure out the details," Raul said as he extracted his hand from the massage and exited his loft's antiseptic front room.

A few weeks into my apprenticeship, days at Raul's studio preparing canvases for art and nights at the restaurant preparing customers for dinner, Andrew called. His hello was like Led Zeppelin playing Bach, infinite and perpetual, familiar yet new. He was back in L.A., wouldn't be in New York after all, did I still love him?

"Yes." Emotions tangled themselves inside me. Euphoria to hear from him, relief he was no longer halfway around the world, but crushed he wasn't at the hotel for me to run over to see.

"Are you learning a lot from Raul?" Andrew's voice slid the question in so easily that it took me a moment to remember I hadn't told him about my apprenticeship. Tory tattling probably. "Interesting artist, isn't he?" Andrew went on. "Not that I've ever bought his work, but I understand why others do. What do you think of him?"

"I'm a bit sequestered off. Another assistant and I stretch and treat the canvases, clean the brushes, that sort of thing, but I'm sure that will change the longer I stay and there'll be time for me to do some of my own work."

"Have you been smoking?" Andrew suddenly said, as if none of my words had been heard by him, only the voice that said them.

"No, why?" I couldn't believe he could tell. And, okay, it was stupid of me to lie and I wasn't even sure why I did, it came out automatically.

"Your voice sounds different than it used to—are you sure you're not smoking? You're not doing drugs, are you?"

"No, I'm not . . . smoking or doing drugs. Maybe the bronchitis changed it."

"It wouldn't do that. Get more sleep; you don't sound good."

I hated and loved that he detected so much. We talked for two hours, and he asked about everything, remembering things we'd discussed that

I'd forgotten myself in all those months. Everything. Except the gallery opening—and that was a relief, but it also made me feel kind of worse. Like it was too horrible for him to mention.

So things at Raul's better go well, I thought when we hung up the phone, and my new work better be great. Though I still hadn't been able to do any because somehow that studio space I was promised never materialized, but I was sure it would, and I'd get new sculptures done, and Tory, please God, would love them, and Andrew would be thrilled.

In almost three months of working at Raul's, I rarely saw the famous artist himself. The assistant I worked with, Todd, who was from Nevada, though we were referred to as one and two by C.A., talked nonstop about his dance club exploits while we stretched and treated the canvases, which were then transferred to assistants three and four who filled in large swatches of color before assistant five painted in subtle multihued lines, finally culminating with them being speckled with a sheer gleaming coat by C.A., and voilà, a painting was done once Raul scrawled his signature on them, something I figured he did at night when we were all gone since none of us but C.A. ever saw him.

I was certain I was missing something. Raul must be aware that the paintings being created weren't really his, but they all bore his signature as if he had slaved over them for months. Though maybe they were reproductions, some kind of self-knockoffs for sale—that must be what it was. But how odd that the public wanted that.

Then one day, I overheard C.A. talking to number five about the deadline we were under for the show of Raul's new work, so in confidence I said to Todd, "But Raul didn't paint a stroke on any of these."

The stillness and silence of Todd's response made it clear I was fucked. I could immediately imagine him whispering my remark to C.A., see C.A.'s birdlike hands rubbing Raul's massive ones as he told him what I'd said, while the Russian model Raul had recently acquired for a girlfriend sat nearby with triumphant boredom on her face.

I was fired that afternoon, so Peg's phone call the next morning was not a surprise when she informed me that my association with the Sexton Space gallery was formally dissolved and my sculptures would be shipped back to my mother's home.

"I appreciate everything you did for me, Peg." I had liked Peg, had given her a compact for Christmas, half sheer powder, half rosy lip gloss—natural and clean like her prettiness. She seemed embarrassed when opening it—because she had nothing for me I'd thought, but now I wondered if she was already seeing what lay ahead.

"Yeah, well, good luck." And she quickly hung up.

I lay on the floor of my room after I hung up the phone, my feet smushed under the three-legged table, as my August-to-April art world whirl crashed down around me and pinned me to the ground. Andrew would definitely find out about this, if he hadn't already. I suspected that Tory had called him first to let him know. I could hear her British vowels enunciating each horrendous word of my demise and dismissal. The dreadfulness of it filled my soul while desperation and despondence ran through my veins. Why had I screwed this up so badly? If only this were a small thing, but it was my dream—my art and Andrew. How could I ever be in his world now? What on earth was there in my life to interest him—my restaurant job? Ha. Without the ascent in the art world he had decided I would have?

I hated that my sculptures were still at the gallery, possibly shoved in the back near the freight door and cleaning supplies. Those people had seen a part of me, sniffed at it, thinly smiled, and turned away. I wanted to slap them and erase all memory of me from Tory and the gallery, the critics and collectors, Raul, C.A., and those stupid numerical assistants. And erase Andrew's knowledge of this. Erase it and have him not need big fucking art star success from me. Then he would love me and I could do my art and it would go well or not, but he'd be in my life and I wouldn't have to see those superior and mean art people again.

I remembered with growing horror that Andrew had never experienced this—being excluded, dismissed, all right, goddamn it, having failed—they were alien concepts to him. One afternoon in February when I was missing him terribly, I went to the Coliseum Bookstore on

Fifty-seventh Street and headed straight to the biography section in search of his name. There were volumes on him; two were rather silly, fluff like fanzines between hard covers, but the other four were thorough.

Andrew had been successful and famous his entire life. In school, every award and honor had been bestowed on him by teachers and classmates alike, then in the outside world, he immediately ascended to heavenly heights. Since the age of twenty, when he was discovered by a talent scout at a hotel pool, his name and visage had been internationally, consistently, swooningly adored.

Since Andrew had achieved that kind of success and fame at the age I would be next year, surely he had expected the same from me. Fuck. Fear knocked the breath out of my chest, and a pit opened up inside me that devoured my abilities to reach him and the him-with-me. I had thought that with Andrew in my life, that pit had been pushed far away. When Daddy left, I had fallen into it for the first time, but before that, I hadn't known it existed—that it was deep inside all of us, only kept at bay by the flimsy fences of parents, home, and school. Not only hadn't I been aware of it, I had thought my fencing was secure, but one phone call from my mother about Daddy's departure had changed all of that for me, as it never did for the rest of the girls in my class. Their eyes reflected light and good times, while a frozen and dark solidity came over mine. Hanging up the phone from Peg's banishment from the gallery and the world that Andrew had expected me to shine in, that frozen and dark solidity took over every part of me.

A couple of days later, after putting it off for as long as I thought I could, I picked up the phone to call Andrew. Not that I didn't think he knew, but it would be weird for me not to tell him myself. Even though we had still never discussed the opening or the review, this one was too big and obvious to ignore. The late afternoon sun was departing from my room, as I lit a cigarette while wishing the smoke had transformative powers to change what I had to say.

Andrew immediately got on the line. "Hi."

"Hi," I said, hoping a comforting chat would somehow miraculously ensue, but only a dismal blankness was on the line.

"Hello?" He sounded annoyed.

"I'm here."

"I'm in the middle of a meeting, Yvette, is there something you wanted to tell me?"

"Oh, sorry. I, uh, well . . . I guess you've heard."

"Heard?"

"About Tory?" Knives pushed in and pulled out of me would have been easier than this.

"Yeah."

Silence again on the line. He clearly hated that, so I said the only thing I genuinely could, "Well."

"I've got people here."

"Right."

"I'll talk to you soon."

"Okay." I tried to sound normal, confident. His "I'll talk to you soon" was a sign to hold on to. I just hoped it were true.

"Bye."

And before I could answer, a click cut the line.

Six weeks passed of few phone calls between us, and those were just exchanges of emptiness. Andrew offered no information about his work or life—I desperately wished he would—and I had nothing to discuss. My restaurant job was of no interest, particularly to him, and my career—I felt embarrassed even using that word—lay splattered on the ground like a body gruesomely ruined.

I lay in my bed each night unable to sleep, as if my mind needed more hours to feel dread in. Hour after hour of each and every day, all I thought about was Andrew and art, art and Andrew. Getting both back in my life the way they used to be, so I could breathe again.

"He's waiting for you to ask," Carrie said one evening over our third glass of wine, after I got home from work. "He'd never offer himself."

I had a feeling she was wrong, but she kept trying to convince me. "It could make all the difference in the world," she said, her tone implying I'd be a fool to pass the chance to ask Andrew to buy one of my sculptures. "He loved your work; he wouldn't have done what he did if he didn't. Just ask him. If he owned one or two of your sculptures, honey, you could get in any gallery in town. It's a public stamp of approval for your art. Hell, you could send out a press release."

That I'd never do, but maybe she was right. He had loved my work and it still looked the same. And he was constantly buying art, okay, only from extremely well established artists and never from newcomers, but maybe he'd break with that pattern just this once.

All week, I rehearsed the question. During runs in the park that were increasingly hard from the cigarettes I was still smoking, and while walking home from work past his hotel—I still thought of the Ritz-Carlton that way. I rehearsed the question constantly, and repeated in my head the things he had said back in the fall about my art like a mentally recorded mantra to shore up my resolve. I picked a Sunday to call him, a little after two, the same day and time of our first great phone call, then spent all of the day before going back and forth about whether it should be ten after two East Coast time or West Coast, but finally decided that later in the day was best.

Dialing his number was like invoking his presence into my room. His overly large persona was there, high above and watching me. As I waited for the operator to put my call through, I remembered that Andrew was always warmer and softer earlier in the day, as if the progressing hours hardened him. I quickly prayed that he'd had a late night and only recently woken up, while I instinctively lit a cigarette.

"Hi." He was there so quickly on the line. My legs started shaking, so I picked up the cigarette I had lit, thinking I would just hold it to provide me with strength.

"How are you?" I immediately wondered why I had asked since he had never answered that question before.

Andrew was actively quiet, then said, "What's new?"

Oh, God, not that. Is there a more horrendous question in all the world? Nothing, actually—how's that for honesty?

"Umm, good." Fuck. I had answered my own question and not his. I took a long drag off my cigarette. "Uh, Andrew? I was wondering . . ."

"Are you smoking?" He made it sound like I was taking an ax to a small child.

"No." I started to put the cigarette out, but changed my mind.

"Right now, you're not smoking?"

"No, I just finished a run; I'm still cooling off."

"Huh." He said nothing for a moment then, "Don't smoke."

"I'm not."

Huge emptiness appeared on the line. I thought of all the states our call was crossing where happy conversations must be taking place. Please, God, make this one of those.

"Andrew, I was wondering if . . . you . . . uh . . ." I had to catch my breath. A strange stoppage had occurred on my last intake, an invisible hand strangling my throat, making my next breath unpleasantly audible. "If you would want to buy one of my sculptures. For not very much, of course, or nothing, really. I'd give you one if you want."

The cigarette was at my lips, kissing my mouth, and the smoke was hugging my throat, holding me inside. His silence was excruciating. I felt as if I were on the edge of a terrifying cliff, the backs of my knees were so weak.

Andrew cleared his throat. "I don't want to be anyone's sponsor."

Oh. Oh, God. Okay. Sponsor. What did that mean? It sounded so involved, active, a thousand times more than one sale. He didn't want to be anyone's—my—sponsor.

"Maybe you should go home," Andrew said. I nearly fell off the bed. Go home? To the muteness of Momma's house; the decrepitude of that life? Maybe I should just kill myself instead. "It doesn't seem to be working there. What do you think?" His dreadful speech was done, but I couldn't believe he expected an answer from me, like an executioner asking if the rope should be in natural or white. The lifeline he had thrown me months before was being retracted.

"I think . . . I think I have to go." I wanted to throw up and my head had begun to spin.

"Yvette."

"Bye, I'm gonna go." And before he could say another word, I hung up.

I found the fifth of Jack Daniel's I had brought with me from Mississippi, grabbed the closest thing we had to a highball glass—a Donald Duck juice cup—and had many Disney-themed drinks full, then curled up on my bed and sobbed myself to sleep. I woke up a little later and sobbed some more. The alternating episodes of sleeping and sobbing became interchangeable—physically engrossing states with wildly precise mental scenes accompanying them.

Carrie must have pushed the curtain back at some point during the night because when I awoke the next morning, the half-empty Jack Daniel's bottle and Disney glass were out of my room and a blanket from the couch was covering me.

Splashing water on my face in the bathroom, I caught a glimpse of myself in the cheap medicine-cabinet mirror. The glow I'd had when Andrew was so on fire about me was gone.

I was preparing for Andrew to get rid of me. The silence from the West Coast was booming; I could barely hear through its din. I made a tentative call to him a few weeks after the internal massacre that was our last conversation. He asked where I was and I answered before realizing he must have thought I'd gone back to the South. It was an exercise in verbal insignificance. I wondered why we were doing it, though he didn't sound ready to be off the phone quickly like he had on our last few calls, but there was little to say. This gangplank of a goodbye was long.

After a few more weeks of silence between us, and nonstop dread about when Andrew was going to call to say never call him again, I finally could bear it no longer and decided to take things into my own hands. I called him on a Thursday afternoon in July, almost a year since we had met. My plan was to end it and lock him out of my life so I could get on with it and my art on my own. Somehow.

"I don't even know why you still talk to me," I told Andrew on our predetermined-by-me expiratory call.

"What?" I could tell he was outraged and shocked.

"Why do you still talk to me?" I derived a strength from saying it twice. "You're just going to drop me. Raul did, Tory did, and you only have people in your life who are famous or are going to be any minute."

"What are you talking about?" His voice had stepped aside as if his body were getting out of the way of a blow.

"You know exactly what I'm talking about, do I have to spell it out to you? I'm not a . . ." I almost said "big fucking art star," but knew I'd lose it if I did, and I had a feeling he knew what I hadn't said. "I fucked up, and all that matters to you is huge, phenomenal success, so let's just end this—whatever the fuck it is—and you can go on with your life and we can forget we ever met because I can't take this anymore." I was free-falling in a descent that had started months ago, and even if it was going to be a crash landing, I wanted it to happen already—I'd been previewing it for too long.

"Yvette, calm down."

"No." I jumped up off my bed. I didn't want any suggestions from him.

"All right, don't calm down. But what you're saying is ridiculous. I'm not going anywhere—I've told you that before and it's true—and neither are you, so just settle down and let's talk about what you need to do."

"About what? You?"

"No, I told you, I don't know what all this stuff about us is that you're going on about. I'm not leaving your life, so you can forget about that. About your art, what you need to do about your art. You're extremely talented."

I was annoyed and comforted by his calm pragmatism, but I suddenly couldn't hear him anymore. I was still in such high gear, all prepared with my big grand "This is over" stand that I wasn't able to suddenly shift and have a "Where I'm going now" father/daughter talk. I said I had to go. He made me promise three times before I got off the phone that I would call him back that night. But I didn't. And when my phone kept ringing, I didn't answer it.

I called Andrew a few days later and told him I was starting School of Visual Arts in the fall, thank you, bossy Suzanne, for making me apply. He was thrilled to hear it and acted like it had been the plan all along, and neither of us brought up that other phone call ever again.

I quit smoking, quit my hostess job at the restaurant, and got a waitressing job at a place in the Village that was closer to SVA and only open at night so it worked with my class schedule. And I made lots of money in tips that the owners didn't think they should be getting. So much that I was finally able to rent part of a loft space down on Elizabeth Street in the Bowery to do my work.

School of Visual Arts was an all-consuming feast. It was heaven being completely saturated—other than on my waiting shifts—with color and shape and technique and history, and I dove into my studies. So much that most of the time I was able to forget about the Tory/Raul episodes. But occasionally, they would come up. I was shocked at how many people had read the review, though maybe I shouldn't have been since I was in art school—but it was weird that so many remembered it. Not everyone obviously, I wasn't paranoid thinking my name was household news, but out of the blue I'd hear, "Weren't you in Tory Sexton's show . . ." And the pit would open up inside me and I'd feel myself falling down, out of sight, my head barely reaching the other person's knees.

I started dating. Guys from class, men from the restaurant or the bars I went to with Lydia, and then I met Tim one day when he came to SVA at the beginning of my sophomore year to speak to a film class about set design, though he was mostly renowned for his work on Broadway. He couldn't find the building that the class he was lecturing was in, so I showed him, then we met for coffee afterward and talked for four hours. That turned into a relationship of three years. And I loved Tim, though still held my heart for Andrew.

Andrew and I talked regularly on the phone the whole time I was in school and seeing Tim. Once I moved in with Tim, I had to call Andrew from pay phones away from the apartment, but since he always came to the phone whenever I called, we talked pretty regularly. He asked about everything, except my art, and was very interested in things about Tim, then always before we hung up, "Do you love me more than him?"

"Yes," I'd tell him. "I do." I loved Tim, but I never had the sense that he'd be around for years to come like Andrew, who was still in my life even though I'd crashed and burned in front of him.

Although what happened with Tory and Raul was never mentioned between Andrew and me, as if it had vanished. I had an odd persistent sense that he had completely forgotten it, as if he were amnesiac about a large part of me, the part that had been the springboard for our relationship. I believed he would have been confounded if I asked him how Tory was, or mentioned those sculptures. Beguilingly confused. No memory of them. Everything else he remembered accurately and questioned extensively, but this large piece was missing, as if it had been a dream we once shared.

Things ended with Tim a few months after I graduated from SVA. He wanted to stay in New York, and I needed to get out. Living there had started to feel as if all the big tall buildings had moved straight into my head and there wasn't any room for my thoughts anymore, as if they were being routed down crowded one-way streets that barely moved, my thinking stuck, unable to get anywhere. And Suzanne, besides being thrilled and probably secretly shocked that I graduated, was dying for me to move to L.A. "We're sisters. We should at least live in the same city," she said, though I had a feeling she wanted to keep a closer eye on me. I guess she had forgotten that big, bad Andrew lived there. But she thought it was over between us since I never mentioned him. And there'd be space in L.A., I thought, and there was the art. David Hockney and Ed Ruscha; Richard Diebenkorn's *Ocean Park*. I could make a fresh start without having to deal with the New York galleries again. Suzanne lived with her music agent boyfriend in a big house in Beverly Hills with a guest room I could stay in until I got on my feet. So, Tim and I broke up, and I moved to L.A.

Without telling Andrew. I don't know why, really. I kept thinking I'd tell him in each conversation we had in the weeks I was preparing to move, but somehow I never brought it up. Not that I didn't want to be in the same city with him again. But I guess I had gotten so used to, and comfortable with, our parental phone relationship that the idea of being in a town where I could see him was unsettling—because what if I didn't. I landed in L.A. with Suzanne waiting for me outside baggage claim, behind the wheel of her silver convertible Saab, and Andrew still thought I was living in New York.

18

I go downtown a lot. Mostly to the jewelry district to buy materials when I run out of gems. Or check on the progress of my jewelry, like I did on Thursday at Dipen's. The new prototype for the necklace was perfect, thank God, although it looks like the order will take longer than Dipen thought because his casting machine broke down. But he promised me he'd have the order ready in two weeks, which puts me at exactly half a week before it is due to Rox, so I'll still meet my deadline easily. I hope. Working with these guys, or let's be honest, being completely dependent on them to make my jewelry, is having to be two parts sugary sweet plus one part hard-core commando, like some kind of chocolate bullet-chip ice cream. I have to stay on them to make sure the work gets done on time, but if I'm not nice about it, they'll keep stalling or even stop doing my orders. I've seen designers at Dipen's in tears, pleading with him to keep doing their work, and him standing on the other side of his counter, his face placid but firm, as he repeatedly tells them to never come there again.

But when I don't have to go downtown for business what I really like to do is drive around downtown a lot, like I did last night when I couldn't get to sleep because I kept thinking about Andrew. It was almost one A.M. on Saturday morning, and Michael had just left because he had to be at the station for the six A.M. show and the freeways are hell in the mornings. "On Saturdays?" I'd asked. But he'd just kissed me and promised to call me later. I couldn't handle being in bed by myself. The stillness was too disturbing. I was just lying there with nothing moving but my thoughts, which were doing swoops in my head, so I finally jumped up, pulled on some clothes, got in my truck, and hit the freeway. Suzanne would have been outraged if she knew. "All those drunk drivers on the road," I could imagine her saying as I got on the 10 heading east. But my truck is big and safe, and it was either drive or tear my hair out thinking about Andrew.

I headed east on the freeway toward downtown and the desert and Texas and what used to be home. But I didn't go that far. I made the loop I like to make from the 10 up the 110 to the 101 that kind of sideswipes me by all those tall downtown buildings, the only really big ones L.A. has. Okay, Century City has a few and there's that corridor of condos on Wilshire Boulevard, but for hard-core New York City–style skyscrapers—they're downtown.

Which is why I went. They make me feel safe, seeing them standing so solid and sure, as if their weight can hold down and secure this slipping, tilting West Coast terrain. And from my truck up on the freeway, they're almost at eye level so they look smaller in a way, like diamond-encrusted jewelry I can touch, even reach out and pick up if I want and put in my pocket to carry with me, like a memory that is there to look at whenever I want to, but isn't the only thing I can see. Like how I wish it were with Andrew.

And don't, honestly.

Usually one loop is enough, but last night, I drove it twice. I took the 110 north to the 101 east until I got off in Hollywood, then I turned back around and got on the freeway, retracing my journey. I passed the buildings a second time, their brightness smiling at me in the dark, I thought I might have to do a triple loop, but once I was completely past them, a lulling feeling kicked in and I knew I could go home. As if the buildings had sung me to sleep.

Some of those buildings it took me a while to like. The DWP building, for instance, on First Street, I could not appreciate at all. Just a tall, simple box of glass and white with black lines running across the front. A big neonothing is what I thought it was. Then one day, driving into downtown on First Street, as I got to the top of the hill, I saw the building there glistening. It was so perfect for its space that I finally understood it couldn't have been anything other than what it was. I suddenly loved it and do still, partly because I disliked it so much before.

But that change of heart has not happened for me with the Pacific Shopping Center, a building I continue to loathe. Particularly Bloomingdale's at the Pacific Shopping Center. Okay, actually the bra department in Bloomingdale's at the Pacific Shopping Center, the locale of the purgatory I am in now.

Suzanne's bridal shower is today, this lovely Saturday, and besides being groggy from not enough sleep thanks to last night's nocturnal drive, I have nothing to wear. A fact that should have me in a clothing department, but if I get a new bra, which I've needed for a while, then the black top with the black pants I am wearing will look fine, though probably wrong. Sheer and floral and soft come to mind for a nuptial event, but after conjuring a blizzard of outfits in my bedroom, I ended up in my favorite black pants and top. The apparel equivalent of eating oatmeal every morning—I don't have to think about choices and I know it's good for my body.

As I stand in front of a rack of bras and flip through the tags on an endless supply of Playmate-appropriate contraptions, I feel like a school-kid who only got three letters of the alphabet: B C C B D D D B.

I walk over to the young, bored, and abundantly endowed salesclerk lounging behind the register, and say, "I'm sorry, I seem to be the last woman in Los Angeles to get breast implants, do you have any A-cup bras at all?"

She regards me as if I am a species she has vaguely heard something about, then points to a wall overflowing with padded built-in-breasts bras.

"Uh, without the matching throw pillows sewn inside."

She gives me an irritated look, then leads me over to a dimly lit corner where, next to a rack of postmastectomy garments, are the brave, the few A-cup bras.

"Maybe you should try one on," she says in what is not a meant-to-be-helpful tone.

"I'm in a hurry, I have to get to a . . ." I suddenly imagine a "Marie Antoinette tits-like-a-champagne-glass" annual convention, but since it is the L.A. chapter, I am all alone. "Just ring it up," I say, taking a bra off the rack that is the same brand and style I've had before, and handing it to her.

As I wait for my purchase, it occurs to me that for my size, a store outside this city might have a bigger selection. I wonder if I have enough frequent flier miles to get some place more . . . flat, I guess, then realize I have no idea where that would be.

The A-cup bra fits perfectly—should that depress me or make me happy?—when I put it on in the second-floor bathroom, wanting to be out of that prejudiced lingerie department. Maybe the ACLU could take them on.

The drive from the shopping center to the Pacific Palisades, where my sister's bridal shower is being held, is easier than I thought it would be considering they are at opposite ends of town. Suzanne's best friend, Mandy, an actress, is hosting it at her Richard Neutra–designed home. When Suzanne told me about it, I vaguely recalled having read an article about the architect, but when I pull up in front of Mandy's house, I quickly recognize its famous style. Very stark, straight, clean lines. As I walk up the sidewalk, the curls of my hair feel like a literal affront to the design. I wonder if Mandy allows any wavy lines on her property at all; then she opens the front door and I see that she has saved them all for herself. She is a series of strategically placed circles: round up-lifted eyes; puffy cloudlike lips; and cleavage that goes on for hours before the nipples even begin to start. I suddenly feel I have more in common with a glass-and-wood structure than a member of my own sex.

Honest to God, it is all I can do to look at her face and not her breasts. Now, growing up, I went to the French Quarter all the time and would see the girls on Bourbon Street with their pasties and twirls, so I've always known that I'm small. I just had no idea until I moved to L.A. how big Big can get. No wonder men stare in incredulous fascination—what this woman had was like nothing on my body at all.

"You must be the sister," Mandy says, moving all of her selves aside to let me in.

Nice to meet you, too, I think, while I force a smile.

Just past the foyer that Mandy has led me into, I can see an austere living room filled with clusters of chattering, tittering women. As I move to join the festivities—Mandy has already entered the room—a waiter intercepts me, blocking my passage with a tray of champagne glasses that he holds in front of my breasts.

My "no" comes out a bit too vehemently, so I soften it with, "I mean, thanks anyway, but do you think I could get a vodka on the rocks with a twist?"

He scrutinizes me, as if trying to predict what other social sins I will commit today.

"No, okay." I brush my request off with a laugh, but he's not buying it. "How about a coffee?"

"Espresso." His tone implies that it is patently obvious I have never attended a bridal shower on the West side.

"Make it a double."

After that delightful tête-à-tête, the party looks like a downright refuge. I see Suzanne sitting next to a building of gifts that appears ready to topple onto her at any moment. Hearts and love and pink and doves decorate the packages, while ribbons cascade down the sides. I immediately envision jewelry of thin multicolored cords dotted with gems encircling necks, arms, and waists, making presents of their wearers. I want to create them.

"There you are," Suzanne yells through the soft and pretty voices of the women in the soft and pretty dresses, as she gestures wildly for me to join her across the room. I immediately regret my outfit, especially the time wasted on the new bra that is making little to no difference on me.

Which reminds me of when I was in first grade and wanting to be like straight-haired Suzanne, I decided to wear headbands. Momma bought one in every color for me, so I could wear a different one each day. The headband was visible in my hair, a happy strip of bright color among my curls, but it had no effect on how my hair looked, though I was certain it did. Certain that by wearing the small binding object, not unlike the one currently on my chest, I had entered the great sorority of life.

On the third day of wearing a headband to school (green was the color du jour), I was walking to the swings at recess to meet my best friend, when a tall blond eighth-grade girl came up to me.

"Why are you wearing that?" She used a tone that I had only heard used by Momma and Daddy when they were really mad. She was in too high a grade to be Suzanne's friend, so why was she talking to me and about what? I was wearing the same plaid pleated uniform as everyone else.

All around us, girls were playing hopscotch, jumping rope, hand patting sing-song games, whispering in groups, or lounging in the sun with their socks rolled down and skirts pushed up until a nun came along.

"That headband. It looks ridiculous in your hair. Curly-haired girls can't wear headbands." Her face contorted from the honey-sweet American dream to a deep ugly sneer. "You look stupid."

The green plastic hair ornament had become tighter and tighter with each of her words. My face felt hot, and I didn't want to look at her anymore. She made a nasty laugh, again said, "You look stupid," then walked away, leaving me standing there. I didn't just feel stupid, I felt dumb, a word Daddy wouldn't let us use about anyone, but there I was using it about me in my head. None of the other girls seemed to have heard her, but I figured they already thought the same thing and just hadn't said it.

I went to the bathroom into the farthest stall, closed and locked the door behind me, and broke the headband with my hands, the sharpness of the plastic hurting me with each break. Pieces of green flew out onto the hexagonal tile floor, as I kept bending and breaking until the headband was just tiny bits of bright shards lying on the dingy white tile. My hair was all wrong and I hadn't even known it. If that wasn't dumb, what was?

I was about four when I noticed that my hair was curly without the pin curls that Momma laboriously put on Suzanne every night before bed. When I asked Momma why I didn't need those, too, she told me that I was blessed, that the angels curled my hair every night while I slept. I tried to stay up a few nights to meet these angels and talk to them, to see if the pin curls they made were the same as the ones Momma did on Suzanne or better—maybe they used golden pins from heaven. But as I stomped on the already broken pieces of green headband on the bathroom floor, I wondered why those angels couldn't've picked on someone else.

"Yvette, Yvette."

My sister was calling me, rescuing me from this memory as she couldn't when it happened.

"Come meet Betsy, my wedding coordinator I've been telling you about."

As I walk down the two steps into the sunken living room, Suzanne turns to the older, conservatively dressed, and professionally happy looking woman sitting on her left and, pointing at me, says, "See her height? Now don't you think her bouquet can be taller?"

I make my way through the ocean of estrogen, hug Suzanne, then move to the empty chair next to them, slipping into it like a life preserver. "It's so nice to meet you," I say to the wedding coordinator. "I'm Suzanne's sister, Yvette."

"Legs apart!" Betsy bellows.

"What?" I jump in my chair, suddenly worried some odd animal is on the loose that only attacks feet that are close together.

"Your legs, you have to keep them uncrossed and apart or you're out of the game." Her silver-haired head is close to me, watery blue eyes peering into my face. She is grinning madly.

"The game."

"Whoever keeps their legs uncrossed during the whole bridal shower wins the prize! Of course, Suzanne here has already won—she's the bride!—but you ladies—"

"Have to—" I smile and nod at her.

"That's right—keep those legs apart!"

"Right, well, lucky for me I'm not wearing a skirt."

Betsy's licensed and official smile quickly turns into a frown as she notices my black pants for the first time. She looks as if someone just told her that the wedding march was legally banned.

"I need to have a fitting with my veil," Suzanne says, leaning past her still-in-shock wedding coordinator. "I've waited long enough; the wedding's just over a month away, for God's sake. How's next week?"

I wake up in a scream. The black clothes I wore to the bridal shower are on the floor next to my bed, and I try to remind myself that nothing else was there, but it feels as though something just left my room. I am still for a few moments, sitting straight up in bed, barely daring to breathe, as I listen, trying to hear anything, anyone, some tangible evidence of what scared me, but the apartment is quiet.

As I sink back onto my pillow, I am relieved no one was really there, but I'm still flipped out. My praying to Mary before going to sleep clearly did nothing to keep the dream away. I consider calling Michael to ask him to come over, but it's after three in the morning, and even though it's Sunday, he probably has a long work day ahead. I don't know where he gets his energy. I wish more of it was spent on me. He almost called me his girlfriend the other night. Kind of, at least. He phoned on Wednesday in the late afternoon, wondering if I wanted to hang out later, then showed up at nine P.M. with Indian food and a video of *The Phantom of the Opera* with Lon Chaney. Even though it was a silent film, Michael insisted we not speak. "The music, after all," he said, which was fine with me. I love Lon Chaney in that role—taped-up nose and dreadful wig, so desperate for the love of someone plainly annoying as hell. Like *Gone With the Wind*, sort of. Though with that story, I had no patience. I couldn't stand Ashley, and found Scarlett a fool for wasting her time and thoughts on him. One rainy summer day when I was ten, in the middle of reading the book in my grandmother's attic-playroom, I literally threw it down in disgust and tramped loudly down the stairs, my critique coming out in my feet. My grandmother was in her sitting room, embroidering pillowcases for a cousin's bridal trousseau.

"I can't stand Ashley," I declared, flouncing onto the couch, but carefully so as not to jar her needlework.

"Ashley Wilkes is a perfect Southern gentleman," she said without looking up from the violet petal she was sewing and knowing exactly whom I was talking about.

"Then I don't like Southern gentlemen."

She pulled the needle taut from the cloth, stopped her embroidery, and looked at me with her gray eyes over her glasses, as if acknowledging my age and deciding that there was still time for this view of mine to be saved. Then she handed me a tea towel, and suggested I help with that, thereby ending the subject.

The Phantom of the Opera video had ended, the credits were rolling by, I was lying on my couch with one of Michael's arms around me, happy, but the movie had made me think of Andrew in a sideways sort of way, and I didn't want to. I had already missed part of what Michael was saying to me, small and low in my ear.

"I mean, we hang out and stuff, isn't that enough? I know there's a label for that, but I'm not into semantics."

By "stuff" I guessed he meant that we have sex. And I didn't exactly want labels, either—though, okay, maybe a little—what I really wanted was the security of "I love you." And to actually feel it for him. Which I think I really will—fully, completely, and truly—once I finally forget about Andrew which surely will happen any day because how long can one interaction, if I can even call it that, which, okay, I am calling it that, an interaction and so much more because he talked to Sydney about me for Christ's sake, and what's that if not the result of an interaction we had, but even so, how much longer can that fuel these constant thoughts of him? He is married, after all, with children, like Suzanne will be soon, but at least Michael will be at her wedding with me, and maybe their love spell will move onto us, so next year we'll be up there. But is that what I want?

It is obvious that I'm not going to fall back asleep, so I get out of bed, put away the clothes I wore to Suzanne's shower, and go to the kitchen for a glass of water and that forces me to pass Suzanne's veil on the iron stand in my living room. I keep moving the damn thing back and forth from my studio to this room, half to force myself to finish it, half to get it out of my sight. I wish it would take flight and my responsibility for it would end. Why in God's name did I ever agree to do this for her? Could there be any bigger emotionally loaded commitment to make? Sure, I'll be completely responsible for what everyone sees around your blushing bridal face on your wedding day. No, that's not too much pressure—okay! I figure I have another week of putting Suzanne off before she tears down my door to see it, but surely I can finish it by then. In fact, I know I can. It's a veil, for Christ's sake, not the *David* I'm meant to create—just get it done. If only I didn't get such ennui whenever I try.

19

I get lost driving in Venice. The streets near this part of the beach angle and cut into one another unlike anywhere else in Los Angeles, so it always surprises me when I am able to find Lizzie's store. She named it Tizzie's, which I thought was charming when I walked in that first time and she bought my jewelry before anyone else. But now as I park my truck, I wonder if the *T* of her sign was less expensive than an *L*. Knowing Lizzie, she got a deal on it somehow, but I guess it's better than a *D*.

The store is the usual customer-challenged turmoil when I walk in, but it's Monday, so I try to pretend to myself it's because of that. The shop is completely rearranged; new items next to retro, any decade fair game.

"Merchandising, that's what they call it." Forgoing a hello, Lizzie has launched into an explanation of her retail method madness. She is sitting on a high stool behind the counter, Santa-suit red hair above pale skin, sipping a diet soda in a to-go cup that looks as though she could dunk her entire head in it. Lizzie is inexplicably attractive in an against-your-will kind of way. I have never seen her in the same pair of glasses twice. Today's are cat eye. For the first time, I wonder if the lenses are fake.

"Suddenly the customer wants to buy, but they have no idea why." She taps her purple-painted fingernail against the jumbled-bright innards of a display case for emphasis. I realize she is directing me to the new location of my jewelry.

Reassuring her what a big change it is (this is true, I just let her interpret it how she likes), I see my earrings and pins in a chaotic clump intermingled with outdated high school rings, forgotten feather earrings, and molded plastic bracelets. My creations look enslaved.

"I need to get that check from you, Lizzie." I smile as I say it, trying to make it pleasant somehow.

"Uh! You never come to visit—just business, business, business with you. Besides, I specifically recall saying—"

"That was three months ago, I can't wait any longer."

"Well, if your stuff sold better in here, hon, maybe I'd have the money for you." She is holding her Goliath-sized beverage cup ominously, as if it were always intended as the weapon it seems. "You know, I've believed in you a real long time. Hell, I've had your trinkets in here since when was it?"

"For a good while, Lizzie, yes, and now I just need to get paid."

"That is not gonna happen today."

I want to grab her drink and throw it in her face, but I am silent for a moment, though wish I weren't. Wish a stream of invectives were pouring forth, covering her with righteousness. For a second, I consider taking the rest of my jewelry back, but that would piss her off so much that I'd never get a check for all the other pieces she sold.

"Okay, three more weeks, can you have it for me then?"

"Of course, Yvette, haven't I always been right as rain with you?" Lizzie's sunny smile is as reassuring as a cloudy day.

Yeah, I think as the bell on the door clangs my departure from the store, *right as a thunderstorm on my economic parade.*

When I get home from Lizzie's, the only messages on my answering machine, besides yet another hang-up, are ones concerning work. One is from an actress who just got back in town and is wondering if the pieces she ordered are ready. They are, so I'll call her to set a time to take them, and I make a mental note to remind myself to somehow work it into our conversation how great they'd be on her when she attends the premiere. Another message is a possible new commission; a woman saw my jewelry on a friend of hers and wants to see what I've got for herself. Why couldn't Michael have called? Just once, I wish he would call to say hey, how are you, I was thinking about you. I haven't seen him since Friday night, and he did call on Saturday, though it wasn't much of a conversation what with radio people talking to him in the background as if the phone to his ear was merely some odd contraption to be ignored. I've been having a small little feeling that I disappear for him if I'm not right in front of him. Like he does for me when I think about Andrew, actually. Stop already. Andrew is out of my life and Michael is here now. Though not enough really somehow. Though maybe he would be more if I could stop thinking about someone I haven't been with in over four years.

But I am relieved that there isn't a phone message from Suzanne asking when she can see her veil. I need to sit down and finish the damn thing. Dipen doesn't have the jewelry ready yet, though there is some invoicing I can do on commissions, but I really should just work on the veil. Talking to Reggie will help me begin even though our conversations have been kind of stilted since Michael's been in the picture again, but work anguish Reggie understands. I know he is at the editing room, so I leave a message on his home number, while wishing for the millionth time that he had a cell phone like everyone else. That and his refusal to watch the Oscars are his two acts of defiance as an Angeleno, which I respect, though it would be a lot easier if Reggie weren't so difficult to reach anytime other than our morning calls. He is usually always out.

One night last year, he came to my apartment, and we ate the Mexican food he'd brought, then pored over a photography book he'd found on turn-of-the-century New Orleans, talking until late about the future filming of his script. Before he left, he used my phone to check his messages, which I found odd since he was heading home, but then realized that there are times when I want to know before I drive home if messages are waiting for me. He pressed some buttons, listened for a bit, hung up, and hugged me goodbye, his body cousin-comfortable with mine, then was out my door.

I went into the kitchen for a glass of water to take to bed. Noticing that I was out of milk for my morning coffee, I headed out to the gas station/convenience store two blocks away. About to cross the street to reach the store, I noticed Reggie's car in the parking lot, but far away from the gas pumps. Then I saw Reggie with his broad back to me, talking on the pay phone. I was just about to shout to him, but a voice in my head stopped me. Why hadn't he used my phone for the call he was making? Traffic was scarce, so I easily could have crossed the street and asked him or just said hello, but I stayed on the corner, letting the situation unfold.

Reggie hung up, got in his car, and took off in the direction opposite his home. It was clear he never saw me. I waited until he was a good distance up the street and out of view, then walked to the store, wondering what it was that was waiting for him? And who? And when, if ever, would he tell me?

Though maybe Reggie's silence about whatever and whoever that was—or is possibly—in his life is no different than the silence I've kept about seeing Andrew a couple of weeks ago. Okay, it will be two weeks ago exactly tomorrow night since I saw Andrew. Like I didn't know. Like he hasn't been in and under and around every thought I've had since then, damn him. And damn you, Michael, for not distracting me enough from him. But I just need to focus more on that relationship, on Michael, because it definitely is moving forward, I can tell, and soon, eventually, the name Andrew will just be one big "Who?" and Michael is the only man I will want to be with.

I hope.
I do?

I cannot figure out how to dress. I am going to a baby shower with Michael. I could tell he really doesn't want to go, mostly because he said, "A baby shower? I'm a guy. I'm not even supposed to go, much less have to." Not that I completely disagree with him. Where I grew up, you'd never catch men at a baby shower. No woman in her right mind wants them around for that. "But," I explained to Michael. "This baby shower is for two men." The music producer I worked for when I first moved here, Bill, and his partner, Tom, adopted a baby, and they aren't women so I guess that throws the whole females-only baby-shower code straight out the window.

As I stand in front of my closet staring into its depths, the only item that keeps popping into my head for me to wear is a pair of breasts. I keep trying to bring my mind back to a pretty skirt versus a dress, but for some reason, all I can think is, *What I really need is a different pair of breasts*. I tell myself that this party is not that thematic—okay, it is about a baby but not how we dress. Bill and Tom definitely don't have breasts. Or need them even for the baby. I suddenly wonder if this body part has finally evolved into scenery—pretty but useless, like the palm trees everywhere. Anyway. I put on a pale pink top that I love with some gray pants, go to the safe in my studio for a necklace, earrings, and bracelets of citrine, amethysts, and gold, grab the baby gift, and go.

I am late, in my truck driving the 101, praying that I get there on time. Michael was supposed to pick me up, but he called half an hour ago to say that things at the station were crazy, the new Sunday-morning talk show had a little blow-up on the air. I had a feeling he was hoping I'd say, "Oh, don't worry about it, I'll go by myself." But no way. Going to a baby shower alone is as bad as going to a wedding solo, in a "Why aren't you further along in your life?" kind of way. So I gave him the address and said he could meet me there.

The baby shower is at a house in the hills of a friend of Bill's, but on the Valley side, which is much less treacherous, but almost as exclusive. As I pull up to the large iron gates in front of the sequestered community and wait while the man in the guardhouse checks his list, I remember a story the nuns used to tell us that if Saint Peter won't let you in the Pearly Gates, run around to the side and Mary will sneak you in the kitchen door. How could I not prefer Mary with promises like that? I always imagined her in a fragrant spotless kitchen, stirring a big pot of gumbo, places at a table ready and set. Then the massive iron gates swing open and a second guard waves me in.

A swarm of valets in pale pink oxford shirts descend upon my car. Michael is standing waiting for me on a meticulously manicured lawn; I am shocked that he is on time. He is surrounded by a forest of giant topiaries depicting every character in *Alice in Wonderland*. The Red Queen's mallet is hovering menacingly over his head. Michael has a look on his face of a man consigned to a circle of hell that he didn't know existed.

"I'm late, I'm late," I say as he kisses me. I wish we could stay at the Mad Hatter's tea party instead of going in, but we stop kissing and turn toward the house, a spectacularly authentic faux French chateau, and walk up a long stone path covered by a continuous archway of pale pink balloons.

"Well, this is nice." I immediately feel like a woman I once overheard exclaiming that the Louvre sure is big.

A pale-pink-shirted man greets us at the door. "Hi! I'm Ken. Everyone's outside."

I put out my hand to introduce myself, thinking he is the host, Bill's friend, but he cuts me off by repeating his lines, and while one hand takes my gift, the other, with a sweeping winglike motion of the arm, guides us along.

Through a bank of open French doors, I see a sea of pale-pink-shirted men moving among a tiny handful of extremely well dressed guests. I realize that I actually have dressed appropriately for this party—as one of the caterers.

"Oh, my God," I say as we step outside. "It looks like a wedding."

"Or bat mitzvah," Michael replies.

Music is wafting from a string quartet playing on a parquet floor laid on the grass. A huge white tent covers ten tables swathed in pink organza and white. Each one is perfectly set for ten guests with a lifelike diaper-clad baby girl doll sitting on every china plate. Trays of mimosas and canapés glide by us, stopping only long enough to be emptied of their wares.

I see Bill and a young woman leaning over a large lace-covered bassinet. A veil of white netting suspended from a tree branch above is streaming down, surrounding the baby's bed. I have an almost irrepressible urge to yank down the veil, throw it on my head, and vow "I do," but I wonder if Michael is the man I want to say that to. Andrew pops into my brain, so I try to get rid of him by quickly taking Michael's arm to walk with him down the carpeted aisle to see the newborn child.

"Here she is," Bill says, pulling aside the veil. The sleeping baby looks just like a cherub. I've heard that before in nursery rhymes and fairy tales, but this one truly does, a sweet little cherub fallen from a cloud.

"She's perfect," I tell Bill, and introduce Michael to him, then Bill introduces us to the baby's mother, Sarah, a seventeen-year-old from the Midwest.

"We took her on a shopping spree on Friday; got her hair cut and colored," Bill gushes as Sarah stands by and blushes. "Malibu beach was yesterday and tomorrow a private tour of the museum. She is having a nonstop great time."

"Oh, that's wonderful," I say to her. "You're really getting to know L.A." But not her own baby, I think, then immediately realize that that may be the point.

"And there's a movie star here!" Sarah suddenly yells, causing the flock of pale-pink-shirted men to stop, turn, stare, then quickly move on.

"Oh," is all I can think to say.

At that moment, Michael, who has said nothing except "Congratulations" to Bill, takes my arm and leads me away.

"Okay, where?" I say to Michael, looking around at the few other guests as I give in to the voyeuristic urge to find the movie star in this extremely sparse crowd. "Him?"

A few feet away stands a blond man that anyone would define as gorgeous. Not that I recognize him, but I figure that has more to do with my box office attendance than his.

"I guess." Michael snags two snacks off one of the ever-roaming trays going by. He has just put one in my mouth when a woman approaches us.

"I thought that was you," she cries, putting a perfectly French-manicured hand on my arm.

Tonette is Bill's personal trainer, has been for a long time, so I knew her when I worked for him. As she leans in for a hug, I remember that I always felt that Tonette and I could have been friends if only I was more . . . L.A. somehow.

"I'm getting married. Did you hear?"

I hadn't, but I can tell. Prenup is written all over her, and I don't mean a contract. Tonette's ring is huge. A mammoth marquis that does not require a lifting of her hand for me to see, so in that sense it's discreet. Her dress is layers of whispering sheer creme chiffon culminating in a moment of silence on her amplified breasts, and tiny sparkly flowers dance in her hair.

"Oh, Tonette, I am so happy for you."

"Are you getting married?" she says, scrutinizing Michael and me. I glance at Michael to see his response. He looks as if he has just gotten on his own personal inner rocket ship that is taking him far, far away.

"No," I say to Tonette while still smiling, but not inside.

"Uh, you have no idea how awful the planning is, but we've only had one fight—which is practically unheard of." Tonette leans in toward me as if she is about to dispense the secret to a long life. "It's 'cause I'm keeping those conversations sexy—that helps."

I cannot imagine what she means. I immediately wonder if whenever I do get to plan that event, the wedding may not even happen because I won't know how to be sexy discussing a guest list. What—something borrowed, something blue, something porno, something new?

At that moment, an annunciation is made by one of the pale-pink-shirted men that luncheon is to begin. Tonette says she'll see me later, and scurries over to unknown-movie-star-man, who I realize is her fiancé. Michael has already started walking over to fix a plate, so I hurry to catch up with him. The buffet table runs the length of the house and is overflowing with dishes of every culinary kind. Guarding it like angels ready to serve are ten of the pale-pink-shirted men, while ten more move about under the tent filling all hundred glasses with champagne. Tom, Bill's partner, is already in line waiting on the carving of a ham when Michael and I join him. After introducing Michael to him, I congratulate Tom on this great event.

"And we're having a second one next month," Tom exults as glistening pork is piled high on his plate.

"Second what?" I ask, while thinking, *Isn't this celebration enough?*

"Baby! We were picked eight times. That's never happened before. The adoption agency kept saying, 'No couple has ever been picked eight times,' so we decided we'd get two—better for her not to grow up alone."

I wonder if this is the start of some new maternal movement—single mothers everywhere choosing only men to raise their young. Maybe they figure that way they won't ever be replaced. Like the way Michael can't replace Andrew? Oh, good God, will you please stop thinking of him? Jesus.

"The other mother's fourteen," Tom is saying as I pick up the conversation again. "Poor thing's having a baby soon because some guy molested her."

Though he probably did a bit more than that unless it's the next baby Jesus they're getting.

"Is any of this kosher?" Sarah asks, appearing in line.

Michael and I take our overfilled plates to sit down and dine. As we settle at the nearest table, moving aside the swaddling-clothed babes,

Tonette and unknown-movie-star-man amble by and sit at a table alone on the tent's far side. The host who owns the home still has not arrived, but the trinity of parents makes a visitation before us.

"Mind if we join you?" Tom says as Bill pulls out a chair for Sarah.

The only other guest at the party—a woman we haven't met—pulls out a chair at our table and plops herself down without saying a word to anyone. Considering how little Michael has contributed to any conversation since we've been here, her behavior seems oddly normal for this event.

"So," Bill says, turning to me. "How long have you two been going out?" He gestures at Michael and smiles, as if I might not be sure who he meant.

"For a little while now, and then a longer while last year, so all combined, I guess a good while now." I glance at Michael to see what he thought of that, but his entire attention is focused on the pork on his plate. He seems to be adopting a strategy of "If I pretend this party isn't happening, it'll go away." It almost makes me wish I hadn't brought him, but then I see Tonette and am glad I did anyway.

"Congratulations! In L.A., the way things go, that is so unusual."

"What's unusual?" says the woman we still haven't met. "You two are engaged?"

"No," I say. "We're usual. I mean, we're dating. Usually. Anyway." I wish the conversation had never started, so I turn my attention to Sarah. "You're having a nice stay?"

"Yeah, it's been great, although I didn't go to temple yesterday," she says, while cutting the pork on her plate, then with a nervous laugh adds, "But what my mother doesn't know won't kill me."

But does she know about any of this? I think.

I actually have gone to temple, once, with Michael, on a High Holy Day the first year we were together. It was nice; a lovely informed—I mean, Reform—service. And I did fine. I didn't genuflect in the aisle, and I even followed along in the prayer book pretty well. I had to keep quiet during the Hebrew lines, but it was all pretty familiar in an Old Testament sort of way. The service was progressing along fine when suddenly during the ram's horn time, it hit me that I was waiting for Mary to arrive. Not Jesus, and God clearly was their Big Guy, but Mary was who I wanted right nearby. Then I remembered that actually Mary was a Jew, and for the first time I wondered who she had prayed to. God? The One who needed her to have His son? I tried to imagine what that must have been like for her—to grow up without a mother figure to give her guidance. Sitting at the baby shower with a madonna soon to be bereft of child, I realize that years from now, the baby in the bassinet will have more of an answer to that than I ever will. Though I guess my own mother's immense and perpetual silence was kind of similar.

The quartet, which had disappeared during lunch, returns and, after getting settled, launches into Brahms's "Lullaby." When they finish, Tom goes to the parquet floor and takes a microphone from a sound man standing nearby. He begins with some of the funnier lines from his last hit TV show, then proceeds to speak eloquently of the great honor he and Bill have received. It is the best acceptance speech I've heard, and God knows there are a lot in this town, although normally the object received isn't alive. As he expresses their deep gratitude to Sarah, none of us can keep a dry eye—his warmth and tenderness toward her are vibrant. But as he continues to glorify her, Sarah suddenly breaks down and deeply cries. As huge engulfing sobs capture her body, all the way over on the lawn's other side, the baby joins her with a wail. The quartet immediately starts playing the lullaby again but louder and faster this time, as Tom practically throws the microphone at the sound man, and he and Bill run to comfort their child, looking for all the world like they want to die.

The still-unintroduced woman at our table scoops Sarah up in her arms and gently leads her inside. Tonette is a blur of creme concern as she flies by, joining them away from our eyes. I look at Michael and the expression on his face says everything I thought it would—he is ready to take this opportunity to flee. We get up from the deserted table and walk over to Bill and Tom to say goodbye. I notice that unknown-movie-star-man is alone on the far side of the tent. All ten baby dolls that were on his table are now sitting on the floor at his feet, like some infantile fan club turned plastic that he can keep.

"Thank you for having us." I kiss each father on the cheek.

"Don't forget your baby," Tom says as he goes to a table, grabs two dolls, and brings them to me, laying one in each of my arms. "In fact, there are so many, take two."

As Michael and I walk back through the house to leave, Ken is still standing at the front door like a heavenly messenger whose announcement never arrived. When we get outside, Michael takes my ticket to the valet, and I see Sarah, the still-unmet female guest, and Tonette sitting on the curb, so I walk over to tell them goodbye.

But what comes blurting out of me instead is nothing I would have planned. To Sarah I say, "Congratulations," then immediately deeply wish that I had not, then in a fluster I turn to the female guest I still have not met and give her a hug. After extricating myself from that mistake, I say to Tonette, "It was so nice to meet you—I mean, see you."

The three of them stare at me as though I am stark raving mad and for a second I wonder if I am, or at least mad from this experience I've had. I briefly consider trying the goodbyes all over again, but I decide it is best to just go away.

Walking over to Michael, who is waiting for me next to my truck, I realize I have spoken to the three women the way I wish they really were: a mother who is happy about the situation with her child, a kind friend who has wished me marital bliss, and a woman I don't know and will never see again.

Michael slips his arms around me and I kiss him, as four fake baby hands dig into my breasts. He helps me into my truck, telling me that he has to get back to the station, but maybe later he'll come by. I start to offer one of the dolls to him, but I know that he doesn't have any use for it. Of course, neither do I.

Michael walks to his car, and as I start to turn the truck around, I see Tom and Bill walk outside with their arms around each other and Bill carrying their now peaceful child. Sarah looks at them and smiles. I suddenly feel a terrible wave of sadness, then decide it is just that lonely

Sunday thing; if Michael were coming with me, I'd be fine. But a voice deep inside me tells me that's a lie.

The guards do not glance up when my truck drives out the tremendous gates. It is like leaving a heaven imagined by someone else. I take a left onto Sepulveda and am traveling a good ten minutes before I realize I am heading the wrong way to get home.

I moved to Los Angeles Labor Day weekend of 1992 when I was twenty-three, a few months after graduating from SVA and breaking up with Tim. Moved and landed in Suzanne's guest room. Or rather the guest room of Marc, her boyfriend at that time, with whom she lived in his Spanish-style house in Beverly Hills. The house was large and cool with a pool I would take dips in on the long hot September afternoons while Suzanne and Marc were at work. Marc was a music agent and he introduced me to Bill, the music producer I worked for as an assistant a few days a week. Marc hooked me up with him right after I got to L.A., sending me up to Bill's home in Silverlake. I liked Bill immediately. He was originally from Detroit with an Ivy League yet groovy vibe about him. He had kind blue eyes, and offered me some of the fresh carrot juice he had just made before we sat outside on his terraced patio to talk about where I was from, the bands he was producing, and the things he needed done.

In my first few days after moving, I started adjusting to the sights of L.A., like the trees. I had never seen such odd ones before. Not that the palm trees were odd—okay, they were out of place, not even indigenous to the city, but they didn't look odd; their gaunt bodies and full plumes on top reminded me of the anorexic yet heavy-chested actresses everywhere. It was the other types of trees, the regular North American kind, that were so odd. They were small. Tiny. I figured maybe the desert climate kept them from growing full because it was hot here, blazing. The sun was at such a close angle—not the rays buffeted through the humidity that I grew up with in the South, or even the curved slant of it you'd get in New York City. This sun was right next to me, literally on my shoulder, like I'd bump into it if I turned around too fast. So a bunch of nice, full, shade-producing, sun-blocking trees would have been a huge help against that heat-inducing foe, but everywhere I went—Sunset Boulevard, Westwood, Beverly Hills—the trees were so curiously small. It made me long for the deep shade and towering fullness of the virtual forests at home in Pass Christian.

Two weeks after I started working for Bill, almost my third week in L.A., I finally called Andrew to let him know I had moved. I had been waiting to call him because I wanted to get more settled somehow, but the longing to hear his voice overpowered me. It had been a month since we had spoken on the phone, and that was in New York, so it was beginning to feel like something that had happened in a far-off distant land that wasn't connected to me but I needed it to be. Needed him to be. It was a Saturday morning, Suzanne and Marc and I had finished breakfast, and I was still sitting at their antique country pine kitchen table while the morning light bounced off the citron walls, studying the book-sized L.A. map to acquaint myself with routes around town. At least streets were clearly marked in this city, with one sign at the corner, and also a larger one a few yards ahead to give a pleasant warning of your future turn. I remembered the small street signs in Pass Christian, mostly hidden by full, luscious trees, and wondered how anyone ever moved there and comfortably got around, but maybe that was the point. Suzanne and Marc came through the kitchen in tennis garb, and told me they'd be back in a few hours. I waved nonchalantly as if I couldn't care less that I had the house again to myself. And the phone.

I waited for the sounds of the garage door opening, the car doors shutting, the car starting and revving (it was a Porsche), and backing out of the drive, before I walked into the den where large sliding doors led out to the pool, sat down on the gargantuan denim-covered couch, picked up the phone on the side table, and dialed Andrew's number that I had known by heart for years, but had always had to dial long distance. Now, for the first time, it was local.

The operator answered, and upon hearing my name, told me to hold, so I knew she was getting him. It seemed as if only one person always answered his phone; no matter what hour it was or day of the week, the voice sounded exactly the same, as if there were a woman put on earth just to handle Andrew's phones. In the years I lived in New York, whenever I called Andrew, I always imagined this operator-woman somewhere in an almost bare, nondescript room, far away from his home, with plastic containers of food and a diet Coke on her desk, always there, never ever gone.

"Where are you?" Andrew said, his concerned voice and large presence suddenly on the line. "Are you okay?"

"Yeah, I'm good; I'm in L.A."

"L.A.? Where?"

I gave him the details, leaving out the length of time I'd been here, until he asked.

"Why haven't you called me before? I've been worried, not hearing from you for weeks, and I couldn't call you because of Tim-my." Andrew exaggerated the last syllable the way he had done since I first started seeing Tim. "Is he here, too?"

"No, that's all over."

"Good." He said it as if Tim were a phase I had needed to go through that he had always known would end, and that having done so it signaled my growth. "Not calling me for weeks, no idea where you were—you are in such big trouble for this."

Thank God.

"Do you still love me?"

"Yes, I do."

"Then why aren't you up here already? Come on." He gave me directions to his home in Bel Air, making sure I knew the right way to go. I almost told him I had a map, but I wanted his instructions. As we hung up, the tingly feeling that had been building in me all during the call settled inside, making me glow stronger than the sun outside. I was going to see Andrew. I hadn't expected that when I called him. I figured we'd just pick up our routine of talking every day, and maybe at some point, one day . . . But this was so immediate. I wondered what it meant and hoped it was huge and would become habitual.

I changed into a little floral dress I had bought on Melrose and put on some makeup, having to keep my hands steady while I thought back to the last time I had seen him. It was in his suite at the Ritz-Carlton, and we had been sitting on the yellow silk couch looking at pictures of Malaysia when that terrible Suzy girl arrived. Maybe seeing him now could be a fresh start, maybe he'd even ask about my art. I looked in the mirror of Marc's guest room one last time before I picked up my bag to go. I was finally going to see Andrew again after five years. Five years that in some ways felt like ten, but also felt like five minutes. I left a note for Suzanne, telling her I had borrowed her car to run some errands, and ran out the door.

On the drive up the road in Bel Air to Andrew's home, I passed huge houses with manicured lawns that became increasing large and more hidden from view the farther up I went. It felt like a dream, being on my way to see him again, real the way dreams feel while I'm having them, yet this one I didn't have to wake up from. The road kept winding around, then wound back one more time, and there at the very top, as if God had saved it for him, was Andrew's property. From the street, all I could see was a dense boundary of trees and shrubbery that I was sure hid a tall and fierce fence topped with barbed wire. A large white gate was closed across a driveway that looked like a small road. I stopped the car on the street before I got any closer—I figured he had security cameras rigged all over the place—and checked my makeup in the rearview mirror, then with an expulsion of air from my gut that was meant to relax the butterflies in there but only made them worse, I drove into the driveway and stopped in front of the gate. I pushed the button on an intercom box that protruded toward my car like a land-bound periscope, and a few seconds later, the wide white gate silently swung open, and a camera swiveled, keeping my car in sight as I drove into the property. Access to Andrew's kingdom had been silently granted.

The curving roadway was flanked by large shady trees and strategically placed groups of shrubs through which I glimpsed tennis courts on the left, then farther up on the right a small house, then the driveway curved once again and his home came into view.

It could have been on the Mediterranean coast, the Italianate architecture was so perfect and grand. Opening the car door, I half expected to smell sea air. It was like an island, a retreat from the intrusion of city life below.

The front door's heavy wood muffled my knock, but I noticed a doorbell, so I pushed that, and a moment later, the door opened by inches and seconds and feet and minutes and Andrew appeared.

"Hi." He said the word as only he could, not so much making it two syllables, but with enough space that there was a sunrise in the first part and a sunset in the last with a day in between for us.

I stood on the step taking him in. I'd seen his face and body in photographs and films countless times in the intervening years, but none of it compared to seeing him live. He was stripped down without the celluloid. Available, raw and real. Then our arms and lips and hands and tongues came together as if they had never not.

He led me through rooms of highly polished dark wood floors, satiny cream walls, and exquisite museum-quality antiques. Kellys, Baselitzes, Lichtensteins, Freuds, Twomblys, Johns, and Richters lined the walls. I thought of my sculptures in Momma's attic and fantasized about one of them being there as we continued through more rooms past more art, then into his bedroom where Andrew sat down on the bed. It was huge. A room of its own. No words were spoken as our garments were removed.

The sex we had didn't feel like only the second time. It was a continuation, an "and then," as if the movement and rhythm and heat had been present all along, just under our skin. We fell in.

After a couple of hours, we got up and went to the kitchen for food, bringing a tray of gourmet dishes his chef had made back to the bed with ice-cold bottles of Pellegrino and beer.

"I'm glad you're here. I've missed seeing your beautiful face," Andrew said. We were lying back on the bed content after feeding each other and devouring the food. I didn't say anything. It was a huge admission from him. One that I knew he might not have said if he'd thought much about it beforehand. It had come out on its own, unable to stay in, and I let it roll over my skin like the sensations of him during sex.

Andrew reached over to the bedside table and pressed a button, making the floor-to-ceiling, wall-to-wall heavy silk cream-colored curtains slowly open, as if the day outside were a performance for us. The slightest cast of shadow was reaching toward his house. I realized it had to be past three and suddenly remembered Suzanne's car sitting outside. It seemed ages ago since I had left that note for her. She was probably frantic, but mostly mad.

"Will I see you again soon or is it going to be years?" I said as I reluctantly got up and started to dress.

"What do you think?" He looked at me from his bed, his eyes on mine as if they had never left.

And I knew what he meant.

He kissed me at the front door. "Call me later, sweet-y-vette."

Despite the annoyance of having to deal with an angry, carless Suzanne, I was ecstatically happy as I flew down the hill in Bel Air. As I turned onto Sunset, speeding into the curves to take them tight and fast, it felt as if Andrew's arms were still holding me close.

And we were back. Not in the way it had been before, because we weren't sexually involved before. Okay, once, I know, but that didn't really count in terms of defining the relationship because the relationship wasn't sexual. It was parental in a way. But now it was going to be different, that was clear. Though I wasn't sure what change had suddenly allowed it. But I didn't care. Andrew was back in my life; that was all that mattered.

Andrew and I started talking a few times every day. He'd call in the morning after Suzanne and Marc had left for work; I'd call him in the afternoon or night. Our New York habit but with the addition that we also talked about the sex we were regularly having. I'd go up to his house late at night, a wind was always high and restless in the trees around his estate even when it had been still as death in L.A. below, and he'd greet me at the front door, the same small "hi" every time before we kissed. Then we'd go into the kitchen if he had to finish up a call he was on with other movie people, I figured, who also conducted business at all hours of the night. The calls sounded important and concerned money or positions of power changing around. I'd sit on a stool waiting for him, listening to him talk and trying to fill in what the other person was saying, clues to Andrew's life and what consumed him.

The kitchen was completely different from the rest of the house with its dark woods, important paintings, and astonishing antiques; it was a modernist's dream. Steel and chrome and white and beams. Reflective surfaces absent of color except for an eternally present, exquisitely fresh bowl of fruit whose type of occupant changed every few days and a David Hockney behind glass, one of the Mulholland Drive series, spreading itself across the large kitchen wall like a bird unable to take full flight. Once the calls were done or would no longer be answered, since calls never ceased to come in for him, we would walk the path to his bedroom, the dark and beautiful art-filled journey into the place where his jeans would come down, my clothes would be taken off, usually with him lying on the bed watching, then I would get on top of him and work my way down to the beginning of bliss for both of us.

After a couple more weeks of living at Marc and Suzanne's when I thought Suzanne and I were going to tear each other's hair out, I bought an old Chevy truck (good for hauling my sculptures, I thought) and put down a deposit plus first month's rent on a five-hundred-dollar-a-month rent-controlled studio apartment on a pretty street in Beverly Hills. I had sold most of the work I did for the graduation show at SVA in New York back in May, so I had that money, and I had gotten a waitressing job at a restaurant to supplement my income since a few days a week working for Bill wasn't covering everything.

The apartment was in an old Spanish-style building from the twenties with huge windows and beautiful tile. It had one large, light-filled room plus an eat-in kitchen, a huge walk-in closet, a decent-sized bathroom, and, the best part, a dressing room that I used as my (tiny) art studio. I had decided to start painting again, wanting to make box-type pieces with objects depicting the juxtaposition of being in two worlds, separate but at once. So the dressing room was messy and full, with a drop cloth covering the hardwood floor and a floodlight clamped onto the door frame so I could work late at night after my restaurant shifts, while I was still wound up from getting customers' gourmand desires while they were under the delusion that sitting in the new hot spot, eating an overly expensive meal, was going to change who they were, or at least fix their unhappiness.

One afternoon when I was home after a morning of working for Bill, Andrew called me from his car. He asked what I was doing, and when I answered, "Working on a new piece," he immediately wanted my address. I had a split second of thinking his motivation was to see what I was working on, then I realized, probably not. I gave the address to him, using the Academy of Motion Pictures, Arts, and Sciences building as a reference point since it was at the corner of my street and I knew he would know where it was at the very least because of all the premieres he must have attended there through the years, not to mention the two Oscars he had won. My downstairs neighbor had told me what the building was soon after I moved in, as I was cooling down from a run early one evening and watching an impeccably hip phalanx walking past our apartment building. A film premiere, she had explained, at the academy. But Andrew had no response to that information. No "That's funny, I'm there for screenings quite a bit." Or "I'm glad you landed on a safe block." Just "I'll be right there." Which was annoying. Was I not supposed to mention that precious part of his world? We didn't talk about his career regularly, and when we did, he was the one who brought it up, and it took the form of him thinking things through out loud while watching my reaction to see how it sounded, sometimes asking what I thought about a particular point or two, then when he was done, we'd have sex.

Andrew walked into my apartment that afternoon, filling up the space with his tall strong frame, the light from his eyes blinding the room. We had sex on the futon that Bill had given me after assuring me that he had bought it to use as a couch, then changed his mind and never did. I had gotten a down-filled mattress pad to cover it, like gold inlay on a plastic watch, I thought every time I lay down, but it was comfortable, I could sleep, and my checkbook hadn't been wrecked by buying a bed.

At Andrew's house, we had a routine, but that afternoon it was altered, the sex a collage of sensations, some motions moved forward, others following while before they had led, and my apartment was the background. Having him there was like a picture of our relationship enlarged. Easier to see, but some things were blurred while others were cut off, as if unnecessary to the subject's essentiality. The sex was different and familiar, and Andrew became imprinted where my life developed most.

Afterward, Andrew got up to use the bathroom. He walked down the short hall and into the dressing room where I heard him stop, his footsteps muffled slightly by the drop cloth. I could imagine him turning his head to look at my pieces, and I wondered what he thought about them and if he would tell me, as he had with my sculptures all those years ago on his bed at the Ritz-Carlton Hotel. A few seconds later I heard more steps, the bathroom door shut, then the faucet turned on. I lay naked on the futon as a soft breeze from the mid-October day blew in through the window, running over my skin the way Andrew's hands just had, and I waited to see if and what he would say about my art and tried not to care if he didn't, but wasn't very successful.

Hopefully, he'd say something. Please, God, say something. I heard water splashing a face, then hands interrupted the spigot's flow. I tried to remember when I had last washed the towels. Two days ago; not great, not horrible. As my grandmother always said, you were clean when you got out of the tub and used them. I thought of his laundry and linens that were whisked away and invisibly replaced. His clothing retained a perfumed cleanliness, the unsullied perfection of being taken care of by many invisible hands. I could smell it on his garments each time I unzipped his jeans, pushed them down, and opened his fly while he stood, sometimes in his kitchen, when our sex started there at the end of a phone call that had been particularly long, or sometimes during one, if it was useless and annoying to him.

Andrew walked back into the room, got onto the futon with me, and put his head on my stomach with his body lying between my legs. As I rubbed his back, he was quiet and so was I as I waited to see if he'd talk about my art. I knew I couldn't casually say, "So what'd you think of what you saw?" My voice would belie the importance behind it and I didn't want him to know that.

"I didn't know if you were going to call me," Andrew said.

"What?"

"When I first met you at the restaurant in New York. You in that uniform and more beautiful than any woman there, including the one I was with." He looked me in the eyes, nodding his head. "You know who

I mean—Lily—and she could tell, too. After you brought me the phone, she kept saying 'You like her, don't you?' over and over all through the rest of our meal. She bitched about you for weeks—you really threatened her."

It was shocking to hear that she had noticed me, much less been worried about what effect I might have on him.

"Then all Sunday morning," Andrew went on. "After I met you the night before at the coat room, I was kicking myself for not getting your phone number. I didn't think you were gonna call me. Thought I'd have to go back to that restaurant for another meal just to talk to you again, which, by the way, was the only reason I went there two weeks in a row was to meet you. I couldn't stop thinking about you that whole time in between."

"Me, too."

"I didn't even need to go to the bathroom, remember, after we talked? You were still in the coat-check room, and I went in the men's room and thought, *Fuck, now what do I do?* So I washed my hands, then had to tip the attendant a dollar for handing me a towel."

It was funny he had remembered the attendant. I had forgotten all about him, a small wiry man who would continually run out of the men's room when no one was in there and stand outside the ladies' room, shouting in to the female attendant to come out and talk to him. Then he'd race back whenever anyone entered the foyer or came down the stairs—shooting in and out of the men's room like a hermit crab from a sand hole.

Andrew wrapped his arms around me, holding me close and kissing me, and I tried to gather in as much of him to last me before I saw him again. It almost made up for him saying nothing about my art.

After Andrew left, as I was working in the dressing room on the new piece, I wondered if he would ever talk to me about my art again—the work he'd seen that afternoon, all of it—the way he had finally spoken to me about his experience when we first met. Maybe I should bring it up, just ask him one day, "So, what did you think of the work you saw at my apartment?" But I didn't think I could do it without caring too much. Especially after all that had happened with it and me and him. Maybe I wouldn't bring it up. Or maybe I wouldn't have to because he would. Dear God, I hoped so. And I hoped it wouldn't take him years, as it had for him to reveal his feelings about when he first met me. I didn't think I'd be able to wait that long.

Early that November, having lived in L.A. a couple of months, I figured I'd embrace the culture, which as far as I could tell meant working out and not eating lots of things in complicated variations that changed with each person I met to the point where it seemed that basic vegetarians had more food options than most Angelenos allowed themselves. Not that there isn't real culture in L.A., there are museums and the Music Center and all that, but they are pushed aside somehow, ignored. Culture in L.A. is like the sidewalks there; nice to have, but not used very much.

I decided to try the working-out part of L.A. culture, so one morning I found a bright and airy but intense-looking workout studio in West Hollywood that offered all sorts of classes. I picked salsa dancing because it sounded fun and was starting in ten minutes. I went into the studio, found a spot in the front row, and looking around at the strategically spandex-clad women, realized I was probably the only person there who at no point in life would ever think I might professionally need that skill.

In the row behind me and just to the left was a famous pop star I recognized named Viv. Her career had started off phenomenally huge a few years back with a Top Ten album that garnered her the Grammy award for best new artist, but then it had stalled midair with her second album's release. She was still in the pantheon, but in the unenviable position of having to prove herself once again to the industry and to her fans. A few minutes later, class began in a burst of ecstatic musical sounds, and I tried to follow the steps that the teacher was exuberantly executing, but didn't do very well. Just keeping count to the fast Latin tempo was a problem, but I was having a good time, so I didn't care and besides, I figured I'd get it sooner or later.

I decided to make the salsa class a regular part of my week. Every Tuesday and Thursday at nine A.M. there I'd be in the front row so I could follow the teacher's moves, which were still not completely easy.

On the Tuesday of my third salsa class, in the middle of a particularly tricky combo, Viv, who had also been going regularly, suddenly sidled over to me, put her hands on my hips, and said in my ear, "Just focus on the legs, forget the arms and hands until you get the footwork down. Two, three, four. One, two, three . . ." As she alternated pressure on my hips with her hands, helping me feel the rhythm change and shift, I remembered her dance-filled videos, then she moved to a spot next to me in the front row for the rest of the class. As unusual as her gesture was, it felt perfectly normal, like a big sister California-style.

At the end of class, Viv asked if I wanted to have a juice with her. There was a sundeck with a health food bar in the back of the studio, far away from the traffic sounds of La Cienega and outfitted with lattice screens and potted palms and hanging ferns to obscure the ugly apartment building that abutted it. Dark green wrought-iron tables with chairs that left crisscross marks on my legs were spread throughout to relax at while we replenished what was burned off.

"You looked like my friend," Viv said, after she downed her shot of wheat grass before settling in with a tall watermelon juice. We were sitting at a table under a heavy Boston fern, its tendrils curling down, reaching toward Viv like the fingers of a fan.

"I did? Who?"

"No, not someone in particular. When you walked into class that first time, my publicist was with me, and a friend of mine had said she might join us, so we were both looking out for her, but my publicist had never seen her before, so she pointed at you thinking you were my friend, and I said, 'No, that's not her.' Then she said, 'She looks like someone who'd be a friend of yours.' Isn't that funny?" Viv made it sound like we had just discovered our grandmothers were first cousins. We stayed for an hour, talking about her music, my art, life in L.A., and before we parted, we traded phone numbers.

Driving home, I was enveloped in the feeling of finding a friend. New school shoes is how it felt. Shiny and pretty with one or two uncomfortable spots maybe, but those would get broken in, as they took me on adventures of many kinds.

A couple of nights later, I arrived at Andrew's house early one evening, and the front door was opened by a slight man with sandy brown hair. Before I could wonder who he was, the man put his hand out and said, "Hello, Yvette, I'm Patrick, I believe we met on the phone." He was as polite and solicitous leading me back to Andrew's office as he had been so many years ago when he arranged for a doctor to come to my apartment, then wired money to me. It was like meeting family, someone I already had a connection to. Andrew got up from his desk when he saw us come in, walked over to kiss me, then handed Patrick a small piece of paper, saying, "These two calls I will take." Then wrapping his arm around me, he said, "C'mon, honey." And we went to his bedroom.

Driving down the hill a few hours later, I realized that I was on a very short list of people whose calls were always put through to Andrew no matter when and no matter what he was doing, and calls constantly came in at Andrew's, like jets lining up at Kennedy with operator-woman and Patrick running traffic control. He always came to the phone for me, and had since the beginning way back in New York. If he was in the middle of a meeting, he'd say, "Where are you?" then, "How are you?" and after hearing that I was okay, he'd tell me he'd call me back. It was the epitome of safety, his attention and concern and time every day. It was like having a million dollars that somehow fit into a back pocket of a garment that I wore daily. Him. Andrew currency. Not that I'd spend it in public. Without him ever saying it, I knew that our relationship was a secret.

Rarely, he'd be unreachable, like when he was at a postproduction studio where he was completing his latest film, *Valiant Hour*, but Patrick would always tell me, or Andrew would himself. Like he would before seeing Stephanie; he'd say he'd be out that night, and I knew what that meant without asking him.

Andrew was seeing Stephanie, a two-time Academy Award–nominated actress who had landed the role of his love interest in *Valiant Hour*, which all the gossip columnists agreed might finally grant her the coveted ultimate award from the industry. Not to mention the award of being on Andrew's arm at every public event and in between his sheets. She was his girlfriend, or that was the word Andrew used when he spoke about her to me.

I had known that Andrew and Stephanie were together long before he said anything about it, thanks to the media chronicling the relationship assiduously from its beginning a year before. When I first read about it I still lived in New York, and I had thought she didn't seem his type. Stephanie was tall and coldly blond and Nordic, like some Viking taking over the land. Then when I moved to L.A. and started seeing Andrew regularly, I really didn't believe in their relationship. The emotional validity of it. I had a feeling Andrew was with her because she was perfect for his film. He generally got involved with his leading women, as if the films he picked to do were some sort of obligatory matchmaking service. And it was impossible for me to believe that Stephanie really cared about him. She looked like a woman who, if she ever pulled herself away from the mirror long enough, would eat her young, so I figured she was just using Andrew to get the trophy that really mattered to her, while she was one on his arm. And he on hers.

A few months before Stephanie had started seeing Andrew, she came into the restaurant I worked at in Greenwich Village. She was in New York promoting a film, the film she had done that must have gotten Andrew's attention and put her on his radar screen as the next girl for him. She had heard about the great little French bistro in the Village that everyone was raving about and had to come in for a meal. But not just any meal. Stephanie was macrobiotic at that point, though God knows what fad she's moved onto since, so the chef was instructed to cook special macro dishes for her that she could eat while her dinner companions chowed down on the regular fare of pâté and cassoulet and tripe and French fries. I guess Stephanie was under the delusion that the chef would be honored to cook for her and us to serve her, but all of us waiters drew straws, with the loser having to take her table, and the chef grumbled and complained the whole time he cooked the brown rice and steamed the sad vegetables and made the soggy beans. He would have been honored if she had eaten a meal he wanted to cook, otherwise, we all wished she had gone to one of those health restaurants in the East Village, but clearly they weren't fabulous enough.

Lying in bed later that night, knowing that Andrew was in bed with Stephanie—he'd told me he had to meet her at some party—I had a wonderful daydream that Stephanie suddenly decided to quit her career and leave Andrew, but I knew that would never happen. And Andrew wouldn't break up with her before their movie came out because that would be bad for box office, so I'd have to wait until after the opening in the spring to see what he'd do, like make another movie with her, or dump her and find someone new. Like me. A part of me hoped *Valiant Hour* would be a big success for him, but another part hoped it wouldn't, but only because of Stephanie, so he'd never see her again and I could move in. Literally.

One morning after salsa class, Viv and I were on the sundeck at our usual table drinking watermelon juice and talking about our weekends. It was late November, but the morning was still warm as if the heat of the summer had saved itself to emerge one final time before withdrawing for the year. I had been jumpy all morning, and had hoped the class would exhaust it out of me, but it hadn't. I needed to talk about Andrew. After seeing him regularly for almost three months and still not telling anyone, I felt about to burst. The impressions of his body on my skin, the daily and multiple phone calls, the withdrawal I went through in between seeing him, all of it was commanding my head nonstop. I needed to get it out to someone. I considered calling Carrie in New York, but we had started drifting apart once I began SVA and was buried in schoolwork. Then when I moved in with Tim, our regular communication ended, so talking to her after so much time wasn't an option. And I needed someone local, a friend, which Viv was, and she was right in front of me, drinking her juice, going on and on about her boyfriend, so for me not to say anything about Andrew felt like being at lunch with her and not eating a meal. Starving, just looking in. I wanted to talk, but in a controlled kind of way, so that Viv would forget all about it afterward, only remembering if I talked about it again. There was no way she could know it was Andrew, so I decided to conceal his identity, and began telling Viv about this guy I was seeing, Andy—a nickname Andrew was never called. I said he went out of town sometimes—my way of talking about not seeing him when he was with Stephanie—and I'd miss him so much, but we talked on the phone all the time and about the sex we had and . . .

It felt good to get it out, and Viv was an attentive listener. She made noises that encouraged me to talk and nodded at other parts; she was completely understanding, even saying things that were dead-on about Andrew, as if we had been speaking about him the whole time I'd known him.

The phone was ringing when I got home. It was Andrew wondering where I'd been, he had come by my apartment, but I wasn't in. I was so happy to have finally been able to talk about him to Viv, even in a veiled way, that I told Andrew about the salsa classes and my friendship with her, though not about the conversation she and I had just had.

"Viv, the pop singer?" Andrew said in a tone I had never heard before.

"Yeah, her." I immediately felt uneasy though I couldn't figure out what could be wrong.

"Viv." Andrew's voice pounced on the word. "Who released a couple of albums, but now is in free fall?"

"Yes, her. What's the big deal?"

"She's Stephanie's best friend."

"Oh, no."

"Oh, yes. You didn't tell her anything about us, did you?"

"Oh, God, no. I wouldn't do that." My mind was scrambling, trying to remember everything I had said to Viv.

"Good, because otherwise we're fucked. Stephanie is pretty vindictive. I can handle her, but I wouldn't want her wrath on your head."

I was quiet for a moment while that horrible thought sank in. "Jesus, how fucking small is this town?"

Which made Andrew laugh, as if I were starting to understand something he had learned before I was born. And actually, I realized, he had.

"As long as you didn't say anything to Viv—who, by the way, has one of the biggest mouths in Hollywood, so don't tell her anything you don't want broadcast on the street—we'll be fine. Call me later," he said, then his voice moved down a few places inside me until it reached exactly where he wanted it to be. "You need to fuck me tonight."

"I sure do."

I hung up the phone thrilled that I was going to see Andrew soon, but flipped out about Stephanie and Viv. Fuck. How could I have been so stupid as to use the name Andy? Daddy had always said that the way people get caught in lies is that they can't remember what they said, so right before I told Viv about Andrew, I thought I'd use a name close to his so I wouldn't get tripped up. But fuck, Stephanie and Viv were best friends. Jesus, I wished I had known that. And how weird was it that of all the people I made friends with, or who had made friends with me, she's removed from Andrew one degree. Though maybe everyone is in

L.A. I prayed Viv wouldn't say anything to Stephanie, though really what could she say? But if Viv had figured it out, and told Stephanie, who then got all over Andrew about it, he would be pissed off and would stop seeing me, and . . . Fuck. I would just have to tell Viv the next time we talked that Andy and I had broken up and pray to God that she forgets everything I'd said.

Two days later, Viv and I were on the patio after salsa class, drinking our watermelon juice while she talked about her boyfriend, Craig Beltram, a music executive for a huge record label she wanted to get on. As she talked, I was mentally rehearsing how to say that Andy and I were over. I had considered telling her that I couldn't stay for juice this time, but I realized that I needed to get the lie about the lie over with, so that I could move on and stop worrying nonstop as I had been for the last forty-eight hours. She was complaining about Craig's habit of being late, so I told her how I just couldn't take Andy's being out of town and had broken up with him last night.

"Good for you," Viv said. "You deserve to have someone who's here when you want him."

Then she started going on about all the cute guys at the parties she went to with Craig, and how I could go with them from now on and meet someone else. I was thrilled she had bought the lie so easily. All that worrying for nothing. But then her topic swerved.

"You know, my best friend, Stephanie, is seeing Andrew Madden, though he still fucks tons of other women on the side," Viv said, looking at me intently. "You're so smart for what you did. I wish she would dump him." She put down her juice and started playing with the wrapper of the straw she had used. "You know, it's funny, but I was thinking the other day about what you said, about your Andy, and in a way, he sounded so much like Andrew Madden."

I nearly choked on my watermelon juice and suddenly wished seeds were in it, so I would have had that excuse. I had given no identifying clues, other than the immense stupidity of shortening his name, though maybe the longing affection in my voice was a clue, as if the encountering of Andrew in that specific sex/love way induced a melody that all reports of him were sung in and Viv had recognized the Andrew tune.

"That is funny. But the Andy I was seeing is nothing like him, from what I hear." Which I knew was true. Andrew with Stephanie was as separate from him with me as alloy to gold.

"Well, that's good," Viv said, looking hard into my eyes. "Because Andrew Madden is the biggest womanizing dirtbag son of a bitch that there is." She paused for a moment, as if considering whether to vilify him further. "But you're too smart to get hooked up with someone like him." Her eyes were on mine, watching my reaction. "I would just love to give Stephanie proof of how badly he treats her so she can dump his ass already. I feel sorry for anyone who is stupid enough to get involved with him, but he just pulls them in. You wouldn't believe the number of women he fucks."

The best I could do was nod noncommittally. Thank God, Viv had to meet her publicist, so she jumped up, kissed me on the cheek, and told me she'd call me that night.

I walked to my truck on La Cienega in a daze. Okay, she definitely somehow had suspected. Fuck. I just hoped she believed that bullshit about my not seeing Andy anymore. But she had no proof that she could go to Stephanie with, so I just needed to let it all blow over. Go to those parties with her and meet other men and pretend that I wanted to date them.

Or maybe I should stop being friends with Viv. It did seem kind of dangerous, and I really didn't want to hear any more stuff like that about Andrew. But it would seem weird to suddenly cut the friendship off, and she had already looked suspicious enough. Besides, I liked Viv. And really, I hadn't said anything that was proof positive about Andrew; she'd probably just forget about it.

But why did Viv hate Andrew so much? Her face had contorted into such intense, ugly vehemence when she talked about him—it was weird. Maybe she had wanted to be his girlfriend and was pissed off that

Stephanie got him first. Viv had sounded like she hated Andrew because he didn't want to be with her. And I didn't know what to think about the "He still fucks tons of women on the side" remark. There couldn't be tons. He and I had been together two or three times a week since I started seeing him and he still had to see Stephanie, so how much time could be left, not to mention his being in postproduction on his film. Probably enough for a few fucks here and there, and okay, I had always known there were other women—Christ, I had met Suzy in New York after all—but they had never bothered me before because I wasn't having sex with Andrew and no one else was in his life the way I was. And all those other women he fucked didn't mean anything to him, so I had never cared about them, but suddenly I did. Okay, I knew he didn't take other women's calls the way he took mine—well, Stephanie's probably, but he had to with her—and with Andrew, phone access was everything. So my status with him was safe. I just had to keep it that way. And pray that after his film opened, he got rid of Stephanie.

22

Suzanne has insisted on coming by to try on her veil. There was no way I could stop her, she was like Sherman through Atlanta, to make a dreadful comparison, when she called me from her car, saying that she was in my neighborhood so was just going to drop by. I haven't seen her in a little over a week, since her bridal shower, when she told me she wanted a fitting, and I know she thinks the veil is finished, which it really should be, so I am madly gluing seed pearls and tiny gems on it while hoping some bridal magic will occur that will transform it into incredibly lovely and finished before she gets here. But I'm not counting on it.

"Good God, I always forget how far east you are," Suzanne says, panting mildly when I open my front door, as if the air over here away from the beach is thinner somehow.

"It's not that far, Suzanne," I say, leaning in for a hug. Instead she brushes an unfelt kiss on my cheek as she walks inside. "Some people even live farther east than me. Imagine."

But Suzanne's mind has moved on to other things. Like her veil. Which is placed neatly on the iron dressmaker's stand in front of the wide living room windows, its backdrop a view of the large tree outside, all pearly green and fluttery leaves in the small April wind. The tree suddenly feels more like family than my sister does.

"Here it is. Finally." Suzanne practically lunges for the soft, white confection, snatches it up, and without the aid of a mirror or an attendant, expertly puts it on her head, arranging it perfectly. I wonder when she learned to do that or if it is a skill that all brides receive along with the engagement ring, a whole host of abilities that see them through this life-changing phase. Suzanne twirls around, looking for a mirror, and upon seeing none, dashes out of the room and down the hall to my office. Her activity is a blur of nuptial beauty. Even with her business suit on, the second the veil touched her head, she became a bride, so lovely and complete, as if the unnatural state was her not being one. I suddenly want to cry. Maybe that spontaneous reaction I should have had upon seeing myself in the veil was saving itself for when the real bride showed up—as if it knew the whole time that it wasn't meant for me.

"It's not finished!" Suzanne suddenly yells from my studio. "Yvette, come in here, there are whole blotches of nothing, and what's with all the pearls? What in Christ's name have you been doing all this time?"

Thinking about Andrew and wishing I'd never told you that I'd make the goddamn thing. I wisely choose not to share that with her, and instead slowly walk myself down the hall to the studio. I feel as if I am going to the dentist, but one where not only will I have all the pain, but will do all the work, too.

"Okay, well," I say, summoning my best soothing-an-irritated-customer tone. Not that I've had any irritated customers for my jewelry, frankly, but pretending my sister is one suddenly helps. "I was just waiting for this fitting to see how it played against your face." Suzanne darts her eyes at me from the mirror, about to question the "played against your face" line, which doesn't surprise me because I'm not even sure what that means, it just sounded designy, but thank God, she decides to accept it. "Because now I can fill in with beading here, and lift the netting up there with a little stiffening so it won't be flat, and . . ." My hands are dancing around Suzanne's head, lightly pinpointing spots on the headpiece, arranging netting, giving her lots of sisterly, maid-of-honor attention, which maybe was the whole point of all this stuff, I realize, so that the bride isn't ever alone with her real fears, but is constantly with someone else who has to be worried about the superficial things that she is, too.

Suzanne starts to say something, then is quiet and looks back in the mirror. I can see her imagining her dress and the flowers and the church and the music and the attendants and the priest and the guests and, most importantly, Matt, waiting for her at the end of the aisle to carry her into a new and perfect life.

"You're going to be a beautiful bride. You already are."

She lets out a sigh of relief. "Thanks, sweetie. I think I just needed to see it, to make sure it was real." She gazes at her reflection one more time, as if confirming the veil is there. "It's going to be great. I'm so glad you're making it. The ones in the stores were beautiful, but none were exactly how I always envisioned it."

I look in the mirror at my sister, who is completely transformed by a few yards of silk netting and a peau-de-soie headpiece with gems and pearls, as if the object with magical powers that we longed for as small girls is finally in her life.

"But now you are going to fix this part, aren't you?" Suzanne says with a small frown, pointing to a section of the veil.

Reggie has convinced me to play hooky by seeing a movie at eleven A.M. I do have some hours to kill before I pick up the order Dipen promised he'd have ready this afternoon, though I could be home working on commissions, getting invoices done, organizing new press kits, or, mainly, finishing Suzanne's veil, particularly since she had the fitting for it only a few days ago, but the idea of escaping from what I should be doing in a dark room in the middle of Wednesday sounds heavenly. And reminds me of what it's like seeing Michael, a little bit, really.

Reggie and I have reached a truce about Michael. I talk about him in a sanitized way, and he says very little, as if waiting for what he is thinking to appear in my brain. It already has; I'm just thinking that future events will prove him wrong. Though Reggie knows that it's already in my brain, so a long silent conversation occurs between us after just a few spoken sentences about Michael.

I am going to a dinner party tonight with Michael. Which actually I was really looking forward to because the last few dates with Michael—the baby shower practically doesn't count because that was more him providing security for me, emotionally at least, or me hoping he would—have all ended rather abruptly with him going home to sleep alone, so since it's a Friday, I feel sure he'll stay this time. I think. He called just a few minutes before he was supposed to pick me up to say that he was running late, could I drive myself and meet him there? Considering that he met me at the baby shower, it would have been churlish to say no, but when he gave me the Hollywood Hills address, what I wanted to say was, "Oops, actually, I can't. In fact, I never would have said yes at all if I had known that the evening included me, alone, on a hill, with my truck." But I didn't. I said, "Yeah, no, that's fine," and jotted down the address.

You see, I don't believe in emergency brakes. I know they exist, I use the one in my truck, but I'm just not convinced that they have any effect at all. I have a very hard time believing that one little lift of my hand on a Fisher Price toy–sounding lever is actually sufficient to keep my truck from careening all the way down a hill and dragging everything else along with it.

Of course, I do make the sign of the cross every time I pass a Catholic church, which is another little lift of my hand, but that actually does prevent my soul from crashing down to hell, so it makes sense. But this—this emergency brake. Even the name cancels itself out; how can it be an emergency, if you're able to use a brake?

But I continue to use it anyway, particularly when I have to visit people up in the hills, which I am supposed to find just charming as hell, but to be totally honest, the two words that instill terror and dread in my heart are "Hollywood Hills," where I am now sitting in my to-a-terrifying-degree-incline-parked truck, hoping it doesn't roll downhill.

I am waiting for Michael, who is running late, in front of his friends' house, which is in that demurely named Greek-god section of the Hollywood Hills, Mt. Olympus. Michael has friends who live in a house that I hate. I am expecting to see Malcolm McDowell walk outside in a toga any minute now. I wonder if they know that their house inspires hate. I decide that they don't. I decide to remember this, this fault Michael has of picking friends with homes like this—I think it will help the next time he doesn't spend the night.

I have changed my shirt a few times now. First into the alternate one that I brought, then back again. Then a few minutes later, I change again.

I had an odd feeling this morning when Michael called to invite me to this dinner party that there is a list. That if I had said no, the next woman would just slide into place, like a bullet in a gun. I know that's not true. Literally. It's probably just those tons-of-women Andrew memories getting to me. I mean, I know Michael has strong feelings for me. I just still don't have any idea what they are. Or what we are to each other. Sometimes I think, *Well, we've been seeing each other altogether for over a year now—we just have big breaks between dates, that's all.* I am trying to think of it more that we're on our own time frame with each other, and I'm sure that at some point we really will progress. I'm choosing to look at our relationship in stages. Though I'm wanting to move forward to the next one. But sometimes I have a little feeling that with Michael there isn't another stage after this. Though clearly, going to this dinner party at his friends' house is some kind of relationship-progressing event. I think. I am waiting to see what he introduces me as.

Finally Michael arrives. I get out of my truck after he parks, and he does that little laugh of his when he sees me, like my presence is some kind of anticipated surprise he feels obligated to pretend he didn't know about. The moon is completely, urgently full. It is hanging above the hills in a rather menacing way. Light is everywhere. It could practically be afternoon, especially with the way sunlight is out here. No hard shadows, just gleaming, glowy, never-landing light, as if it's been decided that we all need to be looked at through a soft-focus lens.

As we embrace for a kiss, I notice more silver in Michael's hair than I ever have and I know that each strand represents deejays and shows and audience numbers, and I wonder if even three concerned hairs are about us.

He actually does not introduce me to his friends at all. I walk in first and am immediately surrounded by the host and hostess, who repeatedly ask me my name while pecking at me with their hands as if I have layers and layers of clothes needing to be shed, which I don't, and I try to find out their names, but for some reason they don't tell me, so I turn to the only other guest there, Kevin, whose name I already do know because years ago I spent three days with him at an odd little film festival in Spain.

He was there with his eight-year-old daughter, and I was there with Tim, who was busy with his professional friends, so I kinda latched onto Kevin's kid, Kitty, who spent the whole time teaching me the Spanish she had learned from her Mexican maid here in L.A.

I haven't seen Kevin since then, but I guess being with Michael in our relative-time relationship, I forget that Kevin and I basically are virtual strangers, so I hug him. A big hug. I think "full body" is the right term for it. Immediately I feel him completely freeze up, but instead of stopping, I commit further like some kind of terrible therapy exercise, then I start patting him on the back, like my grandmother would when you rate a really special hug, and I just cannot seem to stop. Finally, I pull my body back from this very forward motion and see that Kevin looks totally frozen, as if he can only move his mouth.

I ask him about Kitty, who, he says, is away at boarding school. I wonder if the child is ever allowed to stay in L.A., then Kevin locks his eyes onto Michael as if he never wants to look away. I suddenly remember him doing that in Spain to Tim, and for the first time, I understand why I spent all that time there with his daughter. I wish she'd come flying through the door this minute so I'd have someone to talk to.

Instead, there is Slim. The hostess. I have managed to figure out her name, because Michael kept saying it to her, and seeing as how I have never heard him say word one to me or anyone about physical appearance, I figure this must be what she goes by. The pressure of that name leaves me exhausted. I wonder if it does that to her, too. She has very clearly had a face-lift, and I've never been able to tell any of that stuff—nose jobs, eye lifts, I mean, Michael Jackson could get by me—but this one is very noticeable. What strikes me is that her skin actually looks more tired pulled up so tight, as if it was just allowed to fall, it could finally rest. I want to give her skin a Valium.

Slim herds us into the dining room, which she has decorated in the style of old Pompeii. I am feeling profoundly mortal in a way I never have before. We sit down, the five of us, spread around a lap pool of a table. Salads are already at each place.

Kevin, who somehow has managed to find his chair, fork, and plate, all the while staring straight at Michael, announces that he hasn't eaten a raw tomato in over twenty-five years. If it's put under the broiler for even thirty seconds, he'll eat it right up, but not raw, not him. Slim starts in about how a tomato isn't even a vegetable at all, you know, it really is fruit, to which I say, "Yes, in August, I eat them all the time just like an apple. You know, a little salt and you're set."

Then Michael starts waving his hands at Kevin in some pseudo Essa Pekka Salonen motion. "Just relax with the rawness," he says. "Let yourself be open to the firmness of the flavor."

"I think I'm going to do it," Kevin says. "I think I am actually going to do it. My mother would die; she's been trying for years."

"Just experience the tomato in its natural form."

So, as Michael guides him, Kevin puts the piece of tomato into his mouth and we all watch as he succumbs to the flavor, losing his long abstinence from that flesh.

"I think I can eat more," Kevin finally says.

I have a sudden unwelcome image of him as a teenage boy coming up from a very deep dive.

"No, no, don't . . ." Michael says. "That's enough. I feel bad. Don't eat the tomato; you don't like it."

"No, really, maybe just with some bread on it . . ." Kevin pleads.

At this moment, the maid comes in to clear the salads. The two remaining tomato slices on Kevin's plate are squished under the weight of other plates, Kevin's conquest of them thwarted forever.

I have an almost overpowering impulse to start speaking Spanish to the maid, but she is moving too quickly, and I have no idea what I'd say; in fact, I can't remember any of the words Kitty taught me.

After dinner, we move out onto the terrace to look at houses jammed into the hillside. I know they don't have emergency brakes on them, and I am astonished at the people who live in them, these high-rising, stilt-depending structures built on air. Does Isaac Newton mean nothing in this town?

Slim's husband, I think, whose name I still don't know, starts raving about the last kilo of pot he bought, then says, "You'd think the government would take the power back and legalize the goddamn stuff" to which Kevin replies that "pot is for pussies" and "LSD is where it's at."

Michael declares that "everyone should do hallucinogens at least twice in their life. No, make that twice a year, just to keep it fresh." Then the four of them simultaneously expound on their many different trips, when abruptly Kevin looks at me for the second time in the entire evening and says, "What about your acid trip?" and they all stop talking to stare at me.

I have not said word one since my "tomato like an apple" disclosure, but before I can think, I find myself saying, "Oh, well, ever since I was fourteen and my friend took LSD and got gang-raped with a broomstick, I've only tried speed and cocaine. You know, aware and alert."

Slim doesn't skip a beat. "Oh, I've got some coke from the last diet I was on, you want some of that?"

Her husband, I think, says, "There's cocaine in this house right now?"

He is suddenly sounding very Republican, as if it wasn't him who just made a pitch for legalized marijuana. I wonder if his political alliances switch with the drug.

I look at Michael. I do not want any of this woman's cocaine, and I really do not want to be around while her husband or whoever he is finds out about it. Michael takes my hint and we leave the palatial home.

The moon has climbed farther and farther up the sky. Before I get in my truck, I stand looking at it for a moment, wondering what it would be like to rise knowing exactly when and how you would fall.

I follow Michael's car down the hill to my apartment. He has promised me that he'll spend the night, but I'm not getting my hopes up. The street we are driving down angles sharply around blind curves; it is barely wide enough for one vehicle to pass.

L.A. defies gravity. The cars, the skin, the houses, the light. I keep waiting for it all to fall. A day when the cars will crash, the faces will drop, the houses will collapse, and the light will hit hard and direct like a black-and-white film shot in a wintry Midwest. But so far, its emergency brake continues to hold. I know I should be comforted by that; I'm just not.

23

My first winter in Los Angeles, a few months after I moved from New York, was a new experience of that season. December that year was one of stunningly clear mild days with nights that were cold, as if my freezer door had been left open, and I could walk through the frigid air knowing warmth was on the other side. And the mountains all of a sudden were there. In the fall, they had been hidden by haze and smog, but suddenly, miraculously, they appeared closer than ever before. I'd be driving along, up on the freeway or turning a corner, and I'd see them standing out against the sky: near, crisp, photo-ready. God's art department working overtime.

I was juggling my waitress shifts with my job for Bill, while creating new art and learning about L.A.'s gallery scene. Not to mention thinking about Andrew and the sex we were having underneath, centered in, and on top of everything. Life is what I did around thoughts of him. And seeing him.

Which we were doing pretty regularly. Stephanie apparently had no interest in spending every night with him, God knows why, so it was normal for Andrew to call me at eleven P.M., usually our third or fourth call of the day, and say, "What're you doing?" in that low, quiet, inside-of-me way. Then, "Get over here." And I would. Drive the long road to his home in Bel Air, up and up and up to his world that I was part of during our regular hours of eleven at night to one-thirty A.M. The time of night that makes things invisible; we were veiled by everyone else's sleep. The hours a road into the country of us.

One night after a long and deep and wonderful bout of each other while Andrew was being particularly cuddly after I had rubbed his back, I asked him if I could sleep over, and leave very early in the morning. The January night was cold, his bed was layers of soft warmth, and the sweetness of him was too delicious to part from.

"I don't want people asking me who my new wife is," Andrew said, then looked at me gravely, as if hordes of photographers and journalists descended upon him every morning at six A.M., and there was nothing he could do about this lack of privacy.

I almost said, "Who's gonna ask you? Patrick or the maids? They all know I come here anyway, and do they really arrive for work that early?" But I didn't. Though his excuse clearly had no basis in reality, I suddenly understood, as I lay there in his arms, that in his mind it did. That even though media hounds wouldn't actually show up on his extremely private practically-impossible-to-get-onto grounds, he was so used to guarding his life and self from the public for over thirty-two years, that this rule he had come up with that only the "girlfriend" spends the night protected him somehow. And what was even more clear in that moment was that he was trying to protect himself from what he felt. Which made me see that I just needed to break through that wall, slowly and steadily.

That month, Andrew missed my birthday. He knew when it was or I figured he did. I hadn't told him the first time it came around after we had met because he was in Malaysia, but on all of the subsequent ones he knew because I would call him.

"It's my birthday today."

"Happy birthday, sweet-y-vette," he'd say, but nothing ever appeared. All those years in New York, I wanted flowers, roses delivered to my door, a huge bouquet to fill my bedroom, then petals to press between heavy books and laminate onto rice paper—his love in floral form. And it was pretty obvious how easy that would be for him. Patrick could have handled the whole thing. But I decided it just wasn't who Andrew was. Some people don't give birthday presents; they grew up in families where it wasn't a big deal.

But on that birthday in L.A., my twenty-fourth, since we were involved in a deeper way, I was crushed when nothing arrived. And so pissed off that I avoided his calls on that day and the next two; I lay on my futon listening to the phone ring, knowing it was him.

Finally, I gave in and called him. He grilled me about where I'd been, worried I'd disappeared, and I was just happy to hear his voice again. So, he doesn't give gifts. Okay. I knew he loved me. He asked me all the time if I loved him, and though he rarely said it himself, I knew it was what he felt inside. I could see it in his eyes when he looked at me, and could hear it in his voice. And no other woman that he wasn't working with had been in his life for years platonically. And the armor that Andrew wore got heavier with each passing hour. I could hear the changes in his voice as we talked throughout the day, then when I'd see him at night, it wasn't just his clothes that came off, but that solid suit would be removed, revealing a softness inside that very few people knew.

And I felt backed up by him, protected. Loved and adored. His arms holding me, his sweet voice on the phone caressing me, his never vanishing, always taking my calls. Many times in the midst of dealing with an annoying customer at the restaurant, or struggling with an art piece, or a gallery offering me only a maybe and not a definite yes, I would automatically think, *But Andrew loves me*. He was myself. A part of me that I didn't have came from him. And his voice daily and his body frequently sustained that belief.

I started going to parties with Viv. She was still seeing Craig, so I met a lot of his friends, and began recognizing names and faces in the social section of the *L.A. Times*—Craig and his cohorts' parties were covered extensively. Men at the parties would ask me out and I couldn't really say I was already seeing someone because Viv would wonder who that was. So to be able to keep seeing Andrew, undercover in a way, I'd go on some dates, but I'd never have sex with them. We'd just make out a little bit, schoolgirl-in-a-car kind of stuff, then I wouldn't go any further, and after a while, I'd break up with them.

And they were all very nice men. An entertainment lawyer who took me to the best gourmet vegetarian restaurants and gave me a book on Buddhism for Valentine's Day. An actor who was stuck in TV hell, successful by most people's standards, but he only wanted to do films. And an architect who spent three months of each year in Bali acquiring a new tribal tattoo each time and wearing only sarongs there, plus a bunch of kinda-date guys (meet for coffee or a hike in the canyon) thrown in. Interesting, nice men. I just didn't want to be with them. I wanted to be with Andrew. Constantly. The men couldn't say anything without my comparing it in my mind to what Andrew would have said. And who could compare to him? And that was a problem because if it didn't work out with Andrew—but it had to—what would I do? I was dating interesting, attractive, successful men, but none of them compared to Andrew.

And Andrew knew I was dating. He would call; I'd be on my way out. He would call; I'd still be out or would have just gotten home. And he'd want to know who they were and what we did—like he knew them, and sometimes I had a feeling he did or he made it seem that way, that he was having them checked out. There was no piece of information unattainable by him. He never acted jealous (like he had about Tim, derisively calling him Tim-my) and it was pointless to wish that he was. He so fully gathered the men into our experience that they practically weren't people anymore, just fodder for the mill.

So it wasn't a big jump when he asked which of them I was sleeping with. Or fucking, as he said.

"None of them, I'm seeing you."

We were in his bed, it was past one A.M., and a February wind was moving and talking in the trees outside, though I knew it would abandon them by daylight.

"Yvette, you can fuck other men."

I looked up at him from where I was below.

"I think you should," he went on. "It'll be good for you."

How?

Then his movements came harder still.

I drove myself home in the chill quiet dark. My futon was always a depressing refuge after leaving his bed. I lay awake, trying to imagine if that was something I could do. Have sex with two men. I had a feeling it would be like drinking milk and beer in the same sitting. Nice on their own, but stomach-curdling in proximity. It wasn't something I would do. Or wanted to.

But Andrew was pretty persistent. He started asking all the time, so finally . . . I lied. I figured that what Andrew really wanted was an additional barrier, another thing to put between us to protect how he felt. Me with someone else. Like him with Stephanie. And for me to betray him—even though he instigated it—was the only way for me to stay near him. So I pretended I did, but didn't. And even though I wasn't betraying him sexually (the make-outs hardly counted), I was, in fact, betraying him because I lied to him. About being faithful. That I wasn't. But I was. I had known since I moved to L.A. that Andrew wasn't only sleeping with me, he was seeing Stephanie. And supposedly, purportedly a bunch of other women as well, though that part I wasn't sure about and couldn't tell. But even if he was, I didn't care. To be upset about any of that was as futile as moving to the Arctic and throwing a fit about the cold, a condition you knew existed before you went. Wear enough protective layers or move south.

And my lies were simple. It's not like he needed details. Okay, sometimes he wanted them. But a "yes" instead of a "no" to the query usually handled it. He seemed comforted by it somehow. That I'd changed? I didn't know. He'd ask if I loved him the best—that was easy and true. "Yes," I'd say. "I love you the best." I just never wanted to leave his bed, and if pretending to be in other men's helped me stay there, then okay.

A few weeks later, Viv and I were having lunch on the patio of a restaurant on Sunset Boulevard. It was a dumpy little health food place that had a huge following because the food was great, plus they made their own special salad dressing. Tour bus companies paid for the meals of certain celebrities to dine on the patio, which was visible from Sunset Boulevard, so their tourist customers could "unexpectedly" spot stars when they went by, but from what I could tell, Viv wasn't one of them. Viv was going on and on about a meeting she had had the day before with Andrew, while I pretended to need to look intently at my veggie burger to get the tomato and lettuce situated on it just so. I couldn't believe his name was coming up with her again. It had been a nice couple of months since she had complained about how horrible he was, and poor Stephanie, blah, blah, blah. Viv's agent had decided she should do a movie—and how different can that be from the characters she creates for her videos, Viv had told me—so he had arranged a meeting for her with Andrew.

"It went incredibly great," Viv said as she popped vitamins in her mouth. She had a different combination she took with each meal. "Though I still hate him. And it was clear he wanted to fuck me and would have tried to if Stephanie wasn't my best friend."

Then she started her diatribe against him, but it was interspersed with waves of excitement that she would be in Andrew's next film. My appetite was gone from listening to her go on and on. Some of the cheddar cheese on my veggie burger had melted into a hard, shiny surface of orange on my plate. Viv hadn't gotten cheese on hers because she didn't eat any dairy; her nutritionist had told her it goes straight to the hips. I imagined Viv's food lining up in her mouth with marching orders in hand that would direct it to its bodily destinations, like travelers on the mother ship, to enhance her perfect skin, tight body, and soft lips. Viv was going strong with her "poor Stephanie being led astray" monologue. As I sipped my carrot juice, I thought that "poor Stephanie" looked to me like she could take care of herself. She was the epitome of Nordic beauty; I found it frightening. Her physical perfection was so high, it appeared calculated by a force other than God. Finally, an opportunity to end Viv's vitriol presented itself—Viv's ex-boyfriend's current girlfriend walked in, thank God—so I signaled to Viv with my eyes, and we pushed back our chairs, grabbed our purses, went to the parking lot, and said goodbye. Viv was so grateful that I had noticed the new girlfriend so she could make her exit without having to say hello that she forgot all about Andrew.

As I headed west through the sunlit, neon-drenched, billboards-blazing brightness of Sunset Boulevard, I wondered again why Viv disliked Andrew so much. Her anger was so vehement and personal for a man she had only just met. And she had had it before they ever said hello.

But that was only one of countless conversations I found myself in where Andrew was discussed extensively by (*a*) people who kind of knew him, (*b*) people who knew people who knew him, and (*c*) people who knew *People* magazine articles about him. It was excruciating to sit and pretend that I (*a*) didn't know him, (*b*) had little to no interest in him, and (*c*) agreed and/or believed all the crap they said about him. All the women who did it seemed to be inwardly angry that they had never slept with him, and the men appeared jealous of everything he'd gotten. Mostly their conversations were mean, with an undercurrent of reserved awe that I don't think they were even aware of. It was their inability to comprehend doing everything that Andrew had achieved, and it permeated their rumors and stories, disclosing the envy and inferiority they felt. I'd make neutral sounds and facial expressions to keep my true thoughts and feelings opaque, all the while counting the minutes for their gossip to end.

The hardest part was not being able to defend him, to talk about who he really was, about what I liked and loved in him. Keeping quiet and pretending, while they tore him down and chewed him up. It made me want to protect him; I couldn't believe this went on so much. But Andrew seemed to know it did; at least he knew that Viv instigated a lot of it. As I turned onto my street, I wondered how he could have lived with it for so long, but then I realized it must be like underbrush on a path that his boots kick through while he emerges unscathed.

That night at his house, Andrew told me about his meeting with Viv.

"All she did was talk about sex—mine. And practically right from the beginning, so I didn't even try to bring it around to a professional conversation. I figured it was her meeting, she can blow it however she wants."

We were in his kitchen, eating delicacies out of bowls from the fridge that the chef had created, sitting at the marble island on the hard metal stools. I had a feeling someone once had suggested cushions—a decorator maybe, a girlfriend from back when—but Andrew had vetoed it, liking the duality of outward discomfort while luscious food went inward.

"She couldn't shut up about it," Andrew went on. "All the women I'd fucked and how beautiful they were—'What a list,' she said. I told her that she hadn't done too badly herself."

"You mean the men she's been with or . . ."

"What do you think?" Andrew smiled at me.

"Oh." I was silent for a moment. That gave Viv's hatred of Andrew a whole new twist. Maybe it wasn't him she wanted to sleep with, but Stephanie. Or both. Who the fuck knew. "But how do you know who . . ."

"Word gets around."

I should have known. This town really was just one big little high school and all inside information was reported to Andrew.

"And the shit she talks about me—what'd I ever do to her? You'd think she would have thought about that before she tried to get in my next film."

"So why'd you meet with her, then?"

"Because I can, and I'll make sure she never works on my film or anyone else's." He smiled at me quietly and deeply above his dark blue T-shirt, then pulled my head toward his chest and moved it down until it rested in his lap.

Andrew never asked me why Viv and I were friends. Maybe in the midst of his hatred for her, he understood what there was to like. And I did like her. She was vivacious and fun and wonderful one-on-one. We'd meet for coffee or lunch, go to salsa class or get a pedicure, and shopping with her was the best. She knew cool little undiscovered places downtown and in tiny neighborhoods where we could buy cheap, exotic things while we talked the whole time. L.A. was her city and to me she was L.A. The whole way she greeted life: huge smile, cute body, charm talking, and pure drive underneath. Being with Viv helped me understand how the city grew and moved. One-on-one was wonderful; it was when other people were involved that things got weird.

It was the weekend launch of *Valiant Hour*, the film Andrew had produced, directed, and starred in with Stephanie. There was tons of press for months before, and Stephanie was all over the talk shows on the nights leading up to the opening. Even Andrew did an on-camera interview, which usually he avoided. It was with Holly actually. She had moved out to L.A. and was the new entertainment goddess for a national news show and I suppose that's how they met. There was a huge premiere for the film that I read about in the paper the next day, then finally the seventy-two-hour moment that everything had been shooting for arrived—opening weekend. The reviews moved Stephanie's career to a pinnacle higher than it ever had been and Andrew was reaffirmed as the genius he was.

I went to a twelve-thirty feature on the opening Friday. Alone in the dark with my popcorn, watching Stephanie and thinking of Andrew viewing each frame, I tried to interpret the story line as some kind of allegory for them since she died at the end.

I had seen still photographs of the movie in Andrew's kitchen one night. On a table in the corner under the windows, which the dark outside had turned into mirrors, was a light box with color slides spread out on top. Like the mess in a child's room, it looked like it would be there for a while.

Andrew was picking the poster shot and other photos to be used for press. He pulled a chair up close to his so I'd be next to him and able to see his choices and rejects. They all had Stephanie in them. Good Christ, this woman looked like she would never die. She was above death, too full of a singular stunningness to succumb.

Andrew was making small piles; some he'd go back to, others he pushed aside. He would show me one, look at me with an eyebrow raised, then set it down in what he'd determined was its appropriate place.

At one point he said, "Do you know how long I've been doing this?"

I thought he meant looking at the slides that night, so I started to rub his back, which he gave himself into, but then he said, "Longer than you've been alive."

Oh, that. I moved in front of him and removed my dress. The slides and Stephanie became a thing of the past.

I called Andrew when I got home from *Valiant Hour* to tell him how much I loved it. His voice got that formal tone it sometimes had—a combination of embarrassed, polite, and tongue-tied—but it would have been odd not to mention it, this huge thing going on in front of our eyes. And I was proud of him, which sounds silly and hubristic, but there it is. I would've sung his praises to the world if I could. So I said it to him, and he thanked me, simply and rather elegantly, then told me that the next couple of days were going to be crazy with Stephanie and everything.

By the end of the weekend, it was clear his film had done well. Exploded, you could say. I woke up Monday morning and began baking bread. We hadn't seen each other in over a week, but I had known what was taking up his time, the culmination of years of his professional and private life up on the screen.

It had been a while since I had baked for him—that was in the fall, and now it was late spring. I decided to do apple bread, an old recipe of my grandmother's that required two types of apples very finely chopped. I enjoyed the detail work. Cutting each apple slice into a precise amount of minuscule cubes that would almost melt when baked, the membranes of apple dissolving under the heat. I liked tools that create small out of large. A whole represented by a wee part. I remembered an art teacher at the School of Visual Arts who used to say, "If you want an orange, one slice is better than a whole apple." Which was kind of how my relationship was with Andrew—a slice of him, which was better than the whole of someone else, but I knew that wasn't going to be enough for much longer. Hopefully, he'd get rid of Stephanie since the film was finally out.

The bread was cooling when Andrew called. It was almost eleven in the morning, far past the normal time that we spoke. My apartment was warm from the oven, and the open windows were letting in dim sounds from Wilshire Boulevard along with a small breeze.

When I told him what I was doing, he asked how soon I could be there. I had been to his home only a few times during daylight hours, and this was a Monday, a brighter workday than the others, the ravages of the weekend exposed, projects left undone on Friday loudly yelling their impatient needs. In the midst of all that, I entered Andrew's home.

Patrick answered the door, a further signal of the careercentric day. While asking how I was, he led me to the pool where Andrew was sitting on a chaise longue, phone at his ear, notepad and pen on the low table next to him.

I was holding the two loaves of bread. I thought I would go into the kitchen for a knife, but Andrew gave me a silent kiss, while taking a loaf from me. He quietly unwrapped it, and broke pieces off with his hand, silently chewing while listening to the person on the phone. He pantomimed his delight about the bread to me with his face, and reached over and rubbed my leg. I was stretched out on the chaise next to him. The sun was softer up where he lived, muted by an ocean breeze that pushed it through so the harshest rays were dispersed someplace less fortunate. Glaring white towels were stacked on a wrought-iron shelf, and the pool was a miniature Aegean Sea—a fount of pleasure for men and mermaids.

Andrew finished his call and turned to me, but before the kiss was complete, Patrick was at his side with a list.

"Hold everything until I tell you, even Stephanie," Andrew said, without even looking at the paper Patrick proffered. "And would you put these in the kitchen, please?" He handed Patrick the bread, then stood up, and taking my hand, walked me to his bed. It felt as if we were playing hooky from school, but the teacher knew where we were.

Lunch, the result of a call Andrew made to Patrick stating what we wanted, was waiting for us two hours later when we emerged from his bedroom and entered the green-walled, dark wood dining room. Sitting at the large round cherrywood table, I thought how very Andrew it was to not have a rectangular one, bypassing the need to decide who would sit opposite him at the other end.

On the long art-filled walk back to his bed, we passed a maid running a vacuum. She immediately turned it off when she saw Andrew, her body and the machine silent as if that would make them invisible as we went by. In bed again, we napped, then I woke him with my mouth. The room was dark from the wide expanse of drawn curtains, day for night.

Afterward we went down to his screening room, past his gym, and lay on the dove-gray velvet sofa watching the films that had opened against his that past weekend. And still he took no phone calls. Patrick rang in at one point to tell him he was leaving, and I could tell that he asked if Andrew wanted to know who had called, but was told, "No, tomorrow." We were out of town together, gone. Escaping further into home, instead of leaving, but protected as if by great distance. After viewing most of one film, then part of another, and bits of a third, we got bored with them. I was more interested in listening to his reaction to the actors and directors and writers than what was on the screen anyway. One actor he called "a very talented little girl"; an actress was hard on the eyes to watch.

We went upstairs to the kitchen and rooted around in the fridge for food. He definitely had the best "leftovers" of anyone I'd ever known. Whole geographical regions represented by bowls and containers of scrumptious cuisine. It was heaven. The large house was still except for us, other than the constantly flashing light on his phones when there was a call to remind us that the world was outside while we pretended it wasn't.

In his bed again, only sensations of him in me and him through me and me for him were present. It was quiet in the dark, in the almost pitch-blackness, in the inky ravenness, like his Ritz-Carlton room had been that night when we were together in it five and a half years before. As I moved on top of him, Andrew's voice said firmly in my ear, "Why are you the only woman in the world who I believe truly loves me?"

He looked me deep in my eyes when he said it, then his words kept reappearing the longer we looked at each other, coming over and over again. Lying together afterward, each sound, each syllable, each breath they were carried on traveled deep into my heart, then journeyed out along my veins where they would never be separate from me.

24

My sister's living room has successfully completed its transmogrification into an issue of *Modern Bride*. Suzanne is holding forth in italicized verse while flinging yards of net around the room—the yards of net I have labored over to create a bridal-fantasy dream come true for her.

"Impossible for me to get married without a goddamn veil. This isn't what I wanted or drew. I want froufrou without looking complicated or too . . . too . . . I'm getting married in two days and I'm not even going to have a veil." My sister sputters to a stop, her harangue and arms winding down.

"Suzanne, I'm sorry, okay? I'll fix it and it'll look great, I promise."

The veil she is holding is exactly what she drew, or as close to it as I could get. Not to mention that she already saw the damn thing, just a little less finished. I fight the urge to snatch it out of her hands, throw it on the ground, and stomp on it, screaming, "How do you like it now?"

This fantasy allows my breathing to luxuriate in a long, slow exhale, as my body has tired itself out from my imagined tantrum.

Suzanne is staring at me. I have a wild worry that she can read my thoughts, but realize she is just waiting for me to continue reassuring her. "Your new and improved veil will be at the church on Saturday whenever you want."

"Three o'clock."

"Okay, I'll be there, veil in tow."

"Okay."

"Okay. So."

The child bride's dress is hanging over the back of an upholstered chair, the whites of each fabric blending together into a blinding cloud. "This one's nice," I say, lifting the lace-covered frock.

"Coffee?" Suzanne is already leaving the room.

With cyanide for you preferably, but okay.

As I replace the child bride's gown on the chair, I notice my maid-of-honor dress hanging on the wall, like some horrible floral flag. "Well, you cheer me up immensely," I say out loud. I am glad that Suzanne insisted on keeping it here until today. Its proclamation of maidenhood in my apartment all these weeks would have done me in; the veil was depressing enough to have around.

Suzanne and the silver coffee service glide in like the figurehead on a ship.

"So is anyone coming?" I move our mother's prayer book off the coffee table and sit down next to it on the couch, taking small comfort in Momma's presence by proxy.

"Of course anyone is coming." My sister is pouring the coffee we drank growing up; she has bags of it airmailed to her each month. The aroma of all our relatives' kitchens every morning and most afternoons is now wafting toward me in Suzanne's living room so far away on the West Coast. She and I were weaned on this coffee in the form of coffee-milk, which was milk heated on the stove just to the point where the whiteness of it gets really bright, then poured at the same time as the coffee into a cup already waiting with three full spoons of sugar in it. Pouring it was the trick. The milk came out of the open pot faster than the coffee did through the spout, so more milk went in, leaving a beverage that was a beautiful soft ivoried dark. Suzanne and I would sit with our coffee-milk at our relatives' breakfast tables, listening to family news, and watching facial expressions that said everything about who was getting along with whom, while the adults drank their coffee black. It was heresy for the adults to put in sugar, much less milk. But one uncle, who had scandalized the family by moving North, sometimes returned and would tease our grandmother, his momma, by putting a broken spoon handle in his cup, stirring it a few times, then lifting it out, saying, "See, Momma, I told you, the coffee down here just eats spoons right up." Even though it had been many years since I had to drink mine as coffee-milk, I still like the taste of sugar in it.

"Three hundred anyones are coming to the wedding. About a hundred of Matt's relatives from San Francisco, practically his entire firm—"

"No, I meant from home is anyone coming."

"Oh. No. They're not." Suzanne hands me my cup. She has put the sugar cubes in first, the way we were taught growing up so that the heat of the coffee liquefies them, thereby making a spoon unnecessary although it was still used for decorum.

"Aunt Cecile already gave us that engagement party down there, and we decided to go visit in the fall when everyone is back in town, so, no. No one's coming out here for it."

"Oh."

"What?" Suzanne sounds the way she did as a child after she explained the rules of a game she made up that she worried I might not play.

The china cup I am holding has the same delicately balanced weight of hundreds of cups I have held sitting with countless family members in many living rooms as we participate in being flesh and blood. "Is this y'all's pattern?"

My sister nods.

"It's nice." I can imagine her selecting the autumnal floral china, the juxtaposition of blossoms in a season near death—it is very Suzanne to have avoided the exuberance of a spring palette. Beauty with restraint. I have always liked that about her.

"No, it's just . . ." I put my coffee cup down carefully, hoping the action will force me to also be delicate with the fragility I am feeling. "I mean, we have how many first and second and removed and twice-removed cousins, but honest to God, sometimes I feel completely untethered, like a wayward party balloon."

Suzanne stirs her coffee. She must have forgotten that I am probably the only person in L.A. who knows she doesn't need to.

"Would you like some more?" My sister reaches for the pot, my answer decided by her already.

"Not really."

As I drive home from my sister's house, the thought of having to redo her veil by Saturday afternoon (it's Thursday!) makes me want to scream right now. I try to in my truck, but I feel stupid, self-conscious. For the first time, I am grateful to my subconscious for creating my scream dream, allowing me that nocturnal release. And maybe I have finally done it enough for it to end.

I turn my radio on to a station on the far right of the dial that plays classical. One of Bach's Brandenburg Concertos has just begun. That'd be nice to play at my wedding.

What?

Oh, God, no. Do not have thoughts like that. The last thing I need is some unfulfilled bridal fantasy following me around. I will make this veil for Suzanne, be in her wedding, and then consign the entire frightening social institution to the far back regions of my mind where it belongs.

I have my jewelry to think about, like remembering to call Roxanne when I get home to see if she is happy with the order I delivered three days ago, and how could I ever have a husband when Michael won't even spend the night? Of course, Andrew made me leave his bed, too, the jerk. Jesus, I never thought I'd say that he and Michael were alike.

Okay, Michael has had to leave those nights because of work, and that could change. Yeah, like him changing the format of his station to conservative talk radio. I suddenly realize that the many messages coming from him—committed, not, maybe, too-soon-to-tell—are all the same, just like the different shows he broadcasts, supposedly unique in themselves, but really it's only Michael's voice getting through. All Michael all the time without ever really knowing him.

I wonder if one reason I haven't been tons more upset about Michael leaving in the middle of most nights is that I have breakfast with Reggie every morning. Maybe that "nature abhors a vacuum" thing isn't working for me romancewise because a big part of my intimate/love area is taken up with my male best friend. That's worrisome. I wonder if he has ever thought that.

Reggie calls as I am three hours into reconfiguring Suzanne's veil. The message I left for him after I called Roxanne when I got home has elicited an unusually fast response.

"She's a bride, honey, i.e., nuts," Reggie says, after I regale him with my terrible redo-the-veil tale. "Plus, I think most people go a little crazy when they can be demanding in an obscurely specific way. They think they're being creative, meanwhile, they act like a child."

"I guess I've been lucky so far with my commissions, not having to deal with this. Jesus, Reggie, if this is what you go through with your clients, I think I'd throw myself off a bridge."

"It's a little easier to take when they're paying you a lot. All you're getting out of this is—"

"Freedom from sisterly guilt. A small thing."

"No pressure there. Honey, it's going to be beautiful; everything you do is. And if she can't get past her hysteria to appreciate it, there's nothing you can do."

"Thanks, I just don't want her perpetually hating me because I ruined her wedding."

"You're not that powerful, Yvette, even if you're making the veil. Everyone's responsible for their own life—your big sister included."

Reggie always knows exactly what I need to hear. He is able to talk me down off the emotional ledges I climb up on better and faster than anyone else.

"Is Michael going with you?" I am shocked that he asked and can hear in his voice that it is a kind of reconciliation. I know his face looks sweet right now, the way it does when he is about to give me a hug and sing one of his funny made-up songs.

"Yeah, he is."

"You're going to have a great time and the veil's going to be perfect." Reggie sounds so confident of this that I feel renewed energy to tackle Suzanne's headpiece. "Breakfast mañana?"

Manaña is now just a few hours away. I have labored though the night: filling in, taking out, starting over, and covering up, but the headpiece has decided not to work. I have encountered this before when I was doing sculptures with certain metals and various found objects, this refusal to become something else, but none of those had a bride waiting for them who also happens to be my sister. I know that inanimate objects are not alive, but they do, like us, have mass and weight comprised of atoms with space, and they can be pliable or irrefutably static, completely resistant to change. Like us. Or me sometimes, actually. Not changing myself, or refusing to see that something—like this damn headpiece—or someone isn't going to, either. Like Michael, let's be honest.

Anyway. No matter how hard I tried to fix the headpiece, I have finally gotten the message that it was never meant for my sister to wear in her wedding. It was a trial run, practice scales, an opportunity for me to get the kinks out before my efforts really count and become part of something that lasts. I wonder if that describes Michael, as well.

I get into bed to catch a few hours' sleep before Reggie's breakfast phone call will wake me. I know I'll have to make a trip downtown to get new materials, and then will have long hours of work ahead of me on the new headpiece, but I feel clear and clean, like the air after a January storm. As I begin to slip down into sleep, it occurs to me that there is a certain happiness in this relinquishing of the unable-to-do and being ready to embark on the new. Maybe I can have this in other areas of my life, too.

My earthly mother has guided me. I should have turned to her before, but no use crying over spilled milk-colored seed pearls. When I got home from downtown, as I was walking into my apartment, a picture on the living room wall caught my eye. I see it so much that it has become part of the scenery, like the tree you don't notice until it is gone and its protective shade no longer cools you. It is a black-and-white photograph of Momma and Daddy on their wedding day, cutting the tall, proud castle of a wedding cake. My father's hand is gently guiding hers while my mother's face looks young and expectant, as if each layer they are slicing through will provide answers to how her life with my father will go. The picture is slightly blurred. It is just a snapshot, taken by a forgotten family member, but it is the only photograph I have ever seen of my parents' wedding. I know that Suzanne has a copy of it, too.

Momma never spoke about her wedding, nor about a future one that might one day be mine. I wish I had asked her about hers. Maybe brought it up on one of their anniversaries before my father left when that date in the year became like a frozen lake, maintaining its true nature underneath, but with a surface of ice covering it that allowed us to skate over it on top.

The new veil that I have created for my sister appears slightly blurred, just like the one in the wedding photograph of Momma. I finally understood what Suzanne meant about glimmering but not jeweled. I have sewn a layer of white chiffon over the headpiece, muting the tiny seed pearls and sprinkles of jewels underneath, the bridal equivalent of wearing a long strand of pearls inside the deep V-neck of a cocktail dress. A glimpse. Present, but not for show. Suzanne's taste exactly. And just like the photo. I have been giddy since yesterday creating this for her and have an adrenaline rush from working through the night, and from having everything come out right. I can't wait to see the veil on her head.

It is quarter to two on Suzanne's wedding day, and I am all ready to go, though it is much earlier than I need to leave. I decide to forgo a nap—I couldn't fall asleep right now, but if I did, I might not wake up—and clean up the wisps of fine netting, white threads, and minuscule pearls that are scattered everywhere. It feels better to get rid of the nuptial debris than try to put a dent in all the sleep I have missed. Besides, I'm too excited about having Suzanne see her veil.

As I put together a small bag of veil-crisis remedies—knowing that Betsy in her professional bride-soothing role will have everything, but wanting to be prepared just in case—I dial Michael's phone number, and am surprised to get his machine.

"Hey, it's me," I say, while slipping into my shoes. "Well, maybe you're in the shower. I was thinking you might want to go early with me instead of meeting me at the church like we planned, but . . . umm, okay, I think I'm just gonna come by your place, and if you're ready and wanna come with me, I'd love that, and if not, then at least I can see you real quick before I get swallowed up with maid-of-honor duties. And maybe we can swallow each other up first. Okay, I'm on my way, see you soon."

I am driving in my truck with Suzanne's veil pinned to a hanger that is suspended from the clothes hook in front of the passenger window. It's like riding with the ghost of all brides, but a benevolent one, a sort of phantom fairy godmother. I am wearing my maid-of-honor dress. I considered doing the normal thing and wearing something else to the church, then changing there, and I know I will hear a chorus from the bridesmaids: "You didn't wear something comfortable before you have to change into that!" and "Aren't you afraid you'll ruin it before the pictures and ceremony!" But considering that the dress trails around me like an unused parachute and is a jumbled profusion of floral madness, nothing could be more comfortable or less able to show wrinkles or spots. For the first time, I commend my sister's choice, though I suspect Michael might be shocked when he sees me since I wear only solid colors and form-fitting clothes. But that's assuming he'll notice.

It takes three rings of his doorbell before I hear footsteps approach. I know Michael is home because his BMW is parked out front, its great-on-the-outside/a-total-mess-within appearance on full view in the day's bright sunlight.

Finally Michael opens the front door. All he is wearing is cutoff jeans, an unshaved beard, and a peculiar grin on his face. Groovy music that sounds like it was recorded outside is playing inside. He takes a long step backward without saying anything, and as I follow him into the living room's dim light, I see Ivan, a blond dreadlocked deejay from the station, sprawled on the couch. Ivan appears peculiarly specifically cheerful, as well.

"What are y'all—" But my words are suddenly interrupted by Michael's hand touching my mouth.

"The most perfect flower," he says, staring at me. "Your dress and lips and mouth and dress." His fingers are tracing my lips, at first soft, then hard, then gentle, but all annoying, and Ivan is now staring to boot.

"That is so sweet," I say as I try to bat his hand away. "But, um, Michael, shouldn't you be getting ready now?"

Michael's hand is on overdrive. It is grabbing my lips, which can be pulled out much farther than I thought they could, then his hand starts contorting and shaping them with his strong fingers.

"Bloom and die and bloom and die," he chants like the underlying theme of a nursery rhyme.

My attempt to ask what the hell he is doing comes out in gibberish thanks to his hand still having its way with my lips. As I manage to pry his fingers loose, Michael immediately trains his detail-obsessed attention onto my dress, and the general grooviness of his behavior and the scene finally sinks in.

"Oh, God, no. Michael, are you tripping on the day of my sister's wedding?" He is now trying to pick the flowers off my dress, grabbing at the fabric—and ergo, my legs—relentlessly. "Yes, you are. Okay, can I just die now please?"

Michael's face crumples like a punctured balloon. "No, we're going to the Phish concert today."

"Yeah, clearly—you're in great shape for that."

"Wow," he says, eyes blinking hard and fast. "Okay, I really can't handle your dress right now." Michael sits down on the couch and covers his face with his hands.

"Hey, man, don't harsh out his trip." Ivan has moved his feet to the coffee table, and is lying stretched out.

"Oh, no, God forbid I harsh out the Phishing trip."

Michael is now playing some pseudo peekaboo game with himself, his hands flapping open and shut rhythmically over his face.

"Hey, man, seeing as how you're vertical," Ivan says. "Could you hand me the nose-blowing paper?"

"The what?" I suddenly wonder if this is some newfangled acid. And I thought stamps were all kids had to worry about.

"The nose-blowing paper, man." Ivan sounds agitated, and is pointing at a box of tissues, his finger jabbing the air. "I got to blow my nose."

My dress billows around me, a storm of flowers raining in the air, as I pick up the desired object and hand it to him. "Here. Blow away."

A long expanse of white net floats by, then is stopped like a sail catching the wind as Betsy and I place the veil on Suzanne. The three of us stare at the nuptial angel reflected in the full-length mirror of the church's dressing room.

"It's breathtaking," Betsy sighs.

"It's Momma's!" Suzanne ecstatically cries.

"Well, I figured it would definitely match with the prayer book and the music and all."

Betsy squeals with delight.

God is happy with this home. The cathedral my sister is getting married in is gold and ornate, but tasteful in its excess. Baroque music is playing at full steam, filling the air like a teapot about to explode. I am standing at the altar waiting for Suzanne-the-bride to come forth. Six bridesmaids are in a line at my right with Mandy closest to me. Even in her conservative bridesmaid dress, she manages to look like she just posed for a *Cosmo* cover, like some Freudian reminder of what this ceremony is really about.

There is a pause of silence, a crash of chords, then three hundred congregants rise as the wedding march begins and Suzanne effulgently floats down the aisle. Tears immediately start streaming down my face, keeping pace with her steps. My sister is stunningly beautiful as immense joy exudes from her, blinding each row as she walks by.

As I sit in the front pew between Betsy and Mandy during the nuptial mass, my small but audible sobs accompany the vocalist who is glorifying the cathedral with "Ave Maria." The almost-married couple is kneeling at the altar while music swirls around them like fairy dust gracing their union. Betsy looks completely blissed out, not unlike Michael before I harshed out his trip. Without removing her eyes from the bride, she reaches into her voluminous bag and puts a box of tissues on my lap. I blow my nose under cover of "Ave Maria's" final crescendo.

At the reception afterward, I decide the cathedral won the contest for most ornate, but it was close. The hotel ballroom is decorated like a Renaissance court, with two gigantic food-laden tables lining the walls and round white-covered tables festooned with pale soft flowers spread throughout around the dance floor and band.

Guests are making their way through the receiving line, which is missing its customary first greeter, the mother of the bride. I suddenly imagine a spotlight to commemorate her empty spot at the beginning of the line. The place where our father should have stood, between Matt's mother and the bridal couple, is also vacant and therefore closed up, their bodies moved together to where he should stand, as if he never registered in Suzanne's existence. I am next to Suzanne, commencing the attendant portion of the line. Tears are still flowing down my face—they haven't stopped since they started the minute Suzanne walked down the aisle—but I am resigned to them now, like some really bad lipstick I've been forced to wear. I'm not even sure what they are from—happiness, sadness, both at once. Or maybe they are special tears from a reservoir that is marked just for nuptial events—tears to accompany a cacophony of emotion, too loud and jumbled and filled up to be quickly understood. If the guests I am greeting notice my quiet crying, they don't seem to care, or at least no one mentions it, like my neighbors and my screaming at night.

My voice and Suzanne's overlap, singing a roundelay with each other, the repeated phrases and similar angled nods of our heads becoming a sibling social duet.

Suzanne's refrain is, "Thank you so much. Well, simple is what we wanted because it's all about who's here, but once you see the possibilities . . ."

My chorus is a constant underscore of "Hi, so nice to meet you. I'm Yvette, Suzanne's sister. Yes, there is a resemblance. Thank you for being here. Hi, so nice . . ."

A divine intervention must have occurred because my weeping has finally stopped. The band is playing Frank Sinatra covers; the food tables have been ravished, and everyone is dancing. Even people who look like they have not danced in years are caught up in the wedding-love mood. I alone am sitting at one of the round tables, daydreaming about the nice long sleep I could have on the carpet. The child bridal couple darts past, playing hide-and-seek among the empty chairs. Her white lace dress is in tatters, his clip-on bow tie attached to the edge of her sleeve. I suddenly imagine Michael chasing me as persistently as this little groom with his play bride, but that's really a dream.

"Fly me to the moon, and let me sleep among the stars . . ." I like this version I am singing to myself better, a wedding lullaby for the romantically impaired and sleep deprived.

Just as my eyes are starting to nod shut, Suzanne materializes before me, her white silhouette blocking out all other stimuli, like a vision in a dream.

"There you are," she says. I look around at the other empty tables and chairs surrounding the full dance floor, wondering how she possibly could not have seen me. "Where's Michael? Didn't he come?"

It feels like weeks since this afternoon when Michael stood me up or rather grooved out on me, and I had forgotten that my sister doesn't know he never arrived. "No, he went on an unexpected trip."

"Oh, honey, that's too bad. Well, I need you to help me change."

"I mastered that skill at three; haven't you gotten it yet?"

The band has switched to "We Are Family," and the roiling throng is responding with whoops and flailing arms.

"Come on, I need to put on my traveling suit before everyone leaves."

"For what? You and Matt are staying here tonight until your plane leaves tomorrow morning—why are you changing out of your dress?"

"Will you just come help me? God, you are so stubborn sometimes."

Following my sister out the reception hall, I concede that she has a point.

The honeymoon suite where Suzanne and Matt will first slumber as husband and wife is a luxurious peach dream. My sister's empty wedding dress is lying in the middle of the floor like a circus tent dropped at the end, no longer needed to create magic in. I am zipping up Suzanne's cream-colored sheath as she holds her hair out of the way.

"And no one does receiving lines anymore, either, but my God, if I don't get to enjoy all the traditions and costumes that come with a wedding, what's the point." She slips into the matching jacket and examines the result in the mirror.

"Well, I've always considered elevators travel."

Suzanne catches my eye and we laugh ourselves into giggles. I suddenly want to put on our childhood matching nightgowns and play princesses in the backyard among the glowing fireflies that we pretended were fairies until long after dark.

I smooth down the collar of her jacket, letting her hair fall back onto her shoulders. "You look great."

"Thanks."

"I'm really happy for you."

"Thanks, honey."

Suzanne turns around and goes to the dresser, then begins rooting around in our grandmother's burgundy leather traveling valise that she uses as a jewelry case, pulling out pearl studs and a necklace.

"So, how long is y'all's honeymoon again? Bali's going to be great."

Suzanne walks back over to me, holding something in her hand.

"This is yours," she says, and places into my hand our mother's prayer book. The ivory leather is cool and soft on my skin like Momma's cheek was when I'd kiss her good night as a child. "I could tell she wanted you to have it when I asked her for it."

"Oh, Suzanne, I can't."

"Yes, I want you to have it. Now it's from both of us."

A splash of wetness falls from my eye onto the book. I worry what the moisture will do to the leather, but realize mine are not the first tears to be caught and absorbed by the prayers held inside.

"Okay, but . . ." My words are interrupted by more tears emerging from my throat, lungs, and heart. They are fresh and solid, as if they are the first of their kind, not the thousandth that day, but I know that these are from a different place than the others. "I may not be able to use it for what y'all did."

"Hush. You don't know that." Suzanne puts her arms around me and hugs me in a true embrace as my dress gathers in folds between the clinch of our bodies. I feel my sister's arms around me and, through them, every member of our family reaching forward and back through our line.

"So I guess your migration into Matt's family is complete now."

Suzanne pulls back and looks at me. "Is that what you think? Honey, there is family and there's family, but—"

I look into my sister's eyes, eyes the color of Momma's green one while my eyes are the color of Momma's brown one. We are one piece of tourmaline, two colors in the same gem, but split and refracting the light differently.

"You're my only sister. Nothing changes that."

I hug her again, drinking in the safety of our relationship.

"There you two are." Matt's voice enters the room before I see him. "There's a big crowd of people downstairs holding bags of birdseed and staring at me. I feel like I stumbled into the *The Lottery*."

"It's confetti, honey, Betsy doesn't allow—"

"I don't care what it is; are you gonna do this with me?"

Suzanne turns to me one last time. "I'm ready, aren't I?"

"Yeah, you are."

"Come on," my brother-in-law says to me. "You're part of this, too."

Monday morning at 7:02 is not a tranquil time at a radio station. Everything here seems extremely, extremely urgent, so maybe the outgoing message on Michael's cell phone isn't out of line after all.

"What time do you think he'll be done?"

Michael's assistant is like a Doberman pinscher, but one who is perky, blond, and able to look great at this ungodly hour. I, on the other hand, have barely slept. The eleven hours I slept after Matt and Suzanne's wedding brought me straight into Sunday afternoon, and either my sleeping schedule was so screwed up from that or it was the deciding/knowing what I need to do about Michael that kept me up all last night. Whichever it was, I gave in at six A.M. Got out of bed—at least no scream dreams happen on nights without sleep—made coffee, got dressed, jumped in my truck, and now here I am. And Michael was right—the freeway traffic was a bitch.

"It all depends on how long he stays in. It could be—"

Michael charges through the door. "Winter, get me the press clips on that—"

He sees me standing beside her and breaks into a surprised smile. It is the first time that his usual way of greeting me is correct.

"Yvette, hi. What are you doing here? This is great. Did you hear the show? I think we're definitely—"

The look on my face stops him.

"No, forget it, right." Michael takes my hand, and leading me into his office, turns to his assistant. "Winter, buzz Graham, tell him I'll be in a little later, and get the—"

Withdrawing my hand, I enter Michael's office without him.

"Forget it, Winter, I'll give you the rest later."

"You want carrot juice, Michael, or a latte?" Winter says as Michael walks in, but he shuts the door as his answer.

I am half sitting, half leaning on the conference table, figuring the largest object in the room will lend me support.

Michael moves in front of me and straddles me like a chair. "How'd you get so fuckable this early in the day?"

"Michael." I can't help but laugh.

"What? I mean it." He is pressing on me, kissing my mouth and neck and ears. My back becomes diagonal to the table.

"I don't think we should see each other anymore."

Michael straightens up and starts to withdraw his arms, then must realize how that would look, so he keeps them there, arms still around me, but his face so near that it feels uncomfortable considering what I just said. I wonder if he thinks continued physical contact will eradicate it somehow.

"I just think we do a lot better when we're friends."

He drops his arms completely and steps back a little bit. "Uh-huh."

"Don't you, really? I mean, if we could stay friends and still somehow also have sex, but we can't, or I can't, it seems to me."

Winter sticks her face in the door. I always think "rain forest" when I see her; I am certain she spent her junior year abroad there. "Graham said he can wait, and that press clip you wanted—"

"In a minute, thanks."

She looks crushed by Michael's words, then a smile appears on her face, as if she has picked up on the tension in the room and couldn't be happier.

We are quiet as we wait for her to leave, and I suddenly feel we are like divorcing parents with a pet that neither of them liked.

"Do you want to hear about it from my perspective?"

I am almost shocked that he has one about us.

"You know, you've done this before, and it just seems to me like things are going along great when suddenly you have to change it. We hang out, have a good time, isn't that enough? Does everything have to mean something serious?"

"No, everything doesn't, but I don't think this is ever going to mean anything at all, frankly, and maybe it never really has. Not that we don't care about each other, but you know what I mean."

Michael is watching me in a way he hasn't before. Quietly and listening. For the first time, I feel like a complete person to him, not just a response that he needs. It confirms what I am doing even more.

"So let's stop seeing each other now while we're still friends. A lot of it was good; we're just not the One for each other."

"I don't know if the One really exists."

"Yeah, well, I don't either, but I want to find out."

Sounds of the radio station start filtering in. I can hear the cadence of the morning news, and it gives me the same certain yet uneasy feeling I always felt sitting on my parents' bed before kindergarten watching my father prepare for work. As if something big and different were about to happen that would change my life, but I was only just now finding out about it.

"So I guess this means we can't have sex anymore?" Michael says it like he's kidding, but I know him too well.

"Yeah, I think we should finally really not."

He gives me a hug and quick kiss. For the first time, I don't try to feel more from it than is really there.

"Okay, well. I'd better get in gear if I'm gonna make my meeting.

Hey, do you wanna stick around, watch the deejay? I can have breakfast with you in a little bit."

"That's okay, thanks. I need to go."

Winter blows in. I have a feeling she was just outside the door, listening the whole time and waiting to make her entrance.

"Bye, Michael." I pass Winter in the doorway. As I walk away, I can feel his attention shift from me to her to his radio station. A national news program ends and a local one begins as I exit the building and enter the bright, white day.

25

It had ended. Finally the relationship was over. Gossips chattered that Stephanie and Andrew's romance had stopped because their work together was done and there had never been anything real and lasting between them. As opposed to all the other real and lasting celebrity couplings in Hollywood.

Valiant Hour held its top ten box office position well into the summer with public sightings of Andrew and Stephanie as a couple continuing until August when it all disappeared. Theaters replaced the movie with newer fare and Stephanie went on a much-publicized romantic trip to Scotland with the film's cinematographer. Which is how I found out. Andrew hadn't told me and there had been little to no shift in his attitude or time with me; we still saw each other regularly. So I was thrilled it was over, but nervous. I wanted to be the woman who filled Stephanie's place. Or not filled it, because I never believed in her feelings for him anyway. Maybe "take over" would be a better way to say it. I wanted it to be Andrew and me and no one else.

On Labor Day weekend, a few weeks after I found out that Andrew and Stephanie were kaput, I didn't hear from him for a day and a half and I started to get concerned. All right, scared. Okay, terrified. He had met someone else and fallen in love that quickly. Fuck. And this new person probably wasn't just an in-between girl, but someone who would fill every space in him so much that there would no longer be any room or need for me. Panic moved in from the outside of my skin and settled under my breath all day, pushing it up when I tried to inhale, and pulling in when I tried to blow out. I was a wreck.

I bought a bottle of Absolut and some tonic, and drank a lot of it while sitting on my futon wishing my phone would ring.

It finally did at two A.M., but by then I had been passed out—I mean, asleep—for a few hours.

"Hi, sweet-y-vette. I'm in Venice," Andrew said over waves of soft white noise.

I wondered why he was telling me that, but all I cared about was that his voice was on my line calling me.

"Should I meet you at your house?" I was struggling to get my brain and body to match his alertness.

"No, I'm in Italy. Venice, Italy."

"Italy?"

"I'm in Venice, Italy; not Venice, L.A. At the film festival. I'll be home in a few days."

Now I understood. Oh, thank God, he had called and all the way from there.

"Go back to sleep, honey, I'll call you when I get home. If you need me, call Patrick and he'll get me, okay?"

"Okay."

"Do you still love me?"

"Yes."

"Good. I . . ." He was quiet for a moment as if he were going to say the same thing. "I'll talk to you soon. Sweet dreams, Yvette."

"Bye, Andrew."

I hung up the phone and started to put it on the floor, then decided to let it stay on the bed with me, so that his voice it had transported could escort me into sleep. Andrew called. I wondered what time it was in Italy. New York was three hours ahead, and Europe six, so nine would make it eleven A.M. where he was. Jesus, I hoped a woman hadn't just left his bed. Okay, he probably was having sex with other women; they just better be one-time-only things that didn't mean anything to him. At least when he was with Stephanie, as horrible as that was, I knew who she was and I could perform the mental gymnastics required to diminish her threat to me, but these God-knows-who-and-how-many-other women were harder to dispel. Fuck. Oh, Andrew, come home from there and make me the only woman in your life. I fell asleep to that prayer.

For the next month, every time I saw him and every time he called, all I could think about was whether or not Andrew and I were getting closer to being a real couple. To the public, to him, to me. All behavior and conversation between us was looked at through that prism. I was obsessed. It was like some kind of relationship diet. I only felt good on days when the score of promising signs of our togetherness outweighed the bad ones. Seeing him was at the top of the list for making me feel good, but then it would make me feel shitty because why weren't we going out in public? Phone calls, lots of them in one day, were always a good sign, except when was he going to say "I love you" to me?

My art fell by the wayside, completely forgotten. I made mistakes working for Bill and dropped a lot of dishes at the restaurant. I stopped calling friends back—what was the point? I could only think about one thing—Andrew—and I couldn't talk about him with any of them. Especially Viv, who, inspired by Stephanie—all right, maybe not, but I thought of it that way—had broken up with Craig and was just loving her new single status. It made me want to scream. That was the last thing I could hear about, especially from her, since it included more harangues about how great Stephanie was doing now that she was finished with that scumbag Andrew. Though I figured Viv would have to stop trashing him soon since her main conduit for information on him had dried up. Her last diatribe against him sounded like a death rattle.

My days began and ended with the same perpetual thought—were Andrew and I going to be together permanently? It was like some horrible game, like a king with twin sons who takes forever to pick the heir. Someone was going to get picked, but who and when? It was pure hell. And the whole time I tried to appear to him as if I didn't care. As if I wasn't the complete wreck I was inside that made me stop eating and barely sleep through the night. If I hadn't wanted to be with him so much, I would have wanted to die.

One morning in early November, Andrew called me and said, "Why don't you come over tonight and we'll watch the election returns?"

After saying yes in what I hoped was a calm voice, we made a plan, and hung up. I was shocked. Our get-togethers were always last-minute, arranged at the end of the night or as he drove toward my apartment in his car. This was a good ten hours away, and it involved politics, a love of his life, almost as much as collecting art. He had shared some of that world with me, particularly when we first met and my father's Southern Republican opinions still held me in their sway. Andrew taught me about socially responsible government and education instead of arms. I'd ask him the questions that even the forming of confused me, and he would answer at their core, explaining issues and consequences. I wanted to know more about all that for him. I loved his mind and the way he articulated his thoughts. Listening to him talk about politics was like being on an intense-but-intelligent ride—Oh, the places you'll go!—to quote another great, if quite different mind. So to be asked to watch the election returns with him was like an invitation to meet his family—a huge step. I knew he'd have insightful information about each candidate; hell, he knew and was courted by most of the Democrats.

My entire day was about our date at eight. I somehow got through the mundanity of my lunch shift at the restaurant by trying to distance myself from it. As I drove home afterward, still feeling cruddy from handling plates of food, a horrible fear that had been lurking in me for the past few months raised its head and began shouting at me. Over and over it told me that for Andrew to be with me the way he was with those other women, like Lily and Stephanie, completely and publicly, I would have to be famous. Because in the three-plus decades that his romantic life had been fodder for the media, Andrew had never gone out with a woman who wasn't as famous as him, or at least close to it since very, very few ever reached his level. And I was nobody. Hadn't become a big fucking art star in New York and still wasn't one. No matter how many glittering parties I went to with Viv, or how many millionaire men I dated, or how much money I spent that I didn't have on facials and clothes, the reality was the same. I wasn't in his world. Where I grew up, it was the number of decades your family had lived there that mattered—past a century or so and you were in, and mine went back at least two, but in L.A., it was fame and money that mattered. And it looked like it did for Andrew, too.

But maybe that fear was just fucking with me. It had to be. Andrew loved me. And he said that I was the only woman in the world that he believed truly loved him—that had to mean a lot. And, good God, his success and fame were enough for ten. Surely, mine couldn't matter so much to him. We had just never had the chance to really be together, but with Stephanie out of the picture and both of us in the same city, it could finally happen. He had just been taking it slowly, not rushing in, and our date to watch the election returns would be the first step in changing everything.

When I got home, I stripped off my waitress uniform, took a shower, and put on his favorite dress, a small floral-print V-neck with a short pleated skirt. The depth of the neckline, brevity of the skirt, and floral of the fabric were the only differences from my Catholic school uniform. The first time I wore it around him, he opened his door and looked at me for a long while.

"What?" I said.

"You know I'm a sucker for that."

I hadn't, but good.

So I wore that, using everything in my arsenal for a winning campaign.

Andrew had the same reaction to the dress when he opened the door as he had had before. I could tell it made him want to blow off watching the returns. I took it as a good sign about the future of the evening and us.

"Let's miss the beginning," Andrew said as he led me past the kitchen where the TV was blaring and to his bed. I slipped off my dress, and with it all the fears that had been tormenting me. As I knelt on the sheets, I decided that none of that stuff—the fame and success—really mattered to him. It was just him and me. Us. We were completely similar when we were only in our skin and in each other's. And that was what mattered.

The marble counter of the island in Andrew's kitchen was covered with containers and platters of food that Andrew had pulled from his fridge after we finally emerged from his bedroom. We picked through the offerings; giving each other tastes, devouring some, ignoring others. He was into the borscht soup. I thought it looked metallically cold. I was eating sesame noodles. The TV on the counter was still on and the results that were being reported were exactly what Andrew had predicted. He started explaining to me what the party would do and we talked about the different candidates and how they had managed their campaigns—if anyone knew how to handle the media, it was Andrew.

A while later, we were in bed again, right in the middle, when the phone rang. Well, not rang—lit, actually. Andrew's phones didn't ring; they lit up all through his house, like Tinkerbell kept alive by an omnipotent invisible child. Even across a bright room with his back to the instrument, he could tell whenever one of the small transparent plastic buttons began blinking. So I wasn't surprised that in the deep dark of his bedroom—him moving on top of me, I had already had three, but his was still to come—he noticed the sharp small light flashing on the phone on his bedside table.

During the months he was seeing Stephanie, she would sometimes call while we were in his bed and he would have to answer, but he always expected it and would warn me ahead. I'd wait silently while devouring and dissecting every fragment of his side of their conversation. She required tons of shoring up from him. He was constantly having to tell her what a great job she did, and yes, she was the best, no other actress compared to her and on and on. It was shocking. All that animal confidence she exuded was bullshit. Every word she uttered and thing she did needed his constant encouragement.

His bedside phone, like all the others, had a row of buttons, and I knew that only a few persons had the number that lit the one button that would make Andrew pick up, like I did. That was the button that was blinking as he was moving on top of me, speaking into my ear, my hurried breath answering him, together moving forward, so near, but then his arm reached out and the phone was at his ear.

"Hello."

He had stopped moving, which made me stop, but my body inside was a few beats behind. I wanted to continue moving—fuck the caller—but figured I'd better not.

"When does her plane leave?"

"That's obscene," he said to the answer.

"Okay, see you in a little bit."

Before I could register what had just happened, Andrew hung up the phone, kissed my lips, and, withdrawing from bed, said, "Come on, we have people coming over; we're getting dressed."

Fuck. I wanted it to be just me and him. Who were these goddamn people coming over at ten after eleven? Then I realized it was me with him meeting some of his friends. That hadn't happened since the lunch in New York when actor best friend regaled me with funny Andrew tales. If this would be like that—all right, it could be fun. But who was this "she" whose plane was leaving God knows when?

Fuck.

She was a model from Germany. I had seen pictures of her the year before when she had exploded onto *Vogue* and everywhere else. Her beauty was rarified it was so complete, though a bit lupine, I thought. Andrew's friend—the one who had called him and had brought her—was a famous photographer, and I vowed to never again like the hard and beautiful pictures of fashion and celebrities he shot.

We had settled in the kitchen where the stark, brightly lit whiteness seemed to outline the color and flesh of each of us as if we were in a flat cardboard set. I hoped it was hugely obvious that Andrew and I had been having sex. Andrew had wanted me to pull myself together, but I'd let my hair stay a bit mussed, having a feeling I might need the extra armor of our interrupted coitus. Take that, you fucking model.

She was wearing an exquisite dress that I had seen in last month's *Vogue* and loved. If I remembered correctly, it cost over three thousand dollars. Though up close and live, it didn't look as good on her slumping body and had a wine stain near the neck. What a slob. I tried to remind myself that Andrew loved my dress, but I felt small in it, silly, eighty-nine dollars on sale could not compete with that dress, even stained and slumped.

"Where's the bathroom?" the model asked after introductions were made.

She was barely out of the room when the photographer looked at Andrew, turned toward him really, with his back to me like I was more kitchen counter, and said, "So what do you think about her—pretty hot, huh? She'd be nice. And perfect for you."

Andrew was quiet for a second, then said, "She's a very pretty girl." He stated it simply, like the fact it was.

But the photographer's words began furiously reprinting themselves in my head. "*So what do you think about her—pretty hot, huh? She'd be nice. And perfect for you.*" Again and again and again.

Andrew had changed the subject; they were talking about mutual friends, but my mind was reeling.

"Ooo, that bathroom was sssooo cold," the model declared as she entered the kitchen's hot glare. "My pee froze midair before it hit the john."

Andrew looked at me and I looked at him. I knew he knew what I was thinking and I knew he agreed. Growing up in the South, there were some things you just didn't mention because of an implicit understanding that they weren't interesting to anyone else, particularly to people you've just met, like your bodily functions. I wondered if it was her upbringing—it kind of matched how she was with the dress—or a hazard of being that beautiful, the misguided belief that every part of her, refuse included, was a fascinating subject. God, I hated her.

"How about a little food?" Andrew said, practically clapping his hands to help break the moment. "Yvette, will you help me see what's in the fridge?" We both knew exactly what was in the fridge, but I inwardly thanked him for an activity that put me in the hostess role.

"Oh, we're not hungry," the photographer said. Did the model ever allow herself to be? "We just came from Patricia's birthday party—Patricia Alpert." He addressed the last part to me, which I could have believed was a nice inclusion, but instead his tone built a wall around the three of them who knew Patricia already.

"She was so sorry you weren't there," he continued, his focus back on Andrew and the model. "She went on and on about how important you were to her growing up."

That I hadn't known, but could have guessed. Patricia Alpert was the daughter of a legendary studio mogul and had come into success on her own as a film producer, plying her access to her father's movie star friends.

"And what was in that card you wrote?" the photographer asked. "She kept giggling and waving it around like she'd let us see, but she never did."

Andrew was standing next to me holding the refrigerator door open, though it would have stayed open on its own, and I was filling the marble counter of the island with the containers and platters that had provided our recent meal. The photographer and the model were on the other side of the island across from us and I wanted them to stay there, if not leave.

"It said, 'You'll always be eight to me.' "

I knew as he said it that Andrew meant the age, but it registered in my mind as some kind of grammatically incorrect double entendre.

"Love that! And so did she." This goddamn photographer-man would not shut up. "And what you gave her, it was her favorite. And she got loot, lemme tell ya, but those two dozen red roses you sent were the highlight of her evening."

Oh, good God.

Roses. He sent her roses. Or rather, Patrick probably did, following a command from Andrew just that day, maybe even right after Andrew and I had talked on the phone making our plans, once he knew he wouldn't go to Patricia's birthday party. Andrew had had roses sent so she would know how much he cared about her even though he wasn't there. Roses. Twenty-four tall and red and public emissaries of his love. To bloom in front of her and everyone else. And when they started to wilt, she could throw them out or press them or make potpourri and save the memory in her heart for eternity. Roses. For her and everyone to see.

I could feel Andrew looking at me. And I could hear the hum of the photographer's words whirling on and on like a camera motor, but roses was all I could think in my head.

Andrew sends roses. He has sex with other women. And he was looking for a new girlfriend right in front of me.

The bowl of borscht was sweaty from the fridge. Andrew hadn't covered it when he put it in earlier, just pushed it toward the back, and I had wondered if the chef would find it the next day and throw it out or rescue it with plastic wrap. As I lowered the bowl to the counter, it slipped out of my hands, and a long cold wave of bright red liquid went flying over the marble island, spraying, splattering, and covering the model and the photographer and the gleaming, shining room.

I will never know who cleaned it up. Sometimes I think Andrew couldn't possibly have gone to bed with borscht congealing everywhere; other times I know he'd never dirty his hands with that, a damn spot that wouldn't come out. Maybe Miss Lupine licked it up while photographer-man took pictures—Helmut Newton-esque, but real life.

I left without a word. Walked out of the kitchen as if I heard my name being called and wanted to find the source. Got in my truck, and thankfully (or not) didn't hit the photographer's stupid Bentley parked badly behind me as I flew down the winding driveway hill and went out the gate that opened automatically.

Okay, so maybe I was stupid not to see how things were for as long as I did, but I wasn't so stupid as to ever see him again, I thought as I drove through the dark, empty streets in a blur of anger. Roses for one and a pimp-parade from another. Fuck that. And fuck, fuck, fuck him.

I drove around for a couple of hours trying to calm myself down enough to be able to go home and sleep. I considered getting a bottle of Absolut, but realized I might not stop drinking. When I finally got home, the message light on my answering machine was flashing. It seemed to be quite a night for blinking phone lights. There were three messages from Andrew, if you could call them that. Andrew had stopped speaking on my answering machine once we started having sex, as if they'd be evidence, and I guess they would have been, but I could always tell the messages he left by a little sound he would make. A "hunh" noise. Unidentifiable if it was ever used publicly, but I knew it was him and he knew I did. That sound was on each of three messages and nothing else.

Lying on my futon, unable to sleep—I should have gotten the goddamn Absolut—I knew without any doubt that I would never see Andrew Madden again. Fuck him.

My phone rang the next morning at Andrew's usual time to call. I was still in a daze. I had finally fallen asleep around five-thirty A.M., so I felt hungover even without the vodka. I lay on the futon listening to the phone ring, then my machine clicked on when I didn't pick up. I heard a small hesitation, then a hang-up. Fifteen minutes later, it was the same: ring, ring, ring, ring, machine pick up, a hesitation, then hang-up. And on and on every quarter hour all morning long. I guess he thought it would be like that time in New York the morning after Suzy came to the Ritz-Carlton—a pseudoapology and everything back to how it was. But fuck him, I wasn't playing anymore. He could find someone else and I was sure he would. But he was going to be fucked because no one else would love him without wanting to be in one of his stupid goddamn films, no one else would make his back feel new again, would love him in the way I had. But fuck him—he had thrown it all away.

All that afternoon and night, my phone continued to ring. A couple of times, he left the "hunh" message, as if I hadn't known the constant hang-ups were him. My phone continued to ring every morning at his usual time and every night around eleven. It rang and there were no messages. It rang and I didn't pick it up. It rang and I listened to it. It rang like that for a month and then it stopped. It returned to the rhythm it had had before, but without Andrew's melody in it.

When I woke up each morning, it would take me a second to awaken to the Andrew-less reality. It was like having been flung into the ocean on a small dinky craft with no tracking system and the North Star out of sight. Andrew was gone. And my apartment felt empty and quiet, and my life felt colorless, as if it had died inside of me, but had forgotten to notify my body. I carried on, but felt useless.

I tried to hide how I felt when I was with Viv, but she noticed the plunging of my mood. I was sad not to be in a relationship, I said to her. You know, lonely, that's all. I definitely could not tell her the real reason.

She was already involved with someone, the choreographer she was using for her new video. "And it's such a relief not to be with a suit!" Viv said, whenever the subject of Craig came up, though they had stayed friends, and Craig was dating around.

A couple of months after the election-night horror, I was still crying a lot. It wasn't getting any better trying to live without Andrew. How could I ever fall in love with another man? Who could I be with after him? Andrew was the pinnacle, perfect and complete, überman. There was nowhere to go but down. It reminded me of when I left Mississippi at eighteen and had been living in New York for a few months, I realized one day that being up there I had gotten ruined (to ever be able to live in an unfabulous place) and enlightened (as to why I never would) all at the same time. That's what being with Andrew was like in regard to other men—ruined and enlightened all at the same time. I never said any of that to Viv, but she could hear in my voice that I was still down.

"I have a great idea that will cheer you right up," Viv said to me one Friday morning over the phone. "Craig wants to do a little sex-and-drugs blowout in Palm Springs this weekend and is looking for a girl to take for some one-on-one fun. I'll call him and tell him you'll be his date."

I was shocked. I couldn't believe what she was saying. Her ex-boyfriend, for God's sake, lent to me like a dress to lift my spirits, and I lent to him.

"I'm not some good-time girl, Viv. I don't want to be a weekend fuck for your ex-boyfriend."

"Okay, okay, hush." I could imagine Viv's hands flying about, trying to erase our exchange.

"I gotta go," I said. "I'll talk to you later."

We never called each other again. A part of me missed our long talks on her comfy couch, missed discovering great places and getting our nails done. But I couldn't and didn't want to get over the suggestion she had made. Like I had any interest in fucking her ex-boyfriend. Or worse, in being a weekend fling for him. Something to tell the boys about on Monday morning. Was she nuts? Or was she just so used to people fucking their way to the top that she considered an offer of Craig Beltram as manna from heaven?

A few weeks after Viv and I stopped talking, on New Year's Eve afternoon, I met Reggie in the bookstore, and having him made Viv's departure easier to take. And frankly, it was a better exchange.

But I was still ravaged with a depression that I couldn't shake. I stood for hours in the studio I'd made out of the dressing room in my apartment and tried to get back to my art, which I had ignored for months, but nothing came. I dragged myself through my waitressing shifts and my work for Bill. I lost weight and couldn't sleep. Nothing interested me. My mind was a treadmill of thoughts and memories and imagined conversations with Andrew that kept running and running repeatedly, making me feel worse. There were hang-ups on my machine that I wanted to believe were from him, but I also didn't want to kid myself.

In the middle of January, in an effort to break out of my depression, to somehow jump-start my life, I threw myself into my art. I decided that if I got a proper studio, I could work. Maybe the problem was that I was trying to create at home, which held memories of Andrew. I needed someplace new, clean, free of him.

A gallery owner who wanted to see my next batch of work for a planned group show suggested I look into the Santa Fe Art Colony for a space. Which is how I met Steve, by renting part of his studio from him. We became friends through the conversations we had at the end of our work sessions. Or his work sessions, I should say. The change of venue hadn't done anything to change my mood or lift the block I was in. How could I create when I was feeling so dead?

Then the fantasies of driving my truck off a cliff began. Wonderful, exultant crashes of glass and steel, me crumpling within, the sea taking over, pulling the truck and me under, and tearing us up on the hard sand floor. *The Awakening*'s ending with an L.A. twist—driving instead of walking into the ocean.

I started going for long drives along the PCH. It was annoying how hard it was to find a place to drive off. I realized that the places I'd seen in movies, commercials, and magazines of craggy, terrifying cliffs at the edge of Highway 1 were all farther up the coast. That was where the drive-off points that I needed were, high above the surf with sharp rocks below and water swirling in and around, an evil accomplice with an undertow. Malibu and Ventura had nothing as dramatic and lethal as that. So I went through the motions of life while silent and graphic auto-suicides played over and over in my mind. But it was better than the constant thoughts of Andrew. Kind of.

One afternoon in Steve's loft after another very noticeable nonworking session for me and lots of productivity for him, he and I were drinking the green tea he had made and sitting quietly in the large concrete space's fading light. The February day was pressing against the tall windows, its cold gray a match for the color of the floor. Steve was smoking a cigarette, and I was battling with myself about whether to ask him for one. If I was going to drive off a cliff, why worry about lung cancer?

"I started going to a meditation group," Steve said suddenly, as if the thoughts that were in his head were also in mine, so the dive he took into this topic wasn't a complete surprise. "An Intro into Buddhism thing that this Vietnamese monk is doing at his apartment. It's small, just about five of us. And it's free. Why don't you come? Maybe you could use a new view on things."

"That's a nice way of putting it."

Steve laughed with me, then had a deliciously long drag off his cigarette. "We all need to shake things up every once in a while. If you don't like it, don't go back."

I told him thanks, I'd think about it, then we talked about other things until he finished another cigarette and we locked up the studio and left.

A few weeks later, I was home one night flipping through the channels on the TV. It was just after eleven, so I figured I'd catch the evening news, which I rarely do, preferring a newspaper instead, but I turned it on and five minutes later there it was. A nice annunciation story about Andrew Madden's newest life role via Holly McRae's conception. Clearly adding "daddy" to the list of his achievements was a news-making event, particularly at the age of fifty-four when it happened for him. And I guess it was a lot easier for them to have it on the news than to make all those "Guess what?" phone calls to everyone. Sitting on my futon, looking at the grinning photograph of Andrew on the screen while the anchor gave the happy details, felt like getting cut over and over in my gut. As if Holly's full womb were excavating mine. As if the conception I had felt when I first met Andrew had finally died.

I dove into Buddhism classes with Steve. The first time I went I thought I'd try it once and forget about it, but there was so much peace there, such a sense of another way to live. And it wasn't about changing all the outside stuff the way those stadium-renting, bestselling gurus say you have to do, this was quiet and internal. Just between you and you. I liked the independence of it.

One night before we meditated, Dr. En Chuan said that a way to get over a resentment toward someone is to pray for them to have everything you want. That sounded dreadful and difficult enough, but why should I pray for Andrew and Holly when they had everything already? Then En Chuan went on. You don't have to be happy about doing it, he said, in fact, you can still be annoyed at the person, but just pray that they have inner peace and happiness; everyone needs help with that. The prayers will help them, but they will help you the most.

Driving home that night, I thought about what En Chuan had said, but I didn't think I'd be able to do that. Those two had everything in the goddamn world, and besides, the whole point was for me to stop thinking about him. But maybe I'd try it a little. Especially since I didn't have to be happy about doing it.

The meditation and the few prayers I said may have helped, because the depression started lifting and the truck-crashing suicide scenarios fell away. I was able to get back to my art and start a new series of sculptures, and began dating a bit. No one I was seriously interested in, every man still seemed second-rate, but I was participating in life in a way I hadn't for a long time. And the gallery owner who had been interested in my work wanted to put some of my new pieces in her next group show.

So things were going okay when six months later it was announced in the newspapers—and I'm sure on TV, I just didn't watch—that Andrew and Holly were the proud parents of a baby girl. The real daughter he had never had finally appeared. My long-ago stand-in role was officially done.

I started making jewelry—just for birthdays and Christmas presents—crafted from materials that had seemed too delicate to put in a sculpture, along with semiprecious gems I bought downtown in the jewelry district not far from Steve's studio. I must have been making my fifth or sixth set of earrings when I remembered something one of my teachers at the School of Visual Arts had said about my work.

"It almost looks like jewelry."

That sounded small.

"I don't mean that negatively," he went on. "Fine jewelry is an art. Your work is so delicate and personal, very much close-up. It's definitely for the public, but in a personal context which jewelry is—art for a person to wear. An extension of them via you, not work that is left alone in a room. It's just a thought."

I had felt extremely seen when he said that, as if he were explaining a part of me to myself. But back then, I still wanted my work to be how I had envisioned it in Mississippi. Big. Important. Appearing in *ArtForum*. Art that goes into a museum was a powerfully propelling reason to get out of the South, a motivation to pole-vault out of my roots' clinging grasp.

But the painting and sculpting fell away easily a few months after I remembered that, especially since people were buying up my jewelry. Friends loved the pieces I gave them, told their friends, and commissions rolled in. Lizzie started carrying my jewelry, and an actress wore some in a shoot for *Los Angeles Magazine*. I gave up my space in Steve's loft and moved into a nice-sized two-bedroom apartment, so my studio could be at home. And I was happy. The process of creating didn't feel like such a big question mark anymore because once a piece was finished, I knew there was a market for it.

I'd still see items about Andrew in the media; it was impossible not to. And pictures of Holly would pop up; she was he practically. But the stabbing feeling it had engendered in my gut cut down to a low throb, a dull pain that was an automatic response to his name. But I could live with it. Even ignore it sometimes.

Life went on, in its way.

26

There is a concept in Buddhism of "No birth; no death." That all living things continue on in some form. A seed grows into a stem with leaves, then flowers, and dies only to become mulch for new plants in the spring. A cycle of birth and death; everything on the chain continuing, no stopping.

But the Buddhist retreat that I was supposed to go on next week has been stopped. I got a message on my answering machine—after another hang-up—that the Jesuit priest who was going to run it had a medical emergency, so it's been postponed until they aren't sure when. I really could have used the break from everyday life after Suzanne's wedding last weekend, but the Catholic imperative to be forgiving, plus the Buddhist practice of nonattachment are making me feel guilty for my attitude, so I remind myself that the retreat will happen at the time when it will be best.

I have strong faith in Buddhism; I just wish Lizzie played by their rule of continuing. Lizzie probably has not died, but her store, I am sickened to discover, is undeniably, irrevocably kaput. I am standing on a sidewalk under the hot August sun staring at the Closed sign in the door of her store. The empty darkness of the windows is hard to comprehend, so I keep looking up the street and back at them, as if this vision I am having will suddenly change.

"Goddamn you, Lizzie." I glance around to see if anyone heard me, a woman railing at an empty storefront. I don't know why I believe that bellowing her name will somehow make her hear my anger. She is not God, able to divine my thoughts; she is human—closer to Beelzebub, frankly—and skipped out on me without paying and with my jewelry besides.

I get in my truck, start it up, and throw it into gear too quickly, causing it to lurch forward and die. I sit for a moment wondering what birth will arise from this death, but all I feel is anger. The five stages of grief flash in my mind like cards dealt during a magic trick. The joker turns up last and has Lizzie's face on it.

For the first time, I find my way through the Venice streets easily, as if the neighborhood is escorting me out, as if it knows I have no need to go there again. As I get on the 10 freeway heading east to go home, I wonder where Lizzie has disappeared to. In what part of this vast area called Los Angeles is she conjuring a new life. I imagine a trail of fake eyeglasses and packets of red hair dye left in her wake as she discards her store-owner disguise.

And where is my jewelry that was in Lizzie's store? Is she wearing the pieces? Sold them cheap to a friend or maybe gave them to a relative as a seemingly extravagant gift? I want to slap her and wake up from this bad dream. The jewelry is completely lost, gone, given to her with nothing received back except an invoice—a lot of good that will do—and no idea where she or it went. When my pieces in Rox were sold, I didn't know who bought them, but I'd already been given a check for the merchandise, the reciprocal evidence that what I delivered had not disappeared into the ether like a scream never heard.

I had thought Lizzie was permanent, one of those people who will always be right where they are. No change in their life, no growth. One nonmoving thing to count on that will always be in the same spot decades from now. Boy, was I wrong. Lizzie is no longer. Just gone, gone, gone. My father did that once, but he didn't have my jewelry, just my heart. Goddamn him, too.

"It's your father being absent so long, honey," Reggie says during our telephonic breakfast this morning after I tell him about yet another scream dream last night. "You feel unsafe in the world, that's pretty clear."

"It's not because of him." It's too hot this morning for oatmeal and I can hear Reggie sipping on a straw. In an effort to lose weight, he is only drinking protein smoothies for breakfast, he told me, and the rest of his meals are as rigidly mapped out. He's been thrilled for the last month ever since I broke up with Michael, and maybe that euphoria has fueled him to resist his normal fare of sausage, toast, and eggs. "Anyway, I just want the screams to end—it's been six months. Enough already."

"Have you ever thought about finding him?"

"Who?"

"Paul, your father."

"Oh. No, I haven't. Once I did. Years ago when I was still in Mississippi after that dreadful Cousin Elsie woman called, I had daydreams about stealing Momma's car and running away to Florida and somehow connecting with him there, as if our mutual DNA would illuminate my way to him like radar, but I never did. Not only wasn't it realistic, but even if I had miraculously found him, I guess I didn't want to see how he'd respond. Or wouldn't. Sometimes it's better not knowing." I make a point of turning on the water in the kitchen sink. "Can we change the subject, please?"

"I just don't want you waking up screaming anymore."

"Yeah, well, I don't, either." We listen to each other breathe for a moment. I can tell he isn't saying anything in case I want to talk about this some more, which I know he thinks I should, but I don't. "So, what are you up to today?"

Reggie distracts me with tales of his current job. Since I have stopped seeing Michael, my conversations with Reggie have felt more complete, because there is no longer an entire area that I have to leave out. Hanging up the phone, I wonder if or when he will ever start seeing someone.

With Lizzie's shop no longer selling my jewelry—or even in existence, damn her—the solution is to get into another store, a real one that pays on time. And after Suzanne's wedding I began thinking of working with pearls.

As I drive through my neighborhood in the September heat to get downtown, I hear the whir of a small engine growing louder with each block. My stomach instinctively tightens against what I fear the noise is, and I immediately begin praying that it isn't, but I turn the corner and almost run into it. A large truck with a high-sided bed is double-parked in the street and a group of three men wearing straw cowboy hats and long-sleeved shirts despite the heat are the bandits blocking my way. The whirring has become thunderous, like a jetliner taking off, competing only in volume with a radio playing Spanish music that is audible when the buzzsaw one of them is toting isn't cutting, brutalizing, and massacreing a huge California cypress tree.

Trees in Los Angeles are clipped and groomed like a porn star's bush. When I first moved here, I thought the bare branches and small sizes were the trees' reaction to the hot, dry environment, but eventually I understood that that had nothing to do it—people don't let them grow. Drive along Sunset Boulevard or any street in a supposedly well-to-do neighborhood, and the trees are just nubs with small desperate clusters of leaves trying vainly to get some sun. Supposedly it all started with rogue bands that were hired by billboard companies to illegally and under cover of night cut the branches on trees lining commercial streets, so no one will miss an advertisement of yet another terrible movie we all have to see. Then I guess the idiots who move here and buy homes got the impression that that was the L.A. style, and God forbid they not be in on that, so street after street is nothing but brutal, decapitated sticks. Trees, the one thing that would cool down and shade this Saharan land, are desecrated and reduced to nothing. I have never seen anything like it in my life. I want to make everyone in Los Angeles fly en masse to the South and say, "See? This is how a tree is supposed to look, you fucking idiot. Now just leave them alone."

As I drive around the murderers, I have to squelch my impulse to crash into their truck. I know it's not their fault, that they were just hired to do a job, but all I can think about is trying to stop them somehow. I hit the number on my cell phone that automatically dials Reggie. He's already at the editing room, but I can leave him a message about it. He's from Kansas; he understands. At least the tree outside my living room window still looks like one.

The showroom of Vivid Pearls and Gems Company, Importers and Wholesalers, is on the fifth floor of the International Jewelry Center at 550 South Hill Street in downtown. A sad row of tall, sickly palm trees, each trunk barely supporting the fronds, lines the sidewalk in front of the building, which is a large, modern, hulking affair. White horizontal slabs alternate with rows of windows giving the opposite impression of a building you can see into. Transparency and ease of access are not what jewelry vendors want in their place of business. Especially not when the building faces Pershing Square, an elegantly named plaza that holds a few groups of overly pruned trees, but is mostly a small city block of concrete with some permanently installed benches, tables, and chairs that the homeless are periodically roused out of in an effort to show the jewelry businesses that the cops really are doing something about it.

I arrive right on time for my appointment with May Tsou, the owner of Vivid Pearls and Gems, and I have a feeling it is noted and appreciated by her. She buzzes me into the first security door, and I wait inside the chamber for it to click shut behind me, then the inner door is buzzed open, and I push through it into the showroom. May is a small Chinese woman whose easy smile and unlined face hides two decades of her age and her steely-eyed business sense. I have heard stories about her. She gets the best South Sea pearls because her family has been in the business in Asia for generations, so the quality is guaranteed and that makes it worth the hoops one must jump through to buy from her. This is our second appointment. She wanted time to run a credit check on me and, I think, to talk to other wholesalers about dealing with me. When she called the other day to say come down on Thursday, I knew I was in.

She leads me into a small inner room with light dove-gray carpet, walls, and chairs. A dark, sleek table takes up most of the space in front of a doorway that leads to yet another inner room. May walks around the table and into the back room as I sit down in the chair facing her. She soon returns with long, flat black boxes that she stacks on the table. A high-powered lamp, magnifying glass, and scale are already in place. I feel like I am about to buy heroin. Not that I ever have, and I know the normal place of business for that kind of sale is not like this, but my heart is racing as if what I'm about to look at will change my life, or at least how I feel.

Which it does the minute May opens the first box. Lying inside in three segregated chambers and resting on black felt are dozens of gleaming, lustrous, shimmering pearls. Round and full and rich as if the oysters offered not a covered-up glossed-over irritant, but their own wombs. In the midst of this bedazzlement, I realize that May is looking at me with a small smile on her face.

"Beautiful, huh? Tahitian." With a pair of very long tweezers, she picks up a perfect pearl, then holds it to the light under the magnifying glass for me to see. Her deftness with the tool makes me think of her using chopsticks, whereas when I hold tweezers to examine gems, my proficiency is thanks to eyebrow maintenance.

She puts the pearl back on the felt, hands me the tweezers, and lets me look at it for myself. It is a stunning specimen with a peacock-green luster and a pearly glow underneath; large, round, and heavy, it must be fifteen or sixteen millimeters. Without even asking the price, I know it is out of my league, and I have a feeling that May knows that as well, but is showing it to me anyway because she knows the joy that can bring. And wants me to know what is possible if my business keeps growing.

The pearls I am able to buy are a few removed from that first grand one, but still they are beautiful. "Department stores buy regular pearls; dye them. These color real," May says as I put together a group of the ones I will buy in naturally occurring colors of gray, green, pink, and deep brown.

I am in love with them. Each pearl, because of the price range I need to stay in, has a tiny dimple or pit in it, which I wasn't planning on when I sketched the jewelry I will make with them, but as I sit at the table while May totals up my order and writes out an invoice, I start envisioning how to hide that in the designs.

The remains of breakfast lie on the table before us. Or mine does. Reggie is two months into his diet and going strong. I can see a difference in him, but he says all that matters is how great he feels, though I have a feeling he is counting pounds. As we get up to leave, the bagel shop starts filling up. A yoga class has let out from the studio up the street and a serene swarm of stretch fabric clamors into line.

We turn left on the sidewalk, walking down Larchmont toward Reggie's car in the warm morning sun, but he stops us in front of Han's optical shop. "I need some new sunglasses. Wanna help me select?"

Hundreds of frames are on display in the mirrored and dark wood cases of the store. Eyeglasses are folded up like butterfly wings, ready to elongate and light upon a face. Reggie and I quickly set into a rhythm: I find a pair, hand them to him; he tries them on, puts them away. Again and again and again.

A woman dressed casually yet elegantly in Saturday attire enters the store and heads straight to the register. Reggie is peering at himself in a mirror wearing an aggressively hip pair of sunglasses.

"Maybe," I say, trying to imagine them in life every day, then I hand him a very classic frame. "But try these." The glasses emphasize the best parts of Reggie's face. "I think those are great on you."

"Really?" Reggie is doing an odd squinting thing I've never seen him do before.

"Yeah, I like them."

He moves closer to the mirror. "You don't think they . . . I don't know." He takes them off and replaces the hip frames on his face.

"Okay, but these are great frames." I pick them up, admiring the precision of balance and the craftsmanship. "And they were amazing on you."

"They were."

Reggie and I both turn around to see who said this and if it was to us. The woman in the store has stepped closer, appraising Reggie via the mirrors on every wall.

"They're retro, but subtle," she continues. "And on him, you barely notice."

Reggie looks at me for a moment, then takes off the hip pair, so I hand the other frames back to him. The woman moves next to me, and we watch as his face is complemented when he puts the glasses on.

"Yeah, I really like them."

Reggie says nothing and turns around to look in the mirror, then starts turning his head side to side and up and down.

"Those are great pins."

It takes me a second to realize what she is talking about. In the rush to meet Reggie for breakfast, I had pulled on the top I was wearing last night with two of my pins still affixed near the neckline.

"Oh, thanks." I glance down to see which ones they are. "Actually, I made them."

"Really? Do you have a line?"

"Yeah, Broussard's Bijoux," I say as I open my bag and pull out a card for her. "I'm in one store, Rox on Beverly, and I sell privately."

"We should talk." She reaches into her Hermès bag and proffers a business card. "I'm in New York all next week, but call my assistant to set up an appointment—I'd be interested to see your line."

And with that she turns and heads out the door. As she passes in front of the shop's window, her effortlessly sleek appearance stands out amid the yoga-pants and jeans crowd. I look down at the card in my hand, astonished at what I see.

"Reggie, you'll never believe who that woman was." I join him at the register where a salesclerk, who has a hint of a German accent, as if he inherited it not from his motherland but from the store, is asking for his credit card.

"Who?" Reggie puts a worn card down.

"Linda Beckman, head jewelry buyer for Greeley's department store. She wants to see my stuff—I could die."

"That's great, honey. Good thing I needed new sunglasses, huh?"

"Yeah, right? So which ones are you . . ." I stop when I see the hip pair on the counter; the other frames are nowhere in sight. "Well, those looked good, too."

I am sitting on my couch at ten to three in the morning—having been kept awake for the last hour from a scream dream—staring into the tree outside my living room window and thinking about everything I need to do. I called Roxanne to see if she wanted more pieces, but she said check back in January, which is okay because I don't want to show her the new line until after Linda Beckman sees it and has first dibs. My appointment with her at Greeley's is next week and the samples for the new line of jewelry have come out even better than I imagined they would when I took the sketches to Dipen. The pearls shimmer and glow against the braided gold, and the tourmaline, citrine, and peridot that surround them complement and contrast with their natural luminescence. Even Dipen was impressed.

But thinking about this is making me more revved up, not less, so I turn on the television for some barbiturate channel-surfing. If anything will put me to sleep, it's dead-of-night TV. I flip past eighties sitcoms, cable access shows, a John Wayne film my father loved, cop shows, stand-up comics, and . . .

"Well, there he is." The words came out automatically as if they were too large to be contained. On the screen is Andrew. Full color, gorgeous, and close-up. In a classic, quintessential seventies film he did that defined many things, socially and in the movie industry. As I sit watching his face in my living room, with me but not real, like the dreams I've been having, I realize that when he made this movie, he was just a few years older than I am right now. Seeing what he looked like then, it is as if the image of him from back then is reaching toward me now where our difference in age is so much less. His body is moving, walking in his slow panther strides, the same way he walked me to his bedroom all those times. I breathe in and wait for the dull pain in my gut to appear. But it does not. I watch more of the movie, and still the throbbing of anguish doesn't come.

Okay, this is a first. Maybe I'm really done. Maybe seeing him at the theater and all those memories of him were exactly what I needed to get rid of him because here I am watching him, loving how he looks, remembering him gazing at me that very same way, his hand on me that way, smiling at me that way, and no big reaction is coming up. I'm just—okay.

Wow, I am clearly so completely over this man. But in a nice way, like seeing a picture of my favorite teddy bear when I was kid, the one I was sure I could never live without, definitely could not sleep without. Teddy was his name. He was purple and gold, which is a curious choice for a bear, and had only one eye. I loved Teddy. What I loved the most was that in the depths of his softness there was this really hard, solid object. And it would move, so I'd have to search for it in his down each time I held him just to find it. This secret inner core, totally belied by his countenance, that only I knew about. Eventually I realized it was the detached mechanism for a music box. He had been a wind-up toy, and the key must've broken off years before I was even born when my sister had him. But I still knew about his real inner core and no one else did, and what mattered was what he was, not his past, and I was the only one willing to find that part each time.

I pull the tapestry from the back of the couch over me as Andrew's voice moves through my living room surrounding my body, resting in my ears, floating in my head. I fall asleep with his face near, the light behind it illuminating my dreams.

27

I went through three different outfits this morning deciding what to wear to Greeley's, and even called Suzanne for her opinion because Reggie is useless in that area. I needed critical truth about how best to project the creative-yet-business vibe that is essential for this sales call. The outfit Suzanne and I came up with—me describing clothes over the phone, her asking questions about hem lengths and necklines—felt so right that I didn't even feel the need to change in my truck into the backup shirt that I brought along.

In the sales office of Greeley's department store, an older thin-haired receptionist who looks as though she has seen decades of trends and designers come and go tells me to have a seat, she'll buzz Ms. Beckman. I sit down on the low-slung couch. The office is done in peach with touches of chrome, soft but modern. Full-blown photographs of accessories and jewelry from the store's catalogue are framed on the wall like modern art. I suddenly think of Tory. Of waiting in the gallery for her to get off the phone on that day I first met her so long ago in New York, and of Andrew setting the whole thing up. It feels like a memory I've only heard about, like things that happened prekindergarten during that age of not knowing how to do things that in ensuing years were easily learned.

The receptionist tells me I can go in and waves her hand to a door on the left. Linda Beckman is sitting behind her desk in an all-cream room. Her blond hair and pale suit perfectly complement her softly made-up face. She would not be described as beautiful, but has made the most of what God gave her on a level that most women only dream about.

She puts her hand out to me and offers me a seat. "Is that from your new line you were telling me about on the phone?"

She has noticed the necklace I am wearing, as I hoped she would. It is a thin chain of braided eighteen-karat gold from which hangs a large green-gray Tahitian pearl that has an even thinner band of braided gold encircling it with a spray of green peridot dangling on a short chain underneath it. I do what I do with women in their homes; I take the necklace off and hand it to her. I have found that it has the same effect as when a little girl lets a new friend play with her favorite doll. Linda looks surprised for a split second, then I see her eyes light up when the pearl is in her hands. She stands up and moves across the room to put the necklace on in the reflection of the glass of a framed photograph from the store's catalogue.

When she comes back to her desk still wearing my necklace, I pull out the trays of pins and necklaces and bracelets and rings from my faux Vuitton bag, and Linda picks up and plays with or tries on almost everything. She glances through my press kit as she tells me that she wants the order in for January, and I try to contain my euphoria as she explains the terms.

Driving home on Wilshire Boulevard, I pass the other department stores that dominate this section of Beverly Hills, and I can barely believe what's just happened. My jewelry is going to be in one of these, on display and for sale in a national store. And in Greeley's catalogue, *The*

Style Journal, a renowned quarterly that years ago set the bar for all other high-end retail. I have to get the samples of my entire new line of South Sea pearls held with braided gold while peridot, tourmaline, and citrine dance around them to a photography studio next Monday for them to be included in the spring catalogue. Talk about tear sheets for my press kit. The shoots they do are notorious for being beautiful, yet exotically decadent. I can't wait to see my work immortalized that way. I silently bless Suzanne and her wedding for inspiring me to work with pearls.

"That's great, honey, I'm so happy for you. Matt, you have time to squeeze Yvette in tomorrow to look at her contract, don't you, love?" Suzanne has addressed the last part to her financial-whiz husband, but I know it was mostly intended for me.

"Thanks, Suzanne, but I don't need to waste his time. There's not a contract. This is retail, it's an order I'm filling and the terms are what every designer gets the first—"

"Matt, talk to her." And Suzanne hands the phone to my brother-in-law. When my sister has children, I will be a fabulous aunt in terms of empathizing with them on what it is like to be raised by her.

"Congratulations—you're in a national store!"

"Thanks, Matt."

"Now, tell me what your deal is."

"From what I hear from other designers, it's pretty standard for big stores so it's not like I can negotiate. Greeley's policy is that the first time they carry your line, it's on consignment, then they send you checks each month based on what sells, but Linda Beckman, the head jewelry buyer, feels very confident about my line, says it's really different from anything they have so it's just a matter of the money coming later instead of up front."

"Uh-huh."

"And there's the catalogue."

"The catalogue?"

"I have to pay for P and A—that's prints and advertising, all designers do—but when you consider what I'm getting, people all over the country seeing my work, and the top-notch photographs, it's really a good deal."

Matt is quiet for a moment. I can hear Suzanne in the background picking up their dinner plates from the dining room table, the one from the house we grew up in that has been in the family for three generations.

"Keep your own accounting. Don't assume they'll report everything and on time, but it's great news, Yvette, it's a whole new level for your career. I'm proud of you."

Reggie was so ecstatic over my sale that he decided we should take a day off just to celebrate. He pulls his car—late-model El Dorado, which I love because it makes me feel like I'm back in the South—into my driveway to pick me up, and when we hug, I can tell that his tummy that I never thought was a big deal, but was the reason for his diet, I guess, is completely gone. I notice my neighbor Gloria peeking around her curtain, as Reggie opens the car door for me. I am tempted to yell up to her that this isn't a new boyfriend because I know she will ask later on.

"Santa Boo is where I'm taking you." Reggie's infectious cheer is in high gear, or another and the idea of leaving L.A. for a day is heavenly.

As we drive through Malibu up the PCH, we pass houses crammed next to one another on the edge of the highway like a continuous screen hiding the beach and ocean beyond. Coming down the hill past Pepperdine University, we see an expanse of coastline not blocked by development, and the surfless Pacific lies tranquilly under the November typing-paper-white sky. Reggie is playing a cassette he made just for this drive, an hour and a half's worth of music to carry us up the coast, then on the way back, we'll play radio roulette, his term for pushing buttons and never knowing what you'll get. I have a feeling that Michael's station isn't programmed on Reggie's radio and that's fine with me. I haven't listened to Michael's "voice," as Kundalini-cum-collagen woman so accurately identified his station, since I stopped seeing him.

The Santa Barbara Museum of Art is a large two-story white stucco Spanish Mission–style building surrounded by attractive businesses against a backdrop of mountains. It is almost more compelling to stay outside and walk around in the gently sunny day, but the large purple banner hanging on the museum's façade announcing a Picasso exhibit trumps that idea.

Reggie and I step inside the charged quiet of great art on display in the gallery and read the curator's notes on the show, "Weeping Women," which has been traveling the country. The exhibit is composed entirely of portraits of Dora Maar and Marie-Thérèse Walter, his wife and mistress at the time the paintings were done, respectively. When the portraits of Marie-Thérèse were first shown, Dora Maar walked into the gallery, saw the work, and immediately knew Picasso was in love with his model, so infused were they with that truth.

"Prick," Reggie says, when we finish reading the circumstances of the paintings.

"But here you are to enjoy his work."

"That doesn't mean I like him personally."

"You don't know him personally. He wasn't Stalin or Hitler sending millions to the grave." We both know what we are also talking about, or whom, I should say. Even though Reggie and I haven't talked about Andrew in ages, it sometimes feels as if the subject is always there between us, sitting just under the surface.

"Look what he left the world for eternity."

Reggie's eyes stay on mine for a moment defiantly, then he turns and looks around the gallery, as I do. The walls are filled with intense and colorful executions of remorse and desire, sadness and love. The crowds looking at the paintings appear stripped of all outer guise as they stand in their naked desire to view beauty, like babies unable to hide their needs.

Reggie takes my hand and we walk slowly through each room, looking at every portrait, saying few words, and I am struck by Picasso's insistence for honesty. His decision to paint his mistress despite the consequences. It makes me think about the area of my life I have kept from Reggie—Andrew, namely.

At a café near the museum, Reggie pulls a chair out for me at an outside table, but before I can sit down, he gives me a hug. "Maybe we'll make it a perfect road trip and stay over somewhere. The San Ysidro Ranch has got some great bungalows."

"Where the Kennedys honeymooned—yeah, right," I say, playing along with his silly idea.

He presses himself in close, more of him on me than usual. "I'm getting a woody just holding you," he says in my ear.

I can't believe what I just heard. Reggie? A woody? About me? Oh, please tell me I didn't hear him right, but I know I did. And that term. Where'd he get that? The school yard? It quadruples the embarrassment I feel—a woody. Like Pinocchio. Not an association I want with sex. Nor is Reggie. Oh, good God.

I try to laugh, but it comes out like a snort, so I take advantage of that and say, "Gee, I need to blow my nose, be right back."

As I head into the restaurant, my eyes adjusting to the lower lights inside, I try to remember the last time I used the exclamation "gee." I decide I never have and wonder if it came out as the unfulfilled wish of what I hoped our day would be rated. I guess his suggestion of us spending the night was serious. Oh, good Christ. I mean, I love Reggie, he's my best friend, but part of the comfort of him is that since he's not a girl, I don't have to deal with weird female stuff like with Suzanne or Viv, and since he's not really straight, or has never seemed so to me, I could talk to him like a girl. And sexual tension has just never been an issue between us. Or maybe it always was and I just couldn't see it. Or didn't want to.

I suddenly have an urge to take out my cell phone and call . . . well, Reggie, actually, because he's who I call when people behave oddly or confusingly or try to switch their role, all of which he just did. The friend I want to talk to not only isn't home, he's the reason I need to call, as if Reggie could somehow also be a separate person in his apartment for me.

In the bathroom, I wash my hands and put powder on my face. I hope my eyes won't betray me when I go back to the table with their loud conveying of the no-longer-want-to-hang-out-with-him that I feel. Was I wrong to say yes to this day? Maybe I crossed some universal line for friendship that gave him a signal that that was okay. No, I've been behaving exactly as I always have, though now that I think about his diet and this day, maybe he's been planning some kind of relationship change for us ever since I stopped seeing Michael. Oh, good God.

I've powdered my nose five times and can't think of anything else to do to stall my appearance at lunch. Fuck. This is so weird. I make a small prayer to Mary that Reggie was being temporarily weird or got so overcome by all the beauty, sex, and love we saw at the museum that that energy just slipped out at me. But I doubt it. Finally, I join him at our table.

I can tell Reggie knows that he flipped me out because he immediately starts talking about his work, about editing a commercial he actually did like because of the director's vision, a nice neutral topic that makes me sort of relax. "His spots are like short films, really beautiful and telling the story visually. I wouldn't mind him shooting my script."

"I thought you wanted to do it." The pasta I ordered is heavier than I expected, with too much cream. The first few bites were comforting and nice, but now the richness is making me sick.

"Honey, let's be realistic. I've been here too long to not know the score. First-time director without film school or a movie to his credit? Who are we kidding? I need something to happen in my life, it's been the same for way too long. If this guy can get it going, I'd be thrilled. Let him do this one, then maybe some doors will open; otherwise, this wait I've been in will be my whole life."

We walk on the beach together after lunch, and the sun, the sea, the sky, the sand are so encompassing of our senses that we are content not to talk. As we stand at the surf's edge watching the winter sunset's early decline, I wonder how long Reggie's transformation has been going on. Was it a sudden moment of change or an on-going one that started with the protein shakes that made Reggie lose weight and wait diligently?

"I'm going home to visit my father for the weekend," Reggie says on the drive back to L.A. as we head south into the night. We have yielded onto the freeway, becoming one of many commuters, but without the day's work.

"Yeah? Are you looking forward to it?"

"You know, he'll call me 'son.' He's done that for so long, I think he thinks it's my goddamn name. Ever since Mom died, he's called me and my brother 'son' for what, twenty years now, like he needs to reinforce the family bond for fear it'll disappear like she did."

"You're probably right. If so, it's sad and kind of sweet."

We ride along in silence on the rhythm of the miles. Reggie was a godsend when my momma died, flying down to Mississippi to be at the funeral with me and letting me spend the night with him that first week back in L.A. so I wouldn't have to be by myself when the darkness of night came down and I had to adjust my thoughts of Momma being not in her bed but in the ground. He'd known what that was like.

The first time Reggie and I got together after we met, he showed me a black-and-white picture of his mother. She was twenty-one when it was taken, a lovely, young, open-faced woman wearing a gingham shirt. "Ain't she a tomato?" he'd said loudly, causing the other people in the café to all turn and look. He was so comfortable in his exuberance about her, so resolved with her absence in his life that he didn't notice the public reaction, just kept on showing me pictures of her. Riding in his car on the freeway, watching lights speed up close and away, I long to have that about my father, though I know that it's easier when the parent is dead and not just gone.

"I saw Andrew on TV a few weeks ago." I pause for a moment to see if Reggie is receptive, but he is quiet, just smoothly moving into the fast lane. "*Spontaneous* was on, and it was nice, really, just to see him, but especially from that time, L.A. in the seventies. He was so much a part of all that, and I always felt like I got to experience that period by being with him, through him in a way. So it was nice, but the best part was that I felt so okay about him and me. 'Cause, you know, he stepped into my life not long after Daddy was gone, and Andrew was really there for me, like a father to me those years I lived in New York, so it was nice, just to sit there and see him."

Reggie changes lanes again through the steady traffic. The car is moving fast and the highway is streaming past.

"Goddammit, Yvette, you are out of your mind." His voice is at such a pitch and his words so unlike what I thought I'd hear that I almost say, "What?" But his diatribe is spewing on. "He wasn't your father, okay? He was just some man who had sex with you and didn't care enough to do anything more. He probably doesn't even remember your name." Fuck you, I start to say, but Reggie is continuing, his voice filling the car. "You've got to let go of this. You've been dragging him around for years and where has it gotten you? Stuck in the past and ignoring what's in your life today."

Like him trying to make a pass at me? Is that the thing in my life that I'm missing?

"Reggie, I have let Andrew go, that's exactly what the fuck I was saying, if you would listen instead of having a goddamn fit that I mentioned his name. And fuck you, by the way, he was like a father to me, and whether you believe that or not doesn't change anything. What is your goddamn problem about him anyway? Christ, you're the one who's so worked up about this, not me. I'm fine. I have moved on. I've dated a lot since him. It's not my fault none of them have been the one."

I glance over at Reggie and his features look smaller on his face. We pass a few mile markers in silence.

"I just want you to be happy, honey, that's all I'm saying."

"I am."

"Good." Then he turns the radio on loud.

A couple of days after the Santa Boo excursion with Reggie, I am beginning to wonder if this friendship is going to have to end. Not that I want it to, but if I can't tell him what's going on in my life . . . And not even an honest-to-God encounter, just a movie on TV. Christ, I guess he'd really flip his lid if anything real with Andrew happened. Reggie is in Kansas seeing his dad, so we haven't talked much and that's probably for the best. But it's Saturday afternoon, and I can't stay in my apartment thinking about all this another second, so to distract myself I find a matinee to go to.

I decide to wear something upbeat and happy; maybe it will affect my mood. As I put on a deep red sweater, I remember reading somewhere that red cars get hit more than other ones, but only during daylight hours because at night they look gray. I wonder how drivers' eyes under streetlights can transpose vibrant red to dull gray. Self-preservation, maybe, to not be drawn into a nocturnal crash. Then what happens to that instinct during the day?

I arrive at the theater early, so I decide to go to a store three very long blocks down La Brea to try on vintage Levi's that I will never buy. Not because I don't want to buy the Levi's, but whenever I see the way they look on other women I always think, "How do those jeans fit like that on you? That has never happened for me." But still I persist in trying, certain that there is one pair out there that will fit great; it's just a matter of finding it. As I walk the three very long blocks to the store on the empty sidewalk of the busy street, I feel very pioneering to be a pedestrian in L.A.

Half an hour later I emerge from the store jeans-free, but consistent at least. As I head back to the theater, hurrying so I won't be late, I keep thinking about a pair of Levi's I tried on that finally actually maybe did fit but that I still didn't buy, because I was sure that the minute I left the store they suddenly would not, so I'm not noticing very much except that there is a man on the sidewalk—tall, almost young—coming toward me from the other direction. Or veering toward me really. Not drunk, he definitely is not drunk, he's clean looking actually, but just walking diagonally, like San Vicente to Pico kind of. Anyway, I think about moving which is hard. It's a sidewalk, for God's sake, public—moving is such a statement and, other than running into the traffic, where would I go? Then next thing I know, he's near me, in front of me, his arm pulls back, and he punches me hard, right on my left breast.

I am completely shocked. I stand there holding myself and staring at him as the word "clobbered" flashes in my head. Finally, I say, "But I'm a girl." I have no idea why, he clearly can tell that I am. Not that he should be beating up men, but what the hell was that for?

He just looks at me and smiles. With his whole body. Luxuriating, really. I half expect him to light a cigarette and ask how it was for me. Then he does this odd little chuckle and strolls away like he could not be happier with himself if he tried.

The cars on La Brea are blithely driving by. No one has noticed this daylight public bashing. No masked savior has flown down from the sky to stop my perpetrator. It is just me. Walking alone in what should be harmless territory, a sidewalk on a commercial street in a good neighborhood. An activity that appears to be safe, but isn't.

Before I even realize what I am doing, I pull out my cell phone, following my instinct to call Reggie, then I remember the weirdness we are in and that he's out of town, so I hang up. I could call the police. Should probably, but I don't feel like it. I can always do it later, say I was in shock. Frankly, I want to catch the movie and just not think about it.

Driving home in my truck from the movie—which was distracting, but not completely—through the descending darkness of the late afternoon, I think about that guy walking up to me on the sidewalk and hauling one off. And so casually. Easily. As if I had been walking there for the express purpose of letting him take care of his need to express anger. Fuck him. I suddenly am reminded of Reggie blowing up at me in his car on the way home from Santa Barbara. The way his anger came out so completely and unexpectedly. Not that I didn't know he doesn't like hearing about Andrew, but for Christ's sake, yelling at me? What is it with these guys? I realize that I don't want some masked hero coming down from the sky to save me. I want the person who's always there no matter what. Me.

And suddenly I decide to learn how to box. Not that kick-to-get-fit version, I'm talking traditional, in the ring, Ali-is-still-God boxing. So

28

To be totally honest, it wasn't until a couple of years ago that I realized deep down what age I truly am. Not that all this time I've been in some annually recurring version of Alzheimer's—I am aware what year this is and how that relates to my birth—but a few years ago I discovered quite accidentally that in bed I still thought of myself as seventeen.

Not consciously. I wasn't removing my clothes thinking years were being shed at the same time. Other than a vague, off to the side, sort of still-in-my-Catholic-school-uniform feeling, I had no idea I thought of myself as still seventeen until one night right in the middle of having sex, the man I was with said, "Woman." Just "Woman," as if that was expressive enough. Growing up in the South, I was used to being called "sweetie" and "sugar pie," or at least "honey" here in L.A., and, okay, this man was a Yankee, but other than wondering if his last girlfriend was Betty Friedan, it took me a good minute to figure out that he was talking to me. That I was the "Woman." I think I even looked around, worried it was one of those "Surprise! Ménage à trois!" moments—which actually did happen to me once, making me forever doorbellphobic during sex.

Anyway, what I wanted to do was stop what I was doing, climb off him, and say, "Oh, my God, do you know how old I am?" But I did not because he did, in fact, know how old I am, I mean, was then. He was forty-two and well aware of our respective ages. I guess it was just me who wasn't.

But I've never been very clear about all this. When I started seeing widow-man in Pass Christian, I would forget how much older he was than me. Not that he didn't know the real difference in our ages. He did. And I did when prom night came around and I tried to picture how he would look on the dance floor with his wide chest that definitely did not come from high school football practice. He had one of those adult male bodies that just worked for him. I remember one day he decided to go for a five-mile run, just decided and went. He was smoking a pack of cigarettes a day, but he came back, had had a great run, that was it. I will never forget looking at him and wanting that. To be able to just tell my body to perform some physical feat and have it simply comply.

I was still trying to figure out how mine worked. I had only recently started getting my period when I met him, then I immediately went on the pill to stop it. Well, not to stop it, but to stop its effect. Once I could get pregnant, and was doing what you do to get pregnant, I would avoid getting pregnant by making my body think it was pregnant. Which is how I was told the pill works. Like having some constant ghost baby inside my womb, which honest to God, I never even knew I had. I thought only Mary had a womb for Jesus, but clearly I did, too. Just one with nothing in it. Even though my body thought there was, constantly experiencing a false physical reality as if it were true. Like me and my age, I guess. Anyway.

It's my birthday today. On a Monday this year,which is a horrid little day to have a birthday, though it is starting out okay. I went shopping at Barneys, which I rarely do, mostly because I rarely do, so I figured it'd feel special, like Easter Sunday mass after a year of not going. I found some pretty pastel sweaters that I loved, picked out two, then agonized over getting a third with the salesclerk who I immediately liked because she had a name that was unpronounceable when you see it and unspellable when you hear it. I left with only two, but made a silent vow to go back more often—a kind of Lent in reverse—instead of giving up going to Barneys, I decided to give up not going to Barneys.

What I wish I had given up was the massage I am getting now. It is at a natural hot springs spa in Korea Town that I've been to quite a bit, because for some reason I keep forgetting that I don't like it here. The idea of it is so nice—warm water, all naked, hands kneading my body—but the reality is being in a cold echoey room, forced to wear a rubber cap like some cranium version of "socks in the shower," and a rubdown that consists more of slapping and shoving than anything else.

After enduring twenty minutes of this while alternately calculating how many sweaters this session is costing and admonishing myself to get back in the moment and "Enjoy this, goddammit," I sit straight up, look the masseuse in the eye, and say, "Okay, it's my birthday, but stop spanking me." She looks completely shocked, as am I, so I try to diffuse things by laughing, which helps not at all, then I realize that she has in her favor both being fully clothed and able to hit while I do not, so I grab my towel and leave.

Suzanne and Matt are giving me a party this evening, but I don't know if I want to celebrate being thirty. The number sounds frightening, but I can't keep saying I'm twenty-nine because, for one thing, I'm not, and what would I do about the events of whichever year that I'd have to erase? And for another, the whole time I was officially twenty-nine and would tell someone that in response to their horrid question, it always felt like a lie. "I'm twenty-nine" begs the unspoken thought, "She must be thirty."

As I drive to Suzanne and Matt's house in one of my new sweaters, which is not making me feel as fabulous as I had thought it would when I tried it on in the Barneys dressing room, I want to call Suzanne from my cell phone and tell her that I can't make it after all. But I know I can't do that, so I console myself with the fact that at least it's not a surprise party, thank God, just a regular one.

Although, actually, maybe the party should have been a surprise because then everyone who's going to come has arrived by the time you open the door. But with a regular party, guests can show up anytime they want, if they actually remember to come. I spent the entire blessedly short soirée praying that more people would walk through the door, as I tried to be a happy and appreciative birthday girl for Matt, Suzanne, and the few obviously date-book-proficient guests who remembered to attend. Maybe it being on a Monday night confused people and it got erased from their minds somehow. Or Suzanne didn't call everyone, but I doubt that. It was the first time I had seen Reggie since our day two weeks ago in Santa Barbara, and though we've been talking on the phone to try to ease past our blowup, the moment we hugged hello felt weird. Like it was uncomfortable to hug, but also uncomfortable not to hug, so we ended up having one of those don't-know-the-other-person-too-well, quick, sideways hugs. I know he felt it, too.

I considered telling Suzanne that I was too tired for the cake, but I knew that wouldn't fly with her, especially since she had made my favorite German chocolate cake like Momma used to. Even with that, I could not get out of there fast enough when the party was over—rather early, thank God.

Driving home on the PCH to get to the 10, I look out my truck's windshield into the night. There isn't a heavenly body in sight. In fact, the entire sky is completely blank, as if God had dragged a blanket along on His way to bed, catching every object in its hem. I wonder if some huge erasing phenomenon is going on—the entire zodiac of stars and calendars obliterated forever. I decide to feel lucky that the erasing hadn't gotten around to everyone's date book before my party began; at least some people came. And maybe it means that this birthday doesn't have to count. Maybe the universe is giving me a little gift for all my teenage years in bars when I looked older but really wasn't, so now I can truly be younger and not only when I have sex.

It is too early to go to bed when I get home and I have a feeling I won't be tired for a long time anyway, as if I am destined to be awake for every hour of this dreadful birthday. So I sit on my couch, wondering if Momma is thinking of me wherever she is, if her spirit is sending me birthday love. Maybe Daddy thought of me today. But probably not, considering that the last birthday of mine that he was around for was sixteen years ago. It seems more probable that Momma did from beyond the grave.

The ringing of the phone is such a jolt that it makes me jump. As I pick up the receiver, wondering whose date book the erasing possibly could have passed over, I hear "Happy birthday" in my ear. It takes me a minute to believe who it is.

"How did you get this number?"

I realize that isn't the friendliest greeting in the world, but I am in shock. Andrew's perfect vocal shield wraps me in close as he tells me that he's been calling it for quite a while, which really is not an answer, but he has just never left a message. For over two years since I moved into this apartment, I've had a different phone number from the one he used to call me at in my Beverly Hills apartment when we were seeing each other, so the only way he could have gotten this number was if he had called my old Beverly Hills number within six months after I moved to this one and gotten the referral for my new one here. Which means that some of those hang-ups I've heard on my answering machine in the past five years actually have been him, my fantasy confirmed. I can tell he is on a cell phone and driving in his car, moving through the city under the big, empty sky.

"You sure flew out of that theater fast," he says. "Fuckin' FBI couldn't find you."

"Yeah, well, I guess they didn't look very hard."

"I think about you a lot more than you think I do."

"Well, considering that I don't think you think about me at all, I guess you do."

Which makes him laugh, which makes me laugh, and there it is. One second of mutual time between us yielding and spreading until it connects our now with when we were before. A highway in one hello.

"Do you still love me?"

"Still." And I am back, as if the five years apart are five seconds and our breakup had never happened and all I know is that I have to see him, have to have him, have to feel him fill me the way his voice is filling the emptiness inside.

"You wanna come over?" For a split second I worry about his personal obstacles to being with me, but I erase them from my mind when he asks for my address. For all I know, they are separated, I rationalize, though I know they probably aren't because it would have been in the news, but I am like water rushing to Andrew's shore, unable to do anything but be with him.

I give him directions and run around frantically trying to straighten my apartment and myself as he announces over the phone every major intersection he drives through. I feel like a small boat listening to the radar of an oncoming sub. When he pulls onto my street, Andrew sounds completely flummoxed that a parking space isn't waiting for him in front of my building. I suggest he look a bit farther down the block, but for an irrational moment I think he might leave. Maybe it has become standard in L.A. for late night trysts to include valet parking. He declares triumph as he pulls into a space, sounding astonishingly proud for so simple a feat. I tell him that I need to hang up now, but he sounds hurt, so I explain that my line has to be open for him to call me from the gate. How long had he intended for us to stay on the line? Maybe there is some new kind of in-person phone sex he wanted to try.

I can hear his footsteps coming up the stairs and with each step my heart beats faster and faster like it is doing the tarantella inside me. Then a gentle knock is on the door and I open it and Andrew comes in as naturally and majestically as the sun rising on the day. We look at each other as his brightness fills the room.

"Look at you," he finally says. "You look even more beautiful and younger now than you used to." I have to stop myself from running over to a mirror; maybe that erasing thing is doing more than I thought. "I bet you don't look much different than that when you're my age and then—you die."

He makes a little laugh, I think to make me laugh, but I don't think it is funny. I am looking at his great face, and for the first time, I see the age on it and suddenly understand something I never contemplated before—what lines on a face actually lead to. Such an obvious answer—the end for us all—but one I never thought about until he spelled it out to me so clearly. I move to him and bury my face in his neck, kissing him again and again while I take off my clothes and undo his pants.

At first when he keeps his sweater on, I figure he is still warming up, but after a while I wonder if it is his body's temperature or years he is trying to adjust. As much as I want to feel his bare chest against me, the cashmere screen of his sweater becomes another layer of his skin.

Our motions are one, and a kind of multiple time thing happens where past and future and present are here with us, moving with us, coming with us into one endless space where they can always be.

An air pocket of time has filled my apartment, floating us out of the usual dimension, letting us exist in our own realm. Lying with him afterward, rubbing his back as he lies on my stomach, I realize that I had always believed that at a certain predetermined age some other, different older body would descend on top of mine, taking over who I am and rendering me completely gone. That my life and self and sex as I knew it would end and suddenly "old" would begin. That isn't true with Andrew at all. Everything is so much the way it had been, just a deeper, more layered continuum of his body with me and my body with him. I feel I am able to peek ahead at how growing older will be—experiencing through him a physical reality that I had always thought would erase me even before I was gone.

"How're Momma and Suzanne?"

"Momma's dead almost three years now." I had wanted to call him when she died, but never could.

"Good God, how? She was young."

"Yeah, fifty-one."

"Jesus." I know he is thinking that he's seven years older than that.

"Car accident. Drunk driver drove straight into her four blocks from her house. Two o'clock in the afternoon. We couldn't get her to go anywhere once Daddy left, then a drive to the grocery store ended her life."

"I am so sorry. How're you doing with it?"

"Fine now. The grief was horrendous, but—"

"Did your daddy ever show back up?"

"No." We are quiet. The immersion of his time on me is a salve. "Suzanne's married a few months now."

He pulls his head up and looks at me with his chin resting on his hands and his elbows resting on the bed, straddling me. "Why aren't you married?"

He has said it genuinely, but I have no idea how to respond. It reminds me of the times I'm driving my truck on Beverly Boulevard and I stop to offer a ride to one of the older, Jewish women waiting for the bus. They're never going very far, Cedars Hospital usually, so they get in and we ride along, making small talk, but the only thing they ever ask me is, "So, are you married?" Then when I say, "No," the only thing they want to talk about is that I'm not, as if every other part of my life has been erased, never to be seen again.

"I don't know."

"You are going to make a great mother and wife."

That surprises me so much that my hands jump on his back, but I try to incorporate it into his massage so he can't tell.

"When I first met you in New York . . ." I watch him look at the memory of me from back then. There is a kind, soft smile on his face that looks exactly the way it used to feel to speak to him in those days. "You were such a scared little bunny. Big eyes caught in the headlights. That's one reason I didn't have sex with you that whole time. I couldn't, you were so innocent; that was rare. I knew you weren't like all the others."

His kisses my stomach, as my hands on his back rub deeply into him.

"Did you think about me, Andrew, during all these years?"

"What do you think?" He looks at me again, his eyes such a startling shade, peering into a depth of me that I don't like going into alone.

"I don't know. Did you? Miss me?"

"Of course I did."

And all those years without him are gone, like some horrible dream I woke up wrongly believing.

"I had a dream last night that I was making love to you."

When I answered the phone, jumped on it really in hopes it was Andrew, I had been dreamily stumbling around my living room, picking up my discarded clothing and reliving last night. I have forsaken my daily oatmeal—enough with those goddamn grains—but not my coffee and am still in the slip I pulled on after Andrew left around twelve-thirty A.M. I was too keyed up to sleep, too much wanted to feel the aftereffect of him in my bed and on my body before the physical imprints disappeared and while they were ingraining themselves in my memory.

But it is Reggie's voice saying words I never thought I'd hear from him and certainly never wanted to. I wish they were from Andrew and really, really not from Reggie.

"Oh." This comes out like the audio version of sneaking down a hall, trying to get from one room to the next while staying out of view. "Well." I have no idea what to say. A wild fantasy of hanging up pops into my head, then when Reggie calls back, I could explain that I didn't recognize his voice and thought it was some romantic crank caller, but for that to work, I would have had to do it immediately and still it wouldn't have because Reggie knows I know his voice from anyone else's. Fuck. My nonresponse and his obvious waiting for one are going on for too long. I have to say something, but what?

"I had sex with Andrew last night."

It is all I can do to keep from adding, "So I guess he did remember my name after all." And okay, there probably were gentler ways I could have broken the news, but it just jumped out, and even if it hadn't, why can't I tell Reggie like that? Because he goes ballistic and acts personally wounded whenever I have sex with any man, and in particular, stories about Andrew really send him through the roof. But Reggie's my best friend, for God's sake, so he shouldn't tell me he wants to have sex with me and I should be able to tell him anything.

"I can't believe you did that." He sounds hurt, angry, and shocked—everything I don't want him to be. "He's married for Christ's sake, Yvette, with children. How could you be such a common—"

"Don't you dare use that word." It's a toss-up as to which one he was going to fling at me, but I don't want to hear any of them spoken in his voice. I know that it is only a matter of time before my own head starts calling me every name in the book. This morning around five A.M., I finally let myself start wondering where Andrew's wife was while he was with me, thinking of her by name feels too personal and depressing after being with him. I worried about her for a while, feeling guilty and dreadful, then finally fell into a fitful sleep for two hours.

"He's never leaving his wife, he told me that—"

"Oh, well, that's good. So it's okay, then."

"Reggie."

"What?"

"Okay, yes, I made a mistake. I sinned technically—"

"Technically?"

"Jesus, yes, technically and in every other way it was a sin, okay? I admit it. I broke one of the big Ten and I feel horrible about it, but frankly, it wasn't over between Andrew and me, it never really—"

"Here we go again."

"Think what you want, Reggie, but that's the truth. It never really ended with us—it was just put on hold, so maybe both of them should have made sure that what he had with everyone else was definitely over before they settled down." I stop my pacing and sink onto the couch. "Christ, I mean, yes, it was wrong, but it's not like I think he's going to come back to me and we'll live together happily ever after." Though secretly, a part of me does want to think that, and I know Reggie knows that about me and I wish he didn't. "Andrew never left my life and, obviously, I didn't his."

I can hear the protest in Reggie's intake of breath before he can even voice it.

"Look, it happened, and, okay, it shouldn't have, but . . . but . . ." Suddenly huge tears are falling down my face. "But he was like a father to me. For years, Reggie. God knows what I would have done without him; he was always there for me. Why can't I have what other girls got? Why couldn't I have that?"

"Because he wasn't your father, honey. He had sex with you."

"Fuck you." I want to swipe at the air to tear his words out of it so they won't hang in my apartment where they can be real. "Things aren't always so black and white. People don't always have only one set of feelings for someone they love. Sometimes boundaries blur." As the words leave my mouth, I suddenly have a new clarity about Reggie's feelings for me.

An emptiness captures the line. It doesn't feel like our breathing will ever be in sync again. I look out the window at the tree in the courtyard, wishing its brown limbs and silvery leaves against the blue sky could transport me.

"I think we need to not have conversations about this anymore. I can't hear you talk about him. I care about you, Yvette, and all I see is trouble ahead." Reggie's words are like a boat leaving me at the shore.

"That's probably a good idea."

The line is empty. I watch the second hand on my clock sweep through time.

"I'm gonna go; this is uncomfortable."

I start to ask if we'll have breakfast mañana, but it feels inappropriate. "Okay, well, bye."

Reggie hangs up the phone.

"I've been thinking about how beautiful you are."

I was nervous picking up the phone, afraid it was Reggie calling me right back to end our friendship.

"Oh, hey." I immediately am thrilled that it's Andrew, yet something about it feels like I'm running on wet tile around a pool.

"So beautiful. I can't get your face out of my mind—you're all

I've been thinking about." I can feel myself getting warm as his words bathe me.

"I have to leave for the airport to meet my family in New York. But I'll call you when I get back."

"Okay."

"Bye, sweet-y-vette." His voice is sweet and growly just like it used to be.

29

So Andrew is back. In my life again as if he had never gone. Although for the past three weeks, he has been gone in New York City with his family for the holidays, but I feel we're connected. Though I know we shouldn't be. That I shouldn't see him again for all the obvious reasons, but then I tell myself that I don't know where this is going, maybe it will be like when we first met—sex once, then platonic. A friend, he can be. A mentor, someone to guide me. What's wrong with that? So I'll just let things unfold and not worry about where it will go. Though I think about him constantly.

Especially during the holidays, it was impossible to distract myself with anything else. Except I did notice that Reggie didn't call on New Year's Eve, our anniversary, which is the first time that's happened. I know I could've called him, but the tradition was that he did and I wanted to see if he would. I kept checking my messages from the parties I went to, but there was nothing from him. Or from Andrew. Which felt shitty and I tried not to care—he was with his family in New York City—but at that point, it had been two weeks since I'd seen or spoken to him.

Now it's been three and I'm starting to jones pretty badly to hear his voice again. His presence has been hovering over my life all this time like those high and beautiful clouds that never actually rain. The kind I see in the winter particularly when I'm stuck on the 10 freeway like I have been twice a week for over a month to go to boxing. I found a place in Santa Monica right off the 10 before it hits the PCH. An old rock star's gym that he keeps running so he can use it whenever he's in town. It doesn't charge much to train, you just have to know someone to get in, and Bill, my old music-producer boss, hooked me up.

Looking at my jewelry in the display case at Greeley's is how I had always hoped it would feel to be in an art gallery show. My work is displayed perfectly. Each piece is showcased under beautiful light, set against a complementary background with ample space around it, but close enough to the others that while you get a sense of each one's uniqueness, you still see the greater unity. No gallery owner to show it incorrectly.

It is all I can do not to yell out to the shoppers bustling around, "That's my jewelry!" The pearls are dazzling; the lemon citrine, green peridot, and blue tourmaline are winking; and the braided gold is gleaming. None of it existed a few months ago and now here it all is. I have an almost physical urge, like reaching for my morning coffee, to call Reggie to share this with him. I wonder if things will ever stop being weird between us. I miss him.

"What are you doing?"

I had been hoping it'd be Andrew every time the phone rang, but I figured it might be Reggie finally calling me back after I left a message for him two days ago.

"Are you back?" My heart has multiplied and is beating on every part of my body.

"Got in last night." Andrew's voice is like a bed I want to crawl into.

"That's good." Though what I meant was, "Thank God."

"Did you miss me?"

"Every single day."

"So, so, tell me . . ." Then a pause we could lie down in and have sex during. "Who are you fucking?"

Besides you? I think, but don't say. "Uh, no one really." I sit down on my couch, wishing he were next to me. "I was involved with this guy, Michael, for a while—"

"Michael who?"

"Newman, you don't know him, he runs a public radio station, and there've been other guys, but—"

"You are going to make a great wife and mother someday."

After we hang up the phone—Andrew gave me his cell number if I really need to reach him, but it's better if he calls me—his words float in my head. I wonder why he thinks that and am surprised at how much what he said means to me, because it sounds so embarrassingly June Cleaver—a role I don't picture for myself. Except with him, and that was a dream I buried a long time ago. Though part of me still wishes it could live. Fuck. I wish Andrew hadn't unearthed in me this whole wife/mother idea. Suzanne getting married was bad enough, though I thought I did a good job of keeping that longing away from myself, but maybe it has been there waiting to come screaming out. I don't want to want that again with him. But I can't imagine wanting that with someone else. Though at some point, I guess I'll have to.

"Your line has blown out of the store, there's nothing left." Linda Beckman's voice on the phone is like a fairy godmother in my best fantasy. "I want the exact same order in our new Honolulu store, and this time we'll pay up front, but P and A is still on you, of course."

When I hang up with Linda, I immediately call Dipen to tell him that I want the same order, super-rushed. I'll need more pearls and semiprecious stones, but with this windfall, I can stock up and not worry. Life is dreamy.

30

The first thing Andrew does the second time he comes over is search my apartment. He didn't do that the first time he was here, on my birthday. Then he only saw my living room, bedroom, and bathroom, but as I watch him move through my apartment, half peeking in, half peeking out of the doorways, I wonder if this is some famous-person version of seeing someone's home. Either that, or he's checking for intruders. But how dangerous does he think our city is? Okay, we've got our bad neighborhoods, but my bedroom isn't one of them. Anyway.

Being with him again after two months apart was like when we first met, plus our whole relationship all at once. The sex contained every minute of it. The kissing was drinking in every moment we'd been apart, and our moving and touching were like water thrown into the ocean, we were unable to un-merge again.

"Tell me," Andrew says, "I want to hear everything."

We are lying on my bed, his chest is on my stomach, my hands on his back, and I weave for him the story of my line selling out of Beverly Hills and getting into the Hawaii store while I knead the muscles of his back.

"So your art's become jewelry or jewelry is your art, I should say." He pulls his head up and looks at me with his illustrious eyes. "I want to see."

I am glad that my body is held securely beneath his, because otherwise I would have fallen off the bed hearing him finally mention my art. "Now?"

"As opposed to?"

I get up and walk out of the bedroom. In the studio, I crouch in front of the safe and spin the dial. The floor feels refrigerated under my bare feet, the steely-cold February night pressing into the room through the windows, but I am warm and even sweating a little at the thought of what I am doing. Showing Andrew my jewelry reveals my physical nakedness to be the easy exposure that it is. I feel the same prickliness under my skin, the same clenching of my stomach, as when he looked at my slides at the Ritz-Carlton. I put the samples from my new line—earrings and bracelets, rings, necklaces and pins—into a felt-lined tray and arrange them perfectly.

As I walk down the hallway to my bedroom, I look down at the jewelry and their colors begin soothing me, the weight of them in the tray, the work I put into them that can't be taken away. I enter the room and see that Andrew is sitting up in my bed, leaning against the headboard, gazing at me as only he can, way down inside.

He swings his legs around and sits on the side of the bed, and I sit next to him, putting the tray in his lap. As he picks up each piece, he is silent the way he was the only other time he has ever looked at my work.

There are no taxis driving through a park outside my window for me to count, nothing distracting enough in my bedroom to take my attention, so I sit and watch him examining my world. His brow is furrowed as he holds each piece, looking at it from all angles.

"Beauty hanging in the air," he says, and holds a pearl and tourmaline necklace out toward me as if putting it in context. "Like you. You're doing great—I can tell."

I blush. He is the only person who has ever created that response in me, as if certain emotions were staked out and claimed by him.

Andrew puts his hand over mine and looks me in the eyes. "If you and I were where we are now, but just back then—I would never have let you go." And he pauses for a moment, dividing everything before and since. "You're a heavyweight."

The tray of jewelry on his lap holds rings of everlasting gold with wedding-white pearls, as he talks about what could have been for us.

Lying in bed after Andrew has gone, I think about how I was back then, and I finally understand his inability to commit to me. I wouldn't have fit into his world at all. I would have become a kind of mute appendage of him. Would never have discovered creating jewelry and the joy it brings me. So in a weird and wonderful and terrible way, maybe that was for the best. But I go to sleep with the words "if we were where we are now, but just back then . . ." filling my head.

When I awaken the next morning, every inch of my apartment is filled up with him. He's only been here twice, but in the rooms where there aren't memories of us, I have memories of the fantasies of us, so it's all here—a kind of parallel life that happens as soon as I open my eyes to the day.

Andrew and I talked every day for two weeks after that night, but then he went to New York, so the phone calls have stopped for the past week, and since he's with his family, I know we can't talk, but this silence will end as soon as he comes back to L.A. I hope to God that it's soon because I am about to lose my mind not speaking to him. Fortunately, I've been busy getting the order ready for Hawaii, though not distracted enough to not think about him every minute.

I am stuck in four-thirty eastbound traffic on the 10. Cars have surged to a stop, but sitting here isn't bothering me too much because I just shipped off my jewelry to Greeley's receiving warehouse to then be sent to Hawaii in time for my early March delivery. Greeley's has a warehouse in west Texas where every item must go to be processed, then directed to the appropriate store. Even when my jewelry was going across town to Beverly Hills, it first had to make a journey to Texas before it could be shipped here. Getting the order inventoried, packed, and shipped to Greeley's specifications was like doing a tax return with lots of those frightening schedule forms. I wish Andrew were back in town so he could come over tonight to celebrate with me—or even just call me, so I can tell him about it. How long is this damn New York trip going to last? I wish I could fly down to Honolulu and see my jewelry in the store. But even with the check for the sales in Beverly Hills, the amount of inventory I just invested in for this order was large, so I should be conservative until it blows out of the Honolulu store—please, God. The cars in front of me have barely moved. I suddenly realize that I'm not stuck in traffic—I am traffic.

I am also famished. I skipped lunch to make my deadline, so as I inch toward the Robertson Boulevard exit, I decide to get off and find some food.

Daydreaming about my jewelry being in every Greeley's store—there are nine across the country, dotting the map like bright lights of style—keeps me driving north on Robertson and forgetting my hunger until I'm in the fashionable shopping district almost at Beverly Boulevard. I notice that across from Wisteria and its eternally sun-drenched patio is a café I've never seen before. I pull into a parking spot—a miracle on this street after eleven A.M.—and walk in.

The café's interior could have been airlifted from SoHo. There are tons of that very tiny white tile with deep blue accents and heaps of stainless steel. I walk toward the glass-fronted deli case and see to my right a section of white-clothed tables set with deep blue linen napkins and yellow roses in French jelly jars. Light streams in through tall windows that have red geraniums growing in weathered window boxes. Every dish in the deli case is gorgeous. Salads and seafood and tarts and pastas and vegetables with incredible things done to them—the kind of food I like to think I will someday make, but doubt I ever will. There isn't another person in sight. It's that funny nontime for restaurants between lunch and dinner, and as I gaze at the different delicacies, I wonder if they are even open.

"See anything you like?"

I look up into clear blue eyes refracting the light. The man who owns them is tall with dirty-blond hair and looks like he came from the Brittany coast with his strong jaw and cheekbones, rugged but refined.

"Everything looks amazing and I'm starved. What do you suggest?"

"The artichoke pesto penne is really good."

"Sounds great."

"You like salad? I'll put some greens with walnut and mandarin orange in for you."

"Thanks."

"Don't worry about it." As he arranges large portions in a takeout box, his strong back and arms are apparent under the white of his chef's shirt. I look back in the deli case as if fascinated by its contents to keep from staring at him.

"So, when did this place open?"

"Three and a half weeks ago. Do you work around here?"

"No, I design jewelry. My line's not in these stores, but Greeley's just picked it up."

"That's great—that's a big deal."

"Oh, thanks." I look up into his eyes, and they are waiting for mine to join them. For a moment, I have to remember to breathe. "Well. So, what do I owe you?"

"That'll be six dollars and eighty-nine cents."

As I try to figure out if that's right—according to the prices on the large blackboard, it seems he only charged me for one item—I discover that I'm out of cash, so I pull out a credit card.

"Our machine's not hooked up yet." His eyes are still on mine like they belong there.

"Oh, God, well, this is embarrassing, but I'm out of cash and left my checkbook at home. I'm sorry you went to all that trouble."

"Don't worry about it." He puts two pieces of baguette into the bag with the food, folds it closed, and hands it to me. "Here."

"I can't let you do that, bosses and profits and all."

"Take it. Enjoy your dinner."

I will if I think about you during it, I think as I take the bag from his large, strong hand. "That's incredibly sweet of you. Thanks so much."

And he smiles at me. A tangible smile. Like it could leave with me, too.

As I pass the café's large front window, I want to see him one more time, so I look inside, pretending it is for another thank-you in the form of a wave. His eyes are already on mine and he lifts his hand to wave before I do.

It has been five weeks since I have seen Andrew and three weeks since we have spoken on the phone. Every day I have to resist not calling his cell phone. He'll call when he's back, I keep telling myself, just like after his last trip. But maybe he's already back and isn't going to call. No, he wouldn't do that. He's never done that. But maybe he's decided he can't see me anymore, which I guess is best for me and definitely for his wife, but to not even call isn't like him, but maybe that's how he ends things. No, he's just still in New York on some crazy extended trip and I'll hear from him. Please God.

Every day I force myself into my studio to work on commissions, or I drive downtown in a daze of Andrew thoughts to pick up work from Dipen. I found a woman to do a Web site for me, so I need to get pictures of the jewelry together and write copy and I still need to go over Greeley's arcane accounting for the Beverly Hills sales, not to mention see how Honolulu is doing, but my mind is a constant blur about

Andrew. I spend lots of time staring at the phone, like it is my mortal enemy for not ringing with him at the other end of the line, while wishing it would and thinking magical thoughts, like "In this next ten minute period, Andrew will call." Or "If I think about him hard enough, that energy will connect to him and he'll call."

I am screaming at the top of my lungs, staring at the empty spot in my bedroom where the black-clad apparition stood. The vision has already faded before my open eyes, but I still give the scream one last burst of energy as if that will make it go away permanently.

"I finally saw something this time." I am spooning oatmeal into a bowl, the phone is at my ear, and after I pour soy milk in, I take the bowl to the living room and sit on the couch to look at the tree (my tree, as I think of it) outside the window while I talk to Reggie. He isn't sipping through a straw anymore, but the crunchy sounds I'm hearing from his end of the line indicate that he hasn't gone back to sausage and eggs. Grape-Nuts, probably. We have tentatively been having telephonic breakfast together again for the last week and so far it's been okay. As long as I don't talk about Andrew.

"So tell me already, the suspense is killing me."

"Some kind of a figure, a man, all in black, near my bed. And menacing. Then he disappeared."

Reggie is quiet for a moment, then softly says, "Yvette, are you having some kind of a memory come up? About your father, I mean?"

"Oh, God, no. I mean, okay, fine, I have some Daddy issues, who wouldn't with the way he took off." I know Reggie is thinking about my relationship with Andrew as more living proof of that, but I decide to ignore that. "But my father never did anything like that to me. I mean, look, I met a woman once at SVA who was an incest survivor and she told me about this therapy group she was in and convinced me that I should check it out, maybe uncovered stuff would come up. So I went a few times and not only didn't anything come up, but I didn't relate to it. The symptoms they have and everything."

Reggie says nothing, so I know he is still convinced his theory is right.

"I just hope they stop soon, honey."

"So do I."

31

It has gotten to the point that no matter why I am on the 10 freeway, the minute I pass the 405 interchange heading west, I feel it. Fear, really. Dread. A kind of internal backing up. My body thinks it is going to the boxing gym, where I've been going twice a week since November, even if I'm not. Because I am going to get hit at the gym, and my body knows this. I can think all I want about mouth guards and body pads, big pillowy gloves that will never break skin, but the reality is that I am going to get hit. On purpose. Repeatedly.

The fear and dread feels kind of like as a kid when I had to learn how to swim. I was terrified of that. Though I loved playing in the water. I just didn't want to learn how to swim. "Put your face in the water," the swimming teacher would say. But I didn't ever want my face in the water. To this day, I cannot take a shower without a dry cloth nearby. God forbid I am ever on a sinking ship—I'll be grabbing towels to take to the lifeboat. Just keep my face dry. I have no idea why.

And not only am I going to get hit, but I am being trained to stay forward, closer to the hit. To move, certainly, away from the hits—run and hide is what I want to do, but I ignore that logical instinct and choose to believe my coach as he repeatedly yells to me that the closer I am to my opponent, the less effective his punches will be. No time or space for their impact to build up in. "For it to become something," he always says.

So if something happens only once, it could be a fluke, an odd beat out of sync with time, but if that same thing occurs a second time, then a rhythm is established and from that I can kind of tell when it will happen again. This works for anything: scream dreams, right hooks, sex with someone. Andrew and I had been on an eight-week rhythm method thing, established by that first night we were together in December and then the second time in February that made the weeks in between those two dates mean something. Eight weeks without him that moved interminably forward through time suddenly landed and connected me on him. Him on me. Again. But now we have skipped what should have been our third time of seeing each other according to the eight-week rhythm we were on. Now there is a long, silent ten-week pause, which, God knows, rhythms can have—thank you, John Cage—but I am stuck waiting for the beat and hating this rhythm of waiting.

On my third try, I finally get the manager of Greeley's jewelry department in Honolulu on the line.

"Right, Broussard's Bijoux, that's that line of pearls and semiprecious stones?"

That's encouraging—maybe since she's familiar with the line, everything flew out of there, too.

"Well, I hate to tell you this, but your line's just been sitting in the display cases, not budging at all."

For the first time, maybe to distract myself from the horror of her words, I can hear her Chicago accent. I imagine her gladly abandoning that wintery land with fantasies of starting a new life, only to have a similar one, sans snow, on the big island.

"It's not a very sophisticated crowd we get down here. In L.A., I can see how this stuff would work, but Honolulu is mostly tourists and they aren't going to spend upward of five hundred dollars for a piece of jewelry. And the locals, well, pearls are everywhere. Tahiti's so close by, this market's pretty flooded. I don't know what that buyer in the forty-eight was thinking. I told them when they hired me to open this store to let me do my own ordering, but you know how these big stores are."

"So will you put them on sale? What's going to happen?" I want to fly down there and rescue them, as if they were a child who was left at an inappropriate house over night.

"I have to wait and see what they decide. They usually give stock a three-month cycle, so you have a couple more weeks till the end of May. And who knows, one customer could come in and buy the whole thing. Not that I'm counting on it."

I hang up the phone and immediately call Reggie.

Driving on the 10 at one-thirty A.M. is like being among the die-hard dregs of a crowd after a rock concert has ended. Not many other vehicles are around, but the ones that are appear just as needy for this experience not to end as I am. I've made the loop past the downtown skyscrapers three times now and even that hasn't made a dent in the despair and almost physical pain I am in, so I am flying on the 10 heading west to the beach. I'll take the PCH up to Topanga, cut through the canyon, then pick up the 101 in the Valley and take it home. Hopefully that'll be a long enough drive. I told myself that I couldn't sleep because of the godforsaken news from Honolulu, but really it's because I haven't talked to Andrew in eleven weeks.

I can barely face what I am terrified this means. Maybe he isn't ever going to call me again. He can't be in New York this long. I've scoured newspapers and magazines for some hint of a project he or his wife could be doing, but there's been nothing. I could just call his cell phone and hope that he can talk, but that feels risky for his situation and desperate about mine. He's always called before. Even when I walked out on him that night at his house and stopped answering my phone, he called for a month, so why this silence now? Maybe he really did decide that we shouldn't see each other. I just can't believe he didn't say goodbye.

Every time I check my phone messages, I automatically pray to hear that little "hunh" that means that Andrew called. Instead, this morning I get "Hi, Yvette, it's me. There's an opening at the museum tonight and I figured you might wanna go. Call me."

For a split second I think how sweet of Michael to invite me, but then I am wearied by it. I wonder what will have to change in my life for him to stop calling out of the blue. Maybe getting married. If I ever do.

"We think your line will do better in other stores." Linda Beckman's voice over the phone is explaining Greeley's decision to me.

"Stores? So the line's going to be split up?"

"White Plains, Miami, and Houston. Those markets are much better for your work—more sophisticated. I'll figure out who gets what. Don't worry, I won't leave it to the people in Hawaii to ship whichever pieces to whatever store."

"Thanks," I say, trying to sound like that's a relief, though this situation is making my stomach sick.

After finding out from Linda when the stores will each get a third of my line, like a head here, the torso there, arms and legs way over there, I hang up.

Oh, Jesus God. A horrible remembered vision of my jewelry in Lizzie's shop comes to mind. A few pieces in a jumbled display case with no context, just jammed up next to any old jewelry. I tell myself that Greeley's, known for their high-end fashion, is not going to dump pieces somewhere and not display them well. I hope.

I walk into my studio to tackle my work for the day, and decide to check my e-mail while I finish my third cup of coffee. But instead of some wonderful, life-altering news, it is the usual spam, customers checking on commissions, and one "inspirational" note forwarded from Suzanne saying, Don't tell God how big your problems are, tell your problems how big God is. Then it goes on about a little boy in Phoenix who had leukemia and wanted to be a fireman, and how he got to be one for a day, and then a week later as he lay dying, the fire chief came to his hospital bed, held his hand, and told the little boy that he was a real fireman now, because the big chief, Jesus, was waiting for him in heaven.

I feel even worse after I read it. Why does she send me these things? I never know how to respond. "Thanks for the reminder that innocent children are dying terrible, senseless deaths every day—hope your day is going great, too." I don't think Suzanne would appreciate that. Then I feel shitty because I know she means well, and I guess if she were capable of a simple, "Hey sis, what's up?" e-mail she'd send that, so I guess she's not. I suddenly feel so separated from her. And from my jewelry that is being sent all over the country. And a whole, whole, whole lot from Andrew. As I shut down the e-mail program, I have to fight the urge to go to the couch, lie down, and not ever get up.

It has been fourteen weeks since I've heard Andrew's voice and all I want is to see his face in front of me. Instead I am looking at big, pillowy gloves coming straight at my head. Not at the same time. My partner's first combination is right jab, left hook, right hook, which I am supposed to swerve from. Okay, it's not called "swerve." Or "duck," which is the only other word I can think of, but something that I can never remember what they call it when you move out of the way, but in that very specific boxer way where you're gone, but still near, so you can hit them back. It has to do with the rhythm of your weight. How quickly and easily you can shift so you're gone when they're there, but right there before they're gone. I'm still learning.

And the worst part is that I can't hit back. We're taking turns—my partner, Dave, and I. He's on offense, so I'm defense. Dave's a seventeen-year-old . . . kid, I guess you call them. I don't know. I never hung around one that age before because I jumped over that group when

I was fourteen, and going to that all-girl Catholic school, I just never saw one this close up. But here Dave is, with legs like a man, hands still young, every part of his body looking a different age, like someone hit the random button on the CD player of his growth. It's his turn to punch and my turn to shift my rhythm and move my weight toward him, which is the trick, see, because that's when you can switch from just being in the getting-hit-but-trying-to-cover defense role to the yes-your-punches-are-so-in-my-face-but-I'm-moving-toward-you-backing-you-up-while-effortlessly-missing-your-hits-ready-to-make-my-own position.

But that is not happening. What is happening is that Dave's punches are hitting me. Not hard. He's got big, pillowy gloves. I've got a mouth guard. I'm able to do some swerving-duck, but still I am getting hit. Repeatedly. On purpose. And I start getting annoyed. He's seventeen. Energy comes out of nowhere on him like growth spurts shooting out his hands, but I'm trying. I'm stepping forward, shifting the weight, moving my head. It's very hot. My face is melty and wet. I swerve another duck, glance up, and catch Dave smiling at me. Hard. Happy about all this. And suddenly, I start to cry. Silently, but cry. Which I realize is a tactic Tyson and Ali have never used, probably because it doesn't work, although maybe Dave can't tell I'm crying because my face was already quite wet, but now tears are adding lots more, then my nose joins in this liquid fest, but still I try to change my rhythm and shift my weight, which is right when his left hook nails me, busting my lip against the safe mouth guard.

I can tell he feels rotten. So does the coach whose back was turned when it happened. I consider sticking around to make them feel better, but all I want to do is leave and maybe never return. I promise them I'll go to Cedars Hospital, but, honest to God, I just want to go home. I take the towel they give me with the ice wrapped in it, get in my truck, and speed to the 10 where anything can get blotted out if I ride it long enough.

Andrew has been out of my life as fast as he came in. I keep telling myself this is for the best. He's married with two children. Stay away.

He must have come to that decision, too. He told me that first night we were together in December that he had been good, his word for not sleeping around. Until me, I thought. So it's good that he hasn't called me in three and a half godforsaken months. I just wish I completely felt that way.

I skipped my exit. The sign snuck by me like those subliminal ads you hear about in films, so I get off at Hoover to turn back around. I decide to check my messages while pretending to myself that I'm not hoping one from Andrew is miraculously there. I hook back onto the 10 as my answering machine clicks on.

Suzanne's voice is telling me that she tried to reach me on my cell phone, Jesus, she wishes I would leave it on, just call her immediately. I am almost at my exit and consider waiting until I'm home to call her back, but she sounds angry, frantic, and scared all at once so I punch in her number, as trepidation makes a wider space in my stomach than I can hold because Suzanne's voice sounded exactly as it did when she called to tell me about Momma's—

"Hello?" My sister is practically shouting.

"Hey, it's me, what's wrong?" I try to sound normal, hoping my tone will force her answer to be normal, but my words are hindered by the towel-wrapped ice and my enlarged lip getting in the way.

"Why are you talking like that?"

"It's nothing, I'm fine. My lip got hit in boxing tonight, but it's nothing, I'm—"

"Boxing?" Like I said I was in the Arctic, she made it sound that far-fetched.

"Suzanne, what happened, why'd you—"

"Daddy died."

"What?"

"Dad-dy died." She spit the syllables out.

"No, Suzanne, no." The trepidation has kicked itself inside out and is knocking me down from within, as fear, panic, and dread shoot out from it.

My sister is silent as I move my truck over to the shoulder of the 10.

I am astonished that some part of my brain was untouched enough to heed a long-ago-heard safety advice—when in danger on a highway, pull to the side.

"Where? When? From what?" It is too impossible. Time and distance from my father have disappeared, leaving the irrational thought that I was just about to see him, was finally going to get to see him. I suddenly realize I have been dreading this news for years.

"Florida somewhere, a few months ago, I think. Heart attack on the kitchen floor. That woman called to tell me." Suzanne doesn't have to tell me who she means. Ever since Cousin Elsie called Momma to say she saw Daddy in Sarasota, she has been referred to as "that woman."

"Said it had taken her weeks to find me," Suzanne continues. "She wanted to know how Momma died, but I wouldn't say. What a ghoul that woman is—forever calling and bearing bad news."

"Oh, God, oh, God, no. Now I'll never . . ." The silent scream inside me pierces through my skin. I can barely feel my tears. I try to breathe around the panic and fear and dread that are taking all the room inside. Only small areas of my body—fingertips, elbows, heels—have room for my breath to enter and leave. I gasp air in while dispelling sobs, but the two collide. Oxygen squeezes by, just enough to keep me alive. My body is screaming against this information, fighting with punches and hooks and jabs not to know what it has heard.

The silence on the phone is thunderous. If my sister had been speaking, I wouldn't have heard it so clearly.

"I need to finish driving home."

"Are you okay to do that? Maybe you should wait. Where are you anyway?"

I assure her that I'm fine by regulating my breathing to coincide with emitting words—a task so monumental that I have new found awe for our ability to do it without thinking.

I just need to get off the 10, I tell myself as I punch the button to end the call and pull my truck back into the flow of traffic. If I can get home and call her from there, I am sure this news will have changed. A fluke is what it was, like an accident on the highway that will be all cleared up by the time I reach home, the updated report from Suzanne assuring me of Daddy's noninjury.

I immediately listen to my messages again when I get home. I hear Suzanne's first dreadful one that I hung up on without erasing, then I wait to hear a "Call me back; the news I told you was wrong" message from her, but it isn't there. I take the towel off my lip and open it up. The ice has mostly melted; small chips of it are stuck in the white thread among specks of my blood. My lip feels pillowy large, but hard. The pain is forming a concrete mass inside. I dial Suzanne's phone number with a mixture of hope and dread. She picks up on the first ring.

"Good, you made it; I was worried."

I wait for her to say something else, but she doesn't. The news about our father hasn't changed.

"Should we go home?" Then I immediately realize that was dumb.

"Home? Where and to what? He's not there anyway. Who knows what plot of land in Florida he's buried in."

Oh, God. The body. My father's body is no longer him, hasn't been since he died God knows when, yet that is what I want. The body to bury, to watch it go in, to throw myself on it one last time, one last contact since when? To honor it at its end, a goodbye to his physical self. The self that I derive from. I have no idea where my father's spirit is, nor where what it inhabited is. He is displaced in his death from me, just like in life, but I guess not for him and that feels even worse.

"I'm gonna go."

"Do you want us to come over? You don't sound good. Or want to come stay here?"

I can't bear to see Suzanne's face, to see any likeness of him, the likeness I always delighted in: his nose, the shape of his eyes, a certain grin. I can't see them on her, so alive and well, knowing that those on him have been set loose like homing pigeons never to reach their intended end. "No, I'll be fine. I'll call you, okay?"

After a few minutes of convincing my sister that I'll be okay, and assuring her that I am keeping ice on my lip—which I'm not because what's one small injury on my body when my daddy's body is dead?—I call Reggie. My sadness-terror rushes forward to meet him when the phone stops ringing. I'm reassured to hear his voice, but crushed that it's his machine.

"Reggie, it's Yvette." There is small comfort in the facts of our names, though I worry he won't be able to understand my lip-busted speech. I realize I'll have to enunciate each word, and just thinking of that is painful on every level. "My . . ." I can't continue. "Daddydied" has become one word. "My . . ." My mouth twists out to make the next sound, but a noiseless sob catches it, distorting it from saying what I can't. "Dead." Okay, that's part of it. I gulp some air. It hits my lungs for the first time in what feels like years. "Dad." I try to get the "dy" out. I've always hated the word "Dad." It sounds so done with, so obligatorily child-of. I have never wanted to call my father that ever and definitely not now. The "dy" comes out as "me." But at least sounds are escaping, if I pause and say nothing Reggie's machine will cut me off, and I know I won't be able to start this message all over again. "Will you call me?" There is meager relief in getting a full sentence out and the routine sounds of that one helped. "Maybe you could come over or I could come there?" I am begging and hate that I am, but I feel a kind of all encompassing insecurity that I never before have. And he did come over when Momma died. "Please call me, okay? Okay, bye."

I hang up the phone reluctantly. I wish I could just stay on his answering machine, connected to him via the phone line until he comes home and picks it up, then will come here and be with me. But the phone is in its cradle and I am sitting on my couch alone. The clock reads nine-fifteen. What a truly horrendous time to find out my father is gone from this earth. It is too early in the evening for me to know what I know. I am certain that earlier in the day or later at night would have made this manageable somehow.

At least Reggie is fanatical about his phone messages. Maybe before he gets home, he'll check from a pay phone, then drive over here. Please, God. I wish Andrew's arms were holding me in a way that never lets go even when the arms have to.

I curl up on my couch, retreating into it as far back as I can. Like

I'm on a precipice from the world's unendurable drop. The wet, now warm towel is pressed to my lips. It's no longer doing any good, but it's comforting, like holding on to a rail.

I can feel my mind trying to back up and move away from this knowledge that it doesn't want to know. And the knowledge has started moving everywhere inside me, rerouting itself to reach my body's cells, but they are in flight—shooting every which way before this information can catch them. They don't want to know that the two who made them—made me—are dead and gone. Life is not an inextinguishable right. Both of my parents are no longer here, therefore one day, neither will I be and vaporized into where?

I stare across the living room and find minuscule safety in this position, so I hold the gaze, not ever dropping it, while waiting and hoping and praying for my phone to ring, for Reggie to be here, for anything to happen that could somehow obliterate this demise, to see someone who has one parent left, who can still sometimes lie to themselves that the end doesn't come whenever it decides.

I still haven't heard from Reggie. It's been twenty-four hours since I left my swollen-lip jumbled message on his machine. Could something've happened to him, too? Jesus, not a one-two punch of tragedy, I think as I dial. As I leave Reggie another message, the speaking reopens my lip and blood comes pouring out. The Band-Aid I put on feels oppressive, a reminder of the risk from any communication I make.

I have just hung up the phone when it rings, so I answer it quickly, hoping it's him immediately calling back.

"Our father's been dead to me for a very long time," Suzanne says. "This changes nothing as far as I'm concerned."

Then why'd you sound so flipped out when you told me? I want to ask, but don't because it is difficult to keep thoughts in my head long enough for a second sentence to follow a first.

"So, no, I don't want to do some kind of service with you," my sister continues. "I've moved on already."

How very efficient of you, I think as we get off the phone, having nothing more to say to each other, though volumes are being transmitted by the sheer act of our hanging up.

My body is beaten up and stiff from the crumpled pose I stayed in on the couch all night long, and my lips are swollen and throbbing red. I can feel my entire body's internal width and depth fully defined by the aching and soreness. I'm hungry without appetite; exhausted without sleepiness.

My mind is stuck. It recoils from what it knows, then moves awkwardly ahead when I have to speak or perform a task. Backward and forward in a herky-jerky mode. I am frightened that if I don't somehow jar myself, I'll stay in this disconnected to-and-fro groove. I need to talk, to walk, to move through a prescribed course of events, and see the specific sight I never have before, my father in a coffin, for my mind to believe and interpret this event. I need family.

On the fifth day since Daddy died, or since I found out that he died, and having still not heard from Reggie—has he suddenly decided to drop me and is using my father's death as a particularly grisly event to coincide?—so lumping his absence into the barren tundra that is my mind, I decide to go to a funeral from afar. I have no choice. I don't know anyone here who has recently died, and that's a dreadful invitation to want, so it will have to be a stranger's and I'll just keep my distance, like some bad TV movie where the killer appears at the funeral but conspicuously far from the grave.

Which is a bit how this feels—a killer of parts of me that I didn't know even existed before. A cellular longing for my father. An inability to comprehend that he is truly and completely gone. A terror has set in inside me that with him out of this world, I have been unleashed into a void that I won't return from. But at least choosing the outfit for this function is easy: black skirt, black shirt, and black shoes I won't topple over in. Balance has been an issue these past few days, though I guess the lack of sleep and food could have something to do with that. Gloria brought me a fruit salad yesterday. She saw me haggard and bleary at the mailbox, so I told her why before she could imagine the usual reason for that physical state in this town. Though I'd take hungover whore over grieving daughter any day.

I have no idea if there even is a funeral today, but in a city this large, I figure someone has to have died recently. But just the thought of checking the newspaper or making a call to find one exhausts me, so I find a cemetery nearby and hope for the best. Or worst, I should say.

The Normandy cemetery is one of the oldest in Los Angeles. A huge leaping sprawl of land near the 10 by downtown, its sepulture services aren't as fashionable as Forest Lawn's are in Burbank near Warner Brothers and Disney, but giant pine tree branches roam above the graves, a wind is blowing gently, and cobblestone walks twist and sort themselves throughout, taking me past families who have long since dissolved.

The first headstones I study are old and settled into the earth as if the person they represent was meant for nothing more than to claim this land and prevent modernity from growing here. The distance between me here and them there via the death dates is oddly comforting, a silent somber notice of time's impersonal march.

A small black swarm of people catches my eye as they rise on a faraway hill, then vanish over the side. A few stragglers make up the rear. There's one. I head toward them on the winding path, telling myself I'll read more graves later if I feel like it. Driving over, I had the absurd hope of finding a substitute grave for Daddy. One with something similar, the name—Paul's not so hard—or some other sign, to represent Daddy's spirit close by, but at this point, all the tombstones I've read are very much only for the person buried deep inside.

I assume I must be noticeable to the mourners as I walk toward the plot where their ceremony has begun, but hopefully not by much. The purple tent covering the glowing hole in the ground is gaudy above the cemetery's green grass, a flag of grief under the early summer sky.

The funeral I am crashing from a—respectful, I hope—distance has just begun. The gravestones around us are carved in Russian with intricate symbols and letters I can't read. Pictures of the deceased are emblazoned onto the headstones beneath the words, so the dead smile out through glossy marble in the universal language of a countenance.

A wind is blowing the priest's incantations away from me, as traffic noise settles in my ear. I pseudobury my father to the sounds of the 10 freeway.

Bending my head in prayer, I ask Mary to help him find peace and deliver him to rest. My mother's soul I didn't worry about so much, but my father's is a different case.

I suddenly realize that someone is staring at me. I glance up to see an older woman with frazzled hair and a frowning mouth nudge the woman next to her and point at me. My attire is appropriate for the occasion, so it can't be that, though my lip must look really bad—but from this distance, how can she tell? When I was getting dressed I had wished for some kind of hat for my mouth, something to disguise its bad-hair-day-like misshape, but the only thing would have been a gag that really would have been disturbing for mourning.

Then it hits me. I never thought how this might look. An unknown person—a woman, at that—appearing at the graveside. An entirely different TV movie plot than the one I had envisioned spins out in my head. I consider waiting until the end of the funeral and explaining myself to them, but I realize it would sound way too weird, probably even more proof to them that I was sleeping with . . .

Okay, I am feeling guilty for a sin that I didn't commit. At least with him, the deceased. At least, I think it was a him, but maybe souls become sexless, so now he's not any gender.

I feel horrible that I barged into their grief. What was I thinking? Suzanne would be scandalized if she knew. I move toward other graves and look earnestly at names I cannot read. Hopefully that woman won't come over and speak Russian to me. I try to find a marker for someone they won't know that I can pretend to have come to visit and just got distracted by their service. I wish I was a mime, my actions eloquently delivering a new truth I hope they'll believe.

I force myself to sit by a woman's grave—Irina something-I-can't-pronounce, buried in 1934, seems safe—until the funeral ends, then the older, frazzled-hair woman glances surreptitiously at me as the last of the mourning party leaves.

Oh, good God. If Reggie would have called me back this week, he might have come here with me, and I wouldn't have had to worry about all this misinterpretation. Damn him for not calling me; what is his problem? I can't even think about that friendship ending. I never want to visit a cemetery again. I hope Suzanne and Matt aren't buried here. And what if Andrew dies soon and suddenly? He could have a heart attack, too. He's healthy, but who knows? I guess I'd find out the same way I did about his daddy role. That's a funeral I definitely could not attend, especially like I did this one.

Will you stop with these thoughts, please? Let's just keep this to Daddy and stop including everyone else, such as complete strangers burying their kin.

I drive home and fall asleep on the couch. I wake up at five in the afternoon in a room of sadness, a room that springs up and encircles me in its walls wherever I move.

On the one-week anniversary of finding out Daddy died, the only anniversary I will have since his true death date will forever remain unknown to me, like not knowing your birthday and going through life celebrating it when you like, I call Reggie at eight in the morning, our normal time to have breakfast together. I take it as a good/awful sign that he answers his phone. He hasn't the other times I've called thinking I'd leave him another message to pile on top of all the other unanswered ones, but the last few times I hung up.

"Hello." He sounds perfectly casual, so I know he knew it'd be me.

"Hi."

"Hi, Yvette." As if saying my name exemplifies how close we are.

"Why haven't you called me?"

He is quiet for a moment, maybe shocked that I came straight out with it.

"You know, honey, you just expect too much from me. I can't be there for you all the time. Sometimes it has to be about me."

Now I am quiet for a second while this hits me. "My father died." I pronounce each syllable to its fullest sound. The formal noun came out instinctively. "So, yes, I expected you might actually call me back."

"And what am I supposed to do about it?"

That sinks me to the floor; the couch is too high in the air for this. My legs start shaking in anger. "You're right, Reggie, nothing, clearly. Except maybe say hello, ask how I'm doing, hear what happened—the little bit that I know. You could've started by returning my goddamn phone calls and pretending that you give a fuck, since obviously you don't."

"You know that's not true."

"Well, Christ, if this is how you show you care, I hope to God I never have to find out what it's like when you don't. This is brutal enough."

"I'm sorry, all right?"

"I just don't understand why you didn't call me. You showed up for me when Momma died, I can't understand why you wouldn't just call me back. There wasn't even a funeral to fly to."

"This one felt too big for me. I didn't think I could say anything comforting about it. It was your father, for Christ's sake, and now, I mean, both your parents are dead. I had no idea what to say, so I stayed away."

"But anything you say is a comfort to me. All I needed was to know you were there."

Reggie says nothing. The line sounds dead. I wonder if he is back on the protein shakes and has learned to sip them quietly. It still hurts to open my mouth and my appetite isn't back yet anyway.

"Yvette, I'm sorry I didn't call you back when you found out your father died. That must have been horrible. Will you tell me about it now?"

He has asked in the gentle tone that I longed to hear from him a week ago, and as I tell him about it a truce is formed through the information leaving me and becoming part of him, for him to have in his memory, so I don't have to carry it alone.

You just never know with people, I think as I hang up the phone. I had never thought that both of my parents dead might flip Reggie out. When Momma died, I joined a club that he was already in, the club of people with one parent no longer alive. The people I had left outside, the ones still with both parents, had no idea what it was like, so I didn't talk to them about it and I could tell they were glad because they didn't want to hear. I never stopped to think—and now I understand why—that there is an even smaller club to go into, the both-parents-gone tribe, and I guess people with one parent still living don't want to talk to this group, want to stay outside with their last parent standing as long as they can, refusing to believe that this club may actually be home one day to them, and better be home to them because the alternative is their own demise.

I am not going to boxing tonight on this one-week anniversary of finding out about Daddy's death. In fact, I have decided never to go back. Dave and the coach will probably think it is because I got flipped out by being hit, but it's not. It's because my drives home from there will always be associated with discovering that Daddy died and I can't have that memory recurring every time I get on the 10 from that point. I know how to hit now, I have a pretty good right jab, so if anything happens I'm prepared. I mean, obviously, hopefully something won't happen, but I'm prepared if it does, so it probably won't. Those are the odds.

My grief is round and red and jagged inside me. It is exhausting, but I cannot sleep. It has become harder and harder for me to put myself to bed, like a child whose parent has forgotten his job, so I stay on the couch. Push the decorative pillows off, pull the throw down from the back, and settle in. I have stopped attempting to sleep in my bed, and when I fall asleep on the couch, the scream dream follows me there. In the mornings, I peek in at my bedroom, so bright and untouched, like a storeroom display for sleep that can't be bought. I feel like a visitor in there, no longer master of its purpose. I have lost the ability to be in it at night.

In the mornings, I have a truncated conversation with Reggie, sometimes just hello, and not even while we eat. It is hard to know where more pain is emanating from—losing Daddy, Andrew, or Reggie. Though Reggie isn't gone, we just haven't gotten back to where we were. And probably won't. Which I am starting to think is maybe a good thing. Virtual emotional boyfriend is what he was and exactly the problem really.

After a few weeks, I pull myself together enough to think about my jewelry, which has been flung across the country like my father's soul dispersed God knows where.

The last call I make to Greeley's to check on my line is to their Houston store. I figured I'd finish in the South, irrationally hoping that the relative proximity to my birthplace will have a good-luck effect on what they'll tell me.

"I think, yeah, is it the . . . ?" Then the woman's accent gets even more pronounced as she yells away from the phone, "Sally Ann, look over on your side of the case there, hon, is that the Broussard's Bijoux stuff over there? Those pearly necklaces and things. You know, next to the gold add-a-beads."

Pearly necklaces and things. Next to the gold add-a-beads. Oh, good God. Can I fall off a cliff right now?

"Uh-huh, we got 'em. What do ya wanna know?"

We've got all of 'em, she could've said to save her coworker from having to count up the pieces as I waited on the phone while dreading that the numbers were getting higher the longer it took. Not a one had sold. Just like in Miami and White Plains. This was not the news I wanted to hear to cheer me up and give me some security after a godforsaken month of dealing with my father's death. But at least Greeley's had already paid me for them. I just hope Linda will still order more.

I peek at my bank accounts and calculate how much living-time the numbers represent. A couple more months, maybe, but I can already see a sliding-into-broke if nothing comes up. Fuck. Another store is the answer, that is obvious enough. Or new commissions, because I am going to need a cash infusion soon to pay the bills for my business and this apartment that I can't fall asleep in. I pull out my list of private customers and begin addressing envelopes to them that I will put my brochure in, plus a personal note, all the while praying some of them will order new jewelry.

The dream feels real and the scream that accompanies it is real, so it's hard not to believe that they both are, but right before I'm attacked, the vision vanishes and my screaming stops, and I realize it's only the dream, but by then it doesn't matter. I've had the emotions, reacted as if they were real, and the emptiness I'm left with is awful. Maybe the scream dream is trying to wake me up, but to what?

After another night on the couch of not much sleep, I am in my studio doing research on the Internet. The grief I have been in these past five weeks is not ever-present, I do get breaks when I forget my parentlessness, but most of that time, I'm thinking about Andrew, so loss seems to be the general theme. I've decided to embrace this state, which for my new jewelry means jet.

Jet came into prominence during the Victorian era after King Albert died. Queen Victoria went into an extended period of mourning and wore jet jewelry that affected fashion widely. Back then, it was mined in Yorkshire on the coast of England, but the rough jet I can buy downtown to cut into the shapes I want is from Tibet, where the Buddhism I studied originated.

My second cup of coffee is on the table next to me, Beethoven's Third symphony is playing, and I am feeling almost happy to be delving into the realm of a material I've never used before. I draw some designs on my sketch pad, then read on the computer screen about jet's properties. It is a soft material with a hardness factor ranging from two point five to four, which is about what our fingernails have. Every gem is graded on its hardness, which means how resistant it is to being scratched. A diamond has the highest grade of all—a ten—which is why nothing can scratch it, not even steel since it has only a seven. I like that jet doesn't have that superhard quality, especially for my work since part of getting through grief is about not resisting. Though it might be nice to add a semiprecious stone to the jet that would back it up somehow, have a piece of resilience so it isn't all soft. Topaz has a hardness of eight and its smoky brown would be beautiful against jet's soft black.

The Eroica symphony is building to its peak when suddenly a heinous noise cuts through, tearing it in two. I jump off my stool and run out of the studio and down the hall before my mind registers what I've heard—self-preservation if there ever was—but I see it as soon as I turn the corner into my living room. There, through the open windows, in the beautiful silver-green-leafed, silver-brown-barked tree, is a small, dark man wielding a chain saw. Entire branches are falling to the ground. Huge, strong, living limbs are being amputated, and with each mutilating stroke more sunlight comes streaming in. The curtain of green is being torn apart in front of me.

"No!" I shout as I run out the door, and continue shouting as I fly down the stairs, finally stopping at the base of the tree. Two men are standing near me, eyeing me as if I am a crazy woman. "Stop!"

The man in the tree notices the commotion, and turns off his saw while looking down at me. He is in a harness tied to the tree—the tree amicably supporting its destroyer.

"No more cutting," I yell up to him. "It's July. You can't prune a tree right now—it's in the middle of its growth season. You're killing it, don't you see?"

"No comprende," the man says over and over, smiling each time. He looks at his compatriots and smiles more broadly.

I turn to them. One of them has to be some kind of a foreman, has to speak English of some kind. But they smile at me and repeat the other man's line.

I don't even want to think about what this means about the odds of them being licensed arboriculturists, but of course if they were, they wouldn't be pruning a perfectly healthy tree in the middle of summer in a style that can only be described as demolishing.

I yell "Stop" a few more times, but the roar of the saw eats up my words, then branches start falling all around me like the London Blitz, but without a country to fight back with me. I retreat up the stairs, holding my ears against the terrible noise, unable to look at the violence they are waging.

I go into my studio to try to sit down to work, but my entire insides are trembling. Huge waves of anger are roiling back and forth, trapped inside my body. They hit one side of me, then slap up against the other, then back again, like a filled vessel unable to be emptied out. This must be what my boxing coach was always yelling about, wanting me to get some anger out in my hooks. "Goddamn vegetarian," he'd say. "Eat some meat, put some blood in your punches, I can see that tofu in your left hook." I actually don't eat tofu, but I understand now what he meant. I wish that every heavy-bag punch I ever landed could retroactively express what I need to right now. Not that I want to hit these men who are massacring my tree. An Uzi would be much better. No, I don't mean that. Okay, frankly, I am glad there are no weapons around because I feel completely at the mercy of my rage. Goddamn motherfuckers, why is everything being destroyed, never to be seen again?

It is hell sleeping on my couch now that the tree has been desecrated. Light from the street lamp pours into my living room, a horrendous luminous reminder of the brutality that occurred. When I finally do fall asleep around four or five A.M., I awaken a few hours later in that nonremembering slumber state and am shocked each time to see the terrible stubby limbs, the sad absence of leaves, the piece of wood that used to be a tree. And the tree isn't even a ghost of itself because a ghost is all spirit with no form. This tree has lost both.

"Her name's Betty."

Like in *The Glass Menagerie* I almost say but don't since I have a feeling Reggie won't like the comparison, though it's a not a bad one.

The gentleman caller's fiancée in that play was named Betty. The name stuck out at me in the production I saw with Momma and Suzanne at the Saenger in New Orleans, an emotionally redundant afternoon if there ever was one. Betty.

"I met her at the museum," Reggie continues on the phone while I stand over my stove, stirring what must be my millionth pot of oatmeal. "I was wandering around the decorative arts wing, and she came in looking all cool with her clipboard and museum things, and we struck up a conversation and ended up talking for half an hour." Like he and I did when we met, I think. "We've been together since."

"That's great, Reggie."

Years ago, Reggie told me that when he first moved here he used to hang out at the museum hoping to meet a rich dowager (his word) to marry and endure until she died and he inherited all her money. I don't know if I should be surprised at the twist of fate that he's seeing someone he met there, albeit an associate curator, or laugh at the irony.

"And she has great design ideas for my script. Her area is early twentieth-century American, so there's lots of crossover, aesthetically speaking. And we've been working on it with the director for the past few weeks."

I feel simultaneously shut out and relieved. "I'm so glad you found someone."

"Thanks, Yvette." He sounds defensive, embarrassed, and proud. After we hang up the phone, I realize how much this needed to happen and for how long. I just wish it wasn't making me feel so empty.

I take my coffee and oatmeal to the studio, walking through the living room and doing everything I can to not look outside the windows. I might have to get some goddamn draperies. My studio is practically the only habitable room in my apartment now. I put some discs on the CD player, and let my computer boot up while I start eating my breakfast. None of my customers responded to the brochure I sent them, but July is usually a slump for jewelry, though my bank accounts need money fast, thanks to the outlay I had when I bought the jet and materials for my new line. After a few bites, I push the oatmeal away. Losing myself in making this jewelry is the sustenance I want right now. I open the safe and pull out trays of tourmaline, citrine, topaz, peridot, gold chains, and most wonderfully, jet. The pieces of jet lie on the black felt-lined tray like a glistening glass of water floating on a wave, shining and sparkling bright against the same color, as if they alone own it. I stack the trays of semiprecious stones and gold on one side of my desk, Howlin' Wolf is in full moan, and I put the jet in front of me, picking up the largest piece. It is warm to the touch, not cool like gold and stones are, but warmer even than my hand, like someone physically larger enveloping me in a hug.

34

The decision to call Andrew must have formed on its own during the few hours I slept because it was clear as soon as I woke up this morning. It is so completely what I must do that no part of my mind is even bothering with "Should I or shouldn't I?" The only question is "What time?" As I pour water into the coffeemaker, I decide that later mid-morning is probably the best time to catch him on his cell phone away from his house.

I drink a few cups of coffee to kill some time. I try to concentrate on work, but all I can think about are the numbers of Andrew's cell phone and when I can dial them, so I take a long bubble bath, letting the cool water be a contrast to the early August heat.

Finally, it is eleven—that should be late enough. I go into the living room—my studio's too distracting—and sit on the couch with my back to the ruined tree. I rest my hand on the phone for a moment, as if Andrew will get the message and call me himself, then I dial his number.

"Hello." Andrew's voice enters my body, nestling among all the other words it has sown inside me.

"Hey, it's Yvette," I say softly, as if my lowered tone will lessen the possibilities of it being a bad time to call.

"Are you all right?" Andrew sounds frantically concerned.

"Yeah, I'm fine."

"Where have you been?"

"Here, what do you mean?"

"I've been calling and calling you and all I'd get is a message that your phone's been disconnected."

"Disconnected? No, it's what I'm calling you on."

"Your phone hasn't been disconnected?" Then he confidently spiels off a number to me.

Andrew is shocked when I tell him that that's the number for my old apartment in Beverly Hills, where I lived when we were seeing each other years ago. He doesn't write numbers down, just memorizes them, so when he got back from New York last spring, he remembered my old apartment's phone number and had been calling that one.

"And I thought you just didn't want to speak to me anymore," I say, which makes him laugh, letting me know how impossible that would be.

"And I thought you'd gotten married to some really jealous guy who made you give up your old friends."

What is it with him about me getting married? And in six months? Then I remember how fast that happened for him.

"Are you okay?"

"My daddy died."

"Oh, God. I'm so sorry, when?"

I explain how I found out and what Suzanne told me.

"And you hadn't seen him at all since he took off, had you?"

"No."

"How are you doing about it?"

"Umm." Tears form in my eyes, and I realize that I haven't let them out to anyone since it happened. While I cry, Andrew's silence holds me like his strong arms. "It's . . . hard sometimes. Some hours I just lie on the floor and listen to music because I'm too exhausted to do anything else, and I can't think about anything else except that I have no idea where he is, not that I have for sixteen years, but this is worse because when he was in Florida, I could imagine getting a private detective and finding him, or going there myself. Something. But now . . . And then I'll be fine and I can work and do stuff, then it hits me again. And I'm not sleeping much at night. It's like that."

"Yeah, I remember. When my daddy died it was the summer before I went to Malaysia for a film."

"Right before we met."

"You're kidding." We are quiet for a moment as if that time in our lives has come into the rooms with us. "Yeah, I guess it was. Well, the way Lily acted, you would have thought the Chinese food hadn't arrived. She couldn't understand why I was so upset. She was annoyed it affected me."

"Wow, that's pretty harsh."

"I think about him every day," Andrew says. "Mostly small things. How he always drank his orange juice after his breakfast—not with the meal. How he'd fold his newspaper like he was riding a train when he was sitting on the couch. That's what comes back. Not the big moments you were sure mattered."

"I think about mine every day, too, but it's not comforting. It's hard for me to feel that his spirit is benevolent toward me."

"That will change. Give it a while. Your relationship with him isn't over just because he's dead. It continues and gets better, that's what I've found. If anything, now it can be what it never was. I bet in a few months, you'll feel that he's with you all the time in a way you never could feel before."

"I hope that's true." I am silent for a moment as I try to imagine what it'd be like to feel my father with me, to finally have that emptiness filled. "God, it's good talking to you. I've been wanting to tell you."

"You, too, sweet-y-vette. I'm glad you called. I've got some people in the next room waiting for me. Give me your number and I'll call you later, okay, honey?"

After I hang up, Andrew's words about my father take on their own life and are routing themselves to the place inside me where the grief has lived. They attach themselves to it, softening its hard, jagged edges with their presence. My grief is no longer alone. It will always hold Andrew's experience and words of comfort, so that when its sadness hits, it will be tempered by this hope and nonaloneness I finally feel.

My eyes are open wide staring at a large man dressed in black standing over me in my living room. His arms are reaching out, about to grab and attack, then it stops. My scream continues after the image fades, then the nightmare is truly over. The man has disappeared like a special effect in a film, but a horror film I produce and project in the air next to me, no screen needed, the imagined intruder's body blocking out the real wall behind him, until he *poofs* goodbye as magically as he appeared.

"None of your jewelry sold in those other stores," Linda Beckman says, peering over her glasses at me as she sits behind her cluttered and significant desk. "Though I guess you know that. Well, let's see the new line."

There's a nice opening for this sales call, but I refuse to let her words shake me. I pull the samples out of my bag that is on the floor next to me in Linda's extremely cream office. "I'm working in jet now," I say as I place the trays in front of her. "But still with gold and semiprecious stones. It's a similar concept to the pearls, just a different material."

Linda pushes the glasses up her nose and begins lifting jewelry out of the trays. She holds a piece up, scrutinizes it, puts it back, and continues that way for a while. Her expression is inscrutable as she sorts through the trays like it's so much overripe fruit.

I am about to say, "Well, thanks for looking; maybe my next line," when Linda picks up a bracelet and puts it on. She holds her arm out briefly in front of her, then earrings, a necklace, and a pin join her outfit.

She stands up and walks over to one of the framed black-and-white catalogue photographs, checking her reflection in the glass. I wonder why she doesn't just buy a mirror.

"Love them," she says, spinning around and facing me. "The jet is very fresh this way. I love that you're using it for fall and not that black-and-white-for-summer look; I'm so sick of that. Okay, we'll do an order for this store, and if it's a hit, we'll do a shipment to New York. And that one you'd get paid for."

I look at her in confusion.

"It's a charge back. We already paid you for the stock that sat in our stores, so you'll get it back and we'll get your new line in exchange for our money that you've kept. The old stuff will be shipped to you; you should get it next week. And we'll need a check from you for P and A for this line. I want these samples rushed over for the shoot."

Driving away from Greeley's, or Greedy's as I now think of them, I don't know if I should be elated or crushed. I've heard stories from other designers about the department stores playing hardball, I just never thought it would be this hard. Why didn't Greeley's mark the damn jewelry down in a July Fourth sale? Because this way, I realize, they don't lose a dime, the crooks. It's like some terrible wedding contract where the man can keep switching brides under his same vows until he hits upon one he decides to like.

All right, this is the reality of playing in this league, so get a game plan. For this order to be ready for the late-September delivery that Linda wants, I'll have to buy the rest of the materials tomorrow and immediately get them into production, which means that in thirty days I'll have to pay Dipen and the vendors with no money coming in, so I am looking at being in the red with a checking account that is sliding to zero. Fuck. I'll have to sell all of the pieces they are shipping back, plus get some commissions fast, if I want to pay my bills. I'll call Rox, and if she doesn't want it, I'll hit every shop on every boulevard where there are boutiques. Something will come up. I hope.

Andrew and I talk pretty frequently when he is in his car or at his office behind a closed door. Small moments that bind us are etched out of the day, a separate time away from the rest of our lives. But it isn't enough. A hole has been opened in me, a huge gaping desire that bellows and yells from the moment I wake up and continues through my day and into my sleep where, when I'm not screaming, I'm dreaming of him. Being with him, seeing him. Him, him, him. The phone calls we have quench it while making it worse. The days that he doesn't call—I can't call him because of his "situation," there's a euphemism—drag on and on like some dreadful boot camp where if I just live through the next grueling task, then release will come in the form of his voice on the line, but it never does. Until he calls the next day and I am able to breathe again, but it's all I can do not to say, "I have to see you right now. I am going to die if I don't. Get over here." Instead I ask as casually as I can if he can come over, and the answer is always the same. He wants to and will try, but things are crazy right now, then his voice goes down deep inside me to exactly where I want him to be and he talks to me there and I talk to him from there and it's like he's with me and I'm with him and we are together in this perfect place created by our voices that are one and moving together, moving with each other until he and us and this is the only reality there is and it takes over my entire body.

"Broken, Reggie. Probably in transit because it looks like the goddamn salesclerks just threw my jewelry into a box and sent it off. They wrap socks better than this." I am in my living room with the phone cradled against my shoulder as I look through the boxes that just arrived from Greeley's. "Okay, some of the pieces have bubble wrap around them, but not all. It's a fucking mess. I want to kill these stupid people."

"Call that Linda woman and yell."

"Oh, God, I can't do that. This is like the Mafia I'm dealing with.

You play by their rules or they cut you out. I've asked around, and all the department stores are like this with small, individual vendors. It's their retail world; we just want to sell in it." I sit on the floor with my back against the couch in the middle of boxes and invoices and bubble wrap and jewelry that is whole and jewelry that is broken.

"Fuck that. Don't let them have your stuff anymore."

"That's really not a solution. It's like . . . Look, you're letting someone else direct your script even though that was your dream because you'd rather see it on the big screen than only on your computer." I automatically look out the window to be comforted by the tree, but am confronted with its brutalized form, so I quickly turn away. "It's the price of doing business with these people." I pull out a single pearl earring from the bottom of a box; its match is nowhere near. "Oh, good Christ, one of the pearls even looks pocked—is this insane?"

"What are you going to do?"

"Throw myself off a cliff. No, I'll try to sell the pieces that are okay and reuse the broken ones. Melt down the gold; put the gems in other things. You know, move on."

Spending all day going in and out of boutiques on Robertson Boulevard to show them my jewelry reminds me of going around to art galleries years ago in New York City. Cold-calling sucked then and still does. It is the first week of September, and all the managers have told me that they already have their fall inventory; can I come back in January? I want to blow everything off and drive up to Andrew's office, tell his assistant that I have an appointment, he wouldn't say no, walk in, get on his desk, and dive into Andrew-sex-oblivion. Oh, God do I want to do that. I need to do that. He called last night about eleven, and it was like all those times years ago when my phone ringing at that hour meant the coast was clear, Stephanie and her fabulous self had left, and I could go up to his house and crawl into bed with him. For a second last night, I thought I would see him because it felt so much like it had been, us connected and seeing each other all the time, but he had to go home.

I almost close my eyes as I walk down the sidewalk on Robertson because thinking of Andrew makes me lose myself in its deliciousness, but I need to get back on track. I'll get a bite to eat, and drive out to Santa Monica. Maybe the stores there in true beach fashion are more relaxed in their ordering.

I find myself in front of the white and bright SoHo-style café, and as I push open the door, the smell of good food and the sight of people wearing clothes that were probably bought last week envelop me. Coltrane is playing at a pleasant volume and underneath it are the sounds of conversations from the packed tables in the dining area and the customers asking about dishes in the display case. After a good five minutes in line, I order a cappuccino and a grilled-vegetable sandwich. I have paid, gotten my lunch, and am walking outside to sit at one of the wrought-iron tables before I realize that I was hoping I would see that guy who helped me before. At an audition probably.

I almost had a good look this time. As my screaming reached its peak, I almost saw the face of the man about to grab me, but he disappeared.

I sit up on the couch in the glow of the street lamp pouring in. It has been a couple of months since the arboreal massacre and the sad little clumps of leaves growing on the tree almost make it more depressing somehow.

I go to the kitchen to make myself a cup of chamomile tea. As I am waiting for the water to boil, a memory comes to me from when I first started going to meditation sessions at En Chuan's apartment.

It was a night when I got there before the others, so I helped him set up the circle of cushions on his living-room floor. Water for tea was working its way to a boil, and the open windows were letting a breeze in.

"Do you think all this is real?" En Chuan suddenly said to me. We were sitting across the floor from each other. He was on a black meditation cushion with his back so straight and hands so relaxed on his lap that his short thin body seemed to expand in that cross-legged pose as if it were most powerful like that. "Your life and perceptions, experiences and beliefs—are they real?"

I told him I thought so. They certainly felt real.

He nodded, then said, "While you are having a dream, you believe it is real; your nervous system reacts as if it is real; sometimes you even wake up thinking for a moment it is real." He paused and his hands re-folded themselves on his lap like a cat elegantly finding a new pose. "How do you know you won't wake up to discover that none of this was real? That an entirely different reality exists for you to one day awaken and see."

I had no response for that. The kettle began to whistle, so I got up to set out the tea, then Steve and the others arrived. It felt like he had planted something in me, had replaced an organ I didn't know wasn't working, and my body was still deciding if it should reject or welcome the foreign aid.

Curling up with my tea on the couch, I have no idea what this other reality is that En Chuan was speaking of, but just the idea that it may exist is comforting. It isn't heaven he meant, but something else, something here. A way of seeing that is freeing, not limited by dreary reality. I doubt I'll ever have it the way En Chuan probably does, but even just a peek of it—one altered view—would be enough.

35

I have been trying to avoid what I've been thinking lately. I got the order shipped to Greeley's on deadline three weeks ago, so my prayers that it will blow out fast have begun. I asked Dipen and the vendors if I could have an extension on paying my bills, but they need the money, too, and I can't afford to jeopardize those relationships.

All last week, I walked into, then out of, every restaurant on Melrose. They all asked for a picture and a résumé.

"I just want a waitressing job," I said. "I'm not an actress." I had thought that would help—no auditions for me to bail out of a shift for—but they just shrugged and showed me stacks of other applicants' glossy eight-by-tens with smiles and sex abounding within. Who knew never being on TV would handicap me to serve food? Not that any of them were hiring anyway.

I even tried nightclubs. Got dressed up in smallish outfits and went around in the early evening hours. Gloria tried to talk me out of it when I told her what I was doing.

"Those real tall girls can do it, but even they wear the heels, 'cause, hon, you have to keep that tray up and over your head to get through those crowds. You never thought of that, did you? It's hard, hard work. I wouldn't try it if I were you." Like I wanted to.

Every nightclub in town was fully stocked with fully stacked girls and my checkbook was in free fall. I was trying to brace myself for my own personal crash, when the last number would hit and the zero would explode up and out and rain poverty on me, silent nothings crushing me in their wake. Years ago, I met a homeless woman when I was volunteering in a food line on Santa Monica City Hall's front lawn. She was in her early thirties, and I could tell she had been rather pretty once. Long brown hair that she was trying to keep neat, large blue eyes, someone you might meet at a party, not tons of distance between her and me like I always thought there'd be. She was last in line, and as I served her a plate of spaghetti and tomato sauce, she told me about the sliding steps that had gotten her there and how the process back to a rehabilitated life was a sheer vertical cliff. Not that I think I'll end up where she was, but her sunburned face and hopeless eyes have started peering at me from my mind.

I want to jump out of my skin. But each morning I sit at my worktable with coffee, music on, and the jewelry that Greeley's sent back along with what was in the safe—a few tourmalines, peridots, citrines, and jet. I play around with ideas to remake the old pieces while I try not to think about my smashed bank accounts and seeing Andrew. I get caught up in the juxtaposition of color and surface and sparkle and matteness, envisioning a whole new line, and I want to run downtown and scoop up more gems and pearls and jet to create this world, then I remember that I don't have the money, and the panic comes, so I try to get my breath back and look at my options. I could call Matt and Suzanne for a loan, but that's a phone call I really do not want to make.

I couldn't sleep all last night thinking about it, so I got up at two A.M. and drove on the 10 and the 101, going between them on the 110 again and again, looking at the skyscrapers that are always standing no matter what is happening, shiny and bright like perfectly cut jewels, until finally I was sleepy and went home. I woke up at seven and have been waiting until mid-morning when Andrew will be at his office. I tried to limit my caffeine because I am already nervous enough, but not drinking coffee made me edgy, so it was a toss-up as to which was worse.

I am sitting on the couch with my back to the tree. Maybe I should just put the damn couch in front of the windows, but then I'd have to face the butchery head-on whenever I sit down. Draperies may be unavoidable now but that pisses me off because I'm not big on window treatment. Okay, focus on what I have to do. Or have decided to do. I try to form the question in my mind, to rehearse it, but the words slip around, and unrelated ones jump in and join sentences they should never be in, and I realize it is useless to try to make this a comfortable thing to do. I just need to breathe, if I can.

"Are you okay?" is Andrew's hello when he answers his cell phone. He sounds very concerned, like something is terribly wrong. I guess he saw my number on his cell phone, and I don't usually call him.

"Andrew, I'm broke." The words come out so fast that the breath they were on barely left my body.

"Oh." He sounds startled, like someone just handed him a curious prize.

"Can I borrow some money?" I realize that I am clenching my calf hard, like it's the safety latch on a theme-park ride.

"Of course, but I don't want it back."

Relief is pouring into me, but it has to get past the words tumbling out. "I'm sorry to ask, it's just I've been looking for commissions and a new store, but there hasn't been anything, and I told you how Greeley's isn't paying for this order, and I've even looked for waitressing jobs, and I really will pay you back, is it just horrible that I asked?"

"Not at all, don't worry about it, and I don't want money from you. I told you you were like a daughter to me. How much do you need?"

The ease in his voice envelops me and I am able to get a real breath in. "A few thousand? To keep the wolves from the door until something turns up. I'm sorry to—"

"Stop, it's fine. Do you have health insurance?"

"Health insurance?" He could have asked if I had a condo at the beach. "No."

Andrew sighs. I have a feeling I have become a face to a statistic he has fought for and lost.

"I'm happy to get you the money, but this is embarrassing because I don't have any on me. I never do, so it might be a while before I can get any to you. Will you be okay until then?"

"Yeah, I'm not being kicked out, I just don't—" I annoyingly start to cry.

"Yvette, it's okay, don't worry about it. I'm glad you asked. I would've been mad if you hadn't. Now just let me call you later today, okay, honey? I'll call you later."

His protectiveness feels so tangible, I should be able to take that to the bank.

I need to get out of my head. It's been two weeks since I asked Andrew for money, and every day on the phone he says he's getting it, but he hasn't yet. I alternately lambaste myself for asking—maybe Suzanne was the better choice, after all—and wish he would just get it already because my request has been hanging in the air between us all this time, getting distorted in our minds, or mine at least.

Or maybe he's not even going to give it to me. At what point do I stop believing he'll come through? Fuck, I don't want that to happen for so many reasons. I decide to give it another week, and if still nothing's happened, then I'll come up with plan B. Though God only knows what that would be.

But staying in my apartment is making me batty. I need to do something besides pursue work and create jewelry because neither are happening, but "free" is the deciding factor for me and in L.A. that means the Getty. I call Steve to see if he can join me. I considered calling Reggie, but since Betty's been around it's felt better not to. Steve and I are finally going to do that Zen for Christians retreat in a couple of weeks, so it'd be nice to see him before three full days of silence when I can let go of thinking. And worrying.

The late October afternoon at the Getty Museum is God's own artwork, though the land that it is situated on helps. The promontory doesn't jut straight into the ocean, but the area below it, Brentwood, becomes so much scenery as the sea takes all the attention. Steve and I walk through the antiquities, or ancestors as he calls them, then spend our time in a photography exhibit of the Mississippi Delta in the thirties, i.e., dire poverty, but softened by the exposure and printing. Looking at a particularly beautiful bleak view, I am transported to the unforgiving sun and land of my home state. The seasons' sharpness overpowering anyone who lacks the resources for simple body-comforts defense. I have a moment of seeing my being broke as a split second in the hours of my life, a click in time with barely enough import to make a sound. Then the panicky feeling that my breath has been navigating around returns and it is all I can do not to run out of the gallery and call Andrew.

Driving home from the museum, I make it halfway before I am unable to resist any longer. I dial his cell phone and listen to Andrew's silent voice mail message pick up. Fuck. Okay, I shouldn't have called him anyway. I just need to be patient. Or seriously consider a plan B. A mile later, I press the redial button and his voice comes on the line.

"Where are you?" Like he already knew I was driving around, able to meet him.

"On Beverly near Fairfax, why?"

"Come to Crescent Drive at little Santa Monica, I'll meet you at the gas station there."

I turn my truck around. We drive toward each other, describing the rush-hour obstructions we weave through, the web of our words pulling us together at its center point.

I pull in to the gas station, look at the cars at the pumps, but don't see him. Traffic on little Santa Monica is oblivious and insane.

"I'm here, where are you?" I stop my truck a good distance from the pumps. I have no idea what I'll say if a serviceman walks over.

"One street over on Canon—meet me here."

I don't understand what we are meant to do once we meet so publicly.

As I turn onto Canon, Andrew says, "I see you."

"Where?" I swivel around in my truck, searching for him.

"Behind you, the dark Mercedes-Benz."

I spot an "affordable" version of that car just behind me. "That one?"

"No, the fucking big one, you think I'd drive that piece of shit? Two cars back."

"Oh." I look farther back, but still can't find him. I feel pursued, a cops-and-robbers game, but we're on the same team.

"Head north, cross Santa Monica, turn right, and pull in by the park there," he says.

I feel the thrill of a cop forcing my actions, directing my drive. It makes me tremble behind my knees and farther up. And this cop is Andrew.

Life in L.A. is a constant car chase, so having one with Andrew doesn't seem strange. Although really it is more of a car following. When I pull into a space by the park, he comes into view. Behind me. Approaching. Close. I wonder how he was able to stay invisible for so long. He is in my rearview mirror, then next to me in a parking space, his Mercedes engulfing my vision like his force does my life. When he gets out of his car, a giant no longer contained, the air splices into Technicolor, the traffic a soundtrack to his smile. Then he is up in my truck next to me, so close and real and big and I haven't seen him in what feels like years and like seconds. I kiss his lips and neck and face, his well-cared-for skin, so unlike anyone's I have known, as if the years settled like stardust into his cells, plumping them to become a soft radiant shield.

"Let's go somewhere else," he says, glancing around through the windows. "Take Rexford north." I half expect him to duck down.

We are robbers now from the cops, driving through Beverly Hills on a mission whose goal I'm unsure of. Andrew directs me through a series of complicated turns in the hills above Sunset, then stops us at the end of a cul-de-sac in front of a house hidden by a stone wall and a dense line of trees. No one is around.

"Do you know the people who live here?"

"No." He looks startled, as if he might without knowing it. I realize this was a choice of anonymity he made, not the protection of a close-lipped friend. "Here. I know it took weeks to get it, but I hope it'll help." The envelope Andrew hands me is sealed. "It's all I could get for now. Let me know if you—"

"Thanks, Andrew. I really will pay you—"

"Stop, I don't want your money."

A gray cat crossing the street stops upon seeing us, paw suspended midair, then walks on.

"When you asked me, I felt very paternal toward you. I wanted to help you. I always have." He looks embarrassed and proud, like a major highway with a gentle yield that enables you to come on.

Once I can no longer see Andrew's car receding, I stop at the red light at Santa Monica and Crescent, open the envelope and count three thousand dollars in hundred-dollar bills. The light turns green, and I drive with it on my lap, a piece of his protection left for me.

The city is deep into Friday night. Cars are no longer solo-filled for work, but hold pairs and groups. Andrew is driving home to his wife and daughter and son. The daughter whom he won't know when she's my age, I suddenly realize. Unless he reaches eighty-four lucidly, the age he'd be when she's thirty. I wonder if he has thought about that, has let himself imagine how much of her life he'll see and which of her years he'll miss, as I at times in the past sixteen years have tried to imagine my life with my father in it.

And what happened to the dreams my father must have had for me when I was young? Where did he put them when he left and lived in Florida? Underneath, probably, deep down inside where he couldn't find them. But maybe they flew up into the air when he died and merged with the sunlight so they could find me here in California where they have settled into my cells and will redirect their growth correctly.

36

Our phone calls have been platonic since Andrew gave me the money a couple of weeks ago, so I can talk to him without worry that it's hurting anyone, we're friends, there's nothing wrong with that.

But tonight, before I leave for the retreat tomorrow, our conversation got . . . sexual. Which is hard. For it to and for it not to. Hard and easy and soft and dreamy and like we were made for it to. And I didn't resist even though I should have, but it was like easing into a pool where the current is rushing all over me in different ways all at once, and it was so easy to say yes to seeing him when I get back from the retreat, as easy as taking a breath before going under water.

The scream is coming out of me as if the image I am seeing is connected to it. The man is in front of me, black clothes, large body, hands reaching for me, coming closer to the couch, bigger and nearer, I can smell his breath, and no one is coming to save me and he is about to grab, and I look at his face and see it finally. And the scream lets out one last burst, like a death rattle, and he disappears into the night, and I sit here holding myself, shaking quietly.

I can't believe what I saw. Then I wonder why I didn't remember it all this time. I feel pinned to the couch by the memory of the dream that has begun playing in my head. The dream that I had three years in a row when I was a child, always a spring night, and I knew each time that I was going to have it before I went to bed.

The first time, I wanted to leave the hall light on outside my bedroom, which annoyed Suzanne because it shone into her room, too, so she tried to convince my five-year-old self that I wasn't going to have a nightmare that night, it didn't work like that, as if she were so wise at nine that she could explain the mysteries of the dream realm to me, but I knew she was wrong, and once she was asleep, I slid out of bed and turned the light on.

And the nightmare did come, as I had known it would—I just didn't know what it would be about until I had it. I was in the house with Momma, Daddy, and Suzanne. It was a regular spring night, like the real one, and the Wolfman was going to come. He lived in the neighborhood a few blocks away, had a wife and kids, and his job—like my daddy had a job that I also never understood—was to scare the people in Pass Christian. One family one night per year. And it was our turn. It wasn't clear why the Wolfman was only starting to scare us now, but he was coming and no one seemed to care. Momma and Daddy weren't around and Suzanne wasn't fazed by it—the Wolfman, big deal. I was the only one who was scared, waiting for what would happen.

Finally he came. Up our front steps, across the porch and to our front door. His large dark form, black hairy hands and arms, cold mean eyes, all of him scratching at the front door, tearing at it, breaking the wood. I screamed and screamed as he tried to get inside.

I woke myself up screaming, then listened in the semidarkness. He wasn't in my room, and Suzanne seemed to be sleeping peacefully across the hall; at least, I didn't hear any screams from there. My parents were in their room with their door shut at the end of a really dark hall. I was too afraid to go there, so I lay back down and had my first night of insomnia. Held on to Teddy, his small body wedged into my side, and prayed Hail Marys as I stared at the ceiling. I didn't trust that if I went back to sleep the Wolfman wouldn't return, so I waited until sunup before I dozed off.

The next day I told Suzanne, but she brushed it off—a Wolfman, please. I never even thought to tell Momma and Daddy.

The next spring, on the night that I knew the Wolfman was going to come, I again waited until Suzanne was asleep, then turned the hall light on. I got into bed with dread. I didn't know which was worse: the previous year when I knew a nightmare was coming but didn't know what it was about, or knowing the Wolfman would visit again. I considered trying to stay awake, maybe that would keep him away, but I knew it was inevitable—we had to have our turn like every other family in town. Trying to prevent it would only make it worse. I held on tight to Teddy. I said Hail Marys over and over. With her around, I was supposed to have nothing to fear, but it wasn't working. Maybe her power didn't extend to Wolfmen. Then sleep came.

I was in Daddy's work shed looking at a violin and Suzanne was on the swings where I was supposed to be playing when suddenly I heard her yell my name. I ran out and found her outside the shed's door. The Wolfman was walking with determination into our yard. He had a sick grin on his face, like he knew he could get us easily and wasn't going to waste his strength, but Suzanne and I broke into a run and he came after us. We ran around the house, him close on our heels, past the kitchen porch steps, past the den's back door, past the dining room's French doors, past the front porch, and round and round and round again, his breath on our backs, us barely ahead and only because we were familiar with the path, screaming for our parents, hoping they'd appear, until suddenly I woke up and I was in my bed, the sheets turned this way and that, and the house quiet and dark. I stayed up for the rest of the night, holding Teddy in my arms, knowing it was a dream, but also knowing it was somehow real.

The last time the Wolfman came, I asked Suzanne if I could sleep with her that night. I knew she'd say no, but it was a worth a shot. After she refused, I dragged myself into bed. The waiting was excruciating. I held on to Teddy and said lots of prayers, then next thing I knew, I was in the den and Daddy was in his big leather chair, the one from his study, which for some reason was downstairs, and he was listening to his jazz records, his eyes closed and head resting back. I was in my nightgown, the pale pink one with the short sleeves that had its own matching robe that made me feel so grown-up, but I had gotten too tall for it in the past year and Momma had thrown it away. I was at the back door, which was open, and the Wolfman had grabbed hold of my robe and was pulling with all his might, making the fabric taut against the back of my legs, pulling me harder and harder toward him. I screamed for Daddy's help as I pressed my body back so I wouldn't go tumbling out. My screams were louder than the jazz, so I knew he could hear me, but his eyes stayed closed, his head so relaxed, while I screamed and screamed and screamed, then suddenly Daddy disappeared as if he had never been there. The chair was empty, and my father was completely absent. The Wolfman let out a large howling laugh, and with one great tug, started to pull me out, but in a moment of inspiration I took off my robe, and with a startled look on his face, the Wolfman fell back, and I slammed the door shut, locked it tight, then woke up.

The sheet and blanket are wrapped around me as I sit on my couch looking outside at the thwarted yet growing tree and finally I understand that my father was never completely there even when he lived with us. I must have always known that, at least part of me, when I was a child to have had a dream where I had to save myself. Like I've been needing to save myself from the scream dream. And from other things I can't stop seeing. Like my grandfather's secretary, Miss Plauché, constantly walking backward to look at her past that she needed so badly to see and consequently missing her entire future.

I suddenly remember a day the summer I was ten when Suzanne and I went to our grandfather's office to have lunch with him at the top of the big bank building in the private dining room where the maître d' always brought a perfect red rose to Suzanne and me and the bartender would send Shirley Temples to our table as if we ate there regularly. Suzanne and I were waiting in our grandfather's office while he was in the outer room, speaking to Miss Plauché.

"She lost her fiancé and two brothers in World War Two," Suzanne said in a hushed tone, nodding with her head toward the outer room. "Then both her parents died a few years later, and she's walked backward ever since."

My sister spoke with all the romantic drama that only a fourteen-year-old girl can, infusing love and death—almost a longing for a similar fate. As if Miss Plauché's love were more pure because she refused to let it go and move on. Which I guess is what I've been doing with Daddy and Andrew.

I go into the kitchen to fix some tea—I want warmth inside me. As I wait for the water to boil, an image of my father comes to me of him in his leather chair listening to jazz. His eyes are closed, fingers tapping, and he is alone in his study, off in his world. Then I walk in and immediately he makes room for me. I sit on his lap, close my eyes, and join him where he goes in the notes and harmonies and melodious discord and he is there with me as much as he could be. And maybe that was enough really. Or can be. Maybe that was what En Chuan was trying to tell me—that awakening to an entirely different reality is the ability to see my past differently, as a reality that was always true, but that I was asleep to.

As I pour the water into a mug, the chamomile's fragrance is released and it moves toward my face, enveloping me. My father was there as much as he could be and it didn't last as long as I needed, but he had to leave because even when he lived with us, a part of him was already gone or maybe never even moved in. And somehow I knew that and found my own way of reaching him.

I throw the tea bag away, and measure honey into the mug, stirring gold sweetness into the pale green liquid. Maybe what I had with him was enough. Okay, it wasn't what a lot of girls get, but our connection is still valid and now I have it in a way I didn't before—not obscured by memories of need. All this time, he's been with me in my art and jewelry, as surely as I could hear him teaching me how to use his tools in his work shed. I can't not be connected to my father—he is me. Like the 10 freeway from home out here—the same spirit, just farther along in its journey.

I take my tea to the couch and sip it slowly, letting it fill me inside. The aromatic warmth holds me until I fall asleep.

The Zen Compound, in the middle of Korea Town just west of downtown where the Zen for Christians retreat is being held, is a group of small concrete buildings with an eight-foot-high chain-link fence surrounding them—a far cry from the Asian-style house and gurgling brook that I envisioned every time I imagined my three peaceful days here. But Buddhists aren't known for being rich and the whole point of the retreat is to go within, something I definitely will want to do to get away from the aesthetics here, or lack of them.

But after registering in the main gulag-style building and walking into my dorm room, it is all I can do not to turn and run. My room turns out to be a room that I will share with the other five female retreatants. The furnishings are minimal to say the least. Six thin futon pads lie directly on the scarred hardwood floor with a sad pile of sheets, one thin blanket, and a lump that I guess was a pillow in a previous life at the foot of each. There is no other furniture or decoration, as if reminders of our Western life would erase the meditation's effect. A row of hooks runs along one of the chipped green walls, to hang oneself from, I think, but I know it is for our clothing, the few tunics and comfortable pants we were instructed to bring. Who has ever owned a tunic, I thought when I read the confirmation letter's instructions, other than Halston or a monk?

Oh, good God, what have I gotten myself into? Did Steve know it was going to be like this? I fight the urge to run to find him and ask if he has gone completely nuts. I mean, this is clearly going to be very formal Zen and I did learn a lot of this stuff from En Chuan, but that was years ago, and this is looking very intense.

Okay, calm down, I tell myself as I unpack my bag, which means hanging my garments—I can't even think of them as clothes in this forsake-all-worldly-concerns environment—from the hook nearest my futon and putting my toiletries under the blanket. Not out of fear of thievery, I have a feeling any transgression here would cost the perpetrator twice the karmic years, but because the case they are in—the one I got for free when I bought Chanel No. 5 cologne—looks way too materialistic with its white camellias and black ribbons on gold fabric.

I walk downstairs in the late-afternoon November light and locate the building for the meditation sessions. As I enter the anteroom, I can see that the meditation hall it opens into is already filled with the other retreatants. I slip off my shoes and select a plump black zafu cushion from the shelves. At least they spent money on these, considering how much we'll be sitting on them. Carrying it in front of me, I join the group in the hall. Plain wooden platforms slightly raised off the dark hardwood floor line three sides, and on these, the retreatants are sitting deep in meditation. Steve's eyes are shut and he is in full lotus, so I settle into an empty spot a couple of retreatants away from him.

After a thirty-minute meditation that feels like three hours, a short, impossible-to-tell-her-age Japanese monk wearing a deep red robe enters and gives a dharma talk that is mildly challenging and inspiring when I am able to concentrate on it, which isn't much. I figure she is a warm-up act for the Zen Master Jesuit priest, so I let myself wonder why it is that nuns and female monks look so ageless. Is it sex that makes us old? Like that D. H. Lawrence short story—maybe he was right after all. Which makes me think of Andrew; he looks a lot younger than his years and God knows he's fucked a helluva lot. Okay, these are not thoughts to have at a retreat, focus on what she is saying, but the monk suddenly stops. I have an odd feeling that she ended right in the middle of a sentence though I can't be sure since I wasn't paying attention, but with Zen it could have been some odd koan-style kind of lecture. She stands up, bows once, and walks out of the room, then we all get up and silently file out, stopping in the anteroom to recover our shoes, then head across the concrete courtyard to the main building.

The evening meal is exhilarating in its meagerness. The fourteen other retreatants and I are wordless and the reality of how dreadful this could be is hitting me, especially since a few of them are chewing not so silently. I have an improved appreciation for conversation at meals. I imagine a test the Zen Compound could have given—people only able to eat their meals without gestating sounds allowed in. Maybe I'll suggest it. But it would probably be looked down upon as not letting go of worldly concerns like table manners. Though why can't those be enforced? Okay, these also are probably not the kind of thoughts I'm supposed to be having, but keeping myself from pantomiming to Steve, who is down the table from me, my intolerance of the others' eating is taking all of my energy.

At the end of the noisy meal, we proceed noiselessly back to the meditation hall for the day's final za-zen and settle down on our cushions. Steve still has not acknowledged me, and that is just as well since I have a feeling that if he did, words would start flying out of me, so unused am I to this silence emitting from me, this inability to communicate with others, only with myself. No one told me that that was going to be part of this. I mean, I knew about the silence; I just didn't realize that it meant I would only be dealing with myself. That concept is terrifying, frankly. The Zen Master Jesuit priest enters the hall and slowly walks to a special gold zafu that was placed there for him while we were gone. He settles into an intimidating lotus, especially considering that he looks like one of those red-nosed Irish priests I grew up hearing mass from, and agility of body was not a trait I associated with them. Agility with a bottle maybe, but . . . Anyway. Come on, get back to my meditating. I reposition myself on my cushion, pretending that this will help. As I try to feel as comfortable as the rest of the silent sentient beings appear, I think maybe this retreat won't be so bad. The Jesuit priest Zen Master is here. He'll show how Catholicism and Buddhism can cohabit. This is exactly what I need.

The first thirty minutes of meditating only feels like a hundred, and that's an improvement from this afternoon, so I'm doing fine. Okay, my head is going nonstop, but I'm fine. Other than the fact that I keep thinking about . . . And see, just thinking at all is a problem. Of course, I'm not supposed to attach judgment to anything, like labeling something a problem, but if anything is a problem when meditating, then thinking would be it. So I try to bring my mind back to my breathing, but all I keep thinking about is Andrew and . . . Adultery. And I suppose I could have left the Ten Commandments at the Zen Compound's door, but how can I forget them?

So I am in a quandary. And the Catholic guilt suddenly kicks in in preparation for my upcoming mortal sin and the Buddhist loving-kindness for myself and all sentient beings is not working and I am looking at three silent days of thinking about this because I can't speak except within the ceremonies, which so far aren't even Christian, much less Catholic, I mean, a Hail Mary out loud with everyone would really help, but the ceremonies are all very Zen. Then suddenly a little bell sounds—it doesn't ring, it sounds—and everyone gets up, so I get up, and they start walking, but a very specific kind of walking, kind of halfway between sleepwalking and being a bridesmaid, and I've done both, but I'm having a very hard time finding the balance between the two, so my rhythm is totally off, and a line has formed and people are following me, but I start going the wrong way because I can't figure out the damn route, then suddenly the little bell sounds again and somehow everyone has ended up in front of their cushions except for me, like some horrible Zen version of musical chairs, so I rush over to mine, probably causing them to have to bring their minds back to their breathing from being annoyed at me, and we meditate some more, but all I am doing is thinking that Andrew and I had sex before he and his wife even met, so that gives me squatter's rights, and even if it doesn't, I've already committed the red-letter sin with him twice, so surely one more time isn't going to hurt, because my soul's probably already condemned, though it's karma I should be worried about, then that damn little bell sounds again, and we all get up for more weird walking, and I'm a tiny bit better this time, thank God, because it is starting to distract me from the need I am suddenly feeling to confess to everyone, but particularly the Jesuit priest if he would just act like one, then my mind starts very loudly thinking, *Can't we get to the Catholic part? I know how to do those ceremonies. I'm really very good at them, I even remember all the responses. I thought this was supposed to be a combination. Isn't this guy a Jesuit priest?*

Then suddenly Steve, who has been in line behind me, steps forward next to me and, I'm sure with loving-kindness, corrects my hands. It seems I was holding them in prayer, as if I were in line for communion where the priest can see all the way down to my heart, which is becoming a deeper and darker shade of gray with the onslaught of my sin on Monday, and suddenly I lose it. A sound is coming from me that I have never heard before and I am on the floor sobbing while fourteen Christian Buddhists and a Zen Master Jesuit priest all stare at me while standing silently still.

Somehow I manage to stumble mindfully out of the hall, grab my shoes, and get outside where I stand in the concrete courtyard thinking repeatedly, like a mantra with my tears, *How in God's name am I going to be able to do this?*

And then suddenly I know that I can't. I can't stay at the retreat and give up Mary and the way I grew up. And I can't see Andrew or be in touch with him ever again.

I walk silently to the dorm, get my stuff, and leave. My truck has never been such a refuge. I know the sound of the engine starting up is interrupting the retreatants' meditation, but I have to leave in a way that I've never needed to do anything. As I drive out of the compound, I dial Andrew's cell phone.

"Hi."

"It's me."

"Are you okay?" Andrew's voice in my ear gives my pulse a velocity I can't slow down, then I wonder if it is a rush for this to be done, but to always remain in me.

"Yeah, I left the retreat, but I'm fine, I . . . Can I see you, like, immediately?"

I kill an hour at the counter of Jan's Coffee Shop on Beverly. The bright fluorescent lights and garish noise are a relief from the semilit silence of the retreat. An unshaven man in the seat next to me is reading a worn copy of today's paper—it looks as disconnected from the world as he is. I sit still and silent on the stool, a cup of coffee before me, but inside myself, I pace. Counting the minutes, counting my breath. A little bell sounds and I almost jump up, but it is signaling that an order is ready and a wide-hipped waitress goes to fetch it, walking a well-worn route.

I drive around the emptying and indifferent L.A. streets waiting for Andrew to call me. I could only nurse a cup of coffee for so long and I want to be close to his office when he calls.

As I turn onto the street that Andrew's office is on, my cell phone rings and I tell him I'll be right there. He is standing in the open door of the building when I pull into the parking lot, looking godlike in just a T-shirt and jeans. I want to hold this image of him in the palm of my hand, hold it and kiss it and all that has been.

"Hi," Andrew says as I get out of my truck. His chest is large, his shoulders are back, and his height carries his body down to where I start. We don't kiss because even though it's the dark of night and no one is around, we are in public and that is never forgotten with him.

As I follow him into his office, it takes a moment for my eyes to adjust. The lights are on so low that the walls, carpet, and furniture all look the same dusty gray. I wonder if they are like that for atmosphere or as an inventive way to camouflage private papers on his desk. When I get my bearings, I sit down on a low, deep couch; Andrew is standing on the other side of the coffee table, looking ready to pace.

"I need to tell you goodbye, Andrew."

He looks charmingly confused, then he smiles as he comes to sit next to me, and ruffles my hair. It is all I can do to not let my head meld with his hand, fall to his lap, and do what is so natural for us.

"You've been really wonderful to me. You've always been there for me and . . ." And as I say the words, they are true. That terrible time in New York after my art crash, our breakup out here, him acquiring a wife and two children; all of it falls to the ground like pieces in a sculpture that never belonged. Andrew was just being Andrew. "No matter what was happening, underneath it all, I always felt kindly toward you, but I need to tell you goodbye."

Andrew is silent, looking at me. I feel like I am being wrenched up out of too-small skin and my breath has to move past the old barrier to get into this new body where there is more room.

"Don't you think I understand what's happening here?"

I look at him sitting next to me, but bathed in his own light from a spot recessed in the ceiling. A larger but lower sphere of light surrounds us, while the rest of the room recedes into darkness.

"You're saying goodbye to your father figures, growing up. I bet you're about to meet the man you're going to marry, if you haven't already." His calm gaze appraises my face as if he can see a mark that will tell him if that has happened.

"I look at you and I think, I've known her for twelve years. I've loved her all that time; I love her now, and I start feeling romantic toward you and that's not good. For either of us. This has been coming for a while."

I have to fight an impulse to collapse on his chest to delay what he is confirming.

"I think back sometimes on a few of the women who were in my life before, the ones my mind naturally wanders to, the heavyweights, like you." Andrew's eyes are on mine in the way he has looked at me for so long, making sure his thoughts become my own. "I could have married any one of you and been happy. There isn't just one true love for anyone; timing is everything."

I listen as Andrew talks, weaving tales of his past about people and choices he made while time was rolling on, separating him from some, entwining him with others, and it all makes sense. He isn't the only one for me. And never was. But what I had with him still meant something even though it couldn't be defined the way I wanted it to be, thought it had to be, for my life to have a discernible effect on his. And his on mine.

I sit with him in this farewell that began so long ago in the restaurant the first time I saw him when it shot out my heart and through my eyes and dragged me along until here we are at this point where I can let him go.

"I'll always love you, Andrew." I put my hands on his chest, his chest that was such a shield, then slide them around to the armor of his back. I want to pull his body through mine and keep some of it in the spaces between my cells, but I know there isn't room. My holding him turns to tears, and I put my head on his shoulder as the drops fall. I hold him tighter and he rubs my back, speaking low, holding me close. Any sadness I ever had before I met him, during him, and after him washes away.

"I'll walk you out."

Andrew turns off all the lights in his office by flicking one switch, but before we leave, he runs his hand down and around my legs as I wrap my arms tight across his back, holding on one final time.

"Okay. Bye."

My last image of Andrew in my world is in my truck's rearview mirror as I drive off. He is standing in the parking lot, then he takes a few steps, walking backward toward the big building, and his arm moves up and he waves. It is definitive, concluding, and welded onto me. I know if we meet in another space and time that that same wave will reach out toward him from inside of me and I know that I am not leaving behind anything that I still need to see.

"Wow—that's wonderful."

"Thanks, honey, we're really happy, too," Suzanne says on the phone. "So come next May, you'll be an aunt."

"Are you feeling okay?"

As she talks about the nausea and exhaustion, her words making real this soon-to-be member of our family, my other line clicks.

"Will you hang on?" I depress the button. "Hello?"

"Hi."

It takes me a second to connect to the voice that was part of my life for so long, and now only intermittently.

"Hey, Reggie, can I call you back? Suzanne's on the other line."

He sounds slightly nonplussed as he says he'll be around, and I click back to Suzanne.

"Hey, how was that retreat, when was it—"

"Last week," I say, looking at the tree outside my window. Some birds have started nesting in it and there are even enough leaves for the wind to rustle. "It was exactly what I needed it to be."

I know it's way too early to buy baby clothes, and Suzanne's not finding out the gender, but the idea of looking at gifts for my niece or nephew who will arrive in just six months is too delicious. Plus, Suzanne said she'd meet me.

"Oh, fun. It'll be like picking out clothes for our dolls, remember? We'd lay out a different outfit for them for each hour of the day," she'd said on the phone, laughing. "What on earth were we thinking?"

"Of Momma, clearly, and her different ensembles for everything."

"Oh, right." And my sister is quiet for a moment, so I brace myself for her next words to have that sharp, instructive tone, but they are soft and engaging. "I'd forgotten all about that. God, Yvette, what else do you remember that I don't?"

Walking into the café on Robertson Boulevard, I look around for Suzanne, but she is nowhere to be seen. I am a few minutes past our agreed-upon time, so kind of technically on time, but it looks like she is going to be the one who's late for the first time in our lives. Not that I'm going to get mad at a pregnant woman, and with Suzanne, it's refreshing. The café is packed. Outside, the crystalline November day has that autumn in New York energy where everyone is grateful that summer is over, while forgetting the cold it forebodes, although we never get that part in L.A.

After giving the hostess—a friendly one, shockingly, considering the street we are on—my name to go on the list, I step around a clump of women dressed in thin dresses and walk toward the front to wait for Suzanne, when underneath the Miles Davis that is playing I hear a voice in my ear.

"Hey, how's it going with Greeley's?" I turn to see his face, reflected bright from the chef's whites he is wearing over jeans.

"Oh, hey, wow, that's sweet of you to remember. Good, actually, they're putting my line in their New York store and probably San Francisco, too."

"That's great." His smile is like a cloud that will never rain, just hanging in the sky to be illuminated by the sun.

"Thanks." People are moving around us, creating a shelter of space that is only filled with us. "That artichoke pesto you made was incredible. It looks like your place is doing great."

"Glad you liked it. I'm Eric." His hand takes mine and he looks into my eyes as he holds it. It is like sitting in the Y of a great, sturdy tree—I am comfortably encircled and it is easy to stay, like the home I always wanted.

As I lie in bed each night, sleep comes easily. And when I wake up in the mornings, everything I see is real, as if I had finally awakened from a dream.